THE RAZOR'S EDGE

The sharp edge of a razor is difficult to pass over;
thus the wise say the path to Salvation is hard.

KATHA-UPANISHAD

The Razor's Edge

A NOVEL

BY W. SOMERSET MAUGHAM

Doubleday, Doran & Co., Inc.,

GARDEN CITY, NEW YORK

1944

THIS BOOK IS
STANDARD LENGTH,
COMPLETE AND UNABRIDGED,
MANUFACTURED UNDER WARTIME CONDITIONS
IN CONFORMITY WITH ALL GOVERNMENT
REGULATIONS CONTROLLING THE USE
OF PAPER AND OTHER MATERIALS

THE RAZOR'S EDGE

CHAPTER ONE

(i)

I HAVE NEVER BEGUN A NOVEL with more misgiving. If I call it a novel it is only because I don't know what else to call it. I have little story to tell and I end neither with a death nor a marriage. Death ends all things and so is the comprehensive conclusion of a story, but marriage finishes it very properly too and the sophisticated are ill-advised to sneer at what is by convention termed a happy ending. It is a sound instinct of the common people which persuades them that with this all that needs to be said is said. When male and female, after whatever vicissitudes you like, are at last brought together they have fulfilled their biological function and interest passes to the generation that is to come. But I leave my reader in the air. This book consists of my recollections of a man with whom I was thrown into close contact only at long intervals, and I have little knowledge of what happened to him in between. I suppose that by the exercise of invention I could fill the gaps plausibly enough and so make my narrative more coherent; but I have no wish to do that. I only want to set down what I know of my own knowledge.

Many years ago I wrote a novel called *The Moon and Sixpence*. In that I took a famous painter, Paul Gauguin, and, using the novelist's privilege, devised a number of incidents to illustrate the character I had created on the suggestions afforded me by the scanty facts I knew about the French artist. In the present book I have attempted to do nothing of the kind. I have invented nothing. To save embarrassment to people still living I have given to the persons who play a part in this story names of my own contriving, and I have in other ways taken pains to make sure that no one should recognize them. The man I am writing about is not famous. It may be that he never will be. It may be that when his life at last comes to an end he will leave no more trace of his sojourn on earth than a stone thrown into a river leaves on the surface of the water. Then my book, if it is read at all, will be read only for what intrinsic interest it may possess. But it may be that the way of life that he has chosen for himself and the peculiar strength and sweetness of his character may have an ever-growing influence over his fellow men so that, long after his death perhaps, it may be realized that there lived in this age a very remarkable creature. Then it will be quite clear of whom I write in this book and those who want to know at least a little about his early life may find in it something to their purpose. I think my book, within its acknowledged limitations, will be a useful source of information to my friend's biographers.

I do not pretend that the conversations I have recorded can be regarded as verbatim reports. I never kept notes of what was said on this or the other occasion, but I have a good memory for what concerns me, and though I have put these conversations in my own words they faithfully represent, I believe, what was said. I remarked a little while back that I have invented nothing; I want now to modify that statement. I have taken the liberty that historians have taken from the time of Herodotus to put into the mouths of the persons of my narrative speeches that I did not myself hear and could not possibly have heard. I have done this for the same reasons as the historians have, to give liveliness and verisimilitude to scenes that would have been ineffective if they had been merely recounted. I want to be read and I think I am justified in doing what I can to make my book readable. The intelligent reader will easily see for himself where I have used this artifice, and he is at perfect liberty to reject it.

Another reason that has caused me to embark upon this work with apprehension is that the persons I have chiefly to deal with are American. It is very difficult to know people and I don't think one can ever really know any but one's own countrymen. For men and women are not only themselves; they are also the region in which they were born, the city apartment or the farm in which they learnt to walk, the games they played as children, the old wives' tales they overheard, the food they ate, the schools they attended, the sports they followed, the poets they read, and the God they believed in. It is all these things that have made them what they are and these are things that you can't come to know by hearsay, you can only know them if you have lived them. You can only know them if you *are* them. And because you cannot know persons of a nation foreign to you except from observation, it is difficult to give them credibility in the pages of a book. Even so subtle and careful an observer as Henry James, though he lived in England for forty years, never managed to create an Englishman who was through and through English. For my part, except in a few short stories I have never attempted to deal with any but my own countrymen, and if I have ventured to do otherwise in short stories it is because in them you can treat your characters more summarily. You give the reader broad indications and leave him to fill in the details. It

2

may be asked why, if I turned Paul Gauguin into an Englishman, I could not do the same with the persons of this book. The answer is simple: I couldn't. They would not then have been the people they are. I do not pretend that they are American as Americans see themselves; they are American seen through an English eye. I have not attempted to reproduce the peculiarities of their speech. The mess English writers make when they try to do this is only equalled by the mess American writers make when they try to reproduce English as spoken in England. Slang is the great pitfall. Henry James in his English stories made constant use of it, but never quite as the English do, so that instead of getting the colloquial effect he was after, it too often gives the English reader an uncomfortable jolt.

(*ii*)

In 1919 I happened to be in Chicago on my way to the Far East, and for reasons that have nothing to do with this narrative I was staying there for two or three weeks. I had recently brought out a successful novel and being for the moment news I had no sooner arrived than I was interviewed. Next morning my telephone rang. I answered.

"Elliott Templeton speaking."

"Elliott? I thought you were in Paris."

"No, I'm visiting with my sister. We want you to come along and lunch with us today."

"I should love to."

He named the hour and gave me the address.

I had known Elliott Templeton for fifteen years. He was at this time in his late fifties, a tall, elegant man with good features and thick waving dark hair only sufficiently graying to add to the distinction of his appearance. He was always beautifully dressed. He got his haberdashery at Charvet's, but his suits, his shoes and his hats in London. He had an apartment in Paris on the Rive Gauche in the fashionable Rue St. Guillaume. People who did not like him said he was a dealer, but this was a charge that he resented with indignation. He had taste and knowledge, and he did not mind admitting that in bygone years, when he first settled in Paris, he had given rich collectors who wanted to buy pictures the benefit of his advice; and when through his social connections he heard that some impoverished nobleman, English or French, was disposed to sell a picture of first-rate quality he was glad to put him in touch with the directors of American museums who, he happened to know, were on the lookout for a fine example of such and such a master. There were many old families in France and some in England whose circumstances compelled them to part with a signed piece of Buhl or a writing-table made by Chippendale himself if it could be done quietly, and they were glad to know a man of great culture and perfect manners who could arrange the matter with discretion. One would naturally suppose that Elliott profited by the transactions, but one was too well bred to mention it. Unkind people asserted that everything in his apartment was for sale and that after he had invited wealthy Americans to an excellent lunch, with vintage wines, one or two of his valuable drawings would disappear or a marquetry commode would be replaced by one in lacquer. When he was asked why a particular piece had vanished he very plausibly explained that he hadn't thought it quite up to his mark and had exchanged it for one of much finer quality. He added that it was tiresome always to look at the same things.

"Nous autres américains, we Americans," he said, "like change. It is at once our weakness and our strength."

Some of the American ladies in Paris, who claimed to know all about him, said that his family was quite poor and if he was able to live in the way he did it was only because he had been very clever. I do not know how much money he had, but his ducal landlord certainly made him pay a lot for his apartment and it was furnished with objects of value. On the walls were drawings by the great French masters, Watteau, Fragonard, Claude Lorraine and so on; Savonnerie and Aubusson rugs displayed their beauty on the parquet floors; and in the drawing-room there was a Louis Quinze suite in *petit point* of such elegance that it might well have belonged, as he claimed, to Madame de Pompadour. Anyhow he had enough to live in what he considered was the proper style for a gentleman without trying to earn money, and the method by which he had done so in the past was a matter which, unless you wished to lose his acquaintance, you were wise not to refer to. Thus relieved of material cares he gave himself over to the ruling passion of his life, which was social relationships. His business connections with the impecunious great both in France and in England had secured the foothold he had obtained on his arrival in Europe as a young man with letters of introduction to persons of consequence. His origins recommended him to the American ladies of title to whom he brought letters, for he was of an old Virginian family and through his mother traced his descent from one of the signatories of the Declaration of Independence. He was well favoured, bright, a good dancer, a fair shot and a fine tennis player. He was an asset at any party. He was lavish with flowers and expensive boxes of chocolate, and though he entertained little, when he did it was with an originality that pleased. It amused these rich ladies to be taken to bohemian restaurants in Soho or *bistros* in the Latin Quarter. He was always prepared to make himself useful and there was nothing, however tiresome, that you asked him to do for you that he would not do with pleasure. He took an immense amount of trouble to make himself agreeable to ageing women, and it was not long before he was the *ami de la maison,* the household pet, in many an imposing mansion. His amiability was extreme; he never minded being asked at the last moment because someone had thrown you over and you could put him next to a very boring old lady and count on him to be as charming and amusing with her as he knew how.

In two or more years, both in London to which he went for the last part of the season and to pay a round of country house visits in the early autumn, and in Paris, where he had settled down, he knew everyone whom a young American could know. The ladies who had first introduced him into society were surprised to discover how wide the circle of his acquaintance had grown. Their feelings were mixed. On the one hand they were pleased that their young protégé had made so great a success and on the other a trifle nettled that he should be on such intimate terms with persons with whom their own relations had remained strictly formal. Though he continued to be obliging and useful to them, they were uneasily conscious that he had used them as stepping-stones to his social advancement. They were afraid he was a snob. And of course he was. He was a colossal snob. He was a snob without shame. He would put up with any affront, he would ignore any rebuff, he would swallow any rudeness to get asked to a party he wanted to go to or to make a connection with some crusty old dowager of great name. He was indefatigable. When he had fixed his eye on his prey he hunted it with the persistence of a botanist who will expose himself to dangers of flood, earthquake, fever and hostile natives to find an orchid of peculiar rarity. The war of 1914 gave him his final chance. When it broke out he joined an ambulance corps and served first in Flanders and then in the Argonne; he came back after a year with a red ribbon in his buttonhole and secured a position in the Red Cross in Paris. By then he was in affluent circumstances and he contributed generously to the good works patronized by persons of consequence. He was always ready with his exquisite taste and his gift for organization to help in any charitable function that was widely publicized. He became a member of the two most exclusive clubs in Paris. He was *ce cher Elliott* to the greatest ladies in France. He had finally arrived.

When I first met Elliott I was just a young author like another and he took no notice of me. He never forgot a face and when I ran across him here or there he shook hands with me cordially, but showed no desire to further our acquaintance; and if I saw him at the opera, say, he being with a person of high rank, he was apt not to catch sight of me. But then I happened to make a somewhat startling success as a playwright, and presently I became aware that Elliott regarded me with a warmer feeling. One day I received a note from him asking me to lunch at Claridge's, where he lived when in London. It was a small party and not a very smart one, and I conceived the notion that he was trying me out. But from then on, since my success had brought me many new friends, I began to see him more frequently. Shortly after this I spent some weeks of the autumn in Paris and met him at the house of a common acquaintance. He asked me where I was staying and in a day or two I received another invitation to lunch, this time at his apartment; when I arrived I was surprised to see that it was a party of considerable distinction. I giggled to myself. I knew that with his perfect sense of social relations he had realized that in English society as an author I was not of much account, but that in France, where an author just because he is an author has prestige, I was. During the years that followed our acquaintance became fairly intimate without ever developing into friendship. I doubt whether it was possible for Elliott Templeton to be a friend. He took no interest in people apart from their social position. When I chanced to be in Paris or he in London, he continued to ask me to parties when he wanted an extra man or was obliged to entertain travelling Americans. Some of these were, I suspected, old clients and some were strangers sent to him with letters of introduction. They were the cross of his life. He felt he had to do something for them and yet was unwilling to have them meet his grand friends. The best way of disposing of them of course was to give them dinner and take them to a play, but that was often difficult when he was engaged every evening for three weeks ahead, and also he had an inkling that they would scarcely be satisfied with that. Since I was an author and so of little consequence he didn't mind telling me his troubles on this matter.

"People in America are so inconsiderate in the way they give letters. It's not that I'm not delighted to see the people who are sent to me, but I really don't see why I should inflict them on my friends."

He sought to make amends by sending them great baskets of roses and huge boxes of chocolate, but sometimes he had to do more. It was then,

somewhat naïvely after what he had told me, that he asked me to co
to the party he was organizing.

"They want to meet you so much," he wrote to flatter me. "Mrs. So and
So is a very cultivated woman and she's read every word you've written."
Mrs. So and So would then tell me she'd so much enjoyed my book *Mr.
Perrin and Mr. Traill* and congratulate me on my play *The Mollusc*. The
first of these was written by Hugh Walpole and the second by Hubert
Henry Davies.

(iv)

If I have given the reader an impression that Elliott Templeton was a
despicable character I have done him an injustice.

He was for one thing what the French call *serviable,* a word for which,
so far as I know, there is no exact equivalent in English. The dictionary
tells one that *serviceable* in the sense of helpful, obliging and kind is
archaic. That is just what Elliott was. He was generous, and though early
in his career he had doubtless showered flowers, candy and presents on his
acquaintances from an ulterior motive, he continued to do so when it
was no longer necessary. It caused him pleasure to give. He was hospitable. His chef was as good as any in Paris and you could be sure at his
table of having set before you the earliest delicacies of the season. His
wine proved the excellence of his judgment. It is true that his guests were
chosen for their social importance rather than because they were good
company, but he took care to invite at least one or two for their powers
of entertainment, so that his parties were almost always amusing. People
laughed at him behind his back and called him a filthy snob, but nevertheless accepted his invitations with alacrity. His French was fluent and cor-
rect and his accent perfect. He had taken great pains to adopt the manner
of speech as it is spoken in England and you had to have a very sensitive
ear to catch now and then an American intonation. He was a good talker
if only you could keep him off the subject of dukes and duchesses, but even
about them, now that his position was unassailable, he allowed himself,
especially when you were alone with him, to be amusing. He had a pleasantly malicious tongue and there was no scandal about these exalted personages that did not reach his ears. From him I learnt who was the father of
the Princess X's last child and who was the mistress of the Marquis de Y.
I don't believe even Marcel Proust knew more of the inner life of the
aristocracy than Elliott Templeton.

When I was in Paris we used often to lunch together, sometimes at his
apartment and sometimes at a restaurant. I like to wander about the an-

...ity shops, occasionally to buy but more often to look, and Elliott was always enchanted to go with me. He had knowledge and a real love of beautiful objects. I think he knew every shop of the kind in Paris and was on familiar terms with the proprietor. He adored haggling and when we started out would say to me:

"If there's anything you want don't try to buy it yourself. Just give me a hint and let me do the rest."

He would be delighted when he had got for me something I fancied for half the asking price. It was a treat to watch him bargain. He would argue, cajole, lose his temper, appeal to the seller's better nature, ridicule him, point out the defects of the object in question, threaten never to cross his threshold again, sigh, shrug his shoulders, admonish, start for the door in frowning anger and when finally he had won his point shake his head sadly as though he accepted defeat with resignation. Then he would whisper to me in English:

"Take it with you. It would be cheap at double the money."

Elliott was a zealous Catholic. He had not lived long in Paris before he met an abbé who was celebrated for his success in bringing infidels and heretics back to the fold. He was a great diner out and a noted wit. He confined his ministrations to the rich and the aristocratic. It was inevitable that Elliott should be attracted by a man who, though of humble origins, was a welcome guest in the most exclusive houses, and he confided to a wealthy American lady who was one of the abbé's recent converts that, though his family had always been Episcopalian, he had for long been interested in the Catholic Church. She asked Elliott to meet the abbé at dinner one evening, just the three of them, and the abbé was scintillating. Elliott's hostess brought the conversation around to Catholicism and the abbé spoke of it with unction, but without pedantry, as a man of the world, though a priest, speaking to another man of the world. Elliott was flattered to discover that the abbé knew all about him.

"The Duchesse de Vendôme was speaking of you the other day. She told me that she thought you highly intelligent."

Elliott flushed with pleasure. He had been presented to Her Royal Highness, but it had never occurred to him that she would give him a second thought. The abbé spoke of the faith with wisdom and benignity; he was broad-minded, modern in his outlook and tolerant. He made the Church seem to Elliott very like a select club that a well-bred man owed it to himself to belong to. Six months later he was received into it. His conversion, combined with the generosity he showed in his contributions to Catholic charities, opened several doors that had been closed to him before.

8

It may be that his motives in abandoning the faith of his fathers were mixed, but there could be no doubt of his devoutness when he had done so. He attended Mass every Sunday at the church frequented by the best people, went to confession regularly and made periodical visits to Rome. In course of time he was rewarded for his piety by being made a papal chamberlain, and the assiduity with which he performed the duties of his office was rewarded by the order of, I think, the Holy Sepulchre. His career as a Catholic was in fact no less successful than his career as an *homme du monde*.

I often asked myself what was the cause of the snobbishness that obsessed this man who was so intelligent, so kindly and so cultivated. He was no upstart. His father had been president of one of the southern universities and his grandfather a divine of some eminence. Elliott was too clever not to see that many of the persons who accepted his invitations did so only to get a free meal and that of these some were stupid and some worthless. The glamour of their resounding titles blinded him to their faults. I can only guess that to be on terms of intimate familiarity with these gentlemen of ancient lineage, to be the faithful retainer of their ladies gave him a sensation of triumph that never palled; and I think that at the back of it all was a passionate romanticism that led him to see in the weedy little French duke the crusader who had gone to the Holy Land with Saint Louis and in the blustering, fox-hunting English earl the ancestor who had attended Henry the Eighth to the Field of the Cloth of Gold. In the company of such as these he felt that he lived in a spacious and gallant past. I think when he turned the pages of the *Almanach de Gotha* his heart beat warmly as one name after another brought back to him recollections of old wars, historic sieges and celebrated duels, diplomatic intrigues and the love affairs of kings. Such anyhow was Elliott Templeton.

(v)

I was having a wash and a brush up before starting out to go to the luncheon Elliott had invited me to when they rang up from the desk to say that he was below. I was a little surprised, but as soon as I was ready went down.

"I thought it would be safer if I came and fetched you," he said as we shook hands. "I don't know how well you know Chicago."

He had the feeling I have noticed in some Americans who have lived many years abroad that America is a difficult and even dangerous place in which the European cannot safely be left to find his way about by himself.

"It's early yet. We might walk part of the way," he suggested.

There was a slight nip in the air, but not a cloud in the sky, and it was pleasant to stretch one's legs.

"I thought I'd better tell you about my sister before you meet her," said Elliott as we walked along. "She's stayed with me once or twice in Paris, but I don't think you were there at the time. It's not a big party, you know. Only my sister and her daughter Isabel and Gregory Brabazon."

"The decorator?" I asked.

"Yes. My sister's house is awful, and Isabel and I want her to have it done over. I happened to hear that Gregory was in Chicago and so I got her to ask him to lunch today. He's not quite a gentleman, of course, but he has taste. He did Raney Castle for Mary Olifant and St. Clement Talbot for the St. Erths. The duchess was delighted with him. You'll see Louisa's house for yourself. How she can have lived in it all these years I shall never understand. For the matter of that how she can live in Chicago I shall never understand either."

It appeared that Mrs. Bradley was a widow with three children, two sons and a daughter; but the sons were much older and married. One was in a government post in the Philippines and the other, in the diplomatic service as his father had been, was at Buenos Aires. Mrs. Bradley's husband had occupied posts in various parts of the world, and after being first secretary in Rome for some years was made minister to one of the republics on the west coast of South America and had there died.

"I wanted Louisa to sell the house in Chicago when he passed over," Elliott went on, "but she had a sentiment about it. It had been in the Bradley family for quite a long while. The Bradleys are one of the oldest families in Illinois. They came from Virginia in 1839 and took up land about sixty miles from what is now Chicago. They still own it." Elliott hesitated a little and looked at me to see how I would take it. "The Bradley who settled here was what I suppose you might call a farmer. I'm not sure whether you know, but about the middle of last century, when the Middle West began to be opened up, quite a number of Virginians, younger sons of good family, you know, were tempted by the lure of the unknown to leave the fleshpots of their native state. My brother-in-law's father, Chester Bradley, saw that Chicago had a future and entered a law office here. At all events he made enough money to leave his son very adequately provided for."

Elliott's manner, rather than his words, suggested that perhaps it was not quite the thing for the late Chester Bradley to have left the stately mansion and the broad acres he had inherited to enter an office, but the fact that he had amassed a fortune at least partly compensated for it. Elliott was none too pleased when on a later occasion Mrs. Bradley showed me some snapshots of what he called their "place" in the country, and I saw a modest frame house with a pretty little garden, but with a barn and a cowhouse and hog pens within a stone's throw, surrounded by a desolate waste of flat fields. I couldn't help thinking that Mr. Chester Bradley knew what he was about when he abandoned this to make his way in the city.

Presently we hailed a taxi. It put us down before a brownstone house, narrow and rather high, and you ascended to the front door by a flight of steep steps. It was in a row of houses, in a street that led off Lake Shore Drive, and its appearance, even on that bright autumn day, was so drab that you wondered how anyone could feel any sentiment about it. The door was opened by a tall and stout Negro butler with white hair, and we were ushered into the drawing-room. Mrs. Bradley got up from her chair as we came in and Elliott presented me to her. She must have been a handsome woman when young, for her features, though on the large side, were good and she had fine eyes. But her sallowish face, almost aggressively destitute of make-up, had sagged and it was plain that she had lost the battle with the corpulence of middle age. I surmised that she was unwilling to accept defeat, for when she sat down she sat very erect in a straight-backed chair which the cruel armour of her corsets doubtless made more comfortable than an upholstered one. She wore a blue gown, heavily braided, and her high collar was stiff with whalebone. She had a fine head of white hair tightly marcelled and intricately dressed. Her other guest had not arrived and while waiting for him we talked of one thing and another.

"Elliott tells me that you came over by the southern route," said Mrs. Bradley. "Did you stop in Rome?"

"Yes, I spent a week there."

"And how is dear Queen Margherita?"

Somewhat surprised by her question, I said I didn't know.

"Oh, didn't you go and see her? Such a very nice woman. She was so kind to us when we were in Rome. Mr. Bradley was first secretary. Why didn't you go and see her? You're not like Elliott, so black that you can't go to the Quirinal?"

"Not at all," I smiled. "The fact is I don't know her."

"Don't you?" said Mrs. Bradley as though she could hardly believe her ears. "Why not?"

"To tell you the truth authors don't hobnob with kings and queens as a general rule."

"But she's such a sweet woman," Mrs. Bradley expostulated, as though it were very hoity-toity of me not to know that royal personage. "I'm sure you'd like her."

At this moment the door was opened and the butler ushered in Gregory Brabazon.

Gregory Brabazon, notwithstanding his name, was not a romantic creature. He was a short, very fat man, as bald as an egg except for a ring of black curly hair round his ears and at the back of his neck, with a red, naked face that looked as though it were on the point of breaking out into a violent sweat, quick gray eyes, sensual lips and a heavy jowl. He was an Englishman and I had sometimes met him at bohemian parties in London. He was very jovial, very hearty and laughed a great deal, but you didn't have to be a great judge of character to know that his noisy friendliness was merely cover for a very astute man of business. He had been for some years the most successful decorator in London. He had a great booming voice and little fat hands that were wonderfully expressive. With telling gestures, with a spate of excited words he could thrill the imagination of a doubting client so that it was almost impossible to withhold the order he seemed to make it a favour to accept.

The butler came in again with a tray of cocktails.

"We won't wait for Isabel," said Mrs. Bradley as she took one.

"Where is she?" asked Elliott.

"She went to play golf with Larry. She said she might be late."

Elliott turned to me.

"Larry is Laurence Darrell. Isabel is supposed to be engaged to him."

"I didn't know you drank cocktails, Elliott," I said.

"I don't," he answered grimly, as he sipped the one he had taken, "but in this barbarous land of prohibition what can one do?" He sighed. "They're beginning to serve them in some houses in Paris. Evil communications corrupt good manners."

"Stuff and nonsense, Elliott," said Mrs. Bradley.

She said it good-naturedly enough, but with a decision that suggested to me that she was a woman of character and I suspected from the look she gave him, amused but shrewd, that she had no illusions about him. I wondered what she would make of Gregory Brabazon. I had caught the professional look he gave the room as he came in and the involuntary lifting of his bushy eyebrows. It was indeed an amazing room. The paper on the walls, the cretonne of the curtains and on the upholstered furniture were of the same pattern; on the walls were oil paintings in massive gold frames that the Bradleys had evidently bought when they were in Rome. Virgins of the school of Raphael, Virgins of the school of Guido Reni, landscapes of the school of Zuccarelli, ruins of the school of Pannini. There were the trophies of their sojourn in Peking, blackwood tables too profusely carved, huge cloisonné vases, and there were the purchases they had made in Chili or Peru, obese figures in hard stone and earthenware vases. There was a Chippendale writing table and a marquetry vitrine. The lampshades were of white silk on which some ill-advised artist had painted shepherds and shepherdesses in Watteau costumes. It was hideous and yet, I don't know why, agreeable. It had a homely, lived-in air and you felt that that incredible jumble had a significance. All those incongruous objects belonged together because they were part of Mrs. Bradley's life.

We had just finished our cocktails when the door was flung open and a girl came in, followed by a boy.

"Are we late?" she asked. "I've brought Larry back. Is there anything for him to eat?"

"I expect so," smiled Mrs. Bradley. "Ring the bell and tell Eugene to put another place."

"He opened the door for us. I've already told him."

"This is my daughter Isabel," said Mrs. Bradley, turning to me. "And this is Laurence Darrell."

Isabel gave me a rapid handshake and turned impetuously to Gregory Brabazon.

"Are you Mr. Brabazon? I've been crazy to meet you. I love what you've done for Clementine Dormer. Isn't this room terrible? I've been trying to get Mamma to do something about it for years and now you're in Chicago it's our chance. Tell me honestly what you think of it."

I knew that was the last thing Brabazon would do. He gave Mrs. Bradley a quick glance, but her impassive face told him nothing. He decided that Isabel was the person who counted and broke into a boisterous laugh.

"I'm sure it's very comfortable and all that," he said, "but if you ask me point-blank, well, I do think it's pretty awful."

Isabel was a tall girl with the oval face, straight nose, fine eyes and full mouth that appeared to be characteristic of the family. She was comely though on the fat side, which I ascribed to her age, and I guessed that she would fine down as she grew older. She had strong, good hands, though they also were a trifle fat, and her legs, displayed by her short skirt, were fat too. She had a good skin and a high colour, which exercise and the drive back in an open car had doubtless heightened. She was sparkling and vivacious. Her radiant health, her playful gaiety, her enjoyment of life, the happiness you felt in her were exhilarating. She was so natural that she made Elliott, for all his elegance, look rather tawdry. Her freshness made Mrs. Bradley, with her pasty, lined face, look tired and old.

We went down to lunch. Gregory Brabazon blinked when he saw the dining-room. The walls were papered with a dark red paper that imitated stuff and hung with portraits of grim, sour-faced men and women, very badly painted, who were the immediate forbears of the late Mr. Bradley. He was there, too, with a heavy moustache, very stiff in a frock coat and a white starched collar. Mrs. Bradley, painted by a French artist of the nineties, hung over the chimney piece in full evening dress of pale blue satin with pearls round her neck and a diamond star in her hair. With one bejewelled hand she fingered a lace scarf so carefully painted that you could count every stitch and with the other negligently held an ostrich-feather fan. The furniture, of black oak, was overwhelming.

"What do you think of it?" asked Isabel of Gregory Brabazon as we sat down.

"I'm sure it cost a great deal of money," he answered.

"It did," said Mrs. Bradley. "It was given to us as a wedding present by Mr. Bradley's father. It's been all over the world with us. Lisbon, Peking, Quito, Rome. Dear Queen Margherita admired it very much."

"What would you do if it was yours?" Isabel asked Brabazon, but before he could answer, Elliott answered for him.

"Burn it," he said.

The three of them began to discuss how they would treat the room. Elliott was all for Louis Quinze, while Isabel wanted a refectory table and Italian chairs. Brabazon thought Chippendale would be more in keeping with Mrs. Bradley's personality.

"I always think that's so important," he said, "a person's personality." He turned to Elliott. "Of course you know the Duchess of Olifant?"

"Mary? She's one of my most intimate friends."

"She wanted me to do her dining-room and the moment I saw her I said George the Second."

"How right you were. I noticed the room the last time I dined there. It's in perfect taste."

So the conversation went on. Mrs. Bradley listened, but you could not tell what she was thinking. I said little and Isabel's young man, Larry, I'd forgotten his surname, said nothing at all. He was sitting on the other side of the table between Brabazon and Elliott and every now and then I glanced at him. He looked very young. He was about the same height as Elliott, just under six feet, thin and loose-limbed. He was a pleasant-looking boy, neither handsome nor plain, rather shy and in no way remarkable. I was interested in the fact that though, so far as I could remember, he hadn't said half a dozen words since entering the house, he seemed perfectly at ease and in a curious way appeared to take part in the conversation without opening his mouth. I noticed his hands. They were long, but not large for his size, beautifully shaped and at the same time strong. I thought that a painter would be pleased to paint them. He was slightly built but not delicate in appearance; on the contrary I should have said he was wiry and resistant. His face, grave in repose, was tanned, but otherwise there was little colour in it, and his features, though regular enough, were undistinguished. He had rather high cheekbones and his temples were hollow. He had dark brown hair with a slight wave in it. His eyes looked larger than they really were because they were deep set in the orbits and his lashes were thick and long. His eyes were peculiar, not of the rich hazel that Isabel shared with her mother and her uncle, but so dark that the iris made one colour with the pupil and this gave them a peculiar intensity. He had a natural grace that was attractive and I could see why Isabel had been taken by him. Now and again her glance rested on him for a moment and I seemed to see in her expression not only love but fondness. Their eyes met and there was in his a tenderness that was beautiful to see. There is nothing more touching than the sight of young love, and I, a middle-aged man then, envied them, but at the same time, I couldn't imagine why, I felt sorry for them. It was silly because, so far as I knew, there was no impediment to their happiness; their circumstances seemed easy and there was no reason why they should not marry and live happily ever afterwards.

Isabel, Elliott and Gregory Brabazon went on talking of the redecoration of the house, trying to get out of Mrs. Bradley at least an admission that something should be done, but she only smiled amiably.

"You mustn't try to rush me. I want to have time to think it over." She turned to the boy. "What do you think of it all, Larry?"

He looked round the table, a smile in his eyes.

"I don't think it matters one way or the other," he said.

"You beast, Larry," cried Isabel. "I particularly told you to back us up."

"If Aunt Louisa is happy with what she's got what is the object of changing?"

His question was so much to the point and so sensible that it made me laugh. He looked at me then and smiled.

"And don't grin like that just because you've made a very stupid remark," said Isabel.

But he only grinned the more, and I noticed then that he had small and white and regular teeth. There was something in the look he gave Isabel that made her flush and catch her breath. Unless I was mistaken she was madly in love with him, but I don't know what it was that gave me the feeling that in her love for him there was also something maternal. It was a little unexpected in so young a girl. With a soft smile on her lips she directed her attention once more to Gregory Brabazon.

"Don't pay any attention to him. He's very stupid and entirely uneducated. He doesn't know anything about anything except flying."

"Flying?" I said.

"He was an aviator in the war."

"I should have thought he was too young to have been in the war."

"He was. Much too young. He behaved very badly. He ran away from school and went to Canada. By lying his head off he got them to believe he was eighteen and got into the air corps. He was fighting in France at the time of the armistice."

"You're boring your mother's guests, Isabel," said Larry.

"I've known him all my life, and when he came back he looked lovely in his uniform, with all those pretty ribbons on his tunic, so I just sat on his doorstep, so to speak, till he consented to marry me just to have a little peace and quiet. The competition was awful."

"Really, Isabel," said her mother.

Larry leant over towards me.

"I hope you don't believe a word she says. Isabel isn't a bad girl really, but she's a liar."

Luncheon was finished and soon after Elliott and I left. I had told him before that I was going to the museum to look at the pictures and he said he would take me. I don't particularly like going to a gallery with anyone else, but I could not say I would sooner go alone and so accepted his company. On our way we spoke of Isabel and Larry.

"It's rather charming to see two young things so much in love with one another," I said.

"They're much too young to marry."

"Why? It's such fun to be young and in love and to marry."

"Don't be ridiculous. She's nineteen and he's only just twenty. He hasn't got a job. He has a tiny income, three thousand a year Louisa tells me, and Louisa's not a rich woman by any manner of means. She needs all she has."

"Well, he can get a job."

"That's just it. He's not trying to. He seems to be quite satisfied to do nothing."

"I daresay he had a pretty rough time in the war. He may want a rest."

"He's been resting for a year. That's surely long enough."

"I thought he seemed a nice sort of boy."

"Oh, I have nothing against him. He's quite well born and all that sort of thing. His father came from Baltimore. He was assistant professor of Romance languages at Yale or something like that. His mother was a Philadelphian of old Quaker stock."

"You speak of them in the past. Are they dead?"

"Yes, his mother died in childbirth and his father about twelve years ago. He was brought up by an old college friend of his father's who's a doctor at Marvin. That's how Louisa and Isabel knew him."

"Where's Marvin?"

"That's where the Bradley place is. Louisa spends the summer there. She was sorry for the child. Dr. Nelson's a bachelor and didn't know the first thing about bringing up a boy. It was Louisa who insisted that he should be sent to St. Paul's and she always had him out here for his Christmas vacation." Elliott shrugged a Gallic shoulder. "I should have thought she would foresee the inevitable result."

We had now arrived at the museum and our attention was directed to the pictures. Once more I was impressed by Elliott's knowledge and taste. He shepherded me around the rooms as though I were a group of tourists, and no professor of art could have discoursed more instructively than he did. Making up my mind to come again by myself when I could wander at will and have a good time, I submitted; after a while he looked at his watch.

"Let us go," he said. "I never spend more than one hour in a gallery. That is as long as one's power of appreciation persists. We will finish another day."

I thanked him warmly when we separated. I went my way perhaps a wiser but certainly a peevish man.

When I was saying good-bye to Mrs. Bradley she told me that next day Isabel was having a few of her young friends in to dinner and they were going on to dance afterwards and if I would come Elliott and I could have a talk when they had gone.

"You'll be doing him a kindness," she added. "He's been abroad so long, he feels rather out of it here. He doesn't seem able to find anyone he has anything in common with."

I accepted and before we parted on the museum steps Elliott told me he was glad I had.

"I'm like a lost soul in this great city," he said. "I promised Louisa to spend six weeks with her, we hadn't seen one another since 1912, but I'm counting the days till I can get back to Paris. It's the only place in the world for a civilized man to live. My dear fellow, d'you know how they look upon me here? They look upon me as a freak. Savages."

I laughed and left.

(vi)

The following evening, having refused Elliott's telephoned offer to fetch me, I arrived quite safely at Mrs. Bradley's house. I had been delayed by someone who had come to see me and was a trifle late. So much noise came from the sitting-room as I walked upstairs that I thought it must be a large party and I was surprised to find that there were, including myself, only twelve people. Mrs. Bradley was very grand in green satin with a dog collar of seed pearls round her neck, and Elliott in his well-cut dinner jacket looked elegant as he alone could look. When he shook hands with me my nostrils were assailed by all the perfumes of Arabia. I was introduced to a stoutish, tall man with a red face who looked somewhat ill at ease in evening clothes. He was a Dr. Nelson, but at the moment that meant nothing to me. The rest of the party consisted of Isabel's friends, but their names escaped me as soon as I heard them. The girls were young and pretty and the men young and upstanding. None of them made any impression on me except one boy and that only because he was so tall and so massive. He must have been six foot three or four and he had great broad shoulders. Isabel was looking very pretty; she was dressed in white silk, with a long, hobbled skirt that concealed her fat legs; the cut of her frock showed that she had well-developed breasts; her bare arms were a trifle fat, but her neck was lovely. She was excited and her fine eyes sparkled. There was no doubt about it, she was a very pretty and desirable young woman, but it was obvious that unless she took care she would develop an unbecoming corpulence.

At dinner I found myself placed between Mrs. Bradley and a shy drab girl who seemed even younger than the others. As we sat down, to make the way easier Mrs. Bradley explained that her grandparents lived at Marvin and that she and Isabel had been at school together. Her name, the only one I heard mentioned, was Sophie. A lot of chaff was bandied across the table, everyone talked at the top of his voice and there was a great deal of laughter. They seemed to know one another very well. When I was not occupied with my hostess I attempted to make conversation with my neighbor, but I had no great success. She was quieter than the rest. She was not pretty, but she had an amusing face, with a little tilted nose, a wide mouth and greenish blue eyes; her hair, simply done, was of a sandy brown. She was very thin and her chest was almost as flat as a boy's. She laughed at the badinage that went on, but in a manner that was a little forced so that you

18

felt she wasn't as much amused as she pretended to be. I guessed that she was making an effort to be a good sport. I could not make out if she was a trifle stupid or only painfully timid and, having tried various topics of conversation only to have them dropped, for want of anything better to say I asked her to tell me who all the people at table were.

"Well, you know Dr. Nelson," she said, indicating the middle-aged man who was opposite me on Mrs. Bradley's other side. "He's Larry's guardian. He's our doctor at Marvin. He's very clever, he invents gadgets for planes that no one will have anything to do with and when he isn't doing that he drinks."

There was a gleam in her pale eyes as she said this that made me suspect that there was more in her than I had at first supposed. She went on to give me the names of one young thing after another, who their parents were, and in the case of the men what college they had been to and what work they did. It wasn't very illuminating.

"She's very sweet," or: "He's a very good golfer."

"And who is that big fellow with the eyebrows?"

"That? Oh, that's Gray Maturin. His father's got an enormous house on the river at Marvin. He's our millionaire. We're very proud of him. He gives us class. Maturin, Hobbes, Rayner and Smith. He's one of the richest men in Chicago and Gray's his only son."

She put such a pleasant irony into that list of names that I gave her an inquisitive glance. She caught it and flushed.

"Tell me more about Mr. Maturin."

"There's nothing to tell. He's rich. He's highly respected. He built us a new church at Marvin and he's given a million dollars to the University of Chicago."

"His son's a fine-looking fellow."

"He's nice. You'd never think his grandfather was shanty Irish and his grandmother a Swedish waitress in an eating house."

Gray Maturin was striking rather than handsome. He had a rugged, un-finished look; a short blunt nose, a sensual mouth and the florid Irish com-plexion; a great quantity of raven black hair, very sleek, and under heavy eyebrows clear, very blue eyes. Though built on so large a scale he was finely proportioned, and stripped he must have been a fine figure of a man. He was obviously very powerful. His virility was impressive. He made Larry who was sitting next to him, though only three or four inches shorter, look puny.

"He's very much admired," said my shy neighbor. "I know several girls who would stop at nothing short of murder to get him. But they haven't a chance."

"Why not?"

"You don't know anything, do you?"

"How should I?"

"He's so much in love with Isabel, he can't see straight, and Isabel's in love with Larry."

"What's to prevent him from setting to and cutting Larry out?"

"Larry's his best friend."

"I suppose that complicates matters."

"If you're as high-principled as Gray is."

I was not sure whether she said this in all seriousness or whether there was in her tone a hint of mockery. There was nothing saucy in her manner, forward or pert, and yet I got the impression that she was lacking neither in humour nor in shrewdness. I wondered what she was really thinking while she made conversation with me, but that I knew I should never find out. She was obviously unsure of herself and I conceived the notion that she was an only child who had lived a secluded life with people a great deal older than herself. There was a modesty, an unobtrusiveness about her that I found engaging, but if I was right in thinking that she had lived much alone I guessed that she had quietly observed the older persons she lived with and had formed decided opinions upon them. We who are of mature age seldom suspect how unmercifully and yet with what insight the very young judge us. I looked again into her greenish blue eyes.

"How old are you?" I asked.

"Seventeen."

"Do you read much?" I asked at a venture.

But before she could answer, Mrs. Bradley, attentive to her duties as a hostess, drew me to her with some remark and before I could disengage myself dinner was at an end. The young people went off at once to wherever they were going and the four of us who were left went up to the sitting-room.

I was surprised that I had been asked to this party, for after a little desultory conversation they began to talk of a matter that I should have thought they would have preferred to discuss in private. I could not make up my mind whether it would be more discreet in me to get up and go or whether, as a disinterested audience of one, I was useful to them. The question at issue was Larry's odd disinclination to go to work, and it had been brought to a point by an offer from Mr. Maturin, the father of the boy who had been at dinner, to take him into his office. It was a fine opportunity. With ability and industry Larry could look forward to making in due course a great deal of money. Young Gray Maturin was eager for him to take it.

I cannot remember all that was said, but the gist of it is clear in my memory. On Larry's return from France Dr. Nelson, his guardian, had suggested that he should go to college, but he had refused. It was natural that he should want to do nothing for a while; he had had a hard time and had been twice, though not severely, wounded. Dr. Nelson thought that he was still suffering from shock and it seemed a good idea that he should rest till he had completely recovered. But the weeks passed into months and now it was over a year since he'd been out of uniform. It appeared that he had done well in the air corps and on his return he cut something of a figure in Chicago, the result of which was that several businessmen offered him positions. He thanked them, but refused. He gave no reason except that he hadn't made up his mind what he wanted to do. He became engaged to Isabel. This was no surprise to Mrs. Bradley since they had been inseparable for years and she knew that Isabel was in love with him. She was fond of him and thought he would make Isabel happy.

"Her character's stronger than his. She can give him just what he lacks."

Though they were both so young Mrs. Bradley was quite willing that they should marry at once, but she wasn't prepared that they should do so until Larry had gone to work. He had a little money of his own, but even if he had had ten times more than he had she would have insisted on this. So far as I could gather, what she and Elliott wished to find out from Dr. Nelson was what Larry intended to do. They wanted him to use his influence to get him to accept the job that Mr. Maturin offered him.

"You know I never had much authority over Larry," he said. "Even as a boy he went his own way."

"I know. You let him run wild. It's a miracle he's turned out as well as he has."

Dr. Nelson, who had been drinking quite heavily, gave her a sour look. His red face grew a trifle redder.

"I was very busy. I had my own affairs to attend to. I took him because there was nowhere else for him to go and his father was a friend of mine. He wasn't easy to do anything with."

"I don't know how you can say that," Mrs. Bradley answered tartly. "He has a very sweet disposition."

"What are you to do with a boy who never argues with you, but does exactly what he likes and when you get mad at him just says he's sorry and lets you storm? If he'd been my own son I could have beaten him. I couldn't beat a boy who hadn't got a relation in the world and whose father had left him to me because he thought I'd be kind to him."

"That's neither here nor there," said Elliott, somewhat irritably. "The position is this: he's dawdled around long enough; he's got a fine chance of a position in which he stands to make a lot of money and if he wants to marry Isabel he must take it."

"He must see that in the present state of the world," Mrs. Bradley put in, "a man has to work. He's perfectly strong and well now. We all know how after the war between the states there were men who never did a stroke after they came back from it. They were a burden to their families and useless to the community."

Then I added my word.

"But what reason does he give for refusing the various offers that are made him?"

"None. Except that they don't appeal to him."

"But doesn't he want to do anything?"

"Apparently not."

Dr. Nelson helped himself to another highball. He took a long drink and then looked at his two friends.

"Shall I tell you what my impression is? I daresay I'm not a great judge of human nature, but at any rate after thirty-odd years of practice I think I know something about it. The war did something to Larry. He didn't come back the same person that he went. It's not only that he's older. Something happened that changed his personality."

"What sort of thing?" I asked.

"I wouldn't know. He's very reticent about his war experiences." Dr. Nelson turned to Mrs. Bradley. "Has he ever talked to you about them, Louisa?"

She shook her head.

"No. When he first came back we tried to get him to tell us some of his adventures, but he only laughed in that way of his and said there was nothing to tell. He hasn't even told Isabel. She's tried and tried, but she hasn't got a thing out of him."

The conversation went on in this unsatisfactory way and presently Dr. Nelson, looking at his watch, said he must go. I prepared to leave with him, but Elliott pressed me to stay. When he had gone, Mrs. Bradley apologized for troubling me with their private affairs and expressed her fear that I had been bored.

"But you see it's all very much on my mind," she finished.

"Mr. Maugham is very discreet, Louisa; you needn't be afraid of telling him anything. I haven't the feeling that Bob Nelson and Larry are very close, but there are some things that Louisa and I thought we'd better not mention to him."

"Elliott."

"You've told him so much, you may as well tell him the rest. I don't know whether you noticed Gray Maturin at dinner?"

"He's so big, one could hardly fail to."

"He's a beau of Isabel's. All the time Larry was away he was very attentive. She likes him and if the war had lasted much longer she might very well have married him. He proposed to her. She didn't accept and she didn't refuse. Louisa guessed she didn't want to make up her mind till Larry came home."

"How is it that he wasn't in the war?" I asked.

"He strained his heart playing football. It's nothing serious, but the army wouldn't take him. Anyhow when Larry came home he had no chance. Isabel turned him down flat."

I didn't know what I was expected to say to that, so I said nothing. Elliott went on. With his distinguished appearance and his Oxford accent he couldn't have been more like an official of high standing at the Foreign Office.

"Of course Larry's a very nice boy and it was damned sporting of him to run away and join the air corps, but I'm a pretty good judge of character. . . ." He gave a knowing little smile and made the only reference I ever heard him make to the fact that he had made a fortune by dealing in works of art. "Otherwise I shouldn't have at this moment a tidy sum in gilt-edged securities. And my opinion is that Larry will never amount to very much. He has no money to speak of and no position. Gray Maturin is a very different proposition. He has a good old Irish name. They've had a bishop in the family, and a dramatist and several distinguished soldiers and scholars."

"How do you know all that?" I asked.

"It's the sort of thing one knows," he answered casually. "As a matter of fact I happened to be glancing through the Dictionary of National Biography the other day at the club and I came across the name."

I didn't think it was my business to repeat what my neighbor at dinner had told me of the shanty Irishman and the Swedish waitress who were Gray's grandfather and grandmother. Elliott proceeded.

"We've all known Henry Maturin for many years. He's a very fine man and a very rich one. Gray's stepping into the best brokerage house in Chicago. He's got the world at his feet. He wants to marry Isabel and one can't deny that from her point of view it would be a very good match. I'm all in favour of it myself and I know Louisa is too."

"You've been away from America so long, Elliott," said Mrs. Bradley, with a dry smile, "you've forgotten that in this country girls don't marry because their mothers and their uncles are in favour of it."

"That is nothing to be proud of, Louisa," said Elliott sharply. "As the result of thirty years' experience I may tell you that a marriage arranged with proper regard to position, fortune and community of circumstances has every advantage over a love match. In France, which after all is the only civilized country in the world, Isabel would marry Gray without thinking twice about it; then, after a year or two, if she wanted it, she'd take Larry as her lover, Gray would install a prominent actress in a luxurious apartment, and everyone would be perfectly happy."

Mrs. Bradley was no fool. She looked at her brother with sly amusement.

"The objection to that, Elliott, is that as the New York plays only come here for limited periods, Gray could only hope to keep the tenants of his luxurious apartment for a very uncertain length of time. That would surely be very unsettling for all parties."

Elliott smiled.

"Gray could buy a seat on the New York stock exchange. After all, if you must live in America I can't see any object in living anywhere but in New York."

I left soon after this, but before I did Elliott, I hardly know why, asked me if I would lunch with him to meet the Maturins, father and son.

"Henry is the best type of the American businessman," he said, "and I think you ought to know him. He's looked after our investments for many years."

I hadn't any particular wish to do this, but no reason to refuse, so I said I would be glad to.

(vii)

I had been put up for the length of my stay at a club which possessed a good library and next morning I went there to look at one or two of the university magazines that for the person who does not subscribe to them have always been rather hard to come by. It was early and there was only one other person there. He was seated in a big leather chair absorbed in a book. I was surprised to see it was Larry. He was the last person I should have expected to find in such a place. He looked up as I passed, recognized me and made as if to get up.

"Don't move," I said, and then almost automatically: "What are you reading?"

"A book," he said, with a smile, but a smile so engaging that the rebuff of his answer was in no way offensive.

24

He closed it and looking at me with his peculiarly opaque eyes held it so that I couldn't see the title.

"Did you have a good time last night?" I asked.

"Wonderful. Didn't get home till five."

"It's very strenuous of you to be here so bright and early."

"I come here a good deal. Generally I have the place to myself at this time."

"I won't disturb you."

"You're not disturbing me," he said, smiling again, and now it occurred to me that he had a smile of great sweetness. It was not a brilliant, flashing smile, it was a smile that lit his face as with an inner light. He was sitting in an alcove made by jutting out shelves and there was a chair next to him. He put his hand on the arm. "Won't you sit down for a minute?"

"All right."

He handed me the book he was holding.

"That's what I was reading."

I looked at it and saw it was William James's *Principles of Psychology*. It is, of course, a standard work and important in the history of the science with which it deals; it is moreover exceedingly readable; but it is not the sort of book I should have expected to see in the hands of a very young man, an aviator, who had been dancing till five in the morning.

"Why are you reading this?" I asked.

"I'm very ignorant."

"You're also very young," I smiled.

He did not speak for so long a time that I began to find the silence awkward and I was on the point of getting up and looking for the magazines I had come to find. But I had a feeling that he wanted to say something. He looked into vacancy, his face grave and intent, and seemed to meditate. I waited. I was curious to know what it was all about. When he began to speak it was as though he continued the conversation without awareness of that long silence.

"When I came back from France they all wanted me to go to college. I couldn't. After what I'd been through I felt I couldn't go back to school. I learnt nothing at my prep school anyway. I felt I couldn't enter into a freshman's life. They wouldn't have liked me. I didn't want to act a part I didn't feel. And I didn't think the instructors would teach me the sort of things I wanted to know."

"Of course I know that this is no business of mine," I said, "but I'm not convinced you were right. I think I understand what you mean and I can see that, after being in the war for two years, it would have been rather a nuisance to become the sort of glorified schoolboy an undergraduate is during his first and second years. I can't believe they wouldn't have liked you. I don't know much about American universities, but I don't believe American undergraduates are very different from English ones, perhaps a little more boisterous and a little more inclined to horseplay, but on the whole very decent, sensible boys, and I take it that if you don't want to lead their lives they're quite willing, if you exercise a little tact, to let you lead yours. I never went to Cambridge as my brothers did. I had the chance, but I refused it. I wanted to get out into the world. I've always regretted it. I think it would have saved me a lot of mistakes. You learn more quickly under the guidance of experienced teachers. You waste a lot of time going down blind alleys if you have no one to lead you."

"You may be right. I don't mind if I make mistakes. It may be that in one of the blind alleys I may find something to my purpose."

"What is your purpose?"

He hesitated a moment.

"That's just it. I don't quite know it yet."

I was silent, for there didn't seem to be anything to say in answer to that. I, who from a very early age have always had before me a clear and definite purpose, was inclined to feel impatient; but I chid myself; I had what I can only call an intuition that there was in the soul of that boy some confused striving, whether of half-thought-out ideas or of dimly felt emotions I could not tell, that filled him with a restlessness that urged him he did not know whither. He strangely excited my sympathy. I had never before heard him speak much and it was only now that I became conscious of the melodiousness of his voice. It was very persuasive. It was like balm. When I considered that, his engaging smile and the expressiveness of his very black eyes I could well understand that Isabel was in love with him. There was indeed something very lovable about him. He turned his head and looked at me without embarrassment, but with an expression in his eyes that was at once scrutinizing and amused.

"Am I right in thinking that after we all went off to dance last night you talked about me?"

"Part of the time."

"I thought that was why Uncle Bob had been pressed to come to dinner. He hates going out."

"It appears that you've got the offer of a very good job."

"A wonderful job."

"Are you going to take it?"

"I don't think so."

"Why not?"

"I don't want to."

I was butting into an affair that was no concern of mine, but I had a notion that just because I was a stranger from a foreign country Larry was not disinclined to talk to me about it.

"Well, you know when people are no good at anything else they become writers," I said, with a chuckle.

"I have no talent."

"Then what do you want to do?"

He gave me his radiant, fascinating smile.

"Loaf," he said.

I had to laugh.

"I shouldn't have thought Chicago the best place in the world to do that in," I said. "Anyhow, I'll leave you to your reading. I want to have a look at the *Yale Quarterly*."

I got up. When I left the library Larry was still absorbed in William James's book. I lunched by myself at the club and since it was quiet in the library went back there to smoke my cigar and idle an hour or two away, reading and writing letters. I was surprised to see Larry still immersed in his book. He looked as if he hadn't moved since I left him. He was still there when about four I went away. I was struck by his evident power of concentration. He had neither noticed me go nor come. I had various things to do during the afternoon and did not go back to the Blackstone till it was time to change for the dinner party I was going to. On my way I was seized with an impulse of curiosity. I dropped into the club once more and went into the library. There were quite a number of people there then, reading the papers and what not. Larry was still sitting in the same chair, intent on the same book. Odd!

(*viii*)

Next day Elliott asked me to lunch at the Palmer House to meet the elder Maturin and his son. We were only four. Henry Maturin was a big man, nearly as big as his son, with a red fleshy face and a great jowl, and he had the same blunt, aggressive nose, but his eyes were smaller than his son's, not so blue and very, very shrewd. Though he could not have been much more than fifty he looked ten years older and his hair, rapidly thinning, was snow-white. At first sight he was not prepossessing. He looked as though for many years he had done himself too well, and I received the impression of a brutal, clever, competent man who, in business matters at all events, would be pitiless. At first he said little and I had a notion that he

27

was taking my measure. I could not but perceive that he looked upon Elliott as something of a joke. Gray, amiable and polite, was almost completely silent and the party would have been sticky if Elliott, with his perfect social tact, hadn't kept up a flow of easy conversation. I guessed that in the past he had acquired a good deal of experience in dealing with Middle Western businessmen who had to be cajoled into paying a fancy price for an old master. Presently Mr. Maturin began to feel more at his ease and he made one or two remarks that showed he was brighter than he looked and indeed had a dry sense of humour. For a while the conversation turned on stocks and shares. I should have been surprised to discover that Elliott was very knowledgeable on the subject if I had not long been aware that for all his nonsense he was nobody's fool. It was then that Mr. Maturin remarked:

"I had a letter from Gray's friend Larry Darrell this morning."

"You didn't tell me, Dad," said Gray.

Mr. Maturin turned to me.

"You know Larry, don't you?" I nodded. "Gray persuaded me to take him into my business. They're great friends. Gray thinks the world of him."

"What did he say, Dad?"

"He thanked me. He said he realized it was a great chance for a young fellow and he'd thought it over very carefully and had come to the conclusion he'd be a disappointment to me and thought it better to refuse."

"That's very foolish of him," said Elliott.

"It is," said Mr. Maturin.

"I'm awfully sorry, Dad," said Gray. "It would have been grand if we could have worked together."

"You can lead a horse to the water, but you can't make him drink."

Mr. Maturin looked at his son while he said this and his shrewd eyes softened. I realized that there was another side to the hard businessman; he doted on this great hulking son of his. He turned to me once more.

"D'you know, that boy did our course in two under par on Sunday. He beat me seven and six. I could have brained him with my niblick. And to think that I taught him to play golf myself."

He was brimming over with pride. I began to like him.

"I had a lot of luck, Dad."

"Not a bit of it. Is it luck when you get out of a bunker and lay your ball six inches from the hole? Thirty-five yards if it was an inch, the shot was. I want him to go into the amateur championship next year."

"I shouldn't be able to spare the time."

"I'm your boss, ain't I?"

"Don't I know it! The hell you raise if I'm a minute late at the office."

Mr. Maturin chuckled.

"He's trying to make me out a tyrant," he said to me. "Don't you believe him. I'm my business, my partners are no good, and I'm very proud of my business. I've started this boy of mine at the bottom and I expect him to work his way up just like any young fellow I've hired, so that when the time comes for him to take my place he'll be ready for it. It's a great responsibility, a business like mine. I've looked after the investments of some of my clients for thirty years and they trust me. To tell you the truth, I'd rather lose my own money than see them lose theirs."

Gray laughed.

"The other day when an old girl came in and wanted to invest a thousand dollars in a wildcat scheme that her minister had recommended he refused to take the order, and when she insisted he gave her such hell that she went out sobbing. And then he called up the minister and gave him hell too."

"People say a lot of hard things about us brokers, but there are brokers and brokers. I don't want people to lose money, I want them to make it, and the way they act, most of them, you'd think their one object in life was to get rid of every cent they have."

"Well, what did you think of him?" Elliott asked me as we walked away after the Maturins had left us to go back to the office.

"I'm always glad to meet new types. I thought the mutual affection of father and son was rather touching. I don't know that that's so common in England."

"He adores that boy. He's a queer mixture. What he said about his clients was quite true. He's got hundreds of old women, retired service men and ministers whose savings he looks after. I'd have thought they were more trouble than they're worth, but he takes pride in the confidence they have in him. But when he's got some big deal on and he's up against powerful interests there isn't a man who can be harder and more ruthless. There's no mercy there then. He wants his pound of flesh and there's nothing much he'll stop at to get it. Get on the wrong side of him and he'll not only ruin you, but get a big laugh out of doing it."

On getting home Elliott told Mrs. Bradley that Larry had refused Henry Maturin's offer. Isabel had been lunching with girl friends and came in while they were still talking about it. They told her. I gathered from Elliott's account of the conversation that ensued that he had expressed himself with considerable eloquence. Though he had certainly not done a stroke of work for ten years, and the work by which he had amassed an ample competence had been far from arduous, he was firmly of opinion that for the run of mankind industry was essential. Larry was a perfectly ordinary young fellow, of no social consequence, and there was no possible reason why he shouldn't conform with the commendable customs of his country. It was evident to a man as clear-sighted as Elliott that America was entering upon a period of prosperity such as it had never known. Larry had a chance of getting in on the ground floor, and if he kept his nose to the grindstone he might well be many times a millionaire by the time he was forty. If he wanted to retire then and live like a gentleman, in Paris, say, with an apartment in the Avenue du Bois and a château in Touraine, he (Elliott) would have nothing to say against it. But Louisa Bradley was more succinct and more unanswerable.

"If he loves you, he ought to be prepared to work for you."

I don't know what Isabel answered to all this, but she was sensible enough to see that her elders had reason on their side. All the young men of her acquaintance were studying to enter some profession or already busy in an office. Larry could hardly expect to live the rest of his life on his distinguished record in the air corps. The war was over, everyone was sick of it and anxious only to forget about it as quickly as possible. The result of the discussion was that Isabel agreed to have the matter out with Larry once and for all. Mrs. Bradley suggested that Isabel should ask him to drive her down to Marvin. She was ordering new curtains for the living-room and had mislaid the measurements, so she wanted Isabel to take them again.

"Bob Nelson will give you luncheon," she said.

"I have a better plan than that," said Elliott. "Put up a luncheon basket for them and let them lunch on the stoop and after lunch they can talk."

"That would be fun," said Isabel.

"There are few things so pleasant as a picnic lunch eaten in perfect comfort," Elliott added sententiously. "The old Duchesse d'Uzès used to tell me that the most recalcitrant male becomes amenable to suggestion in these conditions. What will you give them for luncheon?"

"Stuffed eggs and a chicken sandwich."

"Nonsense. You can't have a picnic without *pâté de foie gras*. You must give them curried shrimps to start with, breast of chicken in aspic, with a heart-of-lettuce salad for which I'll make the dressing myself, and after the *pâté* if you like, as a concession to your American habits, an apple pie."

"I shall give them stuffed eggs and a chicken sandwich, Elliott," said Mrs. Bradley with decision.

"Well, mark my words, it'll be a failure and you'll only have yourself to blame."

"Larry eats very little, Uncle Elliott," said Isabel, "and I don't believe he notices what he eats."

"I hope you don't think that is to his credit, my poor child," her uncle returned.

But what Mrs. Bradley said they should have was what they got. When Elliott later told me the outcome of the excursion he shrugged his shoulders in a very French way.

"I told them it would be a failure. I begged Louisa to put in a bottle of the Montrachet I sent her just before the war, but she wouldn't listen to me. They took a thermos of hot coffee and nothing else. What would you expect?"

It appeared that Louisa Bradley and Elliott were sitting by themselves in the living-room when they heard the car stop at the door and Isabel come into the house. It was just after dark and the curtains were drawn. Elliott was lounging in an armchair by the fireside reading a novel and Mrs. Bradley was at work on a piece of tapestry that was to be made into a fire screen. Isabel did not come in, but went on up to her room. Elliott looked over his spectacles at his sister.

"I expect she's gone to take off her hat. She'll be down in a minute," she said.

But Isabel did not come. Several minutes passed.

"Perhaps she's tired. She may be lying down."

"Wouldn't you have expected Larry to come in?"

"Don't be exasperating, Elliott."

"Well, it's your business, not mine."

He returned to his book. Mrs. Bradley went on working. But when half an hour had gone by she got up suddenly.

"I think perhaps I'd better go up and see that she's all right. If she's resting I won't disturb her."

She left the room, but in a very short while came down again.

"She's been crying. Larry's going to Paris. He's going to be away for two years. She's promised to wait for him."

"Why does he want to go to Paris?"

"It's no good asking me questions, Elliott. I don't know. She won't tell me anything. She says she understands and she isn't going to stand in his way. I said to her, 'If he's prepared to leave you for two years he can't love you very much.' 'I can't help that,' she said, 'the thing that matters is that I love *him* very much.' 'Even after what's happened today?' I said. 'Today's made me love him more than ever I did,' she said, 'and he does love me, Mamma. I'm sure of that.'"

31

Elliott reflected for a while.

"And what's to happen at the end of two years?"

"I tell you I don't know, Elliott."

"Don't you think it's very unsatisfactory?"

"Very."

"There's only one thing to be said and that is that they're both very young. It won't hurt them to wait two years and in that time a lot may happen."

They agreed that it would be better to leave Isabel in peace. They were going out to dinner that night.

"I don't want to upset her," said Mrs. Bradley. "People would only wonder if her eyes were all swollen."

But next day after luncheon, which they had by themselves, Mrs. Bradley brought the subject up again. But she got little out of Isabel.

"There's really nothing more to tell you than I've told you already, Mamma," she said.

"But what does he want to do in Paris?"

Isabel smiled, for she knew how preposterous her answer would seem to her mother.

"Loaf."

"Loaf? What on earth do you mean?"

"That's what he told me."

"Really I have no patience with you. If you had any spirit you'd have broken off your engagement there and then. He's just playing with you."

Isabel looked at the ring she wore on her left hand.

"What can I do? I love him."

Then Elliott entered the conversation. He approached the matter with his famous tact, "Not as if I was her uncle, my dear fellow, but as a man of the world speaking to an inexperienced girl," but he did no better than her mother had done. I received the impression that she had told him, no doubt politely but quite unmistakably, to mind his own business. Elliott told me all this later on in the day in the little sitting-room I had at the Blackstone.

"Of course Louisa is quite right," he added. "It's all very unsatisfactory, but that's the sort of thing you run up against when young people are left to arrange their marriages on no better basis than mutual inclination. I've told Louisa not to worry; I think it'll turn out better than she expects. With Larry out of the way and young Gray Maturin on the spot—well, if I know anything about my fellow creatures the outcome is fairly obvious. When you're eighteen your emotions are violent, but they're not durable."

"You're full of worldly wisdom, Elliott," I smiled.

"I haven't read my La Rochefoucauld for nothing. You know what Chicago is; they'll be meeting all the time. It flatters a girl to have a man so devoted to her, and when she knows there isn't one of her girl friends who wouldn't be only too glad to marry him—well, I ask you, is it in human nature to resist the temptation of cutting out everyone else? I mean, it's like going to a party where you know you'll be bored to distraction and the only refreshments will be lemonade and biscuits; but you go because you know your best friends would give their eyeteeth to and haven't been asked."

"When does Larry go?"

"I don't know. I don't think that's been decided yet." Elliott took a long, thin cigarette case in platinum and gold out of his pocket and extracted an Egyptian cigarette. Not for him were Fatimas, Chesterfields, Camels or Lucky Strikes. He looked at me with a smile full of insinuation. "Of course I wouldn't care to say so to Louisa, but I don't mind telling you that I have a sneaking sympathy for the young fellow. I understand that he got a glimpse of Paris during the war, and I can't blame him if he was captivated by the only city in the world fit for a civilized man to live in. He's young and I have no doubt he wants to sow his wild oats before he settles down to married life. Very natural and very proper. I'll keep an eye on him. I'll introduce him to the right people; he has nice manners and with a hint or two from me he'll be quite presentable; I can guarantee to show him a side of French life that very few Americans have a chance of seeing. Believe me, my dear fellow, the average American can get into the kingdom of heaven much more easily than he can get into the Boulevard St. Germain. He's twenty and he has charm. I think I could probably arrange a liaison for him with an older woman. It would form him. I always think there's no better education for a young man than to become the lover of a woman of a certain age and of course, if she is the sort of person I have in view, a *femme du monde*, you know, it would immediately give him a situation in Paris."

"Did you tell that to Mrs. Bradley?" I asked, smiling.

Elliott chuckled.

"My dear fellow, if there's one thing I pride myself on it's my tact. I did not tell her. She wouldn't understand, poor dear. It's one of the things I've never understood about Louisa; though she's lived half her life in diplomatic society, in half the capitals of the world, she's remained hopelessly American."

(ix)

That evening I went to dine at a great stone house on Lake Shore Drive which looked as though the architect had started to build a medieval castle

33

and then, changing his mind in the middle, had decided to turn it into a Swiss chalet. It was a huge party and I was glad when I got into the vast and sumptuous drawing-room, all statues, palms, chandeliers, old masters, and overstuffed furniture, to see that there were at least a few people I knew. I was introduced by Henry Maturin to his thin, raddled, frail wife. I said how d'you do to Mrs. Bradley and Isabel. Isabel was looking very pretty in a red silk dress that suited her dark hair and rich hazel eyes. She appeared to be in high spirits and no one could have guessed that she had so recently gone through a harassing experience. She was talking gaily to the two or three young men, Gray among them, who surrounded her. She sat at dinner at another table and I could not see her, but afterwards, when we men, after lingering interminably over our coffee, liqueurs and cigars, returned to the drawing-room I had a chance to speak to her. I knew her too little to say anything directly about what Elliott had told me, but I had something to say that I thought she might be glad to hear.

"I saw your young man the other day in the club," I remarked casually.

"Oh, did you?"

She spoke as casually as I had, but I perceived that she was instantly alert. Her eyes grew watchful and I thought I read in them something like apprehension.

"He was reading in the library. I was very much impressed by his power of concentration. He was reading when I went in soon after ten, he was still reading when I went back after lunch and he was reading when I went in again on my way out to dinner. I don't believe he'd moved from his chair for the best part of ten hours."

"What was he reading?"

"William James's *Principles of Psychology.*"

She looked down so that I had no means of knowing how what I had said affected her, but I had a notion that she was at once puzzled and relieved. I was at that moment fetched by my host to play bridge and by the time the game broke up Isabel and her mother had gone.

(x)

A couple of days later I went to say good-bye to Mrs. Bradley and Elliott. I found them sitting over a cup of tea. Isabel came in shortly after me. We talked about my approaching journey, I thanked them for their kindness to me during my stay in Chicago and after a decent interval got up to go.

"I'll walk with you as far as the drugstore," said Isabel. "I've just remembered there's something I want to get."

The last words Mrs. Bradley said to me were: "You will give my love to dear Queen Margherita the next time you see her, won't you?"

I had given up disclaiming any acquaintance with that august lady and answered glibly that I would be sure to.

When we got into the street Isabel gave me a sidelong smiling glance.

"D'you think you could drink an ice-cream soda?" she asked me.

"I could try," I answered prudently.

Isabel did not speak till we reached the drugstore, and I, having nothing to say, said nothing. We went in and sat at a table on chairs with twisted wire backs and twisted wire legs. They were very uncomfortable. I ordered two ice-cream sodas. There were a few people at the counters buying; two or three couples were seated at other tables, but they were busy with their own concerns; and to all intents and purposes we were alone. I lit a cigarette and waited while Isabel with every appearance of satisfaction sucked at a long straw. I had a notion that she was nervous.

"I wanted to talk to you," she said abruptly.

"I gathered that," I smiled.

For a moment or two she looked at me reflectively.

"Why did you say that about Larry at the Satterthwaites' the night before last?"

"I thought it would interest you. It occurred to me that perhaps you didn't quite know what his idea of loafing was."

"Uncle Elliott's a terrible gossip. When he said he was going to the Blackstone to have a chat with you I knew he was going to tell you all about everything."

"I've known him a good many years, you know. He gets a lot of fun out of talking about other people's business."

"He does," she smiled. But it was only a gleam. She looked at me steadily and her eyes were serious. "What do you think of Larry?"

"I've only seen him three times. He seems a very nice boy."

"Is that all?"

There was a note of distress in her voice.

"No, not quite. It's hard for me to say; you see, I know him so little. Of course, he's attractive. There's something modest and friendly and gentle in him that is very appealing. He's got a lot of self-possession for so young a man. He isn't quite like any of the other boys I've met here."

While I was thus fumblingly trying to put into words an impression that was not distinct in my own mind, Isabel looked at me intently. When I had finished she gave a little sigh, as if of relief, and then flashed a charming, almost roguish smile at me.

35

"Uncle Elliott says he's often been surprised at your power of observation. He says nothing much escapes you, but that your great asset as a writer is your common sense."

"I can think of a quality that would be more valuable," I answered dryly. "Talent, for instance."

"You know, I have no one to talk this over with. Mamma can only see things from her own point of view. She wants my future to be assured."

"That's natural, isn't it?"

"And Uncle Elliott only looks at it from the social side. My own friends, those of my generation, I mean, think Larry's a washout. It hurts terribly."

"Of course."

"It's not that they're not nice to him. One can't help being nice to Larry. But they look upon him as a joke. They josh him a lot and it exasperates them that he doesn't seem to care. He only laughs. You know how things are at present?"

"I only know what Elliott has told me."

"May I tell you exactly what happened when we went down to Marvin?"

"Of course."

I have reconstructed Isabel's account partly from my recollection of what she then said to me and partly with the help of my imagination. But it was a long talk that she and Larry had, and I have no doubt that they said a great deal more than I now propose to relate. I suspect that as people do on these occasions they not only said much that was irrelevant, but said the same things over and over again.

When Isabel awoke and saw that it was a fine day she gave Larry a ring and, telling him that her mother wanted her to go to Marvin to do something for her, asked him to drive her down. She took the precaution to add a thermos of martinis to the thermos of coffee her mother had told Eugene to put in the basket. Larry's roadster was a recent acquisition and he was proud of it. He was a fast driver and the speed at which he went exhilarated them both. When they arrived, Isabel, with Larry to write down the figures, measured the curtains that were to be replaced. Then they set out the luncheon on the stoop. It was sheltered from any wind there was and the sun of the Indian summer was good to bask in. The house, on a dirt road, had none of the elegance of the old frame houses of New England and the best you could say of it was that it was roomy and comfortable, but from the stoop you had a pleasing view of a great red barn with a black roof, a clump of old trees and beyond them, as far as the eye could reach, brown fields. It was a dull landscape, but the sunshine and the glowing tints of the waning year gave it that day an intimate loveliness. There was an exhilaration in the great space that was spread before you. Cold, bleak and dreary as it must have been in winter, dry, sunbaked and oppressive as it may have been in the dog days, just then it was strangely exciting, for the vastness of the view invited the soul to adventure.

They enjoyed their lunch like the healthy young things they were and they were happy to be together. Isabel poured out the coffee and Larry lit his pipe.

"Now go right ahead, darling," he said, with an amused smile in his eyes.

Isabel was taken aback.

"Go right ahead about what?" she asked with as innocent a look as she could assume.

He chuckled.

"Do you take me for a perfect fool, honey? If your mother didn't know perfectly well the measurements of the living-room windows I'll eat my hat. That isn't why you asked me to drive you down here."

Recovering her self-assurance, she gave him a brilliant smile.

"It might be that I thought it would be nice if we spent a day together by ourselves."

"It might be, but I don't think it is. My guess is that Uncle Elliott has told you that I've turned down Henry Maturin's offer."

He spoke gaily and lightly and she found it convenient to continue in the same tone.

"Gray must be terribly disappointed. He thought it would be grand to have you in the office. You must get down to work sometime and the longer you leave it the harder it'll be."

He puffed at his pipe and looked at her, tenderly smiling, so that she could not tell if he was serious or not.

"Do you know, I've got an idea that I want to do more with my life than sell bonds."

"All right then. Go into a law office or study medicine."

"No, I don't want to do that either."

"What do you want to do then?"

"Loaf," he replied calmly.

"Oh, Larry, don't be funny. This is desperately serious."

Her voice quivered and her eyes filled with tears.

"Don't cry, darling. I don't want to make you miserable."

He went and sat down beside her and put his arm around her. There was a tenderness in his voice that broke her and she could no longer hold back her tears. But she dried her eyes and forced a smile to her lips.

"It's all very fine to say you don't want to make me miserable. You are making me miserable. You see, I love you."

"I love you too, Isabel."

She sighed deeply. Then she disengaged herself from his arm and drew away from him.

"Let's be sensible. A man must work, Larry. It's a matter of self-respect. This is a young country and it's a man's duty to take part in its activities. Henry Maturin was saying only the other day that we were beginning an era that would make the achievements of the past look like two bits. He said he could see no limit to our progress and he's convinced that by 1930 we shall be the richest and greatest country in the world. Don't you think that's terribly exciting?"

"Terribly."

"There's never been such a chance for a young man. I should have thought you'd be proud to take part in the work that lies before us. It's such a wonderful adventure."

He laughed lightly.

"I daresay you're right. The Armours and the Swifts will pack more and better meat, the McCormicks will make more and better harvesters, and Henry Ford will turn out more and better cars. And everyone'll get richer and richer."

"And why not?"

"As you say, and why not? Money just doesn't happen to interest me."

Isabel giggled.

"Darling, don't talk like a fool. One can't live without money."

"I have a little. That's what gives me the chance to do what I want."

"Loaf?"

"Yes," he answered, smiling.

"You're making it so difficult for me, Larry," she sighed.

"I'm sorry. I wouldn't if I could help it."

"You can help it."

He shook his head. He was silent for a while, lost in thought. When at last he spoke it was to say something that startled her.

"The dead look so terribly dead when they're dead."

"What do you mean exactly?" she asked, troubled.

"Just that." He gave her a rueful smile. "You have a lot of time to think when you're up in the air by yourself. You get odd ideas."

"What sort of ideas?"

"Vague," he said, smiling. "Incoherent. Confused."

Isabel thought this over for a while.

"Don't you think if you took a job they might sort themselves out and you'd know where you were?"

"I've thought of that. I had a notion that I might go to work with a carpenter or in a garage."

"Oh, Larry, people would think you were crazy."

"Would that matter?"

"To me, yes."

Once more silence fell upon them. It was she who broke it. She sighed.

"You're so different from what you were before you went out to France."

"That's not strange. A lot happened to me then, you know."

"Such as?"

"Oh, just the ordinary casual run of events. My greatest friend in the air corps was killed saving my life. I didn't find that easy to get over."

"Tell me, Larry."

He looked at her with deep distress in his eyes.

"I'd rather not talk about it. After all, it was only a trivial incident."

Emotional by nature, Isabel's eyes again filled with tears.

"Are you unhappy, darling?"

"No," he answered, smiling. "The only thing that makes me unhappy is that I'm making you unhappy." He took her hand and there was something so friendly in the feel of his strong firm hand against hers, something so intimately affectionate, that she had to bite her lips to prevent herself from crying. "I don't think I shall ever find peace till I make up my mind about things," he said gravely. He hesitated. "It's very difficult to put into words. The moment you try you feel embarrassed. You say to yourself: 'Who am I that I should bother my head about this, that and the other? Perhaps it is only because I'm a conceited prig. Wouldn't it be better to follow the beaten track and let what's coming to you come?' And then you think of a fellow who an hour before was full of life and fun, and he's lying dead; it's all so cruel and so meaningless. It's hard not to ask yourself what life is all about and whether there's any sense to it or whether it's all a tragic blunder of blind fate."

It was impossible not to be moved when Larry, with that wonderfully melodious voice of his, spoke, haltingly as though he forced himself to say what he would sooner have left unsaid and yet with such an anguished sincerity; and for a while Isabel did not trust herself to speak.

"Would it help you if you went away for a bit?"

She put the question with a sinking heart. He took a long time to answer.

"I think so. You try to be indifferent to public opinion, but it's not easy. When it's antagonistic it arouses antagonism in you and that disturbs you."

"Why don't you go then?"

"Well, on account of you."

"Let's be frank with one another, darling. There's no place for me in your life just now."

"Does that mean you don't want to be engaged to me any more?"

She forced a smile to her trembling lips.

"No, foolish, it means I'm prepared to wait."

"It may be a year. It may be two."

"That's all right. It may be less. Where d'you want to go?"

He looked at her intently as though he were trying to see into her inmost heart. She smiled lightly to hide her deep distress.

"Well, I thought I'd start by going to Paris. I know no one there. There'd be no one to interfere with me. I went to Paris several times on leave. I don't know why, but I've got it into my head that there everything that's muddled in my mind would grow clear. It's a funny place, it gives you the feeling that there you can think out your thoughts to the end. I think there I may be able to see my way before me."

"And what's to happen if you don't?"

He chuckled.

"Then I shall fall back on my good American horse sense, give it up as a bad job and come back to Chicago and take any work I can get."

The scene had affected Isabel too much for her to be able to tell it to me without getting somewhat emotional, and when she finished she looked at me pitifully.

"Do you think I did right?"

"I think you did the only thing you could do, but what's more I think you've been wonderfully kind, generous and understanding."

"I love him and I want him to be happy. And you know, in a way I'm not sorry he should go. I want him to be out of this hostile atmosphere, and that not only for his sake, but for mine too. I can't blame people when they say he'll never amount to anything; I hate them for it, and yet all the time deep down in me I have an awful fear that they're right. But don't say I'm understanding. I don't begin to understand what he's after."

"Perhaps you understand with your heart rather than with your reason," I smiled. "Why don't you marry him right away and go off to Paris with him?"

The shadow of a smile came into her eyes.

"There's nothing I'd like to do more. But I couldn't. And you know, though I hate to acknowledge it, I do really think he's better off without me. If Dr. Nelson is right and he's suffering from delayed shock surely new surroundings and new interests will cure him, and when he's got his balance again he'll come back to Chicago and go into business like everybody else. I wouldn't want to marry an idler."

Isabel had been brought up in a certain way and she accepted the principles that had been instilled into her. She did not think of money, because she had never known what it was not to have all she needed, but she was instinctively aware of its importance. It meant power, influence and social consequence. It was the natural and obvious thing that a man should earn it. That was his plain life's work.

"It doesn't surprise me that you don't understand Larry," I said, "because I'm pretty sure he doesn't understand himself. If he's reticent about his aims it may be that it's because they're obscure to him. Mind you, I hardly know him and this is only guesswork: isn't it possible that he's looking for something, but what it is he doesn't know, and perhaps he isn't even sure it's there? Perhaps whatever it is that happened to him during the war has left him with a restlessness that won't let him be. Don't you think he may be pursuing an ideal that is hidden in a cloud of unknowing—like an astronomer looking for a star that only a mathematical calculation tells him exists?"

"I feel that something's troubling him."

"His soul? It may be that he's a little frightened of himself. It may be that he has no confidence in the authenticity of the vision that he dimly perceives in his mind's eye."

"He gives me such an odd impression sometimes; he gives me the impression of a sleep-walker who's suddenly wakened in a strange place and can't think where he is. He was so normal before the war. One of the nice things about him was his enormous zest for life. He was so scatter-brained and gay, it was wonderful to be with him; he was so sweet and ridiculous. What can have happened to change him so much?"

"I wouldn't know. Sometimes a very small thing will have an effect on you out of all proportion to the event. It depends on the circumstances and your mood at the time. I remember going to mass on All Saints' Day, which the French called the Day of the Dead, in a village church that the Germans had knocked about a bit on their first advance into France. It was filled with soldiers and with women in black. In the graveyard were rows of little wooden crosses and as the sad, solemn service went on, and women wept and men too, I had a feeling that perhaps those men who lay under the little crosses were better off than we who lived. I told a friend what I felt and he asked me what I meant. I couldn't explain and I saw that he thought me a perfect damned fool. And I remember after a battle seeing a pile of dead French soldiers heaped upon one another. They looked like the marionettes in a bankrupt puppet show that had been cast pell-mell into a dusty corner because they were of no use any more. I thought then just what Larry said to you: the dead look so awfully dead."

I do not want the reader to think I am making a mystery of whatever it was that happened to Larry during the war that so profoundly affected him, a mystery that I shall disclose at a convenient moment. I don't think he ever told anybody. He did, however, many years later tell a woman, Suzanne Rouvier, whom Larry and I both knew, about the young airman who had met his death saving his life. She repeated it to me and so I can only relate it at second hand. I have translated it from her French. Larry had apparently struck up a great friendship with another boy in his squadron. Suzanne knew him only by the ironical nickname by which Larry spoke of him.

"He was a little chap with red hair, an Irishman. We used to call him Patsy," Larry said, "and he had more vitality than anyone I've ever known. Gosh, he was a live wire. He had a funny face and a funny grin, so that it made you laugh just to look at him. He was a harum-scarum devil and he'd do the craziest things; he was always getting hell from the higher-ups. He was absolutely without fear and when he'd escaped death by a hair's breadth he'd grin all over his face as if it was the best joke in the world. But he was a natural-born flyer and up in the air he was cool and wary. He taught me a lot. He was a bit older than me and he took me under his wing; it was rather comic really, because I was a good six inches taller than he was and if it had come to a scrap I could have knocked him out cold. Once in Paris when he was drunk and I was afraid he was going to get into trouble I did.

"I felt a bit out of it when I joined the squadron and I was afraid I wouldn't make good, and he just joshed me into having confidence in myself. He was funny about the war, he had no feeling of hatred for the Jerries; he loved a scrap and to fight them tickled him to death. He simply couldn't look upon bringing down one of their planes as anything but a practical joke. He was impudent and wild and irresponsible, but there was something so genuine about him that you couldn't help liking him. He'd give you his last penny as freely as he'd take yours. And if you were lonely or homesick or scared, and I was sometimes, he'd see it and with his ugly little face puckered up with laughter he'd say just the right thing to make you feel all right again."

Larry puffed at his pipe and Suzanne waited for him to go on.

"We used to wangle it so that we could get our leave together, and when we went to Paris he went wild. We had a grand time. We were due for a spot of leave early in March, in 'eighteen that was, and we made our plans beforehand. There wasn't a thing we weren't going to do. The day before we were to go we were sent up to fly over the enemy lines and bring back reports of what we saw. Suddenly we came bang up against some German planes, and before we knew where we were we were in the middle of a dogfight. One of them came after me, but I got in first. I took a look to see if he was going to crash and then out of the corner of my eye I saw another plane on my tail. I dived to get away from him, but he was on to me like a flash and I thought I was done for; then I saw Patsy come down on him like a streak of lightning and give him all he'd got. They'd had enough and sheered off and we made for home. My machine had got pretty well knocked about and I only just made it. Patsy got in before me. When I got out of my plane they'd just got him out of his. He was lying on the ground and they were waiting for the ambulance to come up. When he saw me he grinned.

" 'I got that blighter who was on your tail,' he said.

" 'What's the matter, Patsy?' I asked.

" 'Oh, it's nothing. He winged me.'

"He was looking deathly white. Suddenly a strange look came over his face. It had just come to him that he was dying, and the possibility of death had never so much as crossed his mind. Before they could stop him he sat up and gave a laugh.

" 'Well, I'm jiggered,' he said.

"He fell back dead. He was twenty-two. He was going to marry a girl in Ireland after the war."

The day after my talk with Isabel I left Chicago for San Francisco, where I was to take ship for the Far East.

CHAPTER TWO

(i)

I DID NOT SEE Elliott till he came to London towards the end of June of the following year. I asked him whether Larry had after all gone to Paris. He had. I was faintly amused at Elliott's exasperation with him.

"I had a kind of sneaking sympathy for the boy. I couldn't blame him for wanting to spend a couple of years in Paris and I was prepared to launch him. I told him to let me know the moment he arrived, but it was only when Louisa wrote and told me he was there that I knew he'd come. I wrote to him care of the American Express, which was the address she gave me, and asked him to come and dine to meet some of the people I thought he ought to know; I thought I'd try him out first with the Franco-American set, Emily de Montadour and Gracie de Château-Gaillard and so on, and d'you know what he answered? He said he was sorry he couldn't come, but he hadn't brought any evening clothes with him."

Elliott looked me full in the face to see the stupefaction with which he expected this communication to fill me. He raised a supercilious eyebrow when he observed that I took it with calm.

"He replied to my letter on a sheet of nasty paper with the heading of a café in the Latin Quarter and when I wrote back I asked him to let me know where he was staying. I felt I must do something about him for Isabel's sake, and I thought perhaps he was shy—I mean I couldn't believe that any young fellow in his senses could come to Paris without evening clothes, and in any case there are tolerable tailors there, so I asked him to lunch and said it would be quite a small party, and would you believe it, not only did he ignore my request to give me some other address than the American Express, but he said he never ate luncheon. That finished him as far as I was concerned."

"I wonder what he's been doing with himself."

"I don't know, and to tell you the truth I don't care. I'm afraid he's a thoroughly undesirable young man and I think it would be a great mistake for Isabel to marry him. After all, if he led a normal sort of life I'd have run across him at the Ritz bar or at Fouquet's or somewhere."

I go sometimes to these fashionable places myself, but I go to others also, and it happened that I spent several days in Paris early in the autumn of that year on my way to Marseilles, where I was proposing to take one of the Messagerie ships for Singapore. I dined one evening with friends in Montparnasse and after dinner we went to the Dôme to drink a glass of beer. Presently my wandering eye caught sight of Larry sitting by himself at a little marble-topped table on the crowded terrace. He was looking idly at the people who strolled up and down enjoying the coolness of the night after a sultry day. I left my party and went up to him. His face lit up when he saw me and he gave me an engaging smile. He asked me to sit down, but I said I couldn't as I was with a party.

"I just wanted to say how d'you do to you," I said.

"Are you staying here?" he asked.

"Only for a very few days."

"Will you lunch with me tomorrow?"

"I thought you never lunched."

He chuckled.

"You've seen Elliott. I don't generally, I can't afford the time, I just have a glass of milk and a brioche, but I'd like you to lunch with me."

"All right."

We arranged to meet at the Dôme next day to have an apéritif and eat at some place on the boulevard. I rejoined my friends. We sat on talking. When next I looked for Larry he had gone.

(ii)

I spent the next morning very pleasantly. I went to the Luxembourg and passed an hour looking at some pictures I liked. Then I strolled in the gardens, recapturing the memories of my youth. Nothing had changed. They might have been the same students who walked along the gravel paths in pairs, eagerly discussing the writers who excited them. They might have been the same children who trundled the same hoops under the watchful eyes of the same nurses. They might have been the same old men who basked in the sunshine reading the morning paper. They might have been the same middle-aged women in mourning who sat on the free benches and gossiped with one another about the price of food and the misdeeds of servants. Then I went to the Odéon and looked at the new books in the galleries and I saw the lads who like myself thirty years before were trying under the petulant eyes of the smock-frocked attendants to read as much as they could of books they could not afford to buy. Then I strolled leisurely along those dear, dingy streets till I came to the Boulevard du Montparnasse and so to the Dôme. Larry was waiting. We had a drink and walked along to a restaurant where we could lunch in the open air.

He was perhaps a little paler than I remembered him and this made his very dark eyes, in their deep orbits, more striking; but he had the same self-possession, curious in one so young, and the same ingenuous smile. When he ordered his lunch I noticed that he spoke French fluently and with a good accent. I congratulated him on it.

"I knew a certain amount of French before, you know," he explained. "Aunt Louisa had a French governess for Isabel, and when they were at Marvin she used to make us talk French with her all the time."

45

I asked him how he liked Paris.

"Very much."

"D'you live in Montparnasse?"

"Yes," he said, after a moment's hesitation which I interpreted into a disinclination to tell exactly where he lived.

"Elliott was rather put out that the only address you gave was the American Express."

Larry smiled but did not answer.

"What do you do with yourself all the time?"

"I loaf."

"And you read?"

"Yes, I read."

"Do you ever hear from Isabel?"

"Sometimes. We're neither of us great letter writers. She's having a grand time in Chicago. They're coming over next year to stay with Elliott."

"That'll be nice for you."

"I don't believe Isabel's ever been to Paris. It'll be fun taking her around."

He was curious to know about my journey in China and listened attentively to what I told him; but when I tried to get him to talk about himself, I failed. He was so uncommunicative that I was forced to the conclusion that he had asked me to lunch with him merely to enjoy my company. I was pleased, but baffled. We had no sooner finished our coffee than he called for the bill, paid it and got up.

"Well, I must be off," he said.

We parted. I knew no more of what he was up to than before. I did not see him again.

(iii)

I was not in Paris in the spring when, sooner than they had planned, Mrs. Bradley and Isabel arrived to stay with Elliott; and again I have to eke out my knowledge of what passed during the few weeks they spent there by the exercise of my imagination. They landed at Cherbourg and Elliott, always considerate, went to meet them. They passed through the customs. The train started. Elliott with some complacency told them that he had engaged a very good lady's maid to look after them and when Mrs. Bradley said that was quite unnecessary, since they didn't need one, he was very sharp with her.

"Don't be tiresome the moment you arrive, Louisa. No one can be well turned out without a maid, and I've engaged Antoinette not only for your

46

sake and Isabel's, but for mine. It would mortify me that you shouldn't be perfectly dressed."

He gave the clothes they were wearing a disparaging glance.

"Of course you'll want to buy some new frocks. On mature consideration I've come to the conclusion that you can't do better than Chanel."

"I always used to go to Worth," said Mrs. Bradley.

She might as well not have spoken, for he took no notice.

"I've talked to Chanel myself and I've made an appointment for you tomorrow at three. Then there are hats. Obviously Reboux."

"I don't want to spend a lot of money, Elliott."

"I know. I am proposing to pay for everything myself. I'm determined that you shall be a credit to me. Oh, and Louisa, I've arranged several parties for you and I've told my French friends that Myron was an ambassador, which, of course, he would have been if he'd lived a little longer, and it makes a better effect. I don't suppose it'll come up, but I thought I'd better warn you."

"You're ridiculous, Elliott."

"No, I'm not. I know the world. I know that the widow of an ambassador has more prestige than the widow of a minister."

As the train steamed into the Gare du Nord, Isabel, who was standing at the window, called out:

"There's Larry."

It had hardly stopped when she sprang out and ran to meet him. He threw his arms round her.

"How did he know you were coming?" Elliott asked his sister acidly.

"Isabel wirelessed him from the ship."

Mrs. Bradley kissed him affectionately, and Elliott gave him a limp hand to shake. It was ten o'clock at night.

"Uncle Elliott, can Larry come to lunch tomorrow?" cried Isabel, her arm in the young man's, her face eager and her eyes shining.

"I should be charmed, but Larry has given me to understand that he doesn't eat lunch."

"He will tomorrow, won't you, Larry?"

"I will," he smiled.

"I shall look forward to seeing you at one o'clock then."

He stretched out his hand once more, intending to dismiss him, but Larry grinned at him impudently.

"I'll help with the luggage and get a cab for you."

"My car is waiting and my man will see to the luggage," said Elliott with dignity.

"That's fine. Then all we've got to do is to go. If there's room for me I'll come as far as your door with you."

"Yes, do, Larry," said Isabel.

They walked down the platform together, followed by Mrs. Bradley and Elliott. Elliott's face bore a look of frigid disapproval.

"*Quelles manières,*" he said to himself, for in certain circumstances he felt he could express his sentiments more forcibly in French.

Next morning at eleven, having finished dressing, for he was not an early riser, he sent a note to his sister, via his man Joseph and her maid Antoinette, to ask her to come to the library so that they could have a talk. When she appeared he closed the door carefully and, putting a cigarette into an immensely long agate holder, lit it and sat down.

"Am I to understand that Isabel and Larry are still engaged?" he asked.

"So far as I know."

"I'm afraid I haven't a very good account to give you of the young man." He told her then how he had been prepared to launch him in society and the plans he had made to establish him in a fit and proper manner. "I even had my eye on a *rez-de-chaussée* that would have been the very thing for him. It belongs to the young Marquis de Rethel and he wanted to sublet is because he'd been appointed to the embassy at Madrid."

But Larry had refused his invitations in a manner that made it quite clear that he did not want his help.

"What the object of coming to Paris is if you're not going to take advantage of what Paris has to give you is beyond my comprehension. I don't know what he does with himself. He doesn't seem to know anybody. Do you know where he lives?"

"The only address we've ever had is the American Express."

"Like a travelling salesman or a school teacher on vacation. I shouldn't be surprised if he was living with some little trollop in a studio in Montmartre."

"Oh, Elliott."

"What other explanation can there be for the mystery he's making of his dwelling place and for his refusal to consort with people of his own class?"

"It doesn't sound like Larry. And last night, didn't you get the impression that he was just as much in love with Isabel as ever? He couldn't be so false."

Elliott by a shrug of the shoulders gave her to understand that there was no limit to the duplicity of men.

"What about Gray Maturin? Is he still in the picture?"

"He'd marry Isabel tomorrow if she'd have him."

Mrs. Bradley told him then why they had come to Europe sooner than they had at first intended. She had found herself in ill-health, and the doctors had informed her that she was suffering from diabetes. It was not serious and by attention to her diet and taking moderate doses of insulin there was no reason why she should not live for a good many years, but the knowledge that she had an incurable disease made her anxious to see Isabel settled. They had talked the matter over. Isabel was sensible. She had agreed that if Larry refused to come back to Chicago at the end of the two years in Paris they had agreed upon and get a job, there was only one thing to do and that was to break with him. But it offended Mrs. Bradley's sense of personal dignity that they should wait till the appointed time and then come to fetch him, like a fugitive from justice, back to his own country. She felt that Isabel would put herself in a humiliating position. But it was very natural that they should spend the summer in Europe, which Isabel had not been to since she was a child. After their visit in Paris they could go to some watering place suitable to Mrs. Bradley's complaint, then on to the Austrian Tyrol for a while and from there travel slowly through Italy. Mrs. Bradley's intention was to ask Larry to accompany them, so that he and Isabel could see whether the long separation had left their feelings unchanged. It would be manifest in due course whether Larry, having had his fling, was prepared to accept the responsibilities of life.

"Henry Maturin was sore with him for turning down the position he offered him, but Gray has talked him round, and he can go into the business the moment he comes back to Chicago."

"Gray's a very nice fellow."

"He certainly is." Mrs. Bradley sighed. "I know he'd make Isabel happy."

Elliott then told her what parties he had arranged for them. He was giving a big luncheon on the following day and at the end of the week a grand dinner party. He was taking them to a reception at the Château-Gaillards and he had got cards for them to a ball that the Rothschilds were giving.

"You'll ask Larry, won't you?"

"He tells me he hasn't any evening clothes," Elliott sniffed.

"Well, ask him all the same. After all, he is a nice boy, and it wouldn't help to give him the cold shoulder. It would only make Isabel obstinate."

"Of course I'll ask him if you wish it."

Larry came to lunch at the appointed time, and Elliott, whose manners were admirable, was pointedly cordial to him. It was not difficult, since Larry was so gay, in such high spirits that it would have needed a much more ill-natured man than Elliott not to be charmed with him. The conversation dealt with Chicago and their common friends there, so that there was not much for Elliott to do other than to look amiable and pretend to be interested in the concerns of persons whom he thought of no social consequence. He did not mind listening; indeed, he thought it rather touching to hear them tell of this young couple's engagement, that young couple's marriage, and another young couple's divorce. Who had ever heard of them? *He* knew that that pretty little Marquise de Clinchant had tried to poison herself because her lover, the Prince de Colombey, had left her to marry the daughter of a South American millionaire. That *was* something to talk about. Looking at Larry, he was obliged to admit that there was something peculiarly attractive in him; with his deep-set, strangely black eyes, his high cheekbones, pale skin and mobile mouth he reminded Elliott of a portrait by Botticelli, and it occurred to him that if he were dressed in the costume of the period he would look extravagantly romantic. He remembered his notion of getting him off with a distinguished Frenchwoman and he smiled slyly on reflecting that he was expecting at dinner on Saturday Marie Louise de Florimond, who combined irreproachable connections with notorious immorality. She was forty, but looked ten years younger; she had the delicate beauty of her ancestress painted by Nattier which, owing to Elliott himself, now hung in one of the great American collections; and her sexual voracity was insatiable. Elliott decided to put Larry next to her. He knew she would waste no time in making her desires clear to him. He had already invited a young attaché at the British Embassy whom he thought Isabel might like. Isabel was very pretty, and as he was an Englishman, and well off, it wouldn't matter that she had no fortune. Mellowed by the excellent Montrachet with which they had started lunch and by the fine Bordeaux that followed, Elliott thought with tranquil pleasure of the possibilities that presented themselves to his mind. If things turned out as he thought they very well might, dear Louisa would have no more cause for anxiety. She had always slightly disapproved of him; poor dear, she was very provincial; but he was fond of her. It would be a satisfaction to him to arrange everything for her by help of his knowledge of the world.

To waste no time, Elliott had arranged to take his ladies to look at clothes immediately after lunch, so as they got up from table he intimated to Larry with the tact of which he was a master that he must make himself scarce, but at the same time he asked him with pressing affability to come to the two grand parties he had arranged. He need hardly have taken so much trouble, since Larry accepted both invitations with alacrity.

But Elliott's plan failed. He was relieved when Larry appeared at the dinner party in a very presentable dinner jacket, for he had been a little nervous that he would wear the same blue suit that he had worn at lunch; and after dinner, getting Marie Louise de Florimond into a corner, he asked her how she had liked his young American friend.

"He has nice eyes and good teeth."

"Is that all? I put him beside you because I thought he was just your cup of tea."

She looked at him suspiciously.

"He told me he was engaged to your pretty niece."

"*Voyons, ma chère,* the fact that a man belongs to another woman has never prevented you from taking him away from her if you could."

"Is that what you want me to do? Well, I'm not going to do your dirty work for you, my poor Elliott."

Elliott chuckled.

"The meaning of that, I presume, is that you tried your stuff and found there was nothing doing."

"Why I like you, Elliott, is that you have the morals of a bawdy-house keeper. You don't want him to marry your niece. Why not? He is well bred and quite charming. But he's really too innocent. I don't think he had the least suspicion of what I meant."

"You should have been more explicit, dear friend."

"I have enough experience to know when I'm wasting my time. The fact is that he has eyes only for your little Isabel, and between you and me, she has twenty years advantage over me. And she's sweet."

"Do you like her dress? I chose it for her myself."

"It's pretty and it's suitable. But of course she has no chic."

Elliott took this as a reflection on himself, and he was not prepared to let Madame de Florimond get away without a dig. He smiled genially.

"One has to have reached your ripe maturity to have *your* chic, dear friend," he said.

Madame de Florimond wielded a bludgeon rather than a rapier. Her retort made Elliott's Virginian blood boil.

"But I'm sure that in your fair land of gangsters [*vôtre beau pays d'apaches*] they will hardly miss something that is so subtle and so inimitable."

But if Madame de Florimond carped, the rest of Elliott's friends were delighted both with Isabel and with Larry. They liked her fresh prettiness, her abounding health and her vitality; they liked his picturesque appearance, his good manners and his quiet, ironic humour. Both had the advantage of speaking good and fluent French. Mrs. Bradley, after living so many years in diplomatic circles, spoke it correctly enough but with an unabashed American accent. Elliott entertained them lavishly. Isabel, pleased with her new clothes and her new hats, amused by all the gaiety Elliott provided and happy to be with Larry, thought she had never enjoyed herself so much.

(iv)

Elliott was of opinion that breakfast was a meal that you should share only with total strangers, and then only if there was no help for it, so Mrs. Bradley, somewhat against her will, and Isabel, far from displeased, were obliged to have theirs in their bedrooms. But Isabel, when she awoke, sometimes told Antoinette, the grand maid Elliott had engaged for them, to take her *café au lait* into her mother's room so that she could talk to her while she had it. In the busy life she led it was the only moment of the day in which she could be alone with her. One such morning, when they had been in Paris nearly a month, after Isabel had done narrating the events of the previous night, most of which she and Larry had spent going the round of the night clubs with a party of friends, Mrs. Bradley let fall the question she had had in mind to ask ever since their arrival.

"When is he coming back to Chicago?"

"I don't know. He hasn't spoken of it."

"Haven't you asked him?"

"No."

"Are you scared to?"

"No, of course not."

Mrs. Bradley, lying on a chaise longue, in a modish dressing-gown that Elliott had insisted on giving her, was polishing her nails.

"What do you talk about all the time when you're alone?"

"We don't talk all the time. It's nice to be together. You know, Larry was always rather silent. When we talk I think I do most of the talking."

"What has he been doing with himself?"

"I don't really know. I don't think anything very much. I suppose he's been having a good time."

"And where is he living?"

"I don't know that either."

"He seems very reticent, doesn't he?"

Isabel lit a cigarette and, as she blew a cloud of smoke from her nostrils, looked coolly at her mother.

"What exactly do you mean by that, Mamma?"

"Your uncle Elliott thinks he has an apartment and is living there with a woman."

Isabel burst out laughing.

"You don't believe that, do you?"

"No, I honestly don't." Mrs. Bradley looked reflectively at her nails. "Don't you ever talk to him about Chicago?"

"Yes, a lot."

"Hasn't he given any sort of indication that he intends to come back?"

"I can't say he has."

"He will have been gone two years next October."

"I know."

"Well, it's your business, dear, and you must do what you think right. But things don't get any easier by putting them off." She glanced at her daughter, but Isabel would not meet her eyes. Mrs. Bradley gave her an affectionate smile. "If you don't want to be late for lunch you'd better go and have your bath."

"I'm lunching with Larry. We're going to some place in the Latin Quarter."

"Enjoy yourself."

An hour later Larry came to fetch her. They took a cab to the Pont St. Michel and sauntered up the crowded boulevard till they came to a café they liked the look of. They sat down on the terrace and ordered a couple of Dubonnets. Then they took another cab and went to a restaurant. Isabel had a healthy appetite and she enjoyed the good things Larry ordered for her. She enjoyed looking at the people sitting cheek by jowl with them, for the place was packed, and it made her laugh to see the intense pleasure they so obviously took in their food; but she enjoyed above all sitting at a tiny table alone with Larry. She loved the amusement in his eyes while she chattered away gaily. It was enchanting to feel so much at home with him. But at the back of her mind was a vague disquiet, for though he seemed very much at home too, she felt it was not so much with her as with the surroundings. She had been faintly disturbed by what her mother had said, and though seeming to prattle so guilelessly she observed his every expression. He was not quite the same as when he had left Chicago, but she couldn't tell in what the difference lay. He looked exactly as she remembered him, as young, as frank, but his expression was changed. It was not that he was more serious, his face in repose had always been serious, it had a calmness that was new to her; it was as though he had settled something with himself and were at ease in a way he had never been before.

When they had finished lunch he suggested that they should take a stroll through the Luxembourg.

"No, I don't want to go and look at pictures."

"All right then, let's go and sit in the gardens."

"No, I don't want to do that either. I want to go and see where you live."

"There's nothing to see. I live in a scrubby little room in a hotel."

"Uncle Elliott says you've got an apartment and are living in sin with an artist's model."

"Come on then and see for yourself," he laughed. "It's only a step from here. We can walk."

He took her through narrow, tortuous streets, dingy notwithstanding the streak of blue sky that showed between the high houses, and after a while stopped at a small hotel with a pretentious façade.

"Here we are."

Isabel followed him into a narrow hall, on one side of which was a desk and behind it a man in shirt sleeves, with a waistcoat in thin black and yellow stripes and a dirty apron, reading a paper. Larry asked for his key, and the man handed it to him from the rack immediately behind him. He gave Isabel an inquisitive glance that turned into a knowing smirk. It was clear that he thought she was going to Larry's room for no honest purpose.

They climbed up two flights of stairs, on which was a threadbare red carpet, and Larry unlocked his door. Isabel entered a smallish room with two windows. They looked out on the gray apartment house opposite, on the ground floor of which was a stationer's shop. There was a single bed in the room, with a night table beside it, a heavy wardrobe with a large mirror, an upholstered but straight-backed armchair and a table between the windows on which were a typewriter, papers and a number of books. The chimney piece was piled with paper-bound volumes.

"You sit in the armchair. It's not very comfortable, but it's the best I can offer."

He drew up another chair and sat down.

"Is this where you live?" asked Isabel.

He chuckled at the look on her face.

"It is. I've been here ever since I came to Paris."

"But why?"

"It's convenient. It's near the Bibliothèque Nationale and the Sorbonne." He pointed to a door she had not noticed. "It's got a bathroom. I can get breakfast here and I generally dine at that restaurant where we had lunch."

"It's awfully sordid."

"Oh no, it's all right. It's all I want."

54

"But what sort of people live here?"

"Oh, I don't know. Up in the attics a few students. Two or three old bachelors in government offices and a retired actress at the Odéon; the only other room with a bath is occupied by a kept woman whose gentleman friend comes to see her every other Thursday; I suppose a few transients. It's a very quiet and respectable place."

Isabel was a trifle disconcerted and because she knew Larry noticed it and was amused she was half inclined to take offence.

"What's that great big book on the table?" she asked.

"That? Oh, that's my Greek dictionary."

"Your what?" she cried.

"It's all right. It won't bite you."

"Are you learning Greek?"

"Yes."

"Why?"

"I thought I'd like to."

He was looking at her with a smile in his eyes and she smiled back at him.

"Don't you think you might tell me what you've been up to all the time you've been in Paris?"

"I've been reading a good deal. Eight or ten hours a day. I've attended lectures at the Sorbonne. I think I've read everything that's important in French literature and I can read Latin, at least Latin prose, almost as fluently as I can read French. Of course Greek's more difficult. But I have a very good teacher. Until you came here I used to go to him three evenings a week."

"And what is that going to lead to?"

"The acquisition of knowledge," he smiled.

"It doesn't sound very practical."

"Perhaps it isn't and on the other hand perhaps it is. But it's enormous fun. You can't imagine what a thrill it is to read the *Odyssey* in the original. It makes you feel as if you only had to get on tiptoe and stretch out your hands to touch the stars."

He got up from his chair, as though impelled by an excitement that seized him, and walked up and down the small room.

"I've been reading Spinoza the last month or two. I don't suppose I understand very much of it yet, but it fills me with exultation. It's like landing from your plane on a great plateau in the mountains. Solitude, and an air so pure that it goes to your head like wine and you feel like a million dollars."

"When are you coming back to Chicago?"

"Chicago? I don't know. I haven't thought of it."

"You said that if you hadn't got what you wanted after two years you'd give it up as a bad job."

"I couldn't go back now. I'm on the threshold. I see vast lands of the spirit stretching out before me, beckoning, and I'm eager to travel them."

"What do you expect to find in them?"

"The answers to my questions." He gave her a glance that was almost playful, so that except that she knew him so well, she might have thought he was speaking in jest. "I want to make up my mind whether God is or God is not. I want to find out why evil exists. I want to know whether I have an immortal soul or whether when I die it is the end."

Isabel gave a little gasp. It made her uncomfortable to hear Larry say such things, and she was thankful that he spoke so lightly, in the tone of ordinary conversation, that it was possible for her to overcome her embarrassment.

"But Larry," she smiled, "people have been asking those questions for thousands of years. If they could be answered, surely they'd have been answered by now."

Larry chuckled.

"Don't laugh as if I'd said something idiotic," she said sharply.

"On the contrary I think you've said something shrewd. But on the other hand you might say that if men have been asking them for thousands of years it proves that they can't help asking them and have to go on asking them. Besides, it's not true that no one has found the answers. There are more answers than questions, and lots of people have found answers that were perfectly satisfactory for them. Old Ruysbroek for instance."

"Who was he?"

"Oh, just a guy I didn't know at college," Larry answered flippantly.

Isabel didn't know what he meant, but passed on.

"It all sounds so adolescent to me. Those are the sort of things sophomores get excited about and then when they leave college they forget about them. They have to earn a living."

"I don't blame them. You see, I'm in the happy position that I have enough to live on. If I hadn't I'd have had to do like everybody else and make money."

"But doesn't money mean anything to you?"

"Not a thing," he grinned.

"How long d'you think all this is going to take you?"

"I wouldn't know. Five years. Ten years."

"And after that? What are you going to do with all this wisdom?"

"If I ever acquire wisdom I suppose I shall be wise enough to know what to do with it."

Isabel clasped her hands passionately and leant forwards in her chair.

"You're so wrong, Larry. You're an American. Your place isn't here. Your place is in America."

"I shall come back when I'm ready."

"But you're missing so much. How can you bear to sit here in a backwater just when we're living through the most wonderful adventure the world has ever known? Europe's finished. We're the greatest, the most powerful people in the world. We're going forwards by leaps and bounds. We've got everything. It's your duty to take part in the development of your country. You've forgotten, you don't know how thrilling life is in America today. Are you sure you're not doing this because you haven't the courage to stand up to the work that's before every American now? Oh, I know you're working in a way, but isn't it just an escape from your responsibilities? Is it more than just a sort of laborious idleness? What would happen to America if everyone shirked as you're shirking?"

"You're very severe, honey," he smiled. "The answer to that is that everyone doesn't feel like me. Fortunately for themselves, perhaps, most people are prepared to follow the normal course; what you forget is that I want to learn as passionately as—Gray, for instance, wants to make pots of money. Am I really a traitor to my country because I want to spend a few years educating myself? It may be that when I'm through I shall have something to give that people will be glad to take. It's only a chance, of course, but if I fail I shall be no worse off than a man who's gone into business and hasn't made a go of it."

"And what about me? Am I of no importance to you at all?"

"You're of very great importance. I want you to marry me."

"When? In ten years?"

"No. Now. As soon as possible."

"On what? Mamma can't afford to give me anything. Besides, she wouldn't if she could. She'd think it wrong to help you to live without doing anything."

"I wouldn't want to take anything from your mother," said Larry. "I've got three thousand a year. That's plenty in Paris. We could have a little apartment and a *bonne à tout faire*. We'd have such a lark, darling."

"But, Larry, one can't live on three thousand a year."

"Of course one can. Lots of people live on much less."

"But I don't want to live on three thousand a year. There's no reason why I should."

"I've been living on half that."

"But how!"

She looked at the dingy little room with a shudder of distaste.

"It means I've got a bit saved up. We could go down to Capri for our honeymoon and then in the fall we'd go to Greece. I'm crazy to go there. Don't you remember how we used to talk about travelling all over the world together?"

"Of course I want to travel. But not like that. I don't want to travel second-class on steamships and put up at third-rate hotels, without a bathroom, and eat at cheap restaurants."

"I went all through Italy last October like that. I had a wonderful time. We could travel all over the world on three thousand a year."

"But I want to have babies, Larry."

"That's all right. We'll take them along with us."

"You're so silly," she laughed. "D'you know what it costs to have a baby? Violet Tomlinson had one last year and she did it as cheaply as she could and it cost her twelve hundred and fifty. And what d'you think a nurse costs?" She grew more vehement as one idea after another occurred to her. "You're so impractical. You don't know what you're asking me to do. I'm young, I want to have fun. I want to do all the things that people do. I want to go to parties, I want to go to dances, I want to play golf and ride horseback. I want to wear nice clothes. Can't you imagine what it means to a girl not to be as well dressed as the rest of her crowd? D'you know what it means, Larry, to buy your friends' old dresses when they're sick of them and being thankful when someone out of pity makes you a present of a new one? I couldn't even afford to go to a decent hairdresser to have my hair properly done. I don't want to go about in street-cars and omnibuses; I want to have my own car. And what d'you suppose I'd find to do with myself all day long while you were reading at the Library? Walk about the streets window-shopping or sit in the Luxembourg Gardens seeing that my children didn't get into mischief? We wouldn't have any friends."

"Oh, Isabel," he interrupted.

"Not the sort of friends I'm used to. Oh yes, Uncle Elliott's friends would ask us now and then for his sake, but we couldn't go because I wouldn't have the clothes to go in, and we wouldn't go because we couldn't afford to return their hospitality. I don't want to know a lot of scrubby, unwashed people; I've got nothing to say to them and they've got nothing to say to me. I want to live, Larry." She grew suddenly conscious of the look in his eyes, tender as it always was when fixed on her, but gently amused. "You think I'm silly, don't you? You think I'm being trivial and horrid."

"No, I don't. I think what you say is very natural."

He was standing with his back to the fireplace, and she got up and went up to him so that they were face to face.

"Larry, if you hadn't a cent to your name and got a job that brought you in three thousand a year I'd marry you without a minute's hesitation. I'd cook for you, I'd make the beds, I wouldn't care what I wore, I'd go without anything, I'd look upon it as wonderful fun, because I'd know that it was only a question of time and you'd make good. But this means living in a sordid beastly way all our lives with nothing to look forward to. It means that I should be a drudge to the day of my death. And for what? So that you can spend years trying to find answers to questions that you say yourself are insoluble. It's so wrong. A man ought to work. That's what he's here for. That's how he contributes to the welfare of the community."

"In short it's his duty to settle down in Chicago and enter Henry Maturin's business. Do you think that by getting my friends to buy the securities that Henry Maturin is interested in I should add greatly to the welfare of the community?"

"There must be brokers and it's a perfectly decent and honorable way of earning a living."

"You've drawn a very black picture of life in Paris on a moderate income. You know, it isn't really like that. One can dress very nicely without going to Chanel. And all the interesting people don't live in the neighborhood of the Arc de Triomphe and the Avenue Foch. In fact few interesting people do, because interesting people generally don't have a lot of money. I know quite a number of people here, painters and writers and students, French, English, American, and what not, whom I think you'd find much more amusing than Elliott's seedy marquises and long-nosed duchesses. You've got a quick mind and a lively sense of humour. You'd enjoy hearing them swap ideas across the dinner table even though the wine was only *vin ordinaire* and you didn't have a butler and a couple of footmen to wait on you."

"Don't be stupid, Larry. Of course I would. You know I'm not a snob. I'd love to meet interesting people."

"Yes, in a Chanel dress. D'you think they wouldn't catch on to it that you looked upon it as a sort of cultured slumming? They wouldn't be at their ease, any more than you would, and you wouldn't get anything out of it except to tell Emily de Montadour and Gracie de Château-Gaillard afterwards what fun you'd had meeting a lot of weird bohemians in the Latin Quarter."

Isabel slightly shrugged her shoulders.

"I daresay you're right. They're not the sort of people I've been brought up with. They're not the sort of people I have anything in common with."

"Where does that leave us?"

"Just where we started. I've lived in Chicago ever since I can remember. All my friends are there. All my interests are there. I'm at home there. It's where I belong and it's where you belong. Mamma's ill and she's never going to get any better. I couldn't leave her even if I wanted to."

"Does that mean that unless I'm prepared to come back to Chicago you don't want to marry me?"

Isabel hesitated. She loved Larry. She wanted to marry him. She wanted him with all the power of her senses. She knew that he desired her. She couldn't believe that when it came to a showdown he wouldn't weaken. She was afraid, but she had to risk it.

"Yes, Larry, that's just what it does mean."

He struck a match on the chimney piece, one of those old-fashioned French sulphur matches that fill your nostrils with an acrid odour, and lit his pipe. Then, passing her, he went over and stood by one of the windows. He looked out. He was silent for what seemed an endless time. She stood as she had stood before, when she was facing him, and looked in the mirror over the chimney piece, but she did not see herself. Her heart was beating madly and she was sick with apprehension. He turned at last.

"I wish I could make you see how much fuller the life I offer you is than anything you have a conception of. I wish I could make you see how exciting the life of the spirit is and how rich in experience. It's illimitable. It's such a happy life. There's only one thing like it, when you're up in a plane by yourself, high, high, and only infinity surrounds you. You're intoxicated by the boundless space. You feel such a sense of exhilaration that you wouldn't exchange it for all the power and glory of the world. I was reading Descartes the other day. The ease, the grace, the lucidity. Gosh!"

"But Larry," she interrupted him desperately, "don't you see you're asking something of me that I'm not fitted for, that I'm not interested in and don't want to be interested in? How often have I got to repeat to you that I'm just an ordinary, normal girl, I'm twenty, in ten years I shall be old, I want to have a good time while I have the chance. Oh, Larry, I do love you so terribly. All this is just trifling. It's not going to lead you anywhere. For your own sake I beseech you to give it up. Be a man, Larry, and do a man's work. You're just wasting the precious years that others are doing so much with. Larry, if you love me you won't give me up for a dream. You've had your fling. Come back with us to America."

"I can't, darling. It would be death to me. It would be the betrayal of my soul."

"Oh, Larry, why d'you talk in that way? That's the way hysterical high-brow women talk. What does it mean? Nothing. Nothing. Nothing."

"It happens to mean exactly what I feel," he answered, his eyes twinkling.

"How can you laugh? Don't you realize this is desperately serious? We've come to the crossroads and what we do now is going to affect our whole lives."

"I know that. Believe me, I'm perfectly serious."

She sighed.

"If you won't listen to reason there's nothing more to be said."

"But I don't think it's reason. I think you've been talking the most terrible nonsense all the time."

"I?" If she hadn't been so miserable she would have laughed. "My poor Larry, you're as crazy as a coot."

She slowly slipped her engagement ring off her finger. She placed it on the palm of her hand and looked at it. It was a square-cut ruby set in a thin platinum band and she had always liked it.

"If you loved me you wouldn't make me so unhappy."

"I do love you. Unfortunately sometimes one can't do what one thinks is right without making someone else unhappy."

She stretched out her hand on which the ruby was resting and forced a smile to her trembling lips.

"Here you are, Larry."

"It's no good to me. Won't you keep it as a memento to our friendship? You can wear it on your little finger. Our friendship needn't stop, need it?"

"I shall always care for you, Larry."

"Then keep it. I should like you to."

She hesitated for an instant, then put it on the finger of her right hand.

"It's too large."

"You can have it altered. Let's go to the Ritz bar and have a drink."

"All right."

She was a trifle taken aback that it had all gone so easily. She had not cried. Nothing seemed to be changed except that now she wasn't going to marry Larry. She could hardly believe that everything was over and done with. She resented the fact a little that they hadn't had a terrific scene. They had talked it all over almost as coolly as though they had been discussing the taking of a house. She felt let down, but at the same time was conscious of a slight sense of satisfaction because they had behaved in such a civilized way. She would have given a lot to know exactly what Larry was feeling. But it was always difficult to know that; his smooth face, his dark eyes were a mask that she was aware even she, who had known him for so many years, could not penetrate. She had taken off her hat and laid it on the bed. Now, standing before the mirror, she put it on again.

"Just as a matter of interest," she said, arranging her hair, "did you want to break our engagement?"

"No."

"I thought it might be a relief to you." He made no reply. She turned round with a gay smile on her lips. "Now I'm ready."

Larry locked the door behind him. When he handed the key to the man at the desk he enveloped them both in a look of conniving archness. It was impossible for Isabel not to guess what he thought they had been up to.

"I don't believe that old fellow would bet much on my virginity," she said.

They took a taxi to the Ritz and had a drink. They spoke of indifferent things, without apparent constraint, like two old friends who saw one another every day. Though Larry was naturally silent, Isabel was a talkative girl, with an ample fund of chit-chat, and she was determined that no silence should fall between them that might be hard to break. She wasn't going to let Larry think she felt any resentment towards him and her pride constrained her to act so that he should not suspect that she was hurt and unhappy. Presently she suggested that he should drive her home. When he dropped her at the door she said to him gaily,

"Don't forget that you're lunching with us tomorrow."

"You bet your life I won't."

She gave him her cheek to kiss and passed through the *porte cochère*.

(*v*)

When Isabel entered the drawing-room she found that some people had dropped in to tea. There were two American women who lived in Paris, exquisitely gowned, with strings of pearls round their necks, diamond bracelets on their wrists and costly rings on their fingers. Though the hair of one was darkly hennaed and that of the other unnaturally golden they were strangely alike. They had the same heavily mascaraed eyelashes, the same brightly painted lips, the same rouged cheeks, the same slim figures, maintained at the cost of extreme mortification, the same clear, sharp features, the same hungry restless eyes; and you could not but be conscious that their lives were a desperate struggle to maintain their fading charms. They talked with inanity in a loud, metallic voice without a moment's pause, as though afraid that if they were silent for an instant the machine would run down and the artificial construction which was all they were would fall to pieces. There was also a secretary from the American Embassy, suave, silent, for he could not get a word in, and very much the man of the world, and a small dark Rumanian prince, all bows and servility, with little darting black eyes and a clean-shaven swarthy face, who was forever jumping up to hand a teacup, pass a plate of cakes, or light a cigarette and who shamelessly dished out to those present the most flattering, the most gross compliments. He was paying for all the dinners he had received from the objects of his adulation and for all the dinners he hoped to receive.

Mrs. Bradley, seated at the tea table and dressed to please Elliott somewhat more grandly than she thought suitable to the occasion, performed her duties as hostess with her usual civil but rather indifferent composure. What she thought of her brother's guests I can only imagine. I never knew her more than slightly and she was a woman who kept herself to herself. She was not a stupid woman; in all the years she had lived in foreign capitals she had met innumerable people of all kinds and I think she summed them up shrewdly enough according to the standards of the small Virginian town where she was born and bred. I think she got a certain amount of amusement from observing their antics and I don't believe she took their airs and graces any more seriously than she took the aches and pains of the characters in a novel which she knew from the beginning (otherwise she wouldn't have read it) would end happily. Paris, Rome, Peking had had no more effect on her Americanism than Elliott's devout Catholicism on her robust, but not inconvenient, Presbyterian faith.

Isabel, with her youth, her strapping good looks and her vitality brought a breath of fresh air into that meretricious atmosphere. She swept in like a young earth goddess. The Rumanian prince leapt to his feet to draw forward a chair for her and with ample gesticulation did his shift. The two American ladies, with shrill amiabilities on their lips, looked her up and down, took in the details of her dress and perhaps in their hearts felt a pang of dismay at being thus confronted with her exuberant youth. The American diplomat smiled to himself as he saw how false and haggard she made them look. But Isabel thought they were grand; she liked their rich clothes and expensive pearls and felt a twinge of envy for their sophisticated poise. She wondered if she would ever achieve that supreme elegance. Of course the little Rumanian was quite ridiculous, but he was rather sweet and even if he didn't mean the charming things he said it was nice to listen to them. The conversation which her entrance had interrupted was resumed and they talked so brightly, with so much conviction that what they were saying was worth saying, that you almost thought they were talking sense. They talked of the parties they had been to and the parties they were going to. They gossiped about the latest scandal. They tore their friends to pieces. They bandied great names from one to the other. They seemed to know everybody. They were in on all the secrets. Almost in a breath they touched upon the latest play, the latest dressmaker, the latest portrait painter, and the latest mistress of the latest premier. One would have thought there was nothing they didn't know. Isabel listened with ravishment. It all seemed to her wonderfully civilized. This really was life. It gave her a thrilling sense of being in the midst of things. This was real. The setting was perfect. That spacious room with the Savonnerie carpet on the floor, the lovely drawings on the richly panelled walls, the *petit-point* chairs on which they sat, the priceless pieces of marquetry, commodes and occasional tables, every piece worthy to go into a museum; it must have cost a fortune, that room, but it was worth it. Its beauty, its discretion struck her as never before because she had still so vividly in her mind the shabby little hotel room, with its iron bed and that hard, comfortless chair in which she had sat, that room that Larry saw nothing wrong in. It was bare, cheerless and horrid. It made her shudder to remember it.

The party broke up and Isabel was left with her mother and Elliott.

"Charming women," said Elliott when he came back from seeing the two poor painted drabs to the door. "I knew them when they first settled in Paris. I never dreamt they'd turn out as well as they have. It's amazing, the adaptability of our women. You'd hardly know they were Americans now and Middle West into the bargain."

Mrs. Bradley, raising her eyebrows, without speaking gave him a look which he was too quick-witted not to understand.

"No one could ever say that of you, my poor Louisa," he continued half acidly and half affectionately. "Though heaven knows, you've had every chance."

Mrs. Bradley pursed her lips.

"I'm afraid I've been a sad disappointment to you, Elliott, but to tell you the truth I'm very satisfied with myself as I am."

"*Tous les goûts sont dans la nature,*" Elliott murmured.

"I think I ought to tell you that I'm no longer engaged to Larry," said Isabel.

"Tut," cried Elliott. "That'll put my luncheon table out for tomorrow. How on earth am I going to get another man at this short notice?"

"Oh, he's coming to lunch all right."

"After you've broken off your engagement? That sounds very unconventional."

Isabel giggled. She kept her gaze on Elliott, for she knew her mother's eyes were fixed upon her and she didn't want to meet them.

"We haven't quarrelled. We talked it over this afternoon and came to the conclusion we'd made a mistake. He doesn't want to come back to America; he wants to stop on in Paris. He's talking of going to Greece."

"What on earth for? There's no society in Athens. As a matter of fact I never thought so much of Greek art myself. Some of that Hellenistic stuff has a certain decadent charm that's rather attractive. But Phidias: no, no."

"Look at me, Isabel," said Mrs. Bradley.

Isabel turned and with a faint smile on her lips faced her mother. Mrs. Bradley gave her a scrutinizing stare, but all she said was, "H'm." The girl hadn't been crying, that she saw; she looked calm and composed.

"I think you're well out of it, Isabel," said Elliott. "I was prepared to make the best of it, but I never thought it a good match. He wasn't really up to your mark, and the way he's been behaving in Paris is a pretty clear indication that he'll never amount to anything. With your looks and your connections you can aspire to something better than that. I think you've behaved in a very sensible manner."

Mrs. Bradley gave her daughter a glance that was not devoid of anxiety. "You haven't done this on my account, Isabel?"

Isabel shook her head decidedly.

"No, darling, I've done it entirely on my own."

(vi)

I had come back from the East and was spending some time in London just then. It was perhaps a fortnight after the events I have just related that Elliott called me up one morning. I was not surprised to hear his voice, for I knew that he was in the habit of coming to England to enjoy the fag end of the season. He told me that Mrs. Bradley and Isabel were with him and if I would drop in that evening at six for a drink they would be glad to see me. They were, of course, staying at Claridge's. I was at that time living not far from there, so I strolled down Park Lane and through the quiet, dignified streets of Mayfair till I came to the hotel. Elliott had his usual suite. It was panelled in brown wood like the wood of a cigar box and furnished with quiet sumptuousness. He was alone when I was ushered in. Mrs. Bradley and Isabel had gone shopping and he was expecting them

65

at any minute. He told me that Isabel had broken her engagement to Larry.

Elliott with his romantic and highly conventional sense of how people should comport themselves under given circumstances had been disconcerted by the young people's behaviour. Not only had Larry come to lunch the very day after the break, but he had acted as though his position were unchanged. He was as pleasant, attentive and soberly gay as usual. He treated Isabel with the same comradely affectionateness with which he had always treated her. He seemed neither harassed, upset nor woebegone. Nor did Isabel appear dispirited. She looked as happy, she laughed as lightly, she jested as merrily as though she had not just taken a decisive and surely searing step in her life. Elliott could not make head or tail of it. From such scraps of their conversation as he caught he gathered that they had no intention of breaking any of the dates they had made. On the first opportunity he talked it over with his sister.

"It's not decent," he said. "They can't run around together as if they were still engaged. Larry really should have more sense of propriety. Besides, it damages Isabel's chances. Young Fotheringham, that boy at the British Embassy, is obviously taken with her; he's got money and he's very well connected; if he knew the coast was clear I wouldn't be at all surprised if he made her an offer. I think you ought to talk to her about it."

"My dear, Isabel's twenty and she has a technique for telling you to mind your own business without offensiveness which I've always found very difficult to cope with."

"Then you've brought her up extremely badly, Louisa. And besides, it *is* your business."

"That is a point on which you and she would certainly differ."

"You're trying my patience, Louisa."

"My poor Elliott, if you'd ever had a grown-up daughter you'd know that by comparison a bucking steer is easy to manage. And as to knowing what goes on inside her—well, it's much better to pretend you're the simple, innocent old fool she almost certainly takes you for."

"But you have talked the matter over with her?"

"I tried to. She laughed at me and told me there was really nothing to tell."

"Is she cut up?"

"I wouldn't know. All I do know is that she eats well and sleeps like a child."

"Well, take my word for it, if you let them go on like this they'll go off one of these days and get married without saying a word to anybody."

Mrs. Bradley permitted herself to smile.

"It must be a relief to you to think that at present we're living in a country where every facility is afforded to sexual irregularity and every obstacle put in the way of marriage."

"And quite rightly. Marriage is a serious matter on which rest the security of the family and the stability of the state. But marriage can only maintain its authority if extraconjugal relations are not only tolerated but sanctioned. Prostitution, my poor Louisa——"

"That'll do, Elliott," interrupted Mrs. Bradley. "I'm not interested in your views on the social and moral value of promiscuous fornication."

It was then he put forward a scheme that would interrupt Isabel's continued intercourse with Larry that was so repugnant to his sense of what was fitting. The Paris season was drawing to a close and all the best people were arranging to go to watering places or to Deauville before repairing for the rest of the summer to their ancestral châteaux in Touraine, Anjou or Brittany. Ordinarily Elliott went to London at the end of June, but his family feeling was strong and his affection for his sister and Isabel sincere; he had been quite ready to sacrifice himself and remain in Paris, if they wished it, when no one who was anyone was there; but he found himself now in the agreeable situation of being able to do what was best for others and at the same time what was convenient to himself. He proposed to Mrs. Bradley that the three of them should go to London immediately, where the season was still in full swing and where new interests and new friends would distract Isabel's mind from her unfortunate entanglement. According to the papers the great specialist on Mrs. Bradley's disease was then in the British capital and the desirability of consulting him would reasonably account for their precipitate departure and override any disinclination to leave Paris that Isabel might have. Mrs. Bradley fell in with the plan. She was puzzled by Isabel. She could not make up her mind whether she was as carefree as she seemed or whether, hurt, angry or heartsick, she was putting on a bold front to conceal her wounded feelings. Mrs. Bradley could only agree with Elliott that it would do Isabel good to see new people and new places.

Elliott got busy on the telephone and when Isabel, who had been spending the day at Versailles with Larry, came home, he was able to tell her that he had made an appointment for her mother to see the celebrated doctor three days from then, that he had engaged a suite at Claridge's and that they were starting on the next day but one. Mrs. Bradley watched her daughter while this intelligence was being somewhat smugly imparted to her by Elliott, but she did not turn a hair.

"Oh, darling, I'm so glad you're going to see that doctor," she cried with her usual rather breathless impetuosity. "Of course, you mustn't miss the chance. And it'll be grand going to London. How long are we going to stay?"

"It would be useless to come back to Paris," said Elliott. "There won't be a soul here in a week. I want you to stay with me at Claridge's for the rest of the season. There are always some good balls in July and of course there's Wimbledon. And then Goodwood and Cowes. I'm sure the Ellinghams will be glad to have us on their yacht for Cowes and the Bantocks always have a large party for Goodwood."

Isabel appeared to be delighted and Mrs. Bradley was reassured. It looked as though she were not giving Larry a thought.

Elliott had just finished telling me all this when mother and daughter came in. I had not seen them for more than eighteen months. Mrs. Bradley was a little thinner than before and more pasty-faced; she looked tired and none too well. But Isabel was blooming. With her high colour, the rich brown of her hair, her shining hazel eyes, her clear skin she gave an impression of such youth, of so much enjoyment of the mere fact of being alive that you felt half inclined to laugh with delight. She gave me the rather absurd notion of a pear, golden and luscious, perfectly ripe and simply asking to be eaten. She radiated warmth so that you thought that if you held out your hands you could feel its comfort. She looked taller than when I had last seen her, whether because she wore higher heels or because the clever dressmaker had cut her frock to conceal her youthful plumpness I don't know, and she held herself with the graceful ease of a girl who has played outdoor games since childhood. She was in short sexually a very attractive young woman. Had I been her mother I should have thought it high time she was married.

Glad of the opportunity to repay some of the kindness I had received from Mrs. Bradley in Chicago, I asked them all three to come to a play with me one evening. I arranged to give a luncheon for them.

"You'll be wise to get in at once, my dear fellow," said Elliott. "I've already let my friends know we're here and I presume that in a day or two we shall be fixed up for the rest of the season."

I understood by this that Elliott meant that then they would have no time for the likes of me and I laughed. Elliott gave me a glance in which I discerned a certain hauteur.

"But of course you'll generally find us here about six o'clock and we shall always be glad to see you," he said graciously, but with the evident intention of putting me, as an author, in my humble place.

But the worm sometimes turns.

"You must try to get in touch with the St. Olpherds," I said. "I hear they want to dispose of their Constable of Salisbury Cathedral."

"I'm not buying any pictures just now."

"I know, but I thought you might dispose of it for them."

A steely glitter came into Elliott's eyes.

"My dear fellow, the English are a great people, but they have never been able to paint and never will be able to paint. I am not interested in the English school."

(vii)

During the next four weeks I saw little of Elliott and his relations. He did them proud. He took them for a week end to a grand house in Sussex and for another week end to an even grander one in Wiltshire. He took them to the royal box at the opera as guests of a minor princess of the House of Windsor. He took them to lunch and dine with the great. Isabel went to several balls. He entertained at Claridge's a series of guests whose names made a fine show in the paper next day. He gave supper parties at Ciro's and the Embassy. In fact he did all the right things and Isabel would have had to be much more sophisticated than she was not to have been a trifle dazzled by the splendour and elegance he provided for her delectation. Elliott could flatter himself that he was taking all this trouble from the purely unselfish motive of distracting Isabel's mind from an unfortunate love affair; but I had a notion he got besides a good deal of satisfaction out of letting his sister see with her own eyes how familiar he was with the illustrious and fashionable. He was an admirable host and he took a delight in displaying his virtuosity.

I went to one or two of his parties myself and now and again I dropped in at Claridge's at six o'clock. I found Isabel surrounded by strapping young men in beautiful clothes who were in the Household Brigade or by elegant young men in less beautiful clothes from the Foreign Office. It was on one of these occasions that she drew me aside.

"I want to ask you something," she said. "D'you remember that evening we went to a drugstore and had an ice-cream soda?"

"Perfectly."

"You were very nice and helpful then. Will you be nice and helpful again?"

"I'll do my best."

"I want to talk to you about something. Couldn't we lunch one day?"

"Almost any day you like."

"Somewhere quiet."

"What d'you say to driving down to Hampton Court and lunching there? The gardens should be at their best just now and you could see Queen Elizabeth's bed."

The notion suited her and we fixed a day. But when the day came the weather, which had been fine and warm, broke; the sky was gray and a drizzling rain was falling. I called up and asked her if she wouldn't prefer to lunch in town.

"We shouldn't be able to sit in the gardens and the pictures will be so dark, we shan't see a thing."

"I've sat in lots of gardens and I'm fed to the teeth with old masters. Let's go anyway."

"All right."

I fetched her and we drove down. I knew a small hotel where one ate tolerably and we went straight there. On the way Isabel talked with her usual vivacity of the parties she had been to and the people she had met. She had been enjoying herself, but her comments on the various acquaintances she had made suggested to me that she had shrewdness and a quick eye for the absurd. The bad weather had kept visitors away and we were the only occupants of the dining room. The hotel specialized in homely English fare and we had a cut off a leg of excellent lamb with green peas and new potatoes and a deep-dish apple pie with Devonshire cream to follow. With a tankard of pale ale it made an excellent lunch. When we had finished I suggested that we should go into the empty coffee room where there were armchairs in which we could sit in comfort. It was chilly in there, but the fire was laid, so I put a match to it. The flames made the dingy room more companionable.

"That's that," I said. "Now tell me what you want to talk to me about."

"It's the same as last time," she chuckled. "Larry."

"So I guessed."

"You know that we've broken off our engagement."

"Elliott told me."

"Mamma's relieved and he's delighted."

She hesitated for a moment and then embarked upon the account of her talk with Larry of which I have done my best faithfully to inform the reader. It may surprise the reader that she should have chosen to tell so much to someone whom she knew so little. I don't suppose I had seen her a dozen times and, except for that one occasion at the drugstore, never alone. It did not surprise me. For one thing, as any writer will tell you, people do tell a writer things that they don't tell others. I don't know why, unless it is that having read one or two of his books they feel on peculiarly

70

intimate terms with him; or it may be that they dramatize themselves and, seeing themselves as it were characters in a novel, are ready to be as open with him as they imagine are to him the characters of his invention. And I think that Isabel felt that I liked Larry and her, and that their youth touched me, and that I was sympathetic to their distresses. She could not expect to find a friendly listener in Elliott who was disinclined to trouble himself with a young man who had spurned the best chance a young man ever had of getting into society. Nor could her mother help her. Mrs. Bradley had high principles and common sense. Her common sense assured her that if you wanted to get on in this world you must accept its conventions, and not to do what everybody else did clearly pointed to instability. Her high principles led her to believe that a man's duty was to go to work in a business where by energy and initiative he had a chance of earning enough money to keep his wife and family in accordance with the standards of his station, give his sons such an education as would enable them on reaching man's estate to make an honest living, and on his death leave his widow adequately provided for.

Isabel had a good memory and the various turns of the long discussion had engraved themselves upon it. I listened in silence till she had finished. She only interrupted herself once to ask me a question.

"Who was Ruysdael?"

"Ruysdael? He was a Dutch landscape painter. Why?"

She told me that Larry had mentioned him. He had said that Ruysdael at least had found an answer to the questions he was asking, and she repeated to me his flippant reply when she had enquired who he was.

"What d'you suppose he meant?"

I had an inspiration.

"Are you sure he didn't say Ruysbroek?"

"He might have. Who was he?"

"He was a Flemish mystic who lived in the fourteenth century."

"Oh," she said with disappointment.

It meant nothing to her. But it meant something to me. That was the first indication I had of the turn Larry's reflection was taking, and while she went on with her story, though still listening attentively, part of my mind busied itself with the possibilities that reference of his had suggested. I did not want to make too much of it, for it might be that he had only mentioned the name of the Ecstatic Teacher to make an argumentative point; it might also have a significance that had escaped Isabel. When he answered her question by saying Ruysbroek was just a guy he hadn't known in college he evidently meant to throw her off the scent.

71

"What do you make of it all?" she asked when she had come to an end. I paused before replying.

"D'you remember his saying that he was just going to loaf? If what he tells you is true his loafing seems to involve some very strenuous work."

"I'm sure it's true. But don't you see that if he'd worked as hard at any productive form of work he'd be earning a decent income?"

"There are people who are strangely constituted. There are criminals who'll work like beavers to contrive schemes that land them in prison and they no sooner get out than they start all over again and again land in prison. If they put as much industry, as much cleverness, resource and patience into honest practices they could make a handsome living and occupy important positions. But they're just made that way. They like crime."

"Poor Larry," she giggled. "You're not going to suggest that he's learning Greek to cook up a bank robbery."

I laughed too.

"No, I'm not. What I'm trying to tell you is that there are men who are possessed by an urge so strong to do some particular thing that they can't help themselves, they've got to do it. They're prepared to sacrifice everything to satisfy their yearning."

"Even the people who love them?"

"Oh, yes."

"Is that anything more than plain selfishness?"

"I wouldn't know," I smiled.

"What can be the possible use of Larry's learning dead languages?"

"Some people have a disinterested desire for knowledge. It's not an ignoble desire."

"What's the good of knowledge if you're not going to do anything with it?"

"Perhaps he is. Perhaps it will be sufficient satisfaction merely to know, as it's a sufficient satisfaction to an artist to produce a work of art. And perhaps it's only a step towards something further."

"If he wanted knowledge why couldn't he go to college when he came back from the war? It's what Dr. Nelson and Mamma wanted him to do."

"I talked to him about that in Chicago. A degree would be of no use to him. I have an inkling that he had a definite idea of what he wanted and felt he couldn't get it at a university. You know, in learning there's the lone wolf as well as the wolf who runs in the pack. I think Larry is one of those persons who can go no other way than their own."

"I remember once asking him if he wanted to write. He laughed and said he had nothing to write about."

"That's the most inconclusive reason for not writing that I've ever heard," I smiled.

Isabel made a gesture of impatience. She was in no mood even for the mildest jest.

"What I can't make out is why he should have turned out like this. Before the war he was just like everybody else. You wouldn't think it, but he plays a very good game of tennis and he's quite a decent golfer. He used to do all the things the rest of us did. He was a perfectly normal boy and there was no reason to suppose he wouldn't become a perfectly normal man. After all you're a novelist, you ought to be able to explain it."

"Who am I to explain the infinite complexities of human nature?"

"That's why I wanted to talk to you today," she added, taking no notice of what I said.

"Are you unhappy?"

"No, not exactly unhappy. When Larry isn't there I'm all right; it's when I'm with him that I feel so weak. Now it's just a sort of ache, like the stiffness you get after a long ride when you haven't been on a horse for months; it's not pain, it's not at all unbearable, but you're conscious of it. I shall get over it all right. I hate the idea of Larry making such a mess of his life."

"Perhaps he won't. It's a long, arduous road he's starting to travel, but it may be that at the end of it he'll find what he's seeking."

"What's that?"

"Hasn't it occurred to you? It seems to me that in what he said to you he indicated it pretty plainly. God."

"God!" she cried. But it was an exclamation of incredulous surprise. Our use of the same word, but in such a different sense, had a comic effect, so that we were obliged to laugh. But Isabel immediately grew serious again and I felt in her whole attitude something like fear. "What on earth makes you think that?"

"I'm only guessing. But you asked me to tell you what I thought as a novelist. Unfortunately you don't know what experience he had in the war that so profoundly moved him. I think it was some sudden shock for which he was unprepared. I suggest to you that whatever it was that happened to Larry filled him with a sense of the transiency of life and an anguish to be sure that there was a compensation for the sin and sorrow of the world."

I could see that Isabel didn't like the turn I had given the conversation. It made her feel shy and awkward.

"Isn't all that awfully morbid? One has to take the world as it comes. If we're here, it's surely to make the most of life."

"You're probably right."

"I don't pretend to be anything but a perfectly normal, ordinary girl. I want to have fun."

"It looks as though there were complete incompatibility of temper between you. It's much better that you should have found it out before marriage."

"I want to marry and have children and live——"

"In that state of life in which a merciful Providence has been pleased to place you," I interrupted, smiling.

"Well, there's no harm in that, is there? It's a very pleasant state and I'm quite satisfied with it."

"You're like two friends who want to take their holiday together, but one of them wants to climb Greenland's snowy mountains while the other wants to fish off India's coral strand. Obviously it's not going to work."

"Anyway I might get a sealskin coat off Greenland's snowy mountains, and I think it's very doubtful if there are any fish off India's coral strand."

"That remains to be seen."

"Why d'you say that?" she asked, frowning a little. "All the time you seem to be making some sort of mental reservation. Of course I know that I'm not playing the star part in this. Larry's got that. He's the idealist, he's the dreamer of a beautiful dream, and even if the dream doesn't come true it's rather thrilling to have dreamt it. I'm cast for the hard, mercenary, practical part. Common sense is never very sympathetic, is it? But what you forget is that it's I who'd have to pay. Larry would sweep along, trailing clouds of glory, and all there'd be left for me would be to tag along and make both ends meet. I want to live."

"I don't forget that at all. Years ago, when I was young, I knew a man who was a doctor, and not a bad one either, but he didn't practice. He spent years burrowing away in the library of the British Museum and at long intervals produced a huge pseudoscientific, pseudophilosophical book that nobody read and that he had to publish at his own expense. He wrote four or five of them before he died and they were absolutely worthless. He had a son who wanted to go into the army, but there was no money to send him to Sandhurst, so he had to enlist. He was killed in the war. He had a daughter too. She was very pretty and I was rather taken with her. She went on the stage, but she had no talent and she traipsed around the provinces playing small parts in second-rate companies at a miserable salary. His wife, after years of dreary, sordid drudgery broke down in health and the girl had to come home and nurse her and take on the drudgery her mother no longer had the strength for. Wasted, thwarted lives and all to no purpose. It's a toss-up when you decide to leave the beaten track. Many are called but few are chosen."

"Mother and Uncle Elliott approve of what I've done. Do you approve too?"

"My dear, what can that matter to you? I'm almost a stranger to you."

"I look upon you as a disinterested observer," she said, with a pleasant smile. "I should like to have your approval. You do think I've done right, don't you?"

"I think you've done right for you," I said, fairly confident that she would not catch the slight distinction I made in my reply.

"Then why have I a bad conscience?"

"Have you?"

With a smile still on her lips, but a slightly rueful smile now, she nodded.

"I know it's only horse sense. I know that every reasonable person would agree that I've done the only possible thing. I know that from every practical standpoint, from the standpoint of worldly wisdom, from the standpoint of common decency, from the standpoint of what's right and wrong, I've done what I ought to do. And yet at the bottom of my heart I've got an uneasy feeling that if I were better, if I were more disinterested, more unselfish, nobler, I'd marry Larry and lead his life. If I only loved him enough I'd think the world well lost."

"You might put it the other way about. If he loved you enough he wouldn't have hesitated to do what you want."

"I've said that to myself too. But it doesn't help. I suppose it's more in woman's nature to sacrifice herself than in a man's." She chuckled. "Ruth and the alien corn and all that sort of thing."

"Why don't you risk it?"

We had been talking quite lightly, almost as if we were having a casual conversation about people we both knew but in whose affairs we were not intimately concerned, and even when she narrated to me her talk with Larry Isabel had spoken with a sort of breezy gaiety, enlivening it with humour, as if she did not want me to take what she said too seriously. But now she went pale.

"I'm afraid."

For a while we were silent. A chill went down my spine as it strangely does when I am confronted with deep and genuine human emotion. I find it terrible and rather awe-inspiring.

"Do you love him very much?" I asked at last.

"I don't know. I'm impatient with him. I'm exasperated with him. I keep longing for him."

Silence again fell upon us. I didn't know what to say. The coffee room in which we sat was small, and heavy lace curtains over the window shut out the light. On the walls, covered with yellow marbled paper, were old sporting prints. With its mahogany furniture, its shabby leather chairs and its musty smell it was strangely reminiscent of a coffee room in a Dickens novel. I poked the fire and put more coal on it. Isabel suddenly began to speak.

"You see, I thought when it came to a showdown he'd knuckle under. I knew he was weak."

"Weak?" I cried. "What made you think that? A man who for a year withstood the disapproval of all his friends and associates because he was determined to go his own way."

"I could always do anything I wanted with him. I could turn him round my little finger. He was never a leader in the things we did. He just tagged along with the crowd."

I had lit a cigarette and watched the smoke ring I had made. It grew larger and larger and then faded away into the air.

"Mamma and Elliott thought it very wrong of me to go about with him afterwards as though nothing had happened, but I didn't take it very seriously. I kept on thinking up to the end that he'd yield. I couldn't believe that when he'd got it into his thick head that I meant what I said he wouldn't give in." She hesitated and gave me a smile of roguish, playful malice. "Will you be awfully shocked if I tell you something?"

"I think it very unlikely."

"When we decided to come to London I called Larry and asked him if we couldn't spend my last evening in Paris together. When I told them, Uncle Elliott said it was most improper and Mamma said she thought it unnecessary. When Mamma says something is unnecessary it means she thoroughly disapproves. Uncle Elliott asked me what the idea was and I said we were going to dine somewhere and then make a tour of the night clubs. He told Mamma she ought to forbid me to go. Mamma said, 'Will you pay any attention if I forbid you to go?' 'No, darling,' I said, 'none.' Then she said, 'That is what I imagined. In that case there doesn't seem to be much point in my forbidding it.'"

"Your mother appears to be a woman of enormous sense."

"I don't believe she misses much. When Larry called for me I went into her room to say good night to her. I'd made up a bit; you know, you have to in Paris or else you look so naked, and when she saw the dress I had on,

I had an uneasy suspicion from the way she took me in from top to toe that she had a pretty shrewd idea what I was after. But she didn't say anything. She just kissed me and said she hoped I'd have a good time."

"What were you after?"

Isabel looked at me doubtfully, as though she couldn't quite decide how frank she was prepared to be.

"I didn't think I was looking too bad and it was my last chance. Larry had reserved a table at Maxim's. We had lovely things to eat, all the things I particularly liked, and we had champagne. We talked our heads off, at least I did, and I made Larry laugh. One of the things I've liked about him is that I can always amuse him. We danced. When we'd had enough of that we went on to the Château de Madrid. We found some people we knew and joined them and we had more champagne. Then we all went to the Acacia. Larry dances quite well, and we fit. The heat and the music and the wine— I was getting a bit lightheaded. I felt absolutely reckless. I danced with my face against Larry's and I knew he wanted me. God knows, I wanted him. I had an idea. I suppose it had been at the back of my mind all the time. I thought I'd get him to come home with me and once I'd got him there, well, it was almost inevitable that the inevitable should happen."

"Upon my word you couldn't put it more delicately."

"My room was quite a way from Uncle Elliott's and Mamma's, so I knew there was no risk. When we were back in America I thought I'd write and say I was going to have a baby. He'd be obliged to come back and marry me, and when I'd got him home I didn't believe it would be hard to keep him there, especially with Mamma ill. 'What a fool I am not to have thought of that before,' I said to myself. 'Of course that'll settle everything.' When the music stopped I just stayed there in his arms. Then I said it was getting late and we had to take the train at noon, so we'd better go. We got into a taxi. I nestled close to him and he put his arms around me and kissed me. He kissed me, he kissed me—oh, it was heaven. It hardly seemed a moment before the taxi stopped at the door. Larry paid it.

" 'I shall walk home,' he said.

"The taxi rattled off and I put my arms round his neck.

" 'Won't you come up and have one last drink?' I said.

" 'Yes, if you like,' he said.

"He'd rung the bell and the door swung open. He switched on the light as we stepped in. I looked into his eyes. They were so trusting, so honest, so—so guileless; he so obviously hadn't the smallest idea that I was laying a trap for him; I felt I couldn't play him such a dirty trick. It was like taking candy off a child. D'you know what I did? I said, 'Oh well, perhaps you'd better not. Mamma's not very well tonight and if she's fallen asleep I don't want to wake her up. Good night.' I put my face up for him to kiss and pushed him out of the door. That was the end of that."

"Are you sorry?" I asked.

"I'm neither pleased nor sorry. I just couldn't help myself. It wasn't me that did what I did. It was just an impulse that took possession of me and acted for me." She grinned. "I suppose you'd call it my better nature."

"I suppose you would."

"Then my better nature must take the consequences. I trust in the future it'll be more careful."

That was in effect the end of our talk. It may be that it was some consolation to Isabel to have been able to speak to someone with entire freedom, but that was all the good I had been able to do her. Feeling I had been inadequate, I tried to say at least some small thing that would give her comfort.

"You know, when one's in love," I said, "and things go all wrong, one's terribly unhappy and one thinks one won't ever get over it. But you'll be astounded to learn what the sea will do."

"What do you mean?" she smiled.

"Well, love isn't a good sailor and it languishes on a sea voyage. You'll be surprised when you have the Atlantic between you and Larry to find how slight the pang is that before you sailed seemed intolerable."

"Do you speak from experience?"

"From the experience of a stormy past. When I suffered from the pangs of unrequited love I immediately got on an ocean liner."

The rain showed no sign of letting up, so we decided that Isabel could survive without seeing the noble pile of Hampton Court or even Queen Elizabeth's bed and drove back to London. I saw her two or three times after that, but only when other people were present, and then, having had enough of London for a while, I set off for the Tyrol.

CHAPTER THREE

(i)

FOR TEN YEARS AFTER THIS I saw neither Isabel nor Larry. I continued to see Elliott and indeed, for a reason that I shall tell later, more frequently than before, and from time to time I learnt from him what was happening to Isabel. But of Larry he could tell me nothing.

"For all I know he's still living in Paris, but I'm not likely to run across him. We don't move in the same circles," he added, not without complacency. "It's very sad that he should have gone so completely to seed. He comes of a very good family. I'm sure I could have made something of him if he'd put himself in my hands. Anyhow it was a lucky escape for Isabel."

My circle of acquaintance was not so restricted as Elliott's and I knew a number of persons in Paris whom he would have thought eminently undesirable. On my brief but not infrequent sojourns I asked one or other of them whether he had run across Larry or had news of him; a few knew him casually, but none could claim any intimacy with him and I could find nobody to give me news of him. I went to the restaurant at which he habitually dined, but found he had not been there for a long time, and they thought he must have gone away. I never saw him at any of the cafés on the Boulevard du Montparnasse which people who live in the neighbourhood are apt to go to.

His intention, after Isabel left Paris, was to go to Greece, but this he abandoned. What he actually did he told me himself many years later, but I will relate it now because it is more convenient to place events as far as I can in chronological order. He stayed on in Paris during the summer and worked without a break till autumn was well advanced.

"I thought I needed a rest from books then," he said, "I'd been working from eight to ten hours a day for two years. So I went to work in a coal mine."

"You did what?" I cried.

He laughed at my astonishment.

"I thought it would do me good to spend a few months in manual labour. I had a notion it would give me an opportunity to sort my thoughts and come to terms with myself."

I was silent. I wondered whether that was the only reason for this unexpected step or whether it was connected with Isabel's refusal to marry him. The fact was, I didn't know at all how deeply he loved her. Most people when they're in love invent every kind of reason to persuade themselves that it's only sensible to do what they want. I suppose that's why there are so many disastrous marriages. They are like those who put their affairs in the hands of someone they know to be a crook, but who happens to be an intimate friend because, unwilling to believe that a crook is a crook first and a friend afterwards, they are convinced that, however dishonest he may be with others, he won't be so with them. Larry was strong enough to refuse to sacrifice for Isabel's sake the life that he thought was the life for him, but it may be that to lose her was bitterer to endure than he had expected. It may be that like most of us he wanted to eat his cake and have it.

"Well, go on," I said.

"I packed my books and my clothes in a couple of trunks and got the American Express to store them. Then I put an extra suit and some linen in a grip and started off. My Greek teacher had a sister who was married to the manager of a mine near Lens and he gave me a letter to him. D'you know Lens?"

"No."

"It's in the North of France, not far from the Belgian border. I only spent a night there, at the station hotel, and next day I took a local to the place where the mine was. Ever been to a mining village?"

"In England."

"Well, I suppose it's much the same. There's the mine and the manager's house, rows and rows of trim little two-story houses, all alike, exactly alike, and it's so monotonous it makes your heart sink. There's a newish, ugly church and several bars. It was bleak and cold when I got there and a thin rain was falling. I went to the manager's office and sent in my letter. He was a little, fat man with red cheeks and the look of a guy who enjoys his food. They were short of labour, a lot of miners had been killed in the war, and there were a good many Poles working there, two or three hundred, I should think. He asked me one or two questions, he didn't much like my being an American, he seemed to think it rather fishy, but his brother-in-law's letter spoke well of me and anyhow he was glad to have me. He wanted to give me a job on the surface, but I told him I wanted to work down below. He said I'd find it hard if I wasn't used to it, but I told him I was prepared for that, so then he said I could be helper to a miner. That was boy's work really, but there weren't enough boys to go round. He was a nice fellow; he asked me if I'd done anything about finding a lodging, and when I told him I hadn't, he wrote an address on a piece of paper and said that if I went there the woman of the house would let me have a bed. She was the widow of a miner who'd been killed and her two sons were working in the mine.

"I took up my grip and went on my way. I found the house, and the door was opened for me by a tall, gaunt woman with graying hair and big, dark eyes. She had good features and she must have been nice-looking once. She wouldn't have been bad then in a haggard way except for two missing front teeth. She told me she hadn't a room, but there were two beds in a room she'd let to a Pole and I could have the other one. Her two sons had one of the upstairs rooms and she had the other. The room she showed me was on the ground floor and supposed, I imagined, to be the living-room; I should have liked a room to myself, but I thought I'd better not be fussy; and the drizzle had turned into a steady, light rain and I was wet already. I didn't want to go further and get soaked to the skin. So I said that would suit me and I settled in. They used the kitchen as a living-room. It had a couple of rickety armchairs in it. There was a coal shed in the yard which was also the bathhouse. The two boys and the Pole had taken their lunch with them, but she said I could eat with her at midday. I sat in the kitchen afterwards smoking and while she went on with her work she told me all about herself and her family. The others came in at the end of their shift. The Pole first and then the two boys. The Pole passed through the kitchen, nodded to me without speaking when our landlady told him I was to share his room, took a great kettle off the hob and went off to wash himself in the shed. The two boys were tall good-looking fellows notwithstanding the grime on their faces, and seemed inclined to be friendly. They looked upon me as a freak because I was American. One of them was nineteen, off to his military service in a few months, and the other eighteen.

"The Pole came back and then they went to clean up. The Pole had one of those difficult Polish names, but they called him Kosti. He was a big fellow, two or three inches taller than me, and heavily built. He had a pale fleshy face with a broad short nose and a big mouth. His eyes were blue and because he hadn't been able to wash the coal dust off his eyebrows and eyelashes he looked as if he was made up. The black lashes made the blue of his eyes almost startling. He was an ugly, uncouth fellow. The two boys after they'd changed their clothes went out. The Pole sat on in the kitchen, smoking a pipe and reading the paper. I had a book in my pocket, so I took it out and began reading too. I noticed that he glanced at me once or twice and presently he put his paper down.

"'What are you reading?' he asked.

"I handed him the book to see for himself. It was a copy of the *Princesse de Clèves* that I'd bought at the station in Paris because it was small enough to put in my pocket. He looked at it, then at me, curiously, and handed it back. I noticed an ironical smile on his lips.

"'Does it amuse you?'

"'I think it's very interesting—even absorbing.'

"'I read it at school at Warsaw. It bored me stiff.' He spoke very good French, with hardly a trace of Polish accent. 'Now I don't read anything but the newspaper and detective stories.'

"Madame Duclerc, that was our old girl's name, with an eye on the soup

81

that was cooking for supper, sat at the table darning socks. She told Kosti that I had been sent to her by the manager of the mine and repeated what else I had seen fit to tell her. He listened, puffing away at his pipe, and looked at me with brilliantly blue eyes. They were hard and shrewd. He asked me a few questions about myself. When I told him I had never worked in a mine before his lips broke again into an ironical smile.

" 'You don't know what you're in for. No one would go to work in a mine who could do anything else. But that's your affair and doubtless you have your reasons. Where did you live in Paris?'

"I told him.

" 'At one time I used to go to Paris every year, but I kept to the Grands Boulevards. Have you ever been to Larue's? It was my favorite restaurant.'

"That surprised me a bit because, you know, it's not cheap."

"Far from it."

"I fancy he saw my surprise, for he gave me once more his mocking smile, but evidently didn't think it necessary to explain further. We went on talking in a desultory fashion and then the two boys came in. We had supper and when we'd finished Kosti asked me if I'd like to come to the *bistro* with him and have a beer. It was just a rather large room with a bar at one end of it and a number of marble-topped tables with wooden chairs around them. There was a mechanical piano and someone had put a coin in the slot and it was braying out a dance tune. Only three tables were occupied besides ours. Kosti asked me if I played belote. I'd learnt it with some of my student friends, so I said I did and he proposed that we should play for the beer. I agreed and he called for cards. I lost a beer and a second beer. Then he proposed that we should play for money. He had good cards and I had bad luck. We were playing for very small stakes, but I lost several francs. This and the beer put him in a good humour and he talked. It didn't take me long to guess, both by his way of expressing himself and by his manners, that he was a man of education. When he spoke again of Paris it was to ask me if I knew so and so and so and so, American women I had met at Elliott's when Aunt Louisa and Isabel were staying with him. He appeared to know them better than I did and I wondered how it was that he found himself in his present position. It wasn't late, but we had to get up at the crack of dawn.

" 'Let's have one more beer before we go,' said Kosti.

"He sipped it and peered at me with his shrewd little eyes. I knew what he reminded me of then, an ill-tempered pig.

" 'Why have you come here to work in this rotten mine?' he asked me.

" 'For the experience.'

" '*Tu es fou, mon petit,*' he said.

" 'And why are you working in it?'

"He shrugged his massive, ungainly shoulders.

" 'I entered the nobleman's cadet school when I was a kid, my father was a general under the Czar and I was a cavalry officer in the last war. I couldn't stand Pilsudski. We arranged to kill him, but someone gave us away. He shot those of us he caught. I managed to get across the frontier just in time. There was nothing for me but the Foreign Legion or a coal mine. I chose the lesser of two evils.'

"I had already told Kosti what job I was to have in the mine and he had said nothing, but now, putting his elbow on the marble-topped table, he said:

" 'Try to push my hand back.'

"I knew the old trial of strength and I put my open palm against his. He laughed. 'Your hand won't be as soft as that in a few weeks.' I pushed with all my might, but I could make no effect against his huge strength and gradually he pressed my hand back and down to the table.

" 'You're pretty strong,' he was good enough to say. 'There aren't many men who keep up as long as that. Listen, my helper's no good, he's a puny little Frenchman, he hasn't got the strength of a louse. You come along with me tomorrow and I'll get the foreman to let me have you instead.'

" 'I'd like that,' I said. 'D'you think he'll do it?'

" 'For a consideration. Have you got fifty francs to spare?'

"He stretched out his hand and I took a note out of my wallet. We went home and to bed. I'd had a long day and I slept like a log."

"Didn't you find the work terribly hard?" I asked Larry.

"Back-breaking at first," he grinned. "Kosti worked it with the foreman and I was made his helper. At that time Kosti was working in a space about the size of a hotel bathroom and one got to it through a tunnel so low that you had to crawl through it on your hands and knees. It was as hot as hell in there and we worked in nothing but our pants. There was something terribly repulsive in that great white fat torso of Kosti's; he looked like a huge slug. The row of the pneumatic cutter in that narrow space was deafening. My job was to gather the blocks of coal that he hacked away and load a basket with them and drag the basket through the tunnel to its mouth, where it could be loaded into a truck when the train came along at intervals on its way to the elevators. It's the only coal mine I've ever known, so I don't know if that's the normal practice. It seemed amateurish to me and it was damned hard work. At half time we knocked off for a rest and ate our lunch and smoked. I wasn't sorry when we were through for the day, and gosh, it was good to have a bath. I thought I'd never get my feet clean; they were as black as ink. Of course my hands blistered and they got as sore as the devil, but they healed. I got used to the work."

"How long did you stick it out?"

"I was only kept on that job for a few weeks. The trucks that carried the coal to the elevators were hauled by a tractor and the driver was a poor mechanic and the engine was always breaking down. Once he couldn't get it going and he didn't seem to know what to do. Well, I'm a pretty good mechanic, so I had a look at it and in half an hour I got it working. The foreman told the manager and he sent for me and asked me if I knew about cars. The result was that he gave me the mechanic's job; of course it was monotonous, but it was easy, and because they didn't have any more engine trouble they were pleased with me.

"Kosti was as sore as hell at my leaving him. I suited him and he'd got used to me. I got to know him pretty well, working with him all day, going to the *bistro* with him after supper, and sharing a room with him. He was a funny fellow. He was the sort of man who'd have appealed to you. He didn't mix with the Poles and we didn't go to the cafés they went to. He couldn't forget he was a nobleman and had been a cavalry officer and he treated them like dirt. Naturally they resented it, but they couldn't do anything about it; he was as strong as an ox, and if it had ever come to a scrap, knives or no knives, he'd have been a match for half a dozen of them together. I got to know some of them all the same, and they told me he'd been a cavalry officer all right in one of the smart regiments, but it was a lie about his having left Poland for political reasons. He'd been kicked out of the Officers' Club at Warsaw and cashiered because he'd been caught cheating at cards. They warned me against playing with him. They said that was why he fought shy of them, because they knew too much about him and wouldn't play with him.

"I'd been losing to him consistently, not much, you know, just a few francs a night, but when he won he always insisted on paying for drinks, so it didn't amount to anything really. I thought I was just having a run of bad luck or that I didn't play as well as he did. But after that I kept my eyes skinned and I was dead sure he was cheating, but d'you know, for the life of me I couldn't see how he did it. Gosh, he was clever. I knew he simply couldn't have the best cards all the time. I watched him like a lynx. He was as cunning as a fox and I guess he saw I'd been put wise to him. One night, after we'd been playing for a while, he looked at me with that rather cruel, sarcastic smile of his which was the only way he knew how to smile, and said:

" 'Shall I show you a few tricks?'

"He took the pack of cards and asked me to name one. He shuffled them and he told me to choose one; I did, and it was the card I'd named. He did two or three more tricks and then he asked me if I played poker. I said I did and he dealt me a hand. When I looked at it I saw I'd got four aces and a king.

" 'You'd be willing to bet a good deal on that hand, wouldn't you?' he asked.

" 'My whole stack,' I answered.

" 'You'd be silly.' He put down the hand he'd dealt himself. It was a straight flush. How it was done I don't know. He laughed at my amazement. 'If I weren't an honest man I'd have had your shirt by now.'

" 'You haven't done so badly as it is,' I grinned.

" 'Chicken feed. Not enough to buy a dinner at Larue's.'

"We continued to play pretty well every night. I came to the conclusion that he cheated not so much for the money as for the fun of it. It gave him a queer satisfaction to know that he was making a fool of me, and I think he got a lot of amusement out of knowing that I was on to what he was doing and couldn't see how it was done.

"But that was only one side of him and it was the other side that made him so interesting to me. I couldn't reconcile the two. Though he boasted he never read anything but the paper and detective stories he was a cultivated man. He was a good talker, caustic, harsh, cynical, but it was exhilarating to listen to him. He was a devout Catholic and had a crucifix hanging over his bed, and he went to Mass every Sunday regularly. On Saturday nights he used to get drunk. The *bistro* we went to was crammed jammed full then, and the air was heavy with smoke. There were quiet, middle-aged miners with their families, and there were groups of young fellows kicking up a hell of a row, and there were men with sweaty faces round tables playing belote with loud shouts, while their wives sat by, a little behind them, and watched. The crowd and the noise had a strange effect on Kosti and he'd grow serious and start talking—of all unlikely subjects—of mysticism. I knew nothing of it then but an essay of Maeterlinck's on Ruysbroek that I'd read in Paris. But Kosti talked of Plotinus and Denis the Areopagite and Jacob Boehme the shoemaker and Meister Eckhart. It was fantastic to hear that great hulking bum, who'd been thrown out of his own world, that sardonic, bitter down-and-out speaking of the ultimate reality of things and the blessedness of union with God. It was all new to me and I was confused and excited. I was like someone who's lain awake in a darkened room and suddenly a chink of light shoots through the curtains and he knows he only has to draw them and there the country will be spread before him in the glory of the dawn. But when I tried to get him on the subject when he was sober he got mad at me. His eyes were spiteful.

"'How should I know what I was talking about when I didn't know what I was saying?' he snapped.

"But I knew he was lying. He knew perfectly well what he was talking about. He knew a lot. Of course he was soused, but the look in his eyes, the rapt expression on his ugly face weren't due only to drink. There was more to it than that. The first time he talked in that way he said something that I've never forgotten, because it horrified me; he said that the world isn't a creation, for out of nothing nothing comes, but a manifestation of the eternal nature; well, that was all right, but then he added that evil is as direct a manifestation of the divine as good. They were strange words to hear in that sordid, noisy café, to the accompaniment of dance tunes on the mechanical piano."

(ii)

To give the reader a moment's rest I am starting here upon a new section, but I am doing it only for his convenience; the conversation was uninterrupted. I may take this opportunity to say that Larry spoke without haste, often choosing his words with care, and though of course I do not pretend to report them exactly, I have tried to reproduce not only the matter, but the manner of his discourse. His voice, rich in tone, had a musical quality that was grateful to the ear; and as he talked, without gesticulation of any kind, puffing away at his pipe and stopping now and again to relight it, he looked you in the face with a pleasant, often whimsical expression in his dark eyes.

"Then the spring came, late in that flat, dismal part of the country, cold and rainy still; but sometimes a fine warm day made it hard to leave the world above ground to go down hundreds of feet in a rickety elevator, crowded with miners in their grimy overalls, into the bowels of the earth. It was spring all right, but it seemed to come shyly in that grim and sordid landscape as though unsure of a welcome. It was like a flower, a daffodil or a lily, growing in a pot on the window sill of a slum dwelling and you wondered what it did there. One Sunday morning we were lying in bed, we always slept late on Sunday morning, and I was reading, when Kosti said to me out of a blue sky:

"'I'm getting out of here. D'you want to come with me?'

"I knew a lot of the Poles went back to Poland in the summer to get the harvest in, but it was early for that, and besides, Kosti couldn't go back to Poland.

86

" 'Where are you going?' I asked.

" 'Tramping. Across Belgium and into Germany and down the Rhine. We could get work on a farm that would see us through the summer.'

"It didn't take me a minute to make up my mind.

" 'It sounds fine,' I said.

"Next day we told the foreman we were through. I found a fellow who was willing to take my grip in exchange for a rucksack. I gave the clothes I didn't want or couldn't carry on my back to the younger of Madame Duclerc's sons who was about my size. Kosti left a bag, packed what he wanted in his rucksack and the day after, as soon as the old girl had given us our coffee, we started off.

"We weren't in any hurry as we knew we couldn't get taken on at a farm at least until the hay was ready to cut, and so we dawdled along through France and Belgium by way of Namur and Liége and got into Germany through Aachen. We didn't do more than ten or twelve miles a day. When we liked the look of a village we stopped there. There was always some kind of an inn where we could get beds and an alehouse where we could get something to eat and beer to drink. On the whole we had fine weather. It was grand to be out in the open air after all those months in the mine. I don't think I've ever realized before how good a green meadow is to look at and how lovely a tree is when the leaves aren't out yet, but when the branches are veiled in a faint green mist. Kosti started to teach me German and I believe he spoke it as well as he spoke French. As we trudged along he would tell me the German for the various objects we passed, a cow, a horse, a man and so on, and then make me repeat simple German sentences. It made the time pass and by the time we got into Germany I could at least ask for the things I wanted.

"Cologne was a bit out of our way, but Kosti insisted on going there, on account of the Eleven Thousand Virgins, he said, and when we got there he went on a bat. I didn't see him for three days and when he turned up at the room we'd taken in a sort of workmen's rooming-house he was very surly. He'd got in a fight and he had a black eye and a cut on his lip. He wasn't a pretty object, I can tell you. He went to bed for twenty-four hours, and then we started to walk down the valley of the Rhine towards Darmstadt, where he said the country was good and we stood the best chance of getting work.

"I never enjoyed anything more. The fine weather held and we wandered through towns and villages. When there were sights to see we stopped off and looked at them. We put up where we could and once or twice we slept in a loft on the hay. We ate at wayside inns and when we got in the wine country we turned from beer to wine. We made friends with the people in the taverns we drank in. Kosti had a sort of rough joviality that inspired them with confidence and he'd play skat with them, that's a German card game, and skin them with such bluff good humour, with the earthy jokes they appreciated, that they hardly minded losing their pfennigs to him. I practised my German on them. I'd bought a little English-German conversation grammar at Cologne and I was getting on pretty well. And then at night, when he'd got a couple of litres of white wine inside him, Kosti would talk in a strange morbid way of the flight from the Alone to the Alone, of the Dark Night of the Soul and of the final ecstasy in which the creature becomes one with the Beloved. But when in the early morning, as we walked through the smiling country, with the dew still on the grass, I tried to get him to tell me more, he grew so angry that he could have hit me.

"'Shut up, you fool,' he said. 'What do you want with all that stuff and nonsense? Come, let's get on with our German.'

"You can't argue with a man who's got a fist like a steam hammer and wouldn't think twice about using it. I'd seen him in a rage. I knew he was capable of laying me out cold and leaving me in a ditch and I wouldn't have put it past him to empty my pockets while I was out. I couldn't make head or tail of him. When wine had loosened his tongue and he spoke of the Ineffable, he shed the rough obscene language that he ordinarily used, like the grimy overalls he wore in the mine, and he was well spoken and even eloquent. I couldn't believe he wasn't sincere. I don't know how it occurred to me, but I got the idea somehow that he'd taken on that hard, brutal labour of the mine to mortify his flesh. I thought he hated that great, uncouth body of his and wanted to torture it and that his cheating and his bitterness and his cruelty were the revolt of his will against—oh, I don't know what you'd call it—against a deep-rooted instinct of holiness, against a desire for God that terrified and yet obsessed him.

"We'd taken our time, the spring was pretty well over and the trees were in full leaf. The grapes in the vineyards were beginning to fill out. We kept to the dirt roads as much as we could and they were getting dusty. We were in the neighbourhood of Darmstadt and Kosti said we'd better start looking for a job. Our money was getting short. I had half a dozen travellers' cheques in my pocket, but I'd made up my mind not to use them if I could possibly help it. When we saw a farmhouse that looked promising we stopped and asked if they wanted a couple of hands. I daresay we didn't look very inviting. We were dusty and sweaty and dirty. Kosti looked a terrible ruffian and I don't suppose I looked much better either. We were turned down time after time. At one place the farmer said he'd take Kosti but couldn't do with me and Kosti said we were buddies and wouldn't separate. I told him to go ahead, but he wouldn't. I was surprised. I knew Kosti had taken a fancy to me, though I couldn't imagine why, as I didn't begin to be the kind of guy he had any use for, but I would never have thought he liked me well enough to refuse a job on my account. I felt rather conscience-stricken as we walked on, because I didn't really like him, in fact I found him rather repulsive, but when I tried to say something to show I was pleased with what he'd done, he bit my head off.

"But at last our luck turned. We'd just gone through a village in a hollow and we came to a rambling farmhouse that didn't look so bad. We knocked at the door and a woman opened it. We offered ourselves as usual. We said we didn't want any wages, but were willing to work for our board and lodging, and to my surprise instead of slamming the door in our face, she told us to wait. She called to someone inside the house and presently a man came out. He had a good stare at us and asked us where we came from. He asked to see our papers. He gave me another stare when he saw I was American. He didn't seem to like it much, but anyhow he asked us to come in and have a glass of wine. He took us into the kitchen and we sat down. The woman brought a flagon and some glasses. He told us that his hired man had been gored by a bull and was in hospital and wouldn't be fit for anything till after the harvest was in. With so many men killed, and others going into the factories that were springing up along the Rhine, it was the devil's own job to get labour. We knew that and had been counting on it. Well, to make a long story short he said he'd take us. There was plenty of room in the house, but I suppose he didn't fancy having us there; anyway he told us there were two beds in the hayloft and that's where we were to sleep.

"The work wasn't hard. There were the cows to look after and the hogs; the machinery was in a bad way, and we had to do something about that; but I had some leisure. I loved the sweet-smelling meadows and in the evenings I used to wander about and dream. It was a good life.

"The household consisted of old Becker, his wife, his widowed daughter-in-law and her children. Becker was a heavy, gray-haired man in the late forties; he'd been through the war and still limped from a wound in the leg. It hurt him a lot and he drank to kill the pain. He was generally high by the time he got to bed. Kosti got on with him fine and they used to go down to the inn together after supper to play skat and swill wine. Frau Becker had been a hired girl. They'd got her out of an orphanage and Becker had married her soon after his wife's death. She was a good many years younger than he was, rather handsome in a way, full-blown, with red cheeks and fair hair and a hungry sensual look. It didn't take Kosti long to come to the con-

89

clusion that there was something doing there. I told him not to be a fool.
We had a good job and we didn't want to lose it. He only jeered at me; he
said Becker wasn't satisfying her and she was asking for it. I knew it was
useless to appeal to his sense of decency, but I told him to be careful; it
might be that Becker wouldn't see what he was after, but there was his
daughter-in-law and she wasn't missing anything.

"Ellie, that was her name, was a thickset, big young woman, well under
thirty, with black eyes and black hair, a sallow square face and a sullen look.
She still wore mourning for her husband killed at Verdun. She was very
devout and on Sunday mornings trudged down to the village to early Mass
and again in the afternoon to vespers. She had three children, one of whom
had been born after her husband's death, and she never spoke at meals
except to scold them. She did a little work on the farm, but spent most of
her time looking after the kids, and in the evening sat by herself in the
sitting-room, with the door open so that she could hear if one of them was
crying, and read novels. The two women hated one another. Ellie despised
Frau Becker because she was a foundling and had been a servant, and bitterly resented her being the mistress of the house and in a position to give
orders.

"Ellie was the daughter of a prosperous farmer and had brought a good
dowry with her. She hadn't gone to the village school, but to Zwingenberg,
the nearest town, where there was a girl's *gymnasium* and she'd got quite a
good education. Poor Frau Becker had come to the farm when she was fourteen and if she could read and write that's about all she could do. That was
another cause of discord between the two women. Ellie lost no opportunity
of showing off her knowledge, and Frau Becker, red in the face with anger,
would ask what use it was to a farmer's wife. Then Ellie would look at her
husband's identification disc which she wore on a steel chain round her
wrist and with a bitter look on her sullen face say:

" 'Not a farmer's wife. Only a farmer's widow. Only the widow of a hero
who gave his life for his country.'

"Poor old Becker had his work cut out to keep the peace between them."

"But what did they make of you?" I interrupted Larry.

"Oh, they thought I'd deserted from the American Army and couldn't go
back to America or I'd be put in jail. That's how they explained that I didn't
care to go down to the inn and drink with Becker and Kosti. They thought
I didn't want to attract attention to myself and have the village constable
asking questions. When Ellie found out I was trying to learn German she
brought out her old schoolbooks and said she'd teach me. So after supper
she and I would go in the sitting-room, leaving Frau Becker in the kitchen,

and I'd read aloud to her while she corrected my accent and tried to make me understand words I couldn't get the sense of. I guessed she was doing it not so much to help me as to put something over on Frau Becker.

"All this time Kosti was trying to make Frau Becker and wasn't getting anywhere. She was a jolly, merry woman and quite prepared to joke and laugh with him, and he had a way with him with women. I guess she knew what he was after and I daresay she was flattered, but when he started pinching her she told him to keep his hands to himself and smacked his face. And I bet it was a good hard smack."

Larry hesitated a little and smiled rather shyly.

"I've never been the sort who thinks women are after me, but it occurred to me that—well, that Frau Becker had fallen for me. It made me rather uncomfortable. For one thing she was a lot older than me, and then old Becker had been very decent to us. She dished out the food at table and I couldn't help noticing that she helped me more liberally than the others, and she seemed to me to look for opportunities of being alone with me. She'd smile at me in what I suppose you'd call a provocative manner. She'd ask me if I had a girl and say that a young fellow like me must suffer for the want of it in a place like that. You know the sort of thing. I only had three shirts and they were pretty well worn. Once she said it was a disgrace that I should wear such rags and if I'd bring them along she'd mend them. Ellie heard her and next time we were alone said that if I had anything to mend she'd do it. I said it didn't matter. But a day or two later I found that my socks had been darned and my shirts patched and put back on the bench in the loft on which we kept our things; but which of them had done it I didn't know. Of course I didn't take Frau Becker seriously; she was a good-natured old soul and I thought it might be just motherliness on her part; but then one day Kosti said to me:

" 'Listen, it's not me she wants; it's you. I haven't got a chance.'

" 'Don't talk such nonsense,' I said to him. 'She's old enough to be my mother.'

" 'What of it? You go ahead, my boy, I won't stand in your way. She's not so young as she might be, but she's a fine figure of a woman.'

" 'Oh, shut up.'

" 'Why d'you hesitate? Not on my account, I hope. I'm a philosopher and I know there are as good fish in the sea as ever came out. I don't blame her. You're young. I've been young too. *Jeunesse ne dure qu'un moment.*'

"I wasn't too pleased that Kosti was so sure of what I didn't want to believe. I didn't quite know how to deal with the situation, and then I recalled various things that hadn't struck me at the time. Things said by Ellie that I hadn't paid much attention to. But now I understood them and I was pretty sure that she too knew what was happening. She'd turn up suddenly in the kitchen when Frau Becker and I happened to be alone. I got the impression that she was watching us. I didn't like it. I thought she was out to catch us, I knew she hated Frau Becker, and if she had half a chance she'd make trouble. Of course I knew she couldn't catch us, but she was a malevolent creature and I didn't know what lies she mightn't invent and pour into old Becker's ears. I didn't know what to do except to pretend I was such a fool I didn't see what the old girl was up to. I was happy at the farm and enjoying the work and I didn't want to go till after we'd got the harvest in."

I couldn't help smiling. I could imagine what Larry had looked like then, in his patched shirt and shorts, his face and neck burnt brown by the hot sun of the Rhine valley, with his lithe slim body and his black eyes in their deep sockets. I could well believe that the sight of him set the matronly Frau Becker, so blond, so full-breasted, all of a flutter with desire.

"Well, what happened?" I asked.

"Well, the summer wore on. We worked like demons there. We cut and stacked the hay. Then the cherries were ripe, Kosti and I got up on ladders and picked them, and the two women put them in great baskets and old Becker took them into Zwingenberg and sold them. Then we cut the rye. And of course there were always the animals to look after. We were up before dawn and we didn't stop work till nightfall. I supposed Frau Becker had given me up as a bad job; as far as I could without offending her, I kept her at arm's length. I was too sleepy to read much German in the evenings and soon after supper I'd take myself off to our loft and fall into bed. Most evenings Becker and Kosti went to the inn down in the village, but I was fast asleep by the time Kosti came back. It was hot in the loft and I slept naked.

"One night I was awakened. At the first moment I couldn't make out what it was; I was only half awake. I felt a hot hand on my mouth and I realized somebody was in bed with me. I tore the hand away and then a mouth was pressed to mine, two arms were thrown round me and I felt Frau Becker's great breasts against my body.

"'*Sei still*,' she whispered. 'Be quiet.'

"She pressed up against me and kissed my face with hot, full lips and her hands travelled over my body and she twined her legs in mine."

Larry stopped. I giggled.

"What did you do?"

He gave me a deprecating smile. He even flushed a little.

"What could I do? I could hear Kosti breathing heavily in his sleep in the bed next to mine. The situation of Joseph has always seemed to me faintly ridiculous. I was only just twenty-three. I couldn't make a scene and kick her out. I didn't want to hurt her feelings. I did what was expected of me.

"Then she slipped out of bed and tiptoed out of the loft. I can tell you, I heaved a sigh of relief. You know, I'd been scared. 'Gosh,' I said, 'what a risk to take!' I thought it likely that Becker had come home drunk and fallen asleep in a stupor, but they slept in the same bed, and it might be that he'd woken up and seen his wife wasn't there. And there was Ellie. She always said she didn't sleep well. If she'd been awake she'd have heard Frau Becker go downstairs and out of the house. And then, suddenly, something struck me. When Frau Becker was in bed with me I'd felt a piece of metal against my skin. I'd paid no attention, you know one doesn't in those circumstances, and I'd never thought of asking myself what the devil it was. And now it flashed across me. I was sitting on the side of my bed thinking and worrying about the consequences of all this and it was such a shock that I jumped up. The piece of metal was Ellie's husband's identification disc that she wore round her wrist and it wasn't Frau Becker that had been in bed with me. It was Ellie."

I roared with laughter. I couldn't stop.

"It may seem funny to you," said Larry. "It didn't seem funny to me."

"Well, now you look back on it, don't you think there is just a faint element of the humorous about it?"

An unwilling smile played on his lips.

"Perhaps. But it was an awkward situation. I didn't know what it was going to lead to. I didn't like Ellie. I thought her a most unpleasant female."

"But how could you mistake one for the other?"

"It was pitch dark. She never said a word except to tell me to keep my trap shut. They were both big stout women. I thought Frau Becker had her eye on me. It never occurred to me for a moment that Ellie gave me a thought. She was always thinking of her husband. I lit a cigarette and thought the position over and the more I thought of it the less I liked it. It seemed to me that the best thing I could do was to get out.

"I'd often cursed Kosti because he was so hard to wake. When we were at the mine I used to have to shake the life out of him to get him up in time to go to work. But I was thankful now that he slept so heavily. I lit my lantern and dressed, bundled my things into my rucksack—I hadn't got much, so it didn't take a minute—and slipped my arms through the straps. I walked across the loft in my stocking feet and didn't put my shoes on till I got to the bottom of the ladder. I blew out the lantern. It was a dark night, with no moon, but I knew my way to the road and I turned in the direction of the village. I walked fast as I wanted to get through it before anyone was up and about. It was only twelve miles to Zwingenberg and I got there just as it was stirring. I shall never forget that walk. There wasn't a sound except my footsteps on the road and now and then the crowing of a cock in a farm. Then the first grayness when it wasn't yet light and not quite dark, and the first hint of dawn, and the sunrise with the birds all starting to sing, and that lush green country, meadows and woods and the wheat in the fields silvery gold in the cool light of the beginning day. I got a cup of coffee at Zwingenberg and a roll, then I went to the post office and sent a wire to the American Express to have my clothes and my books sent to Bonn."

"Why Bonn?" I interrupted.

"I'd taken a fancy to it when we stopped off there on our tramp down the Rhine. I liked the way the light shone on the roofs and the river, and its old narrow streets, and its villas and gardens and avenues of chestnut trees and the rococo buildings of the university. It struck me then it wouldn't be a bad place to stay in for a bit. But I thought I'd better present a respectable appearance when I got there, I looked like a tramp and I didn't think I'd inspire much confidence if I went to a pension and asked for a room, so I took a train to Frankfurt and bought myself a grip and a few clothes. I stayed in Bonn off and on for a year."

"And did you get anything out of your experience, at the mine, I mean, and on the farm?"

"Yes," said Larry, nodding his head and smiling.

But he didn't tell me what it was and I knew him well enough by then to know that when he felt like telling you something he did, but when he didn't he would turn off questions with a cool pleasantry that made it useless to insist. For I must remind the reader that he narrated all this to me ten years after it happened. Till then, when I once more came in contact with him, I had no notion where he was or how he was engaged. For all I knew he might be dead. Except for my friendship with Elliott, who kept me posted with the course of Isabel's life and so reminded me of Larry, I should doubtless have forgotten his existence.

(iii)

Isabel was married to Gray Maturin early in the June of the year after the termination of her engagement to Larry. Though Elliott hated leaving Paris at a moment when the season was at its height and he must miss a number of grand parties, his family feeling was too strong to allow him to neglect what he thought a social duty. Isabel's brothers were unable to leave their distant posts and so it behooved him to make the irksome journey to Chicago to give his niece away. Remembering that French aristocrats had gone to the guillotine in all their finery, he made a special journey to London to get himself a new morning coat, a dove-gray double-breasted waistcoat and a silk hat. On his return to Paris he invited me to come and see them on. He was in a state of perturbation because the gray pearl he usually wore in his necktie would not make any sort of effect against the pale gray tie he had chosen as suitable to the festive occasion. I suggested his emerald-and-diamond pin.

"If I were a guest—yes," he said. "But in the particular position I shall occupy I *feel* that a pearl is indicated."

He was much pleased with the marriage, which concorded with all his ideas of propriety, and he spoke of it with the unctuousness of a dowager duchess expressing herself on the suitability of a union between a scion of the La Rochefoucaulds with a daughter of the Montmorencys. As a visible mark of his satisfaction he was taking over as a wedding present, sparing no expense, a fine portrait by Nattier of a princess of the House of France.

It appeared that Henry Maturin had bought for the young couple a house in Astor Street so that they should be close to where Mrs. Bradley lived and not too far from his own palatial residence on Lake Shore Drive. By a happy chance, in which I suspected the deft complicity of Elliott, Gregory Brabazon was in Chicago at the time the purchase was made and the decoration was entrusted to him. When Elliott returned to Europe and, throwing in his hand so far as the season in Paris was concerned, came straight to London he brought photographs of the result. Gregory Brabazon had let himself go. In the drawing-room and dining-room he had gone all George the Second and it was very grand. In the library, which was to be Gray's den, he had been inspired by a room in the Amalienburg Palace at Munich, and except that there was no place in it for books it was perfect. Save for the twin beds, Louis Quinze visiting Madame de Pompadour would have found himself perfectly at home in the bedroom Gregory had provided for this young American couple, but Isabel's bathroom would have been an eye-opener to him; it was all glass—walls, ceiling and bath—and on the walls silver fish meandered profusely among gilded aquatic plants.

"Of course it's a tiny house," said Elliott, "but Henry told me the decoration set him back a hundred thousand dollars. A fortune to some people."

The ceremony was performed with such pomp as the Episcopal church could afford.

"Not like a wedding at Nôtre Dame," he told me complacently, "but for a Protestant affair it didn't lack style."

The press had behaved very handsomely and Elliott negligently tossed the cuttings to me. He showed me photographs of Isabel, hefty but handsome in her wedding dress, and Gray, a massive but fine figure of a man, a trifle self-conscious in his formal clothes. There was a group of the young couple with the bridesmaids and another group with Mrs. Bradley in a sumptuous garment and Elliott holding his new silk hat with a grace that only he could have achieved. I asked how Mrs. Bradley was.

"She's lost a good deal of weight and I don't like her colour, but she's pretty well. Of course the whole thing was a strain on her, but now it's all over she'll be able to rest up."

A year later Isabel was delivered of a daughter, to whom, following the fashion of the moment, she gave the name of Joan; and after an interval of two years she had another daughter whom, following another fashion, she called Priscilla.

One of Henry Maturin's partners died and the other two under pressure soon afterwards retired, so that he entered into sole possession of the business over which he had always exercised despotic control. He realized the ambition he had long entertained and took Gray into partnership with him. The firm had never been so prosperous.

"They're making money hand over fist, my dear fellow," Elliott told me. "Why, Gray at the age of twenty-five is making fifty thousand a year, and that's only a beginning. The resources of America are inexhaustible. It isn't a boom, it's just the natural development of a great country."

His chest swelled with an unwonted patriotic fervor.

"Henry Maturin can't live forever, high blood pressure, you know, and by the time Gray's forty he should be worth twenty million dollars. Princely, my dear fellow, princely."

Elliott kept up a fairly regular correspondence with his sister and from time to time as the years went on passed on to me what she told him. Gray and Isabel were very happy, and the babies were sweet. They lived in a style that Elliott gladly admitted was eminently suitable; they entertained lavishly and were lavishly entertained; he told me with satisfaction that Isabel and Gray hadn't dined by themselves once in three months. Their whirl of gaiety was interrupted by the death of Mrs. Maturin, that colourless, highborn lady whom Henry Maturin had married for her connection when he was making a place for himself in the city to which his father had come as a country bumpkin; and out of respect for her memory for a year the young couple never entertained more than six people to dinner.

"I've always said that eight was the perfect number," said Elliott, determined to look on the bright side of things. "It's intimate enough to permit

96

of general conversation and yet large enough to give the impression of a party."

Gray was wonderfully generous to his wife. On the birth of their first child he gave her a square-cut diamond ring and on the birth of her second a sable coat. He was too busy to leave Chicago much, but such holidays as he could take they spent at Henry Maturin's imposing house at Marvin. Henry could deny nothing to the son whom he adored and one Christmas gave him a plantation in South Carolina so that he could get a fortnight's duck shooting in the season.

"Of course our merchant princes correspond to those great patrons of the arts of the Italian Renaissance who made fortunes by commerce. The Medici, for instance. Two kings of France were not too proud to marry the daughters of that illustrious family and I foresee the day when the crowned heads of Europe will seek the hands of our dollar princesses. What was it Shelley said? 'The world's great age begins anew, The golden years return.' "

Henry Maturin had for many years looked after Mrs. Bradley's and Elliott's investments and they had a well-justified confidence in his acumen. He had never countenanced speculation and had put their money into sound securities, but with the great increase in values they found their comparatively modest fortunes increased in a manner that both surprised and delighted them. Elliott told me that, without stirring a finger, he was nearly twice as rich in 1926 as he had been in 1918. He was sixty-five, his hair was gray, his face lined and there were pouches under his eyes, but he bore his years gallantly; he was as slim and held himself as erectly as ever; he had always been moderate in his habits and taken care of his appearance. He had no intention of submitting to the ravages of time so long as he could have his clothes made by the best tailor in London, his hair dressed and his face shaved by his own particular barber and a masseur to come in every morning to keep his elegant body in perfect condition. He had long forgotten that he had ever so far demeaned himself as to engage in a trade, and without ever saying so outright, for he was not so stupid as to tell a lie that might be found out, he was inclined to suggest that in his youth he had been in the diplomatic service. I must admit that if I had ever had occasion to draw a portrait of an ambassador I would without hesitation have chosen Elliott as my model.

But things were changing. Such of the great ladies who had advanced Elliott's career as were still alive were well along in years. The English peeresses, having lost their lords, had been forced to surrender their mansions to daughters-in-law, and had retired to villas at Cheltenham or to modest houses in Regent's Park. Stafford House was turned into a museum, Curzon House

97

became the seat of an organization, Devonshire House was for sale. The yacht on which Elliott had been in the habit of staying at Cowes had passed into other hands. The fashionable persons who occupied the stage had no use for the elderly man that Elliott now was. They found him tiresome and ridiculous. They were still willing to come to his elaborate luncheon parties at Claridge's, but he was quick-witted enough to know that they came to meet one another rather than to see him. He could no longer pick and choose among the invitations that once had littered his writing-table, and much more often than he would have liked anyone to know he suffered the humiliation of dining by himself in the privacy of his suite. Women of rank in England, when a scandal has closed the doors of society to them, develop an interest in the arts and surround themselves with painters, writers and musicians. Elliott was too proud thus to humiliate himself.

"The death duties and the war profiteers have ruined English society," he told me. "People don't seem to mind who they know. London still has its tailors, its bootmakers and its hatters, and I trust they'll last my time, but except for them it's finished. My dear fellow, do you know that the St. Erths have women to wait at table."

This he said when we were walking away from Carlton House Terrace after a luncheon party at which an unfortunate incident had occurred. Our noble host had a well-known collection of pictures and a young American, Paul Barton by name, who was there for the first time expressed a desire to see them.

"You've got a Titian, haven't you?"

"We had. It's in America now. Some old Jew offered us a packet of money for it and we were damned hard up at the time, so my governor sold it."

I noticed that Elliott, bristling, threw a venomous glance at the jovial marquess and guessed that it was he that had bought the picture. He was furious at hearing himself, Virginian born and the descendant of a signatory of the Declaration, thus described. He had never in his life suffered so great an affront. And what made it worse was that Paul Barton was the object of his virulent hatred. He was a young man who had appeared in London soon after the war. He was twenty-three, blond, very good-looking, charming, a beautiful dancer and with an ample fortune. He had brought a letter of introduction to Elliott, who with the kindness of heart natural to him had presented him to various of his friends. Not content with this he had given him some valuable hints on conduct. Delving back into his own experience, he had shown him how it was possible, by paying small attentions to old ladies and by lending a willing ear to distinguished men, however tedious, for a stranger to make his way in society.

But it was a different world that Paul Barton entered from that into which, a generation before, Elliott Templeton had penetrated by means of dogged perseverance. It was a world bent on amusing itself. Paul Barton's high spirits, pleasing exterior and engaging manner did for him in a few weeks what Elliott had achieved only after years of industry and determination. Soon he no longer needed Elliott's help and took small pains to conceal the fact. He was pleasant to him when they met, but in an offhand way that deeply offended the older man. Elliott did not ask people to a party because he liked them, but because they helped to make it go, and since Paul Barton was popular he continued to invite him on occasion to his weekly luncheons; but the successful young man was generally engaged and twice he threw Elliott over at the last moment. Elliott had done this himself too often not to know it was because he had just had a more tempting invitation.

"I don't ask you to believe it," Elliott told me, fuming, "but it's God's truth that when I see him now he patronizes me. ME. Titian. Titian," he spluttered. "He wouldn't know a Titian if he saw one."

I had never seen Elliott so angry and I guessed his wrath was caused by his belief that Paul Barton had asked about the picture maliciously, having somehow learnt that Elliott had bought it, and would make a funny story at his expense out of the noble lord's reply.

"He's nothing but a dirty little snob, and if there's one thing in the world I detest and despise it's snobbishness. He'd have been nowhere except for me. Would you believe it, his father makes office furniture. Office furniture." He put withering scorn into the two words. "And when I tell people he simply doesn't exist in America, his origins couldn't be more humble, they don't seem to care. Take my word for it, my dear fellow, English society is as dead as the dodo."

Nor did Elliott find France much better. There the great ladies of his youth, if still alive, were given over to bridge (a game he loathed), piety and the care of their grandchildren. Manufacturers, Argentines, Chileans, American women separated or divorced from their husbands, inhabited the stately houses of the aristocracy and entertained with splendour, but at their parties Elliott was confounded to meet politicians who spoke French with a vulgar accent, journalists whose table manners were deplorable, and even actors. The scions of princely families thought it no shame to marry the daughters of shopkeepers. It was true Paris was gay, but with what a shoddy gaiety! The young, devoted to the mad pursuit of pleasure, thought nothing more amusing than to go from one stuffy little night club to another, drinking champagne at a hundred francs a bottle and dancing close-packed with the riffraff of the town till five o'clock in the morning. The smoke, the heat, the noise made Elliott's head ache. This was not the Paris that he had accepted thirty years before as his spiritual home. This was not the Paris that good Americans went to when they died.

(iv)

But Elliott had a flair. An inner monitor suggested to him that the Riviera was on the point of becoming once more the resort of rank and fashion. He knew the coast well from having often spent a few days in Monte Carlo at the Hôtel de Paris on his way back from Rome to which his duties at the papal court had called him or at Cannes at the villa of one or the other of his friends. But that was in the winter, and of late rumours had reached him that it was beginning to be well spoken of as a summer resort. The big hotels were remaining open; their summer visitors were listed in the social columns of the Paris *Herald* and Elliott read their familiar names with approval.

"The world is too much with me," he said. "I have now reached a time of life when I am prepared to enjoy the beauties of nature."

The remark may seem obscure. It isn't really. Elliott had always felt that nature was an impediment to the social life, and he had no patience with people who could bother to go to see a lake or a mountain when they had before their eyes a Regency commode or a painting by Watteau. He had at the time a considerable sum of money to spend. Henry Maturin, urged by his son and exasperated by the sight of his friends on the stock exchange who were making fortunes overnight, had surrendered at last to the current of events and, abandoning little by little his old conservatism, had seen no reason why he too should not get on the band wagon. He wrote to Elliott that he was as much opposed to gambling as he had ever been, but this was not gambling, it was an affirmation of his belief in the inexhaustible resources of the country. His optimism was based on common sense. He could see nothing to halt the progress of America. He ended by saying that he had bought on margin a number of sound securities for dear Louisa Bradley and was glad to be able to tell Elliott that she now had a profit of twenty thousand dollars. Finally, if Elliott wanted to make a little money and would allow him to act according to his judgement, he was confident that he would not be disappointed. Elliott, apt to use hackneyed quotations, remarked that he could resist anything but temptation; the consequence of which was that from then on, instead of turning to the social intelligence as he had done for many years when the *Herald* was brought him with his breakfast, he gave his first attention to the reports of the stock market. So successful were Henry Maturin's transactions on his behalf that now Elliott found himself with the tidy sum of fifty thousand dollars which he had done nothing to earn.

He decided to take his profit and buy a house on the Riviera. As a refuge from the world he chose Antibes, which held a strategic position between Cannes and Monte Carlo so that it could be conveniently reached from either; but whether it was the hand of Providence or his own sure instinct that led him to choose a spot that was soon to become the centre of fashion, it is impossible to say. To live in a villa with a garden had a suburban vulgarity that revolted his fastidious taste, so he acquired two houses in the old town looking on the sea, knocked them into one, and installed central heating, bathrooms and the sanitary conveniences that American example has forced on a recalcitrant continent. Pickling was all the rage just then, so he furnished the house with old Provençal furniture duly pickled and, surrendering discreetly to modernity, with modern fabrics. He was still unwilling to accept such painters as Picasso and Braque—"horrors, my dear fellow, horrors"—whom certain misguided enthusiasts were making such a fuss about, but felt himself at long last justified in extending his patronage to the Impressionists and so adorned his walls with some very pretty pictures. I remember a Monet of people rowing on a river, a Pissarro of a quay and a bridge on the Seine, a Tahitian landscape by Gauguin and a charming Renoir of a young girl in profile with long yellow hair hanging down her back. His house when finished was fresh and gay, unusual, and simple with that simplicity that you knew could only have been achieved at great expense.

Then began the most splendid period of Elliott's life. He brought his excellent chef down from Paris and it was soon acknowledged that he had the best cuisine on the Riviera. He dressed his butler and his footman in white with gold straps on their shoulders. He entertained with a magnificence that never overstepped the bounds of good taste. The shores of the Mediterranean were littered with royalties from all parts of Europe. Some lured there on account of the climate, some in exile, and some because a scandalous past or an unsuitable marriage made it more convenient for them to inhabit a foreign country. There were Romanoffs from Russia, Hapsburgs from Austria, Bourbons from Spain, the two Sicilys and Parma; there were princes of the House of Windsor and princes of the House of Bragança; there were Royal Highnesses from Sweden and Royal Highnesses from Greece: Elliott entertained them. There were princes and princesses not of royal blood, dukes and duchesses, marquesses and marchionesses from Austria, Italy, Spain, Russia and Belgium: Elliott entertained them. In winter the King of Sweden and the King of Denmark made sojourns on the coast; now and then Alfonso of Spain paid a hurried visit: Elliott entertained them. I never ceased to admire the way in which, when he bowed with courtly grace to these exalted personages, he managed to maintain the independent demeanor of the citizen of a country in which all men are said to be born equal.

I had then, after some years of travel, bought a house on Cap Ferrat and thus saw a good deal of Elliott. I had risen so high in his good graces that sometimes he invited me to his very grandest parties.

"Come as a favour to me, my dear fellow," he would say. "Of course I know just as well as you do that royalties ruin a party. But other people like to meet them and I think one owes it to oneself to show the poor things some attention. Though heaven knows they don't deserve it. They're the most ungrateful people in the world; they'll use you, and when they have no further use for you they'll cast you aside like a frayed shirt; they'll accept innumerable favours from you, but there's not one of them who'd cross the road to do the smallest thing for you in return."

Elliott had taken pains to get on good terms with the local authorities, and the prefect of the district and the bishop of the diocese, accompanied by his vicar general, often graced his table. The bishop had been a cavalry officer before entering the Church and in the war had commanded a regiment. He was a rubicund, stoutish man, who affected the rough-and-ready language of the barracks, and his austere, cadaverous vicar general was always on pins and needles lest he should say something scandalous. He listened with a deprecating smile when his superior told his favourite stories. But the bishop conducted his diocese with remarkable competence and his eloquence in the pulpit was no less moving than his sallies at the luncheon table were amusing. He approved of Elliott for his pious generosity to the Church and liked him for his amiability and the good food he provided; and the two became good friends. Elliott could thus flatter himself that he was making the best of both worlds and, if I may venture so to put it, effecting a very satisfactory working arrangement between God and Mammon.

Elliott was house-proud and he was anxious to show his new house to his sister; he had always felt a certain reserve in her approval of him and he wanted her to see the style in which he now lived and the friends he hobnobbed with. It was the definitive answer to her hesitations. She would have to admit that he had made good. He wrote and asked her to come over with Gray and Isabel, not to stay with him, for he had no room, but to stay as his guests at the near-by Hôtel du Cap. Mrs. Bradley replied that her travelling days were over, for her health was indifferent and she thought she was better off at home; and in any case it was impossible for Gray to absent himself from Chicago; business was booming and he was making a great deal of money and had to stay put. Elliott was attached to his sister and her letter alarmed him. He wrote to Isabel. She replied by cable that, though her mother was so far from well that she had to stay in bed one day a week, she was in no immediate danger and indeed with care might be expected to live a long time yet; but that Gray needed a rest and, with his father there to look after things, there was no reason why he should not take a holiday; so, not that summer but the next, she and Gray would come over.

On October the 23d, 1929, the New York market broke.

(v)

I was in London then and at first we in England did not realize how grave the situation was nor how distressing its results would be. For my own part though chagrined at losing a considerable sum, it was for the most part paper profits that I lost, and when the dust had settled I found myself little the poorer in cash. I knew that Elliott had been gambling heavily and feared that he was badly hit, but I did not see him till we both returned to the Riviera for Christmas. He told me then that Henry Maturin was dead and Gray ruined.

I know little of business matters and I daresay that my account of the events, told me by Elliott, will seem confused. So far as I could make out the catastrophe that had befallen the firm was due in part to Henry Maturin's self-will and in part to Gray's rashness. Henry Maturin at first would not believe that the break was serious, but persuaded himself that it was a plot of the New York brokers to put a quick one over their provincial brethren, and setting his teeth he poured forth money to support the market. He raged against the Chicago brokers who were letting themselves be stampeded by those scoundrels in New York. He had always prided himself on the fact that none of his smaller clients, widows with settled incomes, retired officers and such like, had ever lost a penny by following his advice, and now, instead of letting them take a loss, he supported their accounts out of his own pocket. He said he was prepared to go broke, he could make another fortune, but he could never hold up his head again if the little people who trusted him lost their all. He thought he was magnanimous; he was only vain. His great fortune melted and one night he had a heart attack. He was in his sixties, he had always worked hard, played hard, eaten too much and drunk heavily; after a few hours of agony he died of coronary thrombosis.

Gray was left to deal with the situation alone. He had been speculating extensively on the side, without the knowledge of his father, and was personally in the greatest difficulty. His efforts to extricate himself failed. The banks would not lend him money; older men on the exchange told him that the only thing was to throw in the sponge. I am not clear about the rest of the story. He was unable to meet his obligations and was, I understand, declared bankrupt; he had already mortgaged his own house and was glad to hand it over to the mortgagees; his father's house on Lake Shore Drive and the house at Marvin were sold for what they would fetch; Isabel sold her jewels: all that was left them was the plantation in South Carolina, which was settled on Isabel but for which a purchaser could not be found. Gray was wiped out.

"And what about you, Elliott?" I asked.

"Oh, I'm not complaining," he answered airily. "God tempers the wind to the shorn lamb."

I did not question him further, for his financial affairs were no business of mine, but whatever his losses were I presumed that like the rest of us he had suffered.

The depression did not at first hit the Riviera badly. I heard of two or three people who had lost a good deal, many villas remained closed for the winter and several were put up for sale. The hotels were far from full and the Casino at Monte Carlo complained that the season was poor. But it was not for a couple of years that the draught made itself felt. Then an estate agent told me that on the stretch of coast that reaches from Toulon to the Italian border there were forty-eight thousand properties, large and small, to be sold. The shares of the Casino slumped. The great hotels put down their prices in a vain attempt to attract. The only foreigners to be seen were those who had always been so poor that they couldn't be poorer, and they spent no money because they had no money to spend. The shopkeepers were in despair. But Elliott neither diminished his staff nor lessened their wages as many did; he continued to provide choice food and choice wines to royal and titled persons. He bought himself a large new car, which he imported from America and on which he had to pay a tremendous duty. He gave generously to the charity the bishop had organized to provide free meals for the families of the workless. In fact he lived as though there had never been a crisis and half the world were not staggering from its effects.

I discovered the reason by chance: Elliott had by this time ceased to go to England except for a fortnight once a year to buy clothes, but he still transferred his establishment to his apartment in Paris for three months in the autumn and for May and June, these being the periods when the Riviera was deserted by Elliott's friends; he liked the summer there, partly on account of the bathing, but chiefly, I think, because the hot weather gave him the opportunity to indulge in a gaiety of dress that his sense of decorum had always forced him to eschew. He would appear then in trousers of startling colour, red, blue, green or yellow, and with them wear singlets of contrasting hue, mauve, violet, puce or harlequin, and would accept the compliments his attire clamoured for with the deprecating grace of an actress who is told that she has played a new role divinely.

I happened to be spending a day in Paris in the spring on my way back to Cap Ferrat and had asked Elliott to lunch with me. We met in the Ritz bar, no longer thronged with college boys come from America to have a good time, but as deserted as a playwright after the first night of an unsuccessful play. We had a cocktail, a transatlantic habit with which Elliott had at last become reconciled, and ordered our lunch. When we had finished, he suggested that we should go round the curio shops, and though I told him I had no money to spend I was glad enough to accompany him. We walked through the Place Vendôme and he asked if I would mind going into Charvet's for a moment; he had ordered some things and wanted to know if they were ready. It appeared that he was having some undershirts made, and some drawers, and he was having his initials embroidered on them. The undershirts had not come in yet, but the drawers were there and the shop assistant asked Elliott if he would like to see them.

"I would," said he, and when the man had gone to fetch them added to me: "I have them made to order on a pattern of my own."

They were brought, and to me, except that they were of silk, looked exactly like the drawers I had frequently bought for myself at Macy's; but what caught my eye was that above the intertwined E. T. of the initials was a count's crown. I did not say a word.

"Very nice, very nice," said Elliott. "Well, when the undershirts are ready you'll send them along."

We left the shop and Elliott, as he walked away, turned to me with a smile.

"Did you notice the crown? To tell you the truth, I'd forgotten about it when I asked you to come in to Charvet's. I don't think I've had occasion to tell you that His Holiness has been graciously pleased to revive in my favour my old family title."

"Your what?" I said, startled out of my politeness.

Elliott raised a disapproving eyebrow.

"Didn't you know? I am descended in the female line from the Count de Lauria who came over to England in the suite of Philip the Second and married a maid of honour of Queen Mary."

"Our old friend Bloody Mary?"

"That, I believe, is what heretics call her," Elliott answered, stiffly. "I don't think I ever told you that I spent September of '29 in Rome. I thought it a bore having to go because of course Rome is empty then, but it was fortunate for me that my sense of duty prevailed over my desire for worldly pleasures. My friends at the Vatican told me that the crash was coming and strongly advised me to sell all my American securities. The Catholic Church has the wisdom of twenty centuries behind it and I didn't hesitate for a moment. I cabled to Henry Maturin to sell everything and buy gold, and I cabled to Louisa to tell her to do the same. Henry cabled back asking me if I was crazy and said he'd do nothing until I confirmed the instructions. I immediately cabled in the most peremptory manner, telling him to carry them out and to cable me that he had done so. Poor Louisa paid no attention to my advice and suffered for it."

"So when the crash came you were sitting pretty?"

"An Americanism, my dear fellow, which I see no occasion for you to use, but it expresses my situation with a good deal of accuracy. I lost nothing; in fact I had made what you would probably call a packet. I was able some time later to buy back my securities for a fraction of their original cost, and since I owed it all to what I can only describe as the direct interposition of Providence I felt it only right and proper that I should do something for Providence in return."

"Oh, and how did you set about that?"

"Well, you know that the Duce has been reclaiming great tracts of land in the Pontine Marshes and it was represented to me that His Holiness was gravely concerned at the lack of places of worship for the settlers. So, to cut a long story short, I built a little Romanesque church, an exact copy of one I knew in Provence, and perfect in every detail, which, though I say it myself, is a gem. It is dedicated to St. Martin because I was lucky enough to find an old stained-glass window representing St. Martin in the act of cutting his cloak in two to give half of it to a naked beggar, and as the symbolism seemed so apt I bought it and placed it over the high altar."

I didn't interrupt Elliott to ask him what connection he saw between the Saint's celebrated action and the rake-off on the pretty penny he had made by selling out in the nick of time which, like an agent's commission, he was paying a higher power. But to a prosaic person like me symbolism is often obscure. He went on.

"When I was privileged to show the photographs to the Holy Father, he was gracious enough to tell me that he could see at a glance that I was a man of impeccable taste, and he added that it was a pleasure to him to find in this degenerate age someone who combined devotion to the Church with such rare artistic gifts. A memorable experience, my dear fellow, a memorable experience. But no one was more surprised than I when shortly afterwards it was intimated to me that he had been pleased to confer a title upon me. As an American citizen I feel it more modest not to use it, except of course at the Vatican, and I have forbidden my Joseph to address me as *Monsieur le Comte,* and I trust you will respect my confidence. I don't wish it bruited abroad. But I would not like His Holiness to think that I do not value the honour that he has done me and it is purely out of respect for him that I have the crown embroidered on my personal linen. I don't mind telling you that I take a modest pride in concealing my rank under the sober pin stripe of an American gentleman."

We parted. Elliott told me he would come down to the Riviera at the end of June. He did not do so. He had just made his arrangements to transfer his staff from Paris, intending to drive down leisurely in his car so that everything should be in perfect order on his arrival, when he received a cable from Isabel to say that her mother had suddenly taken a turn for the worse. Elliott, besides being fond of his sister, had, as I have said, a strong sense of family feeling. He took the first ship out of Cherbourg and from New York went to Chicago. He wrote to tell me that Mrs. Bradley was very ill and grown so thin that it was a shock to him. She might last a few weeks longer or even a few months, but in any case he felt it his sad duty to remain with her till the end. He said he found the great heat more supportable than he had expected, but the lack of congenial society only tolerable because at such a moment he had in any case no heart for it. He said he was disappointed with the way his fellow-countrymen had reacted to the depression; he would have expected them to take their misfortune with more equanimity. Knowing that nothing is easier than to bear other people's calamities with fortitude, I thought that Elliott, richer now than he had ever been in his life, was perhaps hardly entitled to be severe. He ended by giving me messages to several of his friends and bade me by no means to forget to explain to everyone I met why it was that his house must remain closed for the summer.

Little more than a month later I received another letter from him to tell me that Mrs. Bradley had died. He wrote with sincerity and emotion. I would never have thought him capable of expressing himself with such dignity, real feeling and simplicity, had I not long known that notwithstanding his snobbishness and his absurd affectations Elliott was a kindly, affectionate and honest man. In the course of this letter he told me that Mrs. Bradley's affairs appeared to be in some disorder. Her elder son, a diplomatist, being *chargé d'affaires* in Tokyo during the absence of the ambassador, had been of course unable to leave his post. Her second son,

Templeton, who had been in the Philippines when I first knew the Bradleys, had been in due course recalled to Washington and occupied a responsible position in the State Department. He had come with his wife to Chicago when his mother's condition was recognized as hopeless, but had been obliged to return to the capital immediately after the funeral. In these circumstances Elliott felt that he must remain in America until things were straightened out. Mrs. Bradley had divided her fortune equally between her three children, but it appeared that her losses in the crash of '29 had been substantial. Fortunately they had found a purchaser for the farm at Marvin. Elliott in his letter referred to it as dear Louisa's country place.

"It is always sad when a family has to part with its ancestral home," he wrote, "but of late years I have seen this forced upon so many of my English friends that I feel that my nephews and Isabel must accept the inevitable with the same courage and resignation that *they* have. *Noblesse oblige.*"

They had been lucky too in disposing of Mrs. Bradley's house in Chicago. There had long been a scheme afoot to tear down the row of houses in one of which Mrs. Bradley lived and build in their stead a great block of apartments, but it had been held up by her obstinate determination to die in the house in which she had lived. But no sooner was the breath out of her body than the promoters came forward with an offer and it was promptly accepted. But even at that Isabel was left very ill provided for.

After the crash Gray had tried to get a job, even as a clerk in the office of such of the brokers as had weathered the storm, but there was no business. He applied to his old friends to give him something to do, however humble and however badly paid, but he applied in vain. His frenzied efforts to stave off the disaster that finally overwhelmed him, the burden of anxiety, the humiliation, resulted in a nervous breakdown and he began to have headaches so severe that he was incapacitated for twenty-four hours and as limp as a wet rag when they ceased. It had appeared to Isabel that they could not do better than go down with the children to the plantation in South Carolina till Gray regained his health. In its day it had brought in a hundred thousand dollars a year for its rice crop, but for long now had been no more than a wilderness of marsh and gumwood, useful only to sportsmen who wanted to shoot duck, and no purchaser could be found for it. There they had lived off and on since the crash and there they proposed to return till conditions improved and Gray could find employment.

"I couldn't allow that," Elliott wrote. "Why, my dear fellow, they live like pigs. Isabel without a maid, no governess for the children, and only a couple of coloured women to look after them. So I've offered them my apartment in Paris and proposed that they should stay there till things change in this fantastic country. I shall provide them with a staff, as a matter of fact my kitchen maid is a very good cook, so I shall leave her with them and I can easily find someone to take her place. I shall arrange to settle the accounts myself so that Isabel can spend her small income on her clothes and the *menus plaisirs* of the family. This means of course that I shall spend much more of my time on the Riviera and so hope to see a great deal more of you, my dear fellow, than I have in the past. London and Paris being now what they are I'm really more at home on the Riviera. It's the only place remaining where I can meet people who speak my own language. I daresay I shall go to Paris now and then for a few days, but when I do, I don't in the least mind pigging it at the Ritz. I'm glad to say that I've at long last persuaded Gray and Isabel to accede to my wishes and I'm bringing them all over as soon as the necessary arrangements can be made. The furniture and the pictures (very poor in quality, my dear fellow, and of the most doubtful authenticity) are being sold the week after next and meanwhile, as I thought to live in the house till the last moment would be painful to them, I have brought them to stay with me at the Drake. I shall settle them in when we get to Paris and then come down to the Riviera. Don't forget to remember me to your royal neighbour."

Who could deny that Elliott, that arch-snob, was also the kindest, most considerate and generous of men?

CHAPTER FOUR

(i)

Elliott, having installed the Maturins in his spacious apartment on the Left Bank, returned to the Riviera at the end of the year. He had planned his house to suit his own convenience and there was no room in it for a family of four, so that, even if he had wanted to, he could not have had them to stay with him there. I do not think he regretted it. He was well aware that as a man by himself he was a more desirable asset than if he must be accompanied by a niece and a nephew, and he could hardly expect to arrange his own distinguished little parties (a matter over which he took immense trouble) if he had to count invariably on the presence of two house guests.

"It's much better for them to settle down in Paris and accustom themselves to civilized life. Besides, the two girls are old enough to go to school and I've found one not far from my apartment which I'm assured is very select."

In consequence of this I did not see Isabel till the spring when, because I had some work to do that made it desirable for me to spend some weeks there, I went to Paris and took a couple of rooms in a hotel just out of the Place Vendôme. It was a hotel I frequented, not only for its convenient situation, but because it had an air. It was a big old house built around a courtyard and it had been an inn for close upon two hundred years. The bathrooms were far from luxurious and the plumbing far from satisfactory; the bedrooms with their iron beds, painted white, their old-fashioned white counterpanes and their huge *armoires à glace* had a poverty-stricken look; but the parlours were furnished with fine old furniture. The sofa, the arm-chairs, dated from the gaudy reign of Napoleon the Third, and, though I could not say they were comfortable, they had a florid charm. In that room I lived in the past of the French novelists. When I looked at the Empire clock under its glass case I thought that a pretty woman in ringlets and a flounced dress might have watched the minute hand move as she waited for a visit from Rastignac, the well-born adventurer whose career in novel after novel Balzac followed from his humble beginnings to his ultimate grandeur. Dr. Bianchon, the physician who was so real to Balzac that when he lay dying he said: "Only Bianchon can save me," might well have come into that room to feel the pulse and look at the tongue of a noble dowager from the provinces who had come to Paris to see an attorney about a lawsuit and had called in a doctor for a passing ailment. At that bureau a lovesick woman in a crinoline, her hair parted in the middle, may have written a passionate letter to her faithless lover or a peppery old gentleman in a green frock coat and a stock indited an angry epistle to his extravagant son.

The day after my arrival I called up Isabel and asked if she would give me a cup of tea if I came along at five. It was ten years since I'd seen her. She was reading a French novel when I was ushered into the drawing-room by a staid butler and getting up she took both my hands and greeted me with a warm and winning smile. I had never seen her more than a dozen times, and only twice alone, but she made me feel at once that we were not casual acquaintances but old friends. The ten years that had passed had reduced the gulf that separated the young girl from the middle-aged man and I was no longer conscious of the disparity of age between us. With the delicate flattery of a woman of the world she treated me as if I were her contemporary, and in five minutes we were chatting as frankly and as unconstrainedly as though we were playmates who had been in the habit of meeting without interruption. She had acquired ease, self-possession and assurance.

But what chiefly struck me was the change in her appearance. I remembered her as a pretty, bouncing girl who threatened to run to fat; I do not know whether, realizing this she had taken heroic measures to reduce her weight or whether it was an unusual, though happy, accident of childbearing; but now she was as slender as anyone could wish. The mode of the moment accentuated this. She was in black, and at a glance I noticed that her silk dress, neither too plain nor too fancy, had been made by one of the best dressmakers in Paris, and she wore it with the careless confidence of a woman to whom it is second nature to wear expensive clothes. Ten years before, even with Elliott to advise, her frocks had been somewhat on the showy side and she had worn them as though she were not quite at home in them. Marie Louise de Florimond could not have said now that she lacked chic. She had chic to the tips of her rose-painted nails. Her features had fined down and it occurred to me that she had as pretty and as straight a nose as I had ever seen on a woman's face. There was not a line on her forehead or under her hazel eyes, and though her skin had lost the fresh bloom of extreme youth, its texture was as fine as ever; it obviously owed something now to lotions, creams and massage, but they had given it a soft, transparent delicacy that was singularly attractive. Her thin cheeks were very faintly rouged and her mouth was painted with discretion. She wore her bright brown hair bobbed as was the fashion of the moment and marcelled. She had no rings on her fingers, and I remembered that Elliott had told me that she had sold her jewellery; her hands, though not remarkably small, were well made. At that period women wore short frocks in the daytime and I saw that her legs in champagne-coloured stockings were shapely, long and slender. Legs are the undoing of many a comely woman; Isabel's legs, as a girl her most unfortunate trait, were now uncommonly good. In fact from the pretty girl whose glowing health, high spirits and brilliant colour had given her attractiveness she was become a beautiful woman. That she owed her beauty in some degree to art, discipline and mortification of the flesh did not seem to matter. The result was vastly satisfactory. It might be that the grace of her gestures, the felicity of her carriage, had been acquired by taking thought, but they had a look of perfect spontaneity. I conceived the notion that these four months in Paris had put the finishing touches to a work of conscious art that had been years in the making. Elliott, even in his most censorious mood, could not but have approved of her; I, a person less difficult to please, found her ravishing.

Gray had gone to Mortefontaine to play golf, but she told me he would be in presently.

"And you must see my two little girls. They've gone to the Tuileries Gardens, but they ought to be in soon. They're sweet."

We talked of one thing and another. She liked being in Paris and they were very comfortable in Elliott's apartment. Before leaving them he had made them acquainted with such of his friends as he thought they would like and they had already a pleasant circle of acquaintances. He had pressed them to entertain as abundantly as he had been in the habit of doing.

"You know, it tickles me to death to think that we're living like quite rich people when really we're absolutely broke."

"Is it as bad as that?"

She chuckled, and now I remembered the light, gay laugh that I had found so pleasing in her ten years before.

"Gray hasn't a penny and I have almost exactly the income Larry had when he wanted me to marry him and I wouldn't because I thought we couldn't possibly live on it and now I've got two children besides. It's rather funny, isn't it?"

"I'm glad you can see the joke of it."

"What news have you of Larry?"

"I? None. I haven't set eyes on him since before you were last in Paris. I knew slightly some of the people he used to know and I did ask them what had become of him, but that was years ago. No one seemed to know anything about him. He just vanished."

"We know the manager of the bank in Chicago where Larry has his account and he told us that every now and then he got a draft from some queer place. China, Burma, India. He seems to have been getting around."

I did not hesitate to put the question that came to the tip of my tongue. After all, if you want to know something the best way is to ask.

"D'you wish now that you had married him?"

She smiled engagingly.

"I've been very happy with Gray. He's been a wonderful husband. You know, until the crash came we had a grand time together. We like the same people, and we like doing the same things. He's very sweet. And it's nice being adored; he's just as much in love with me now as when we first married. He thinks I'm the most wonderful girl in the world. You can't imagine how kind and considerate he is. It was quite absurd how generous he was; you see, he thought nothing was too good for me. D'you know, he's never said an unkind or harsh thing to me all these years we've been married. Oh, I've been very lucky."

I asked myself if she thought she'd answered my question. I changed the conversation.

"Tell me about your little girls."

As I spoke the doorbell rang.

"Here they are. You shall see for yourself."

In a moment they came in followed by a nursery governess and I was introduced first to Joan, the elder, and then to Priscilla. Each in turn gave a polite little knick as she took my hand. One was eight and the other six. They were tall for their age; Isabel of course was tall and Gray, I remembered, was immense; but they were pretty only in the way all children are pretty. They looked frail. They had their father's black hair and their mother's hazel eyes. The presence of a stranger did not make them shy, and they talked eagerly to her of their doings in the gardens. They cast eager eyes on the dainties Isabel's cook had provided for tea, but which neither of us had touched, and being given permission to have one thing were thrown into a small agony of doubt as to which to choose. It was pleasant to see the demonstrative affection they had for their mother and the three of them clustered together made a charming picture. When they had eaten the little cake each had selected, Isabel sent them away and they went without a word of expostulation. I received the impression that she was bringing them up to do as they were told.

When they were gone I said the usual things one says to a mother about her children and Isabel accepted my compliments with evident, but somewhat casual, pleasure. I asked her how Gray was liking Paris.

"Well enough. Uncle Elliott left us a car so he can go and play golf almost every day and he's joined the Travellers Club and he plays bridge there. Of course, Uncle Elliott's offer to support us in this apartment has been a godsend. Gray's nerves went all to pieces and he still has those terrible headaches; even if he could get a job he isn't really fit to take it; and naturally that worries him. He wants to work, he feels he ought to, and it humiliates him not to be wanted. You see, he feels it's a man's business to work and if he can't work he may just as well be dead. He can't bear his feeling of being a drug on the market, and I only got him to come here by persuading him that rest and change would bring him back to normalcy. But I know he won't be really happy till he gets back into harness."

"I'm afraid you've had a very rough time these last two and a half years."

"Well, you know, when the crash came at first I simply couldn't believe it. It seemed inconceivable to me that we should be ruined. I could understand that other people should be ruined, but that we should be—well, it just seemed impossible. I went on thinking that something would happen to save us at the last moment. And then, when the final blow came, I felt that life wasn't worth living any more, I didn't think I could face the future; it was too black. For a fortnight I was absolutely miserable. God, it was awful, having to part with everything, knowing there wouldn't be any fun any more, having to do without everything I liked—and then at the end of a fortnight I said: 'Oh, to hell with it, I'm not going to give it another thought,' and I promise you I never have. I don't regret anything. I had a lot of fun while it lasted and now it's gone, it's gone."

"It's obvious that ruin is easier to bear in a luxurious apartment in a fashionable quarter, with a competent butler and an excellent cook free and for nothing, and when one can cover one's haggard bones with a dress by Chanel, isn't it?"

"Lanvin," she giggled. "I see you haven't changed much in ten years. I don't suppose you'll believe me, being a cynical brute, but I'm not sure if I'd have accepted Uncle Elliott's offer except for Gray and the children. On my twenty-eight hundred a year we could have managed perfectly well on the plantation and we'd have grown rice and rye and corn and kept pigs. After all I was born and raised on a farm in Illinois."

"In a manner of speaking," I smiled, knowing that in point of fact she had been born in an expensive clinic in New York.

At this point Gray came in. It is true that I had only seen him two or three times twelve years before, but I had seen a photograph of him with his bride (Elliott kept it in a splendid frame on his piano along with signed photographs of the King of Sweden, the Queen of Spain and the Duc de Guise) and I had a fair recollection of him. I was taken aback. His hair had receded on the temples and there was a small bald patch on the crown, his face was puffy and red, and he had a double chin. He had put on a lot of weight during years of good living and hard drinking and only his great height saved him from being grossly obese. But the thing I most noticed was the expression of his eyes. I remembered quite well the trusting, open frankness of their Irish blue, when the world was before him and he hadn't a care in the world; now I seemed to see in them a sort of puzzled dismay, and even if I hadn't known the facts I think I might have guessed that something had occurred to destroy his confidence in himself and in the ordered course of events. I felt a kind of diffidence in him, as though he had done wrong, though unwittingly, and were ashamed. It was plain that his nerve was shaken. He greeted me with pleasant cordiality and indeed seemed as glad to see me as if I were an old friend, but I had the impression that his rather noisy heartiness was a habit of manner that scarcely corresponded with his inner feeling.

Drinks were brought in and he mixed us a cocktail. He'd played a couple of rounds of golf and was satisfied with his game. He went into somewhat verbose detail over the difficulties he had surmounted over one of the holes and Isabel listened with an appearance of lively interest. After a few minutes, having made a date to take them to dine and see a play, I left.

(ii)

I fell into the habit of dropping in to see Isabel three or four times a week in the afternoon after my day's work was over. She was generally alone at that hour and glad to have a gossip. The persons to whom Elliott had introduced her were much older than she and I discovered that she had few friends of her own generation. Mine were for the most part busy till dinnertime and I found it more agreeable to talk with Isabel than to go to my club and play bridge with rather grouchy Frenchmen who did not particularly welcome the intrusion of a stranger. Her charming way of treating me as if she and I were of an age made conversation easy and we joked and laughed and chaffed one another, chatting now about ourselves, now about our common acquaintances, now about books and pictures, so that the time passed very agreeably. One of the defects of my character is that I can never grow used to the plainness of people; however sweet a disposition a friend of mine may have, years of intimacy can never reconcile me to his bad teeth or lopsided nose: on the other hand I never cease to delight in his comeliness and after twenty years of familiarity I am still able to take pleasure in a well-shaped brow or the delicate line of a cheekbone. So I never came into Isabel's presence without feeling anew a little thrill of pleasure in the perfection of her oval face, in the creamy delicacy of her skin and in the bright warmth of her hazel eyes.

Then a very unexpected thing happened.

(iii)

In all big cities there are self-contained groups that exist without intercommunication, small worlds within a greater world that lead their lives, their members dependent upon one another for companionship, as though they inhabited islands separated from each other by an unnavigable strait. Of no city, in my experience, is this more true than of Paris. There high society seldom admits outsiders into its midst, the politicians live in their own corrupt circle, the bourgeoisie, great and small, frequent one another, writers congregate with writers (it is remarkable in André Gide's *Journal* to see with how few people he seems to have been intimate who did not follow his own calling), painters hobnob with painters and musicians with musicians. The same thing is true of London, but in a less marked degree; there birds of a feather flock much less together, and there are a dozen houses where at the same table you may meet a duchess, an actress, a painter, a member of Parliament, a lawyer, a dressmaker and an author.

The events of my life have led me at one time and another to dwell transitorily in pretty well all the worlds of Paris, even (through Elliott) in the closed world of the Boulevard St. Germain; but that which I like best, better than the discreet circle that has its centre in what is now called the Avenue Foch, better than the cosmopolitan crew that patronized Larue's and the Café de Paris, better than the noisy sordid gaiety of Montmartre, is that section of which the artery is the Boulevard du Montparnasse. In my youth I spent a year in a tiny apartment near the Lion de Belfort, on the fifth floor, from which I had a spacious view of the cemetery. Montparnasse has still for me the tranquil air of a provincial town that was characteristic of it then. When I pass through the dingy narrow Rue d'Odessa I remember with a pang the shabby restaurant where we used to foregather to dine, painters and illustrators and sculptors, I, but for Arnold Bennett on occasion, the only writer, and sit late discussing excitedly, absurdly, angrily painting and literature. It is still a pleasure to me to stroll down the boulevard and look at the young people who are as young as I was then and invent stories for myself about them. When I have nothing better to do I take a taxi and go and sit in the old Café du Dôme. It is no longer what it was then, the meeting place exclusively of Bohemia; the small tradesmen of the neighbourhood have taken to visiting it, and strangers from the other side of the Seine come to it in the hope of seeing a world that has ceased to exist. Students come to it still, of course, painters and writers, but most of them are foreigners; and when you sit there you hear around you as much Russian, Spanish, German and English as French. But I have a notion that they are saying very much the same sort of things as we said forty years ago, only they speak of Picasso instead of Manet and of André Breton instead of Guillaume Apollinaire. My heart goes out to them.

When I had been in Paris about a fortnight I was sitting one evening at the Dôme and since the terrace was crowded I had been forced to take a table in the front row. It was fine and warm. The plane trees were just bursting into leaf and there was in the air that sense of leisure, lightheartedness and alacrity that was peculiar to Paris. I felt at peace with myself, but not lethargically, with exhilaration rather. Suddenly a man, walking past me, stopped and with a grin that displayed a set of very white teeth said: "Hello!" I looked at him blankly. He was tall and thin. He wore no hat and he had a mop of dark brown hair that badly needed cutting. His upper lip and his chin were concealed by a thick brown beard. His forehead and his neck were deeply tanned. He wore a frayed shirt, without a tie, a brown, threadbare coat and a pair of shabby gray slacks. He looked a bum and to the best of my belief I had never seen him before. I put him down for one of those good-for-nothings who have gone to the devil in Paris and I expected him to pull a hard-luck story to wheedle a few francs out of me for a dinner and a bed. He stood in front of me, his hands in his pockets, showing his white teeth, with a look of amusement in his dark eyes.

"You don't remember me?" he said.

"I've never set eyes on you in my life."

I was prepared to give him twenty francs, but I wasn't prepared to let him get away with the bluff that we knew one another.

"Larry," he said.

"Good God! Sit down." He chuckled, stepped forward and took the empty chair at my table. "Have a drink." I beckoned to the waiter. "How could you expect me to recognize you with all that hair on your face?"

The waiter came and he ordered an orangeade. Now that I looked at him I remembered the peculiarity of his eyes, which came from the black of the iris being as black as that of the pupil and which gave them at once intensity and opaqueness.

"How long have you been in Paris?" I asked.

"A month."

"Are you going to stay?"

"For a while."

While I asked these questions my mind was busy. I noticed that the cuffs of his trousers were ragged and that there were holes in the elbows of his coat. He looked as destitute as any beachcomber I had ever met in an Eastern port. It was hard in those days to forget the depression and I wondered whether the crash of '29 had left him penniless. I didn't much like the thought of that and not being a person to beat about the bush I asked him outright:

"Are you down and out?"

"No, I'm all right. What makes you think that?"

"Well, you look as if you could do with a square meal and the things you've got on are only fit for the garbage can."

"Are they as bad as all that? I never thought about it. As a matter of fact I have been meaning to get myself a few odds and ends, but I never seem able to get down to it."

I thought he was shy or proud and I didn't see why I should put up with that sort of nonsense.

"Don't be a fool, Larry. I'm not a millionaire, but I'm not poor. If you're short of cash let me lend you a few thousand francs. That won't break me."

He laughed outright.

"Thanks a lot, but I'm not short of cash. I've got more money than I can spend."

"Notwithstanding the crash?"

"Oh, that didn't affect me. Everything I had was in government bonds. I don't know whether they went down in value, I never enquired, but I do know that Uncle Sam went on paying up on the coupons like the decent old party he is. In point of fact I've been spending so little during the last few years, I must have quite a bit in hand."

"Where have you come from now then?"

"India."

"Oh, I heard you'd been there. Isabel told me. She apparently knows the manager of your bank in Chicago."

"Isabel? When did you last see her?"

"Yesterday."

"She's not in Paris?"

"She is indeed. She's living in Elliott Templeton's apartment."

"That's grand. I'd love to see her."

Though I was watching his eyes pretty closely while we were exchanging these remarks I could discern only a natural surprise and pleasure, but no feeling more complicated.

"Gray's there too. You know they're married?"

"Yes, Uncle Bob—Dr. Nelson, my guardian—wrote and told me, but he died some years ago."

It occurred to me that with this break in what appeared his only link with Chicago and his friends there he probably knew nothing of what had happened. I told him of the birth of Isabel's two daughters, of the death of Henry Maturin and Louisa Bradley, of Gray's complete ruin and of Elliott's generosity.

"Is Elliott here too?"

"No."

For the first time in forty years Elliott was not spending the spring in Paris. Though looking younger he was now seventy and as usual with men

118

of that age there were days when he felt tired and ill. Little by little he had given up taking any but walking exercise. He was nervous about his health and his doctor came to see him twice a week to thrust into an alternate buttock a hypodermic needle with the fashionable injection of the moment. At every meal, at home or abroad, he took from his pocket a little gold box from which he extracted a tablet which he swallowed with the reserved air of one performing a religious rite. His doctor had recommended him to take the cure at Montecatini, a watering place in the north of Italy, and after this he proposed to go to Venice to look for a font of a design suitable to his Romanesque church. He was less unwilling to leave Paris unvisited since each year he found it socially more unsatisfactory. He did not like old people, and resented it when he was invited to meet only persons of his own age, and the young he found vapid. The adornment of the church he had built was now a main interest of his life and here he could indulge his ineradicable passion for buying works of art with the comfortable assurance that he was doing it to the glory of God. He had found in Rome an early altar of honey-coloured stone and had been dickering in Florence for six months for a triptych of the Siennese school to put over it.

Then Larry asked me how Gray was liking Paris.

"I'm afraid he's feeling rather lost here."

I tried to explain to him how Gray had struck me. He listened to me with his eyes fixed on my face with a meditative, unblinking gaze that suggested to me, I don't know why, that he was listening to me not with his ears, but some inner, more sensitive organ of hearing. It was queer and not very comfortable.

"But you'll see for yourself," I finished.

"Yes, I'd love to see them. I suppose I shall find the address in the phone book."

"But if you don't want to scare them out of their wits and drive the children into screaming hysterics, I think you'd be wise to have your hair cut and your beard shaved."

He laughed.

"I've been thinking of it. There's no object in making myself conspicuous."

"And while you're about it you might get yourself a new outfit."

"I suppose I am a bit shabby. When I came to leave India I found that I had nothing but the clothes I stand up in."

He looked at the suit I was wearing and asked me who my tailor was. I told him, but added that he was in London and so couldn't be of much use to him. We dropped the subject and he began to talk again of Gray and Isabel.

"I've been seeing quite a lot of them," I said. "They're very happy together. I've never had a chance of talking to Gray alone, and anyway I daresay he wouldn't talk to me about Isabel, but I know he's devoted to her. His face is rather sullen in repose and his eyes are harassed, but when he looks at Isabel such a gentle, kind look comes into them, it's rather moving. I have a notion that all through their trouble she stood by him like a rock and he never forgets how much he owes her. You'll find Isabel changed." I didn't tell him she was beautiful as she had never been before. I wasn't sure he had the discernment to see how the pretty, strapping girl had made herself into the wonderfully graceful, delicate and exquisite woman. There are men who are affronted by the aids that art can supply to feminine nature. "She's very good to Gray. She's taking infinite pains to restore his confidence in himself."

But it was growing late and I asked Larry if he would come along the boulevard and dine with me.

"No, I don't think I will, thanks," he answered. "I must be off."

He got up, nodded in a friendly way, and stepped out onto the pavement.

(iv)

I saw Gray and Isabel next day and told them that I had seen Larry. They were as surprised as I had been.

"It'll be wonderful to see him," said Isabel. "Let's call him up at once."

Then I remembered that I hadn't thought of asking him where he was staying. Isabel gave me hell.

"I'm not sure he'd have told me if I had," I protested, laughing. "Probably my subconscious had something to do with it. Don't you remember, he never liked telling people where he lived. It was one of his oddities. He may walk in at any moment."

"That would be like him," said Gray. "Even in the old days you could never count on his being where you expected him to be. He was here today and gone tomorrow. You'd see him in a room and think in a moment you'd go and say hello to him and when you turned round he'd disappeared."

"He always was the most exasperating fellow," said Isabel. "It's no good denying that. I suppose we shall just have to wait till it suits him to turn up."

He didn't come that day, nor the next, nor the day after. Isabel accused me of having invented the story to annoy. I promised her I hadn't and sought to give her reasons why he hadn't shown up. But they were implausible. Within myself I wondered whether on thinking it over he hadn't made up his mind that he just didn't want to see Gray and Isabel and had wandered off somewhere or other away from Paris. I had a feeling already that he never took root anywhere, but was always prepared at a moment's notice, for a reason that seemed good to him or on a whim, to move on.

He came at last. It was a rainy day and Gray hadn't gone to Mortefontaine. The three of us were together, Isabel and I drinking a cup of tea, Gray sipping a whiskey and Perrier, when the butler opened the door and Larry strolled in. Isabel with a cry sprang to her feet and throwing herself into his arms kissed him on both cheeks. Gray, his fat red face redder than ever, warmly wrung his hand.

"Gee, I'm glad to see you, Larry," he said, his voice choked with emotion. Isabel bit her lip and I saw she was constraining herself not to cry.

"Have a drink, old man," said Gray unsteadily.

I was touched by their delight at seeing the wanderer. It must have been pleasant for him to perceive how much he meant to them. He smiled happily. It was plain to me that he was, however, completely self-possessed. He noticed the tea things.

"I'll have a cup of tea," he said.

"Oh gosh, you don't want tea," cried Gray. "Let's have a bottle of champagne."

"I'd prefer tea," smiled Larry.

His composure had on the others the effect he may have intended. They calmed down, but looked at him still with fond eyes. I don't mean to suggest that he responded to their natural exuberance with an ungracious coldness; on the contrary, he was as cordial and charming as one could wish; but I was conscious in his manner of something that I could only describe as remoteness and I wondered what it signified.

"Why didn't you come and see us at once, you horror?" cried Isabel, with a pretence of indignation. "I've been hanging out of the window for the last five days to see you coming and every time the bell rang my heart leapt to my mouth and I had all I could do to swallow it again."

Larry chuckled.

"Mr. M. told me I looked so tough that your man would never let me through the door. I flew over to London to get some clothes."

"You needn't have done that," I smiled. "You could have got a reach-me-down at the Printemps or the Belle Jardinière."

"I thought if I was going to do it at all, I'd better do the thing in style.

I haven't bought any European clothes for ten years. I went to your tailor and said I wanted a suit in three days. He said it would take a fortnight, so we compromised on four. I got back from London an hour ago."

He wore a blue serge that nicely fitted his slim figure, a white shirt with a soft collar, a blue silk tie and brown shoes. He had had his hair cut short and shaved off the hair on his face. He looked not only neat, but well-groomed. It was a transformation. He was very thin; his cheekbones were more prominent, his temples hollower and his eyes in the deep sockets larger than I remembered them; but notwithstanding he looked very well; he looked, indeed, with his deeply sunburnt, unlined face, amazingly young. He was a year younger than Gray, they were both in their early thirties, but whereas Gray looked ten years more than his age, Larry looked ten years less. Gray's movements, owing to his great bulk, were deliberate and rather heavy; but Larry's were light and easy. His manner was boyish, gay and debonair, but withal it had a serenity that I was peculiarly conscious of and that I did not recollect in the lad I had known before. And as the conversation proceeded, flowing without difficulty as was natural in old friends with so many common memories, with bits of news about Chicago thrown in by Gray and Isabel, trivial gossip, one thing leading to another, with airy laughter, my impression persisted that in Larry, though his laughter was frank and he listened with evident pleasure to Isabel's breezy chatter, there was a very singular detachment. I did not feel that he was playing a part, he was too natural for that and his sincerity was obvious; I felt that there was something within him, I don't know whether to call it an awareness or a sensibility or a force, that remained strangely aloof.

The children were brought in, made known to Larry and gave him their polite little knicks. He held out his hand, looking at them with an engaging tenderness in his soft eyes, and they took it, staring at him gravely. Isabel brightly told him they were getting on nicely with their lessons, gave them a cookie each and sent them away.

"I'll come and read to you for ten minutes when you're in bed."

She did not at that moment want to be interrupted in her pleasure at seeing Larry. The little girls went up to say good night to their father. It was charming to see the love that lit up the red face of that gross man as he took them in his arms and kissed them. No one could help seeing that he proudly adored them and when they were gone he turned to Larry and with a sweet slow smile on his lips said:

"They're not bad kids, are they?"

Isabel gave him an affectionate glance.

"If I let Gray have his way he'd spoil them to death. He'd let me starve to death, that great brute, to feed the children on caviar and *pâté de foie gras.*"

He looked at her with a smile and said: "You're a liar and you know it. I worship the ground you tread on."

There was a responsive smile in Isabel's eyes. She knew that and was glad of it. A happy couple.

She insisted that we should stay to dinner. I, thinking they would prefer to be by themselves, made excuses, but she would not listen to them.

"I'll tell Marie to put another carrot in the soup and there'll be plenty for four. There's a chicken and you and Gray can eat the legs while Larry and I eat the wings, and she can make the soufflé large enough for all of us."

Gray too seemed to want me to stay, so I let myself be persuaded to do what I wanted to.

While we waited Isabel told Larry at length what I had already told him in brief. Though she narrated the lamentable story as gaily as possible Gray's face assumed an expression of sullen melancholy. She tried to cheer him up.

"Anyhow it's all over now. We've fallen on our feet and we've got the future before us. As soon as things improve, Gray's going to get a splendid job and make millions."

Cocktails were brought in and a couple did something to raise the poor fellow's spirits. I saw that Larry, though he took one, scarcely touched it, and when Gray, unobservant, offered him another he refused. We washed our hands and sat down to dinner. Gray had ordered a bottle of champagne, but when the butler began to fill Larry's glass he told him he didn't want any.

"Oh, but you must have some," cried Isabel. "It's Uncle Elliott's best and he only gives it to very special guests."

"To tell you the truth I prefer water. After having been in the East so long it's a treat to drink water that's safe."

"This is an occasion."

"All right, I'll drink a glass."

The dinner was excellent, but Isabel noticed, as I did too, that Larry ate very little. It struck her, I suppose, that she had been doing all the talking and that Larry had had no chance to do more than listen, so now she began to question him on his actions during the ten years since she had seen him. He answered with his cordial frankness, but so vaguely as not to tell us much.

"Oh, I've been loafing around, you know. I spent a year in Germany and some time in Spain and Italy. And I knocked about the East for a bit."

"Where have you just come from now?"

"India."

"How long were you there?"

"Five years."

"Did you have fun?" asked Gray. "Shoot any tigers?"

"No," Larry smiled.

"What on earth were you doing with yourself in India for five years?" said Isabel.

"Playing about," he answered, with a smile of kindly mockery.

"What about the Rope Trick?" asked Gray. "Did you see that?"

"No, I didn't."

"What did you see?"

"A lot."

I put a question to him then.

"Is it true that the Yogis acquire powers that would seem to us supernatural?"

"I wouldn't know. All I can tell you is that it's commonly believed in India. But the wisest don't attach any importance to powers of that sort; they think they're apt to hinder spiritual progress. I remember one of them telling me of a Yogi who came to the bank of a river; he hadn't the money to pay the ferryman to take him across and the ferryman refused to take him for nothing, so he stepped on the water and walked upon its surface to the other side. The Yogi who told me shrugged his shoulders rather scornfully. 'A miracle like that,' he said, 'is worth no more than the penny it would have cost to go on the ferryboat.'"

"But d'you think the Yogi really walked over the water?" asked Gray.

"The Yogi who told me implicitly believed it."

It was a pleasure to hear Larry talk, because he had a wonderfully melodious voice; it was light, rich without being deep, and with a singular variety of tone. We finished dinner and went back to the drawing-room to have our coffee. I had never been to India and was eager to hear more of it.

"Did you come in contact with any writers and thinkers?" I asked.

"I notice that you make a distinction between the two," said Isabel to tease me.

"I made it my business to," Larry answered.

"How did you communicate with them? In English?"

"The most interesting, if they spoke at all, didn't speak it very well and understood less. I learnt Hindustani. And when I went south I picked up enough Tamil to get along pretty well."

"How many languages d'you know now, Larry?"

"Oh, I don't know. Half a dozen or so."

"I want to know more about the Yogis," said Isabel. "Did you get to know any of them intimately?"

"As intimately as you can know persons who pass the best part of their time in the Infinite," he smiled. "I spent two years in the Ashrama of one."

"Two years? What's an Ashrama?"

"Well, I suppose you might call it a hermitage. There are holy men who live alone, in a temple, in the forest or on the slopes of the Himalayas. There are others who attract disciples. A charitable person to acquire merit builds a room, large or small, for a Yogi whose piety has impressed him to live in, and the disciples live with him, sleeping on the veranda or in the cookhouse if there is one or under the trees. I had a tiny hut in the compound just big enough for my camp bed, a chair and a table, and a bookshelf."

"Where was this?" I inquired.

"In Travancore, a beautiful country of green hills and valleys and soft flowing rivers. Up in the mountains there are tigers, leopards, elephants and bison, but the Ashrama was on a lagoon and all around it grew coconuts and areca palms. It was three or four miles from the nearest town, but people used to come from there, and even from much further, on foot or by bullock cart, to hear the Yogi talk when he was inclined to, or just to sit at his feet and share with one another the peace and blessedness that was irradiated from his presence as its fragrance is wafted upon the air by the tuberose."

Gray moved uneasily in his chair. I guessed that the conversation was taking a turn that he found uncomfortable.

"Have a drink?" he said to me.

"No, thanks."

"Well, I'm going to have one. What about you, Isabel?"

He raised his great weight from the chair and went over to the table on which stood whiskey and Perrier and glasses.

"Were there other white men there?"

"No. I was the only one."

"How could you stand it for two years?" cried Isabel.

"They passed like a flash. I've spent days that seemed to be unconscionably longer."

"What did you do with yourself all the time?"

"I read. I took long walks. I went out in a boat on the lagoon. I meditated. Meditation is very hard work; after two or three hours of it you're as exhausted as if you'd driven a car five hundred miles, and all you want to do is to rest."

Isabel frowned slightly. She was puzzled and I'm not sure that she wasn't a trifle scared. I think she was beginning to have a notion that the Larry who had entered the room a few hours before, though unchanged in appearance and seemingly as open and friendly as he had ever been, was not the same as the Larry, so candid, easy and gay, wilful to her mind but delightful, that she had known in the past. She had lost him before, and on seeing him again, taking him for the old Larry, she had a feeling that, however altered the circumstances, he was still hers; and now, as though she had sought to catch a sunbeam in her hand and it slipped through her fingers as she grasped it, she was a trifle dismayed. I had looked at her a good deal that evening, which was always a pleasant thing to do, and had seen the fondness in her eyes as they rested on his trim head, with the small ears close to the skull, and how the expression in them changed when they dwelt on his hollow temples and the thinness of his cheek. She glanced at his long, lean hands, which notwithstanding their emaciation were strong and virile. Then her gaze lingered on his mobile mouth, well shaped, full without being sensual, and on his serene brow and clean-cut nose. He wore his new clothes not with the bandbox elegance of Elliott, but with a sort of loose carelessness as though he had worn them every day for a year. I felt that he aroused in Isabel motherly instincts I had never felt in her relation with her children. She was an experienced woman; he still looked a boy; and I seemed to read in her air the pride of a mother for her grown-up son because he is talking intelligently and others are listening to him as if he made sense. I don't think the import of what he said penetrated her consciousness.

But I was not done with my questioning.

"What was your Yogi like?"

"In person, d'you mean? Well, he wasn't tall, neither thin nor fat, palish brown in colour and clean-shaven, with close-cropped white hair. He never wore anything but a loincloth, and yet he managed to look as trim and neat and well dressed as a young man in one of Brooks Brothers' advertisements."

"And what had he got that particularly attracted you?"

Larry looked at me for a full minute before answering. His eyes in their deep sockets seemed as though they were trying to pierce to the depths of my soul.

"Saintliness."

I was slightly disconcerted by his reply. In that room, with its fine furniture, with those lovely drawings on the walls, the word fell like a plop of water that has seeped through the ceiling from an overflowing bath.

"We've all read about the saints, St. Francis, St. John of the Cross, but that was hundreds of years ago. I never thought it possible to meet one who was alive now. From the first time I saw him I never doubted that he was a saint. It was a wonderful experience."

"And what did you gain from it?"

"Peace," he said casually, with a light smile. Then, abruptly, he rose to his feet. "I must go."

"Oh, not yet, Larry," cried Isabel. "It's quite early."

"Good night," he said, smiling still, taking no notice of her expostulation. He kissed her on the cheek. "I'll see you again in a day or two."

"Where are you staying? I'll call you."

"Oh, don't bother to do that. You know how difficult it is to get a call through in Paris, and in any case our telephone is generally out of order."

I laughed inwardly at the neatness with which Larry had got out of giving an address. It was a queer kink of his to make a secret of his abode. I suggested that they should all dine with me next evening but one in the Bois de Boulogne. It was very pleasant in that balmy spring weather to eat out-of-doors, under the trees, and Gray could drive us there in the coupé. I left with Larry and would willingly have walked a way with him, but as we got into the street he shook hands with me and walked quickly off. I got into a taxi.

(v)

We had arranged to meet at the apartment and have a cocktail before starting. I arrived before Larry. I was taking them to a very smart restaurant and expected to find Isabel arrayed for the occasion; with all the women dressed up to the nines I was confident she would not wish to be outshone. But she had on a plain woolen frock.

"Gray's got one of his headaches," she said. "He's in agony. I can't possibly leave him. I told the cook she could go out when she'd given the children their supper and I must make something for him myself and try to get him to take it. You and Larry had better go alone."

"Is Gray in bed?"

"No, he won't ever go to bed when he has his headaches. God knows, it's the only place for him, but he won't. He's in the library."

This was a little panelled room, brown and gold, that Elliott had found in an old château. The books were protected from anyone who wanted to read them by gilt latticework, and locked up, but this was perhaps as well, as they consisted for the most part of illustrated pornographic works of the eighteenth century. In their contemporary morocco, however, they made a very pretty effect. Isabel led me in. Gray was sitting humped up in a big leather chair, with picture papers scattered on the floor beside him. His eyes were closed and his usually red face had a gray pallor. It was evident that he was in great pain. He tried to get up, but I stopped him.

"Have you given him any aspirin?" I asked Isabel.

"That never does any good. I have an American prescription, but that doesn't help either."

"Oh, don't bother, darling," said Gray. "I shall be all right tomorrow." He tried to smile. "I'm sorry to make such a nuisance of myself," he said to me. "You all go out to the Bois."

"I wouldn't dream of it," said Isabel. "D'you think I should enjoy myself when I knew you were suffering the tortures of the damned?"

"Poor slut, I think she loves me," said Gray, his eyes closed.

Then his face was suddenly contorted and you could almost see the lancinating pain that pierced his head. The door was softly opened and Larry stepped in. Isabel told him what was the matter.

"Oh, I am sorry," he said, giving Gray a look of commiseration. "Isn't there anything one can do to relieve him?"

"Nothing," said Gray, his eyes still closed. "The only thing you can any of you do for me is to leave me alone; go off and have a good time by yourselves."

I thought myself that was really the only sensible course to take, but I didn't suppose Isabel could square it with her conscience.

"Will you let me see if I can help you?" asked Larry.

"No one can help me," said Gray wearily. "It's just killing me and sometimes I wish to God it would."

"I was wrong in saying that perhaps I could help you. What I meant was that perhaps I could help you to help yourself."

Gray slowly opened his eyes and looked at Larry.

"How can you do that?"

Larry took what looked like a silver coin out of his pocket and put it in Gray's hand.

"Close your fingers on it tightly and hold your hand palm downwards. Don't fight against me. Make no effort, but hold the coin in your clenched fist. Before I count twenty your hand will open and the coin will drop out of it."

Gray did as he was told. Larry seated himself at the writing table and began to count. Isabel and I remained standing. One, two, three, four. Till he got up to fifteen there was no movement in Gray's hand, then it seemed to tremble a little and I had the impression, I can hardly say I saw, that the clenched fingers were loosening. The thumb moved away from the fist. I distinctly saw the fingers quiver. When Larry reached nineteen the coin fell out of Gray's hand and rolled to my feet. I picked it up and looked at it. It was heavy and misshapen, and in bold relief on one side of it was a youthful head which I recognized as that of Alexander the Great. Gray stared at his hand with perplexity.

"I didn't let the coin drop," he said. "It fell out of itself."

He was sitting with his right arm resting on the arm of the leather chair.

"Are you quite comfortable in that chair?" asked Larry.

"As comfortable as I can be when my head's giving me hell."

"Well, let yourself go quite slack. Take it easy. Do nothing. Don't resist. Before I count twenty your right arm will rise from the arm of the chair until your hand is above your head. One, two, three, four."

He spoke the numbers slowly in that silver-toned, melodious voice of his, and when he had reached nine we saw Gray's hand rise, only just perceptibly, from the leather surface on which it rested until it was perhaps an inch above it. It stopped for a second.

"Ten, eleven, twelve."

There was a little jerk and then slowly the whole arm began to move upwards. It wasn't resting on the chair any more. Isabel, a little scared, took hold of my hand. It was a curious effect. It had no likeness to a voluntary movement. I've never seen a man walking in his sleep, but I can imagine that he would move in just the same strange way that Gray's arm moved. It didn't look as though the will were the motive power. I should have thought it would be hard to raise the arm so slowly and so evenly by a conscious effort. It gave the impression that a subconscious force, independent of the mind, was raising it. It was the same sort of movement as that of a piston moving very slowly back and forth in a cylinder.

"Fifteen, sixteen, seventeen."

The words fell, slow, slow, slow, like drops of water in a basin from a defective faucet. Gray's arm rose, rose, till his hand was above his head, and as Larry reached the number he had said it fell of its own weight on to the arm of the chair.

"I didn't lift my arm," said Gray. "I couldn't help its rising like that. It did it of its own accord."

Larry faintly smiled.

"It's of no consequence. I thought it might give you confidence in me. Where's that Greek coin?"

I gave it to him.

"Hold it in your hand." Gray took it. Larry glanced at his watch. "It's thirteen minutes past eight. In sixty seconds your eyelids will grow so heavy that you'll be obliged to close them and then you'll sleep. You'll sleep for six minutes. At eight twenty you'll wake and you'll have no more pain."

Neither Isabel nor I spoke. Our eyes were on Larry. He said nothing more. He fixed his gaze on Gray, but did not seem to look at him; he seemed rather to look through and beyond him. There was something eery in the silence that fell upon us; it was like the silence of flowers in a garden at nightfall. Suddenly I felt Isabel's hand tighten. I glanced at Gray. His eyes were closed. He was breathing easily and regularly; he was asleep. We stood there for a time that seemed interminable. I badly wanted a cigarette, but did not like to light one. Larry was motionless. His eyes looked into I knew not what distance. Except that they were open he might have been in a trance. Suddenly he appeared to relax; his eyes took on their normal expression and he looked at his watch. As he did so, Gray opened his eyes.

"Gosh," he said, "I believe I dropped off to sleep." Then he started. I noticed that his face had lost its ghastly pallor. "My headache's gone."

"That's fine," said Larry. "Have a cigarette and then we'll all go out to dinner."

"It's a miracle. I feel perfectly swell. How did you do it?"

"I didn't do it. You did it yourself."

Isabel went to change and meanwhile Gray and I drank a cocktail. Though it was plain that Larry did not wish it, Gray insisted on talking of what had just happened. He couldn't make it out at all.

"I didn't believe you could do a thing, you know," he said. "I just gave in because I felt too lousy to argue."

He went on to describe the onset of his headaches, the anguish he endured and the wreck he was when the attack subsided. He could not understand how it was that just then he felt his usual robust self. Isabel came back. She was wearing a dress I had not seen before; it reached to the ground, a white sheath of what I think is called marocain, with a flare of black tulle, and I could not but think she would be a credit to us.

It was very gay at the Château de Madrid and we were in high spirits. Larry talked amusing nonsense in a way I had not heard him do before and he made us laugh. I had a notion he was doing this with the idea of diverting our minds from the exhibition of his unexpected power. But Isabel was a determined woman. She was prepared to play ball with him as long as it suited her convenience, but she did not lose sight of her desire to satisfy her curiosity. When we had finished dinner and were drinking coffee and liqueurs and she might well have supposed that the good food, the one glass of wine he drank and the friendly talk had weakened his defences she fixed her bright eyes on Larry.

"Now tell us how you cured Gray's headache."

"You saw for yourself," he answered, smiling.

"Did you learn to do that sort of thing in India?"

"Yes."

"He suffers agonies. D'you think you could cure him permanently?"

"I don't know. I might be able to."

"It would make a difference to his whole life. He couldn't expect to hold a decent job when he may be incapacitated for forty-eight hours. And he'll never be happy till he's at work again."

"I can't work miracles, you know."

"But it was a miracle. I saw it with my own eyes."

"No, it wasn't. I merely put an idea in old Gray's head and he did the rest himself." He turned to Gray. "What are you doing tomorrow?"

"Playing golf."

"I'll look in at six and we'll have a talk." Then, giving Isabel his winning smile: "I haven't danced with you for ten years, Isabel. Would you care to see if I still know how to?"

(vi)

After that we saw a good deal of Larry. For the next week he came to the apartment every day and for half an hour shut himself up with Gray in the library. It appeared that he wanted to persuade him—that was how he smilingly put it—out of having those shattering megrims, and Gray conceived a childlike trust in him. From the little Gray said I got the idea that he was trying besides to restore his broken confidence in himself. About ten days later Gray had another headache, and it so happened that Larry was not to come till the evening. It was not a very bad one, but Gray was so confident now in Larry's odd power that he thought if Larry could be got hold of he could take it away in a few minutes. But neither I, whom Isabel called on the phone, nor they knew where he lived. When Larry at last came and relieved Gray of his pain, Gray asked him for his address so that in case of need he could summon him at once. Larry smiled.

"Call the American Express and leave a message. I'll call them every morning."

Isabel asked me later why Larry made a secret of his address. He had done that before and then it had turned out that he lived without any mystery in a third-rate hotel in the Latin Quarter.

"I haven't a notion," I said in answer. "I can only suggest something very fanciful and there's probably nothing in it. It may be that some queer instinct urges him to carry over to his dwelling place some privacy of his spirit."

"What in God's name d'you mean by that?" she cried rather irritably.

"Hasn't it struck you that when he's with us, easy as he is to get on with, friendly and sociable, one's conscious of a sort of detachment in him, as though he weren't giving all of himself, but withheld in some hidden part of his soul something, I don't know what it is—a tension, a secret, an aspiration, a knowledge—that sets him apart?"

"I've known Larry all my life," she said impatiently.

"Sometimes he reminds me of a great actor playing perfectly a part in a trumpery play. Like Eleanora Duse in *La Locandièra*."

Isabel pondered over this for a moment.

"I suppose I know what you mean. One's having fun, and one thinks he's just like one of us, just like everybody else, and then suddenly you have the feeling that he's escaped you like a smoke ring that you try to catch in your hands. What do you think it can be that makes him so queer?"

"Perhaps something so commonplace that one simply doesn't notice it."

"Such as?

"Well, goodness, for instance."

Isabel frowned.

"I wish you wouldn't say things like that. It gives me a nasty feeling in the pit of my stomach."

"Or is it a little pain in the depth of your heart?"

Isabel gave me a long look as though she were trying to read my thoughts. She took a cigarette from the table beside her and, lighting it, leant back in her chair. She watched the smoke curl up into the air.

"Do you want me to go?" I asked.

"No."

I was silent for a moment, watching her, and I took my pleasure in the contemplation of her shapely nose and the exquisite line of her jaw.

"Are you very much in love with Larry?"

"God damn you, I've never loved anyone else in all my life."

"Why did you marry Gray?"

"I had to marry somebody. He was mad about me and Mamma wanted me to marry him. Everybody told me I was well rid of Larry. I was very fond of Gray; I'm very fond of him still. You don't know how sweet he is. No one in the world could be so kind and so considerate. He looks as though he had an awful temper, doesn't he? With me he's always been angelic.

When we had money, he wanted me to want things so that he could have the pleasure of giving them to me. Once I said it would be fun if we could have a yacht and go round the world, and if the crash hadn't come he'd have bought one."

"He sounds almost too good to be true," I murmured.

"We had a grand time. I shall always be grateful to him for that. He made me very happy."

I looked at her, but did not speak.

"I suppose I didn't really love him, but one can get on all right without love. At the bottom of my heart I hankered for Larry, but as long as I didn't see him it didn't really bother me. D'you remember saying to me that with three thousand miles of ocean between, the pangs of love become quite tolerable? I thought it a beastly cynical remark then, but of course it's true."

"If it's a pain to see Larry, don't you think it would be wiser not to see him?"

"But it's a pain that's heaven. Besides, you know what he is. Any day he may vanish like a shadow when the sun goes in and we may not see him again for years."

"Have you never thought of divorcing Gray?"

"I've got no reason for divorcing him."

"That doesn't prevent your countrywomen from divorcing their husbands when they have a mind to."

She laughed.

"Why d'you suppose they do it?"

"Don't you know? Because American women expect to find in their husbands a perfection that English women only hope to find in their butlers."

Isabel gave her head such a haughty toss that I wondered she didn't get a crick in the neck.

"Because Gray isn't articulate you think there's nothing to him."

"You're wrong there," I interrupted quickly. "I think there's something rather moving about him. He has a wonderful faculty of love. One only has to glance at his face when he's looking at you to see how deeply, how devotedly he's attached to you. He loves his children much more than you do."

"I suppose you're going to say now that I'm not a good mother."

"On the contrary I think you're an excellent mother. You see that they're well and happy. You watch over their diet and take care that their bowels act regularly. You teach them to behave nicely and you read to them and make them say their prayers. If they were sick you'd send for a doctor at once and nurse them with care. But you're not wrapped up in them as Gray is."

"It's unnecessary that one should be. I'm a human being and I treat them as human beings. A mother only does her children harm if she makes them the only concern of her life."

"I think you're quite right."

"And the fact remains that they worship me."

"I've noticed that. You're their ideal of all that's graceful and beautiful and wonderful. But they're not cosy and at their ease with you as they are with Gray. They worship you, that's true; but they love him."

"He's very lovable."

I liked her for saying that. One of her most amiable traits was that she was never affronted by the naked truth.

"After the crash Gray went all to pieces. For weeks he worked at the office till midnight. I used to sit at home in an agony of fear, I was afraid he'd blow his brains out, he was so ashamed. You see, they'd been so proud of the firm, his father and Gray, they were proud of their integrity and the sureness of their judgement. It wasn't so much that we'd lost all our money, what he couldn't get over was that all those people who'd trusted him had lost theirs. He felt that he ought to have had more foresight. I couldn't get him to see that he wasn't to blame."

Isabel took a lipstick out of her bag and painted her lips.

"But that's not what I wanted to tell you. The one thing we had left was the plantation and I felt that the only chance for Gray was to get away, so we parked the children with Mamma and went down there. He'd always liked it, but we'd never been there by ourselves; we'd taken a crowd with us and had a grand time. Gray's a good shot, but he hadn't the heart to shoot then. He used to take a boat and go out on the marsh by himself for hours at a time and watch the birds. He'd wander up and down the canals with the pale rushes on each side of him and only the blue sky above. On some days the canals are as blue as the Mediterranean. He used not to say much when he came back. He'd say it was swell. But I could see what he felt. I knew that his heart was moved by the beauty and the vastness and the stillness. There's a moment just before sunset when the light on the marsh is lovely. He used to stand and look at it and it filled him with bliss. He took long rides in those solitary, mysterious woods; they're like the woods in a play of Maeterlinck's, so gray, so silent, it's almost uncanny; and there's a moment in spring—it hardly lasts more than a fortnight—when the dogwood bursts into flower, and the gum trees burst into leaf, and their young fresh green against the gray of the Spanish moss is like a song of joy;

the ground is carpeted with great white lilies and wild azalea. Gray couldn't say what it meant to him, but it meant the world. He was drunk with the loveliness of it. Oh, I know I don't put it well, but I can't tell you how moving it was to see that great hulk of a man uplifted by an emotion so pure and so beautiful that it made me want to cry. If there is a God in heaven Gray was very near Him then."

Isabel had grown a trifle emotional while she told me this and taking a tiny handkerchief she carefully wiped away a tear that glistened at the corner of each eye.

"Aren't you romanticising?" I said, smiling. "I have a notion that you're ascribing to Gray thoughts and emotions that you would have expected him to have."

"How should I have seen them if they hadn't been there? You know what I am. I'm never really happy unless I feel the cement of a sidewalk under my feet and there are large plate-glass windows all along the street with hats to look at and fur coats and diamond bracelets and gold-mounted dressingcases."

I laughed and we were silent for a moment. Then she went back to what we had been talking of before.

"I'd never divorce Gray. We've been through too much together. And he's absolutely dependent upon me. It's rather flattering, you know, and it gives you a sense of responsibility. And besides . . ."

"Besides what?"

She gave me a sidelong glance and there was a roguish twinkle in her eyes. I had a notion she didn't quite know how I would take what she had in mind to say.

"He's wonderful in bed. We've been married for ten years and he's as passionate a lover as he was at the beginning. Didn't you say in a play once that no man wants the same woman longer than five years? Well, you didn't know what you were talking about. Gray wants me as much as when we were first married. He's made me very happy in that way. Although you wouldn't think it to look at me, I'm a very sensual woman."

"You're quite wrong, I would think it."

"Well, it's not an unattractive trait, is it?"

"On the contrary." I gave her a searching look. "Do you regret you didn't marry Larry ten years ago?"

"No. It would have been madness. But of course if I'd known then what I know now I'd have gone away and lived with him for three months, and then I'd have got him out of my system for good and all."

"I think it's lucky for you you didn't make the experiment; you might have found yourself bound to him by bonds you couldn't break."

"I don't think so. It was merely a physical attraction. You know, often the best way to overcome desire is to satisfy it."

"Has it ever struck you that you're a very possessive woman? You've told me that Gray has a deep strain of poetic feeling and you've told me that he's an ardent lover; and I can well believe that both mean a lot to you; but you haven't told me what means much more to you than both of them put together—your feeling that you hold him in the hollow of that beautiful but not so small hand of yours. Larry would always have escaped you. D'you remember that Ode of Keats'? 'Bold Lover, never, never canst thou kiss, though winning near the goal.'"

"You often think you know a great deal more than you do," she said, a trifle acidly. "There's only one way a woman holds a man and you know it. And let me tell you this: it's not the first time she goes to bed with him that counts, it's the second. If she holds him then she holds him for good."

"You do pick up the most extraordinary bits of information."

"I get around and I keep my eyes and ears open."

"May I enquire how you acquired that one?"

She gave me her most teasing smile.

"From a woman I made friends with at a dress show. The *vendeuse* told me she was the smartest kept woman in Paris, so I made up my mind I'd got to know her. Adrienne de Troye. Ever heard of her?"

"Never."

"How your education has been neglected. She's forty-five and not even pretty, but she looks much more distinguished than any of Uncle Elliott's duchesses. I sat down beside her and put on my impulsive little-American-girl act. I told her I had to speak to her because I'd never seen anyone more ravishing in my life. I told her she had the perfection of a Greek cameo."

"The nerve you've got."

"She was rather stiff at first and stand-offish, but I ran on in my simple naïve way and she thawed. Then we had quite a nice little chat. When the show was over I asked her if she wouldn't come to lunch with me at the Ritz one day. I told her I'd always admired her wonderful chic."

"Had you ever seen her before?"

"Never. She wouldn't lunch with me, she said they had such malicious tongues in Paris, it would compromise me, but she was pleased that I'd asked her, and when she saw my mouth quiver with disappointment she asked me if I wouldn't come and lunch with her in her house. She patted my hand when she saw I was simply overwhelmed by her affability."

"And did you go?"

"Of course I went. She has a dear little house off the Avenue Foch and we were waited on by a butler who's the very image of George Washington. I stayed till four o'clock. We took our hair down and our stays off, and had a thorough girls' gossip. I learnt enough that afternoon to write a book."

"Why don't you? It's just the sort of thing to suit the *Ladies' Home Journal*."

"You fool," she laughed.

I was silent for a moment. I pursued my thoughts.

"I wonder if Larry was ever *really* in love with you," I said presently.

She sat up. Her expression lost its amenity. Her eyes were angry.

"What are you talking about? Of course he was in love with me. D'you think a girl doesn't know when a man's in love with her?"

"Oh, I daresay he was in love with you after a fashion. He didn't know any girl so intimately as he knew you. You'd played around together since you were children. He expected himself to be in love with you. He had the normal sexual instinct. It seemed such a natural thing that you should marry. There wouldn't have been any particular difference in your relations except that you lived under the same roof and went to bed together."

Isabel, to some extent mollified, waited for me to go on and, knowing that women are always glad to listen when you discourse upon love, I went on.

"Moralists try to persuade us that the sexual instinct hasn't got so very much to do with love. They're apt to speak of it as if it were an epiphenomenon."

"What in God's name is that?"

"Well, there are psychologists who think that consciousness accompanies brain processes and is determined by them, but doesn't itself exert any influence on them. Something like the reflection of a tree in water; it couldn't exist without the tree, but it doesn't in any way affect the tree. I think it's all stuff and nonsense to say that there can be love without passion; when people say love can endure after passion is dead they're talking of something else, affection, kindliness, community of taste and interest, and habit. Especially habit. Two people can go on having sexual intercourse from habit in just the same way as they grow hungry at the hour they're accustomed to have their meals. Of course there can be desire without love. Desire isn't passion. Desire is the natural consequence of the sexual instinct and it isn't of any more importance than any other function of the human animal. That's why women are foolish to make a song and dance when their husbands have an occasional flutter when the time and the place are propitious."

"Does that apply only to men?"

I smiled.

"If you insist I'll admit that what is sauce for the gander is sauce for the goose. The only thing to be said against it is that with a man a passing connection of that sort has no emotional significance, while with a woman it has."

"It depends on the woman."

I wasn't going to let myself be interrupted.

"Unless love is passion, it's not love, but something else; and passion thrives not on satisfaction, but on impediment. What d'you suppose Keats meant when he told the lover on his Grecian urn not to grieve? 'Forever wilt thou love, and she be fair!' Why? Because she was unattainable and however madly the lover pursued she still eluded him. For they were both imprisoned in the marble of what I suspect was an indifferent work of art. Your love for Larry and his for you were as simple and natural as the love of Paolo and Francesca and Romeo and Juliet. Fortunately for you it didn't come to a bad end. You made a rich marriage and Larry roamed the world to seek out what song the Sirens sang. Passion didn't enter into it."

"How d'you know?"

"Passion doesn't count the cost. Pascal said that the heart has its reasons that reason takes no account of. If he meant what I think, he meant that when passion seizes the heart it invents reasons that seem not only plausible but conclusive to prove that the world is well lost for love. It convinces you that honour is well sacrificed and that shame is a cheap price to pay. Passion is destructive. It destroyed Antony and Cleopatra, Tristan and Isolde, Parnell and Kitty O'Shea. And if it doesn't destroy it dies. It may be then that one is faced with the desolation of knowing that one has wasted the years of one's life, that one's brought disgrace upon oneself, endured the frightful pang of jealousy, swallowed every bitter mortification, that one's expended all one's tenderness, poured out all the riches of one's soul on a poor drab, a fool, a peg on which one hung one's dreams, who wasn't worth a stick of chewing gum."

Before I finished this harangue I knew very well that Isabel wasn't paying any attention to me, but was occupied with her own reflections. But her next remark surprised me.

"Do you think Larry is a virgin?"

"My dear, he's thirty-two."

"I'm certain he is."

"How can you be?"

"That's the kind of thing a woman knows instinctively."

138

"I knew a young man who had a very prosperous career for some years by convincing one beautiful creature after another that he'd never had a woman. He said it worked like a charm."

"I don't care what you say. I believe in my intuition."

It was growing late, Gray and Isabel were dining with friends, and she had to dress. I had nothing to do and so walked in the pleasant spring evening up the Boulevard Raspail. I have never believed very much in women's intuition; it fits in too neatly with what they want to believe to persuade me that it is trustworthy; and as I thought of the end of my long talk with Isabel I couldn't but laugh. It put me in mind of Suzanne Rouvier and it occurred to me that I had not seen her for several days. I wondered if she was doing anything. If not, she might like to dine with me and go to a movie. I stopped a prowling taxi and gave the address of her apartment.

(vii)

I mentioned Suzanne Rouvier at the beginning of this book. I had known her for ten or twelve years and at the date which I have now reached she must have been not far from forty. She was not beautiful; in fact she was rather ugly. She was tall for a Frenchwoman, with a short body, long legs and long arms; and she held herself gawkily as though she didn't know how to cope with the length of her limbs. The colour of her hair changed according to her whim, but most often was of a reddish brown. She had a small square face, with very prominent cheekbones vividly rouged, and a large mouth with heavily painted lips. None of this sounds attractive, but it was; it is true that she had a good skin, strong white teeth and big, vividly blue eyes. They were her best features and she made the most of them by painting her eyelashes and her eyelids. She had a shrewd, roving, friendly look and she combined great good nature with a proper degree of toughness. In the life she had led she needed to be tough. Her mother, the widow of a small official in the government, had on his death returned to her native village in Anjou to live on her pension and when Suzanne was fifteen had apprenticed her to a dressmaker in the neighbouring town, which was near enough for her to be able to come home on Sundays. It was during her fortnight's holiday, when she had reached the age of seventeen, that she was seduced by an artist who was spending his summer in the village to paint landscape. She already knew very well that without a penny to bless herself with her chance of marriage was remote and when the painter, at the end of the summer, proposed taking her to Paris she consented with alacrity. He took her to live with him in a rabbit warren of studios in Montmartre, and she spent a very pleasant year in his company.

At the end of this he told her that he had not sold a single canvas and could no longer afford the luxury of a mistress. She had been expecting the news for some time and was not disconcerted by it. He asked her if she wanted to go home and when she said she didn't, told her that another painter in the same block would be glad to have her. The man he named had made a pass at her two or three times and though she had rebuffed him it had been with so much good humour that he was not affronted. She did not dislike him and so accepted the proposition with placidity. It was convenient that she did not have to go to the expense of taking a taxi to transport her trunk. Her second lover, a good deal older than the first, but still presentable, painted her in every conceivable position, clothed and in the nude; and she passed two happy years with him. She was proud to think that with her as a model he had made his first real success and she showed me a reproduction cut out of an illustrated paper of the picture that had brought it about. It had been purchased by an American gallery. It was a nude, life-size, and she was lying in something of the same position as Manet's *Olympe*. The artist had been quick to see that there was something modern and amusing in her proportions, and, fining down her thin body to emaciation, he had elongated her long legs and arms, he had emphasised her high cheekbones and made her blue eyes extravagantly large. From the reproduction I naturally could not tell what the colour was like, but I was sensible of the elegance of the design. The picture brought him sufficient notoriety to enable him to marry an admiring widow with money, and Suzanne, well aware that a man had to think of his future, accepted the rupture of their cordial relations without acrimony.

For by now she knew her value. She liked the artistic life, it amused her to pose, and after the day's work was over she found it pleasant to go to the café and sit with painters, their wives and mistresses, while they discussed art, reviled dealers, and told bawdy stories. On this occasion, having seen the break coming, she had made her plans. She picked out a young man who was unattached and who, she thought, had talent. She chose her opportunity when he was alone at the café, explained the circumstances and without further preamble suggested that they should live together.

"I'm twenty and a good housekeeper. I'll save you money there and I'll save you the expense of a model. Look at your shirt, it's a disgrace, and your studio is a mess. You want a woman to look after you."

He knew she was a good sort. He was amused at her proposal and she saw he was inclined to accept.

"After all, there's no harm in trying," she said. "If it doesn't work we shall neither of us be worse off than we are now."

He was a non-representative artist and he painted portraits of her in squares and oblongs. He painted her with one eye and no mouth. He painted her as a geometrical arrangement in black and brown and gray. He painted her in a crisscross of lines through which you vaguely saw a human face. She stayed with him for a year and a half and left him of her own accord.

"Why?" I asked her. "Didn't you like him?"

"Yes, he was a nice boy. I didn't think he was getting any further. He was repeating himself."

She found no difficulty in discovering a successor. She remained faithful to artists.

"I've always been in painting," she said. "I was with a sculptor for six months, but I don't know why, it said nothing to me."

She was pleased to think that she had never separated.from a lover with unpleasantness. She was not only a good model, but a good housewife. She loved working about the studio she happened for a while to be living in and took pride in keeping it in apple-pie order. She was a good cook and could turn out a tasty meal at the smallest possible cost. She mended her lovers' socks and sewed buttons on their shirts.

"I never saw why because a man was an artist he shouldn't be neat and tidy."

She only had one failure. This was a young Englishman who had more money than anyone she had known before and he had a car.

"But it didn't last long," she said. "He used to get drunk and then he was tiresome. I wouldn't have minded that if he'd been a good painter, but, my dear, it was grotesque. I told him I was going to leave him and he began to cry. He said he loved me.

" 'My poor friend,' I said to him. 'Whether you love me or not isn't of the smallest consequence. What is of consequence is that you have no talent. Return to your own country and go into the grocery business. That is all you're fit for.' "

"What did he say to that?" I asked.

"He flew into a passion and told me to get out. But it was good advice I gave him, you know. I hope he took it, he wasn't a bad fellow; only a bad artist."

Common sense and good nature will do a lot to make the pilgrimage of life not too difficult to a light woman, but the profession Suzanne had adopted has its ups and downs like any other. There was the Scandinavian for instance. She was so imprudent as to fall in love with him.

"He was a god, my dear," she told me. "He was immensely tall, as tall as the Eiffel Tower, with great broad shoulders and a magnificent chest, a waist that you could almost put your hands round, a belly flat, but flat like the palm of my hand, and muscles like a professional athlete's. He had golden, wavy hair and a skin of honey. And he didn't paint badly. I liked his brush work, it was bold and dashing, and he had a rich vivid palette."

She made up her mind to have a child by him. He was against it, but she told him she would take the responsibility of it.

"He liked it well enough when it was born. Oh, such a lovely baby, rosy, fair-haired and blue-eyed like her papa. It was a girl."

Suzanne lived with him for three years.

"He was a little stupid and sometimes he bored me, but he was very sweet and so beautiful that I didn't really mind."

Then he got a telegram from Sweden to say his father was dying and he must come back at once. He promised to return, but she had a premonition that he never would. He left her all the money he had. She didn't hear from him for a month and then she got a letter from him saying that his father had died, leaving his affairs in confusion, and that he felt it his duty to remain by his mother and go into the lumber business. He enclosed a draft for ten thousand francs. Suzanne was not the woman to give way to despair. She came to the conclusion very quickly that a child would hamper her activities and so took the baby girl down to her mother's and left her, along with the ten thousand francs, in her care.

"It was heart-rending, I adored that child, but in life one has to be practical."

"What happened then?" I asked.

"Oh, I got along. I found a friend."

But then came her typhoid. She always spoke of it as "my typhoid" as a millionaire might speak of "my place at Palm Beach" or "my grouse moor." She nearly died of it and was in the hospital for three months. When she left she was nothing but skin and bones, as weak as a rat, and so nervous that she could do nothing but cry. She wasn't much use to anyone then, she wasn't strong enough to pose and she had very little money.

"*Oh la, la,*" she said, "I passed through some hard times. Luckily I had good friends. But you know what artists are, it's a struggle for them to make both ends meet anyway. I was never a pretty woman, I had something of course, but I wasn't twenty any more. Then I ran into the cubist I'd been with; he'd been married and divorced since we lived together, he'd given up cubism and become a surrealist. He thought he could use me and said he was lonely; he said he'd give me board and lodging and I promise you, I was glad to accept."

Suzanne stayed with him till she met her manufacturer. The manufacturer was brought to the studio by a friend on the chance that he might buy one of the ex-cubist's pictures, and Suzanne, anxious to effect a sale, set herself out to be as agreeable to him as she knew how. He could not make up his mind to buy on the spur of the moment, but said he would like to come and see the pictures again. He did, a fortnight later, and this time she received the impression that he had come to see her rather than works of art. When he left, still without buying, he pressed her hand with unnecessary warmth. Next day the friend who had brought him waylaid her when she was on her way to market to buy the day's provisions and told her that the manufacturer had taken a fancy to her and wanted to know if she would dine with him next time he came to Paris, because he had a proposition to make to her.

"What does he see in me, d'you suppose?" she asked.

"He's an amateur of modern art. He's seen portraits of you. You intrigue him. He's a provincial and a businessman. You represent Paris to him, art, romance, everything that he misses in Lille."

"Has he money?" she asked in her sensible way.

"Plenty."

"Well, I'll dine with him. There's no harm hearing what he's got to say."

He took her to Maxim's, which impressed her; she had dressed very quietly, and she felt as she looked at the women around her that she could pass very well for a respectable married woman. He ordered a bottle of champagne and this persuaded her that he was a gentleman. When they came to coffee he put his proposition before her. She thought it very handsome. He told her that he came to Paris regularly once a fortnight to attend a board meeting and it was tiresome in the evening to dine alone and if he felt the need of feminine society to go to a brothel. Being a married man with two children he thought that an unsatisfactory arrangement for a man in his position. Their common friend had told him all about her and he knew she was a woman of discretion. He was no longer young and he had no wish to get entangled with a giddy girl. He was something of a collector of the modern school and her connection with it was sympathetic to him. Then he came down to brass tacks. He was prepared to take an apartment for her and furnish it and provide her with an income of two thousand francs a month. In return for this he wished to enjoy her company for one night every fourteen days. Suzanne had never had the spending of so much money in her life and she quickly reckoned that on such a sum she could not only live and dress as such an advancement in the world evidently demanded, but provide for her daughter and put away something for a rainy day. But she hesitated for a moment. She had always been "in painting," as she put it, and there was no doubt in her mind that it was a come down to be the mistress of a businessman.

"*C'est à prendre ou à laisser*," he said. "You can take it or leave it."

He was not repulsive to her and the rosette of the Legion of Honour in his buttonhole proved that he was a man of distinction. She smiled.

"*Je prends*," she replied. "I'll take it."

(*viii*)

Though Suzanne had always lived in Montmartre she decided that it was necessary to break with the past and so took an apartment in Montparnasse in a house just off the boulevard. It consisted of two rooms, a tiny kitchen and a bathroom; it was on the sixth floor, but there was a lift. To her a bathroom and a lift, even though it only held two persons and moved at a snail's pace and you had to walk downstairs, represented not only luxury but style.

For the first few months of their union Monsieur Achille Gauvain, for such was his name, put up at a hotel on his fortnightly visits to Paris and, after spending such part of the night with Suzanne as his amorous inclination demanded, returned to it to sleep by himself till it was time for him to get up and catch his train to return to his business affairs and the sober pleasures of family life; but then Suzanne pointed out to him that he was throwing away money to no purpose and it would be both more economical and more comfortable if he stayed in the apartment till morning. He could not but see the force of this. He was flattered at Suzanne's thoughtfulness for his comfort—it was true, there was nothing agreeable in going out into the street and finding a taxi on a cold winter night—and he approved of her disinclination to put him to useless expense. It was a good woman who counted not only her own pennies but her lover's.

Monsieur Achille had every reason to feel pleased with himself. In general they went to dine at one of the better restaurants in Montparnasse, but now and then Suzanne prepared dinner for him in the apartment. The tasty food she gave him was very much to his liking. On warm evenings he would dine in his shirt sleeves and feel deliciously wanton and bohemian. He had always had an inclination for buying pictures, but Suzanne would let him buy nothing that she did not approve of and he soon found reason to trust her judgement. She would have no truck with dealers, but took him to the studios of the painters and thus enabled him to buy pictures for half the money he would otherwise have had to pay. He knew that she was putting something aside and when she told him that year by year she was buying a bit of land in her native village he felt a thrill of pride. He knew the desire to own land that is in the heart of every person of French blood, and his esteem for her was increased because she possessed it too.

On her side Suzanne was well satisfied. She was neither faithful to him nor unfaithful; that is to say, she took care not to form any permanent connection with another man, but if she came across one who took her fancy she was not averse to going to bed with him. But it was a point of honour with her not to let him stay all night. She felt she owed that to the man of means and position who had settled her life in such an assured and respectable manner.

I had come to know Suzanne when she was living with a painter who happened to be an acquaintance of mine and had often sat in his studio while she posed; I continued to see her now and then at infrequent intervals, but did not enter upon terms of any intimacy with her till she moved to Montparnasse. It appeared then that Monsieur Achille, for this was how she always spoke of him and how she addressed him, had read one or two of my books in translation and one evening he invited me to dine with them at a restaurant. He was a little man, half a head shorter than Suzanne, with iron-gray hair and a neat gray moustache. He was on the plump side, and he had a potbelly, but only to the extent of giving him an air of substance. He walked with the short fat man's strut and it was plain that he was not displeased with himself. He gave me a fine dinner. He was very polite. He told me he was glad I was a friend of Suzanne's, he could see at a glance that I was *comme il faut* and he would be glad to think that I should see something of her. His affairs, alas! kept him tied to Lille and the poor girl was too often alone; it would be a comfort to him to know that she was in touch with a man of education. He was a businessman, but he had always admired artists.

"*Ah, mon cher monsieur,* art and literature have always been the twin glories of France. Along with her military prowess, of course. And I, a manufacturer of woolen goods, have no hesitation in saying that I put the painter and the writer on a level with the general and the statesman."

No one could say handsomer than that.

Suzanne would not hear of having a maid to do the housework, partly for economy's sake and partly because (for reasons best known to herself) she didn't want anyone poking her nose into what was nobody's business but her own. She kept the tiny apartment, furnished in the most modern style of the moment, clean and neat and she made all her own underclothes. But even then, now that she no longer posed, time hung heavily on her hands, for she was an industrious woman; and presently the idea occurred to her that, after having sat to so many painters, there was no reason why she should not paint too. She bought canvases, brushes and paints and forthwith set to work. Sometimes when I was to take her out to dinner I would go early and find her in a smock busily at work. Just as the embryo in the womb recapitulates in brief the evolution of the species, so did Suzanne recapitulate the styles of all her lovers. She painted landscape like the landscape painter, abstractions like the cubist and with the help of picture postcards sailing boats lying at anchor like the Scandinavian. She could not draw, but she had an agreeable sense of colour and if her pictures were not very good she got a lot of fun out of painting them.

Monsieur Achille encouraged her. It gave him a sense of satisfaction that his mistress should be an artist. It was on his insistence that she sent a canvas to the autumn salon and they were both very proud when it was hung. He gave her one bit of good advice.

"Don't try to paint like a man, my dear," he said. "Paint like a woman. Don't aim to be strong; be satisfied to charm. And be honest. In business sharp practice sometimes succeeds, but in art honesty is not only the best but the only policy."

At the time of which I write the connection had lasted for five years to their mutual content.

"Evidently he doesn't thrill me," said Suzanne. "But he's intelligent and in a good position. I've reached an age when it's necessary for me to think of my situation."

She was sympathetic and understanding and Monsieur Achille conceived a high opinion of her judgement. She lent a willing ear when he discussed with her his business and domestic affairs. She condoled with him when his daughter failed in an examination and rejoiced with him when his son got engaged to a girl with money. He had himself married the only child of a man in his own line of business and the amalgamation of two rival firms had been a source of profit to both parties. It was naturally a satisfaction to him that his son was sensible enough to see that the soundest basis of a happy marriage is community of financial interests. He confided to Suzanne his ambition to marry his daughter into the aristocracy.

"And why not, with her fortune?" said Suzanne.

Monsieur Achille made it possible for Suzanne to send her own daughter to a convent where she would receive a good education, and he promised that at the proper age he would pay to have her suitably trained to earn her living as a typist and stenographer.

"She's going to be a beauty when she grows up," Suzanne told me, "but evidently it won't hurt her to have an education and to be able to pound a typewriter. Of course she's so young it's too soon to tell, it may be that she'll have no temperament."

Suzanne had delicacy. She left it to my intelligence to infer her meaning. I inferred it all right.

(ix)

A week or so after I had so unexpectedly run into Larry, Suzanne and I one night, having dined together and gone to a movie, were sitting in the Sélect on the Boulevard du Montparnasse, having a glass of beer, when he strolled in. She gave a gasp and to my surprise called out to him. He came up to the table, kissed her and shook hands with me. I could see that she could hardly believe her eyes.

"May I sit down?" he said. "I haven't had any dinner and I'm going to have something to eat."

"Oh, but it's good to see you, *mon petit,*" she said, her eyes sparkling. "Where have you sprung from? And why have you given no sign of life all these years? My God, how thin you are. For all I know you might have been dead."

"Well, I wasn't," he answered, his eyes twinkling. "How is Odette?"

That was the name of Suzanne's daughter.

"Oh, she's growing a big girl. And pretty. She still remembers you."

"You never told me you knew Larry," I said to her.

"Why should I? I never knew you knew him. We're old friends."

Larry ordered himself eggs and bacon. Suzanne told him all about her daughter and then about herself. He listened in his smiling, charming way while she chattered. She told him that she had settled down and was painting. She turned to me.

"I'm improving, don't you think? I don't pretend I'm a genius, but I have as much talent as many of the painters I've known."

"D'you sell any pictures?" asked Larry.

"I don't have to," she answered airily. "I have private means."

"Lucky girl."

"No, not lucky: clever. You must come and see my pictures."

She wrote down her address on a piece of paper and made him promise to go. Suzanne, excited, went on talking nineteen to the dozen. Then Larry asked for his bill.

"You're not going?" she cried.

"I am," he smiled.

He paid and with a wave of the hand left us. I laughed. He had a way that always amused me of being with you one moment and without explanation gone the next. It was so abrupt; it was almost as if he had faded into the air.

"Why did he want to go away so quickly?" said Suzanne with vexation.

"Perhaps he's got a girl waiting for him," I replied mockingly.

"That's an idea like another." She took her compact out of her bag and powdered her face. "I pity any woman who falls in love with him. *Oh la, la.*"

"Why do you say that?"

She looked at me for a minute with a seriousness I had not often seen in her.

"I very nearly fell in love with him myself once. You might as well fall in love with a reflection in the water or a ray of sunshine or a cloud in the sky. I had a narrow escape. Even now when I think of it I tremble at the danger I ran."

Discretion be blowed. It would have been inhuman not to want to know what this was all about. I congratulated myself that Suzanne was a woman who had no notion of reticence.

"How on earth did you ever get to know him?" I asked.

"Oh, it was years ago. Six years, seven years, I forget. Odette was only five. He knew Marcel when I was living with him. He used to come to the studio and sit while I was posing. He'd take us out to dinner sometimes. You never knew when he'd come. Sometimes not for weeks and then two or three days running. Marcel used to like to have him there; he said he painted better when he was there. Then I had my typhoid. I went through a bad time when I came out of the hospital." She shrugged her shoulders. "But I've already told you all that. Well, one day I'd been round the studios trying to get work and no one wanted me, and I'd had nothing but a glass of milk and a croissant all day and I didn't know how I was going to pay for my room, and I met him accidentally on the Boulevard Clichy. He stopped and asked me how I was and I told him about my typhoid and then he said to me: 'You look as if you could do with a square meal.' And there was something in his voice and in the look of his eyes that broke me; I began to cry.

"We were next door to La Mère Mariette and he took me by the arm and sat me down at a table. I was so hungry I was ready to eat an old boot, but when the omelette came I felt I couldn't eat a thing. He forced me to take a little and he gave me a glass of burgundy. I felt better then and I ate some asparagus. I told him all my troubles. I was too weak to hold a pose. I was just skin and bone and I looked terrible; I couldn't expect to get a man. I asked him if he'd lend me the money to go back to my village. At least I'd have my little girl there. He asked me if I wanted to go and I said of course not, Mamma didn't want me, she could hardly live on her pension with prices the way they were, and the money I'd sent for Odette had all been spent, but if I appeared at the door she could hardly refuse to take me in, she'd see how ill I looked. He looked at me for a long time, and I thought he was going to say he couldn't lend me anything. Then he said:

" 'Would you like me to take you down to a little place I know in the country, you and the kid? I want a bit of a holiday.'

"I could hardly believe my ears. I'd known him for ages and he'd never made a pass at me.

" 'In the condition I'm in?' I said. I couldn't help laughing. 'My poor friend,' I said, 'I'm no use to any man just now.'

"He smiled at me. Have you ever noticed what a wonderful smile he's got? It's as sweet as honey.

" 'Don't be so silly,' he said. 'I'm not thinking of that.'

"I was crying so hard by then, I could hardly speak. He gave me money to fetch the child and we all went to the country together. Oh, it was charming, the place he took us to."

Suzanne described it to me. It was three miles from a little town the name of which I have forgotten and they took a car out to the inn. It was a ramshackle building on a river with a lawn that ran down to the water. There were plane trees on the lawn and they had their meals in their shade. In summer artists came there to paint, but it was early for that yet and they had the inn to themselves. The fare was famous and on Sundays people used to drive from here and there to lunch with abandon, but on weekdays their peace was seldom disturbed. With the rest, the good food and wine, Suzanne grew stronger, and she was happy to have her child with her.

"He was sweet with Odette and she adored him. I had to prevent her from making a nuisance of herself, but he never seemed to mind how much she pestered him. It used to make me laugh, they were like two children together."

"What did you do with yourselves?" I asked.

"Oh, there was always something to do. We used to take a boat and fish and sometimes we'd get the *patron* to lend us his Citroën and we'd go into town. Larry liked it. The old houses and the *place*. It was so quiet that your footsteps on the cobblestones were the only sound you heard. There was a Louis Quatorze *hôtel de ville* and an old church and at the edge of the town was the château with a garden by Le Notre. When you sat at the café on the *place* you had the feeling that you had stepped back three hundred years and the Citroën at the curb didn't seem to belong to this world at all."

It was after one of these outings that Larry told her the story of the young airman which I narrated at the beginning of this book.

"I wonder why he told you," I said.

"I haven't an idea. They'd had a hospital in the town during the war and in the cemetery there were rows and rows of little crosses. We went to see it. We didn't stay long, it gave me the creeps—all those poor boys lying there. Larry was very silent on the way home. He never ate much, but at dinner he hardly touched a thing. I remember so well, it was a beautiful, starry night and we sat on the riverbank, it was pretty with the poplars silhouetted against the darkness, and he smoked his pipe. And suddenly, *à propos de bottes,* he told me about his friend and how he died to save him." Suzanne took a swig of beer. "He's a strange creature. I shall never understand him. He used to like to read to me. Sometimes in the daytime, while I sewed things for the little one, and in the evening after I'd put her to bed."

"What did he read?"

"Oh, all sorts of things. Letters of Madame de Sévigné and bits of Saint-Simon. *Imagine toi,* I who'd never read anything before but the newspaper and now and then a novel when I heard them talk about it in the studios and didn't want them to think me a fool! I had no idea reading could be so interesting. Those old writers, they weren't such fatheads as one would think."

"Who would think?" I chuckled.

"Then he made me read with him. We read *Phèdre* and *Bérénice.* He took the men's parts and I took the women's. You can't think how amusing it was," she added naïvely. "He used to look at me so strangely when I cried at the pathetic parts. Of course it was only because I hadn't got my strength. And you know, I've still got the books. Even now I can't read some of the letters of Madame de Sévigné that he read to me without hearing his lovely voice and without seeing the river flowing so quietly and the poplars on the opposite bank, and sometimes I can't go on, it gives me such a pain in my heart. I know now that those were the happiest weeks I ever spent in my life. That man, he's an angel of sweetness."

Suzanne felt she was growing sentimental and feared (wrongly) that I should laugh at her. She shrugged her shoulders and smiled.

"You know, I've always made up my mind that when I've reached the canonical age and no man wants to sleep with me any more I shall make my peace with the Church and repent of my sins. But the sins I committed with Larry nothing in the world will ever induce me to repent of. Never, never, never!"

"But as you've described it I can see nothing you can possibly have to repent of."

"I haven't told you the half of it yet. You see, I have a naturally good constitution and being out in the air all day, eating well, sleeping well, with not a care in the world, in three or four weeks I was as strong as ever I'd been. And I was looking well; I had colour in my cheeks and my hair had recovered its sheen. I felt twenty. Larry swam in the river every morning and I used to watch him. He has a beautiful body, not an athlete's like my Scandinavian, but strong and of an infinite grace.

"He'd been very patient while I was so weak, but now that I was perfectly well I saw no reason to keep him waiting any longer. I gave him a hint or two that I was ready for anything, but he didn't seem to understand. Of course you Anglo-Saxons are peculiar, you're brutal and at the same time you're sentimental; there's no denying it, you're not good lovers. I said to myself, 'Perhaps it's his delicacy, he's done so much for me, he's let me have the child here, it may be that he hasn't the heart to ask me for the return that is his right.' So one night, as we were going to bed, I said to him, 'D'you want me to come to your room tonight?'"

I laughed.

"You put it a bit bluntly, didn't you?"

"Well, I couldn't ask him to come to mine, because Odette was sleeping there," she answered ingenuously. "He looked at me with those kind eyes of his for a moment, then he smiled. 'D'you want to come?' he said.

"'What do you think—with that fine body of yours?'

"'All right, come then.'

"I went upstairs and undressed and then I slipped along the passage to his room. He was lying in bed reading and smoking a pipe. He put down his pipe and his book and moved over to make room for me."

Suzanne was silent for a while and it went against my grain to ask her questions. But after a while she went on.

"He was a strange lover. Very sweet, affectionate and even tender, virile without being passionate, if you understand what I mean, and absolutely without vice. He loved like a hotblooded schoolboy. It was rather funny and

151

rather touching. When I left him I had the feeling that I should be grateful to him rather than he to me. As I closed the door I saw him take up his book and go on reading from where he had left off."

I began to laugh.

"I'm glad it amuses you," she said a trifle grimly. But she was not without a sense of humour. She giggled. "I soon discovered that if I waited for an invitation I might wait indefinitely, so when I felt like it I just went into his room and got into bed. He was always very nice. He had in short natural human instincts, but he was like a man so preoccupied that he forgets to eat, yet when you put a good dinner before him he eats it with appetite. I know when a man's in love with me, and I should have been a fool if I'd believed that Larry loved me, but I thought he'd get into the habit of me. One has to be practical in life and I said to myself that it would suit me very well if when we went back to Paris he took me to live with him. I knew he'd let me have the child and I should have liked that. My instinct told me I'd be silly to fall in love with him, you know women are very unfortunate, so often when they fall in love they cease to be lovable, and I made up my mind to be on my guard."

Suzanne inhaled the smoke of her cigarette and blew it out through her nose. It was growing late and many of the tables were now empty, but there was still a group of people hanging around the bar.

"One morning, after breakfast, I was sitting on the riverbank sewing, and Odette was playing with some bricks he'd bought her when Larry came up to me.

" 'I've come to say good-bye to you,' he said.

" 'Are you going somewhere?' I said, surprised.

" 'Yes.'

" 'Not for good?' I said.

" 'You're quite well now. Here's enough money to keep you for the rest of the summer and to start you off when you get back to Paris.'

"For a moment I was so upset I didn't know what to say. He stood in front of me, smiling in that candid way of his.

" 'Have I done something to displease you?' I asked him.

" 'Nothing. Don't think that for a moment. I've got work to do. We've had a lovely time down here. Odette, come and say good-bye to your uncle.'

"She was too young to understand. He took her up in his arms and kissed her; then he kissed me and walked back into the hotel; in a minute I heard the car drive away. I looked at the banknotes I had in my hand. Twelve thousand francs. It came so quickly I hadn't time to react. 'Zut alors,' I said to myself. I had at least one thing to be thankful for, I hadn't allowed myself to fall in love with him. But I couldn't make head or tail of it."

I was obliged to laugh.

"You know, at one time I made quite a little reputation for myself as a humorist by the simple process of telling the truth. It came as such a surprise to most people that they thought I was being funny."

"I don't see the connection."

"Well, Larry is, I think, the only person I've ever met who's completely disinterested. It makes his actions seem peculiar. We're not used to persons who do things simply for the love of God whom they don't believe in."

Suzanne stared at me.

"My poor friend, you've had too much to drink."

CHAPTER FIVE

(i)

I DAWDLED OVER MY WORK in Paris. It was very agreeable in the springtime, with the chestnuts in the Champs Elysées in bloom and the light in the streets so gay. There was pleasure in the air, a light transitory pleasure, sensual without grossness, that made your step more springy and your intelligence more alert. I was happy in the various company of my friends and, my heart filled with amiable memories of the past, I regained in spirit at least something of the glow of youth. I thought I should be a fool to allow work to interfere with a delight in the passing moment that I might never enjoy again so fully.

Isabel, Gray, Larry and I went for excursions to places of interest within convenient distance. We went to Chantilly and Versailles, to St. Germain and Fontainebleau. Wherever we went, we lunched well and copiously. Gray ate largely to satisfy his enormous frame and was apt to drink a little too much. His health, whether owing to Larry's treatment or merely to the course of time, was certainly improved. He ceased to have racking headaches and his eyes were losing the look of bewilderment that when first I saw him on coming to Paris had been so distressing. He did not talk much except now and then to tell a long-winded story, but laughed with great loud guffaws at the nonsense Isabel and I talked. He enjoyed himself. Though not amusing, he was so good-humoured and so easily pleased that it was impossible not to like him. He was the kind of man with whom one would have hesitated to pass a lonely evening, but with whom one might cheerfully have looked forward to spending six months.

His love for Isabel was a delight to see; he adored her beauty and thought her the most brilliant, fascinating creature in the world; and his devotion, his doglike devotion to Larry was touching. Larry appeared to enjoy himself too; I had a notion that he looked upon this time as a holiday that he was taking from whatever projects he had in mind and was serenely making the most of it. He did not talk very much either, but it didn't matter, his company was sufficient conversation; he was so easy, so pleasantly cheerful that you did not ask more of him than what he gave, and I well knew that if the days we spent together were so happy it was due to his being with us. Though he never said a brilliant or a witty thing, we'd have been dull without him.

It was on the return from one of these jaunts that I witnessed a scene that somewhat startled me. We had been to Chartres and were on our way back to Paris. Gray was driving and Larry was sitting beside him; Isabel and I were at the back. We were tired after the long day. Larry sat with his arm stretched out along the top of the front seat. His shirt cuff was pulled back by his position and displayed his slim, strong wrist and the lower part of his brown arm lightly covered with fine hairs. The sun shone goldly upon them. Something in Isabel's immobility attracted my attention, and I glanced at her. She was so still that you might have thought her hypnotized. Her breath was hurried. Her eyes were fixed on the sinewy wrist with its little golden hairs and on that long, delicate, but powerful hand, and I have never seen on a human countenance such a hungry concupiscence as I saw then on hers. It was a mask of lust. I would never have believed that her beautiful features could assume an expression of such unbridled sensuality. It was animal rather than human. The beauty was stripped from her face; the look upon it made her hideous and frightening. It horribly suggested the bitch in heat and I felt rather sick. She was unconscious of my presence; she was conscious of nothing but the hand, lying along the rim so negligently, that filled her with frantic desire. Then as it were a spasm twitched across her face, she gave a shudder and shutting her eyes sank back into the corner of the car.

"Give me a cigarette," she said in a voice I hardly recognized, it was so raucous.

I got one out of my case and lit it for her. She smoked it greedily. For the rest of the drive she looked out of the window and never said a word.

When we arrived at their house Gray asked Larry to drive me back to my hotel and then take the car to the garage. Larry got into the driver's seat and I sat myself beside him. As they crossed the pavement Isabel took Gray's arm and, snuggling up to him, gave him a look which I could not see, but whose sense I could divine. I guessed that he would have a passionate bedfellow that night, but would never know to what prickings of conscience he owed her ardor.

June was approaching its end and I had to get back to the Riviera. Friends of Elliott, who were going to America, had lent the Maturins their villa at Dinard and they were going there with the children as soon as their school closed. Larry was staying in Paris to work, but was buying himself a second-hand Citroën and had promised to spend a few days with them in August. On my last night in Paris I asked the three of them to dine with me.

It was on that night that we met Sophie Macdonald.

(ii)

Isabel had conceived the desire to make a tour of the tough joints and because I had some acquaintance with them she asked me to be their guide. I did not much like the notion, because in places of that sort in Paris they are apt to make their disapproval of sightseers from another world unpleasantly obvious. But Isabel insisted. I warned her that it would be very boring and begged her to dress plainly. We dined late, went to the Folies Bergères for an hour and then set out. I took them first to a cellar near Notre Dame frequented by gangsters and their molls where I knew the proprietor, and he made room for us at a long table at which were sitting some very disreputable people, but I ordered wine for all of them and we drank one another's healths. It was hot, smoky and dirty. Then I took them to the Sphynx where women, naked under their smart, tawdry evening dresses, their breasts, nipples and all, exposed, sit in a row on two benches opposite one another and when the band strikes up dance together listlessly with their eyes on the lookout for the men who sit round the dance hall at marble-topped tables. We ordered a bottle of warm champagne. Some of the women gave Isabel the eye as they passed us and I wondered if she knew what it meant.

Then we went on to the Rue de Lappe. It is a dingy, narrow street and even as you enter it you get the impression of sordid lust. We went into a café. There was the usual young man, pale and dissipated, playing the piano, while another man, old and tired, scraped away on a fiddle and a third made discordant noise on a saxophone. The place was packed and it looked as though there wasn't a vacant table, but the *patron,* seeing that we were customers with money to spend, unceremoniously turned a couple out, making them take seats at a table already occupied, and settled us down. The two persons who were hustled away did not take it well and they made remarks about us that were far from complimentary. A lot of people were dancing, sailors with the red pompon on their hats, men mostly with their caps on and handkerchiefs round their necks, women of mature age and young girls, painted to the eyes, bareheaded, in short skirts and coloured blouses. Men danced with podgy boys with made-up eyes; gaunt, hard-featured women danced with fat women with dyed hair; men danced with women. There was a froust of smoke and liquor and of sweating bodies. The music went on interminably and that unsavory mob proceeded round the room, the sweat shining on their faces, with a solemn intensity in which there was something horrible. There were a few big men of brutal aspect, but for the most part they were puny and ill-nourished. I watched the three who were playing. They might have been robots, so mechanical was their performance, and I asked myself if it was possible that at one time, when they were setting out, they had thought they might be musicians whom people would come from far to hear and to applaud. Even to play the violin badly you must take lessons and practice: did that fiddler go to all that trouble just to play fox trots till the small hours of the morning in that stinking squalor? The music stopped and the pianist wiped his face with a dirty handkerchief. The dancers slouched or sidled or squirmed back to their tables. Suddenly we heard an American voice.

"For Christ's sake."

A woman got up from one of the tables across the room. The man she was with tried to stop her, but she pushed him aside and staggered across the floor. She was very drunk. She came up to our table and stood in front of us, swaying a little and grinning stupidly. She seemed to find the sight of us vastly amusing. I glanced at my companions. Isabel was staring at her blankly, Gray had a sullen frown on his face and Larry gazed as though he couldn't believe his eyes.

"Hello," she said.

"Sophie," said Isabel.

"Who the hell did you think it was?" she gurgled. She grabbed the waiter who was passing. "Vincent, fetch me a chair."

"Fetch one yourself," he said, snatching himself away from her.

"*Salaud,*" she cried, spitting at him.

"*T'en fais pas, Sophie,*" said a big fat fellow with a great head of greasy hair, who was sitting next to us in his shirt sleeves. "Here's a chair."

"Fancy meeting you all like this," she said, still swaying. "Hello, Larry.

156

Hello, Gray." She sank into the chair which the man who had spoken placed behind her. "Let's all have a drink. *Patron,*" she screamed.

I had noticed that the proprietor had his eye on us and now he came up.

"You know these people, Sophie?" he asked, addressing her in the familiar second person singular.

"*Ta gueule,*" she laughed drunkenly. "They're my childhood's friends. I'm buying a bottle of champagne for them. And don't you bring us any *urine de cheval*. Bring us something one can swallow without vomiting."

"You're drunk, my poor Sophie," he said.

"To hell with you."

He went off, glad enough to sell a bottle of champagne—we for safety's sake had been drinking brandy and soda—and Sophie stared at me dully for a moment.

"Who's your friend, Isabel?"

Isabel told her my name.

"Oh? I remember, you came to Chicago once. Bit of a stuffed shirt, aren't you?"

"Maybe," I smiled.

I had no recollection of her, but that was not surprising, since I had not been to Chicago for more than ten years and had met a great many people then and a great many since.

She was quite tall and, when standing, looked taller still, for she was very thin. She wore a bright green silk blouse, but it was crumpled and spotted, and a short black skirt. Her hair, cut short and loosely curled, but tousled, was brightly hennaed. She was outrageously made up, her cheeks rouged to the eyes, and her eyelids, upper and lower, heavily blued; her eyebrows and eyelashes were thick with mascara and her mouth scarlet with lipstick. Her hands, with their painted nails, were dirty. She looked more of a slut than any woman there and I had a suspicion that she was not only drunk but doped. But one couldn't deny that there was a certain vicious attractiveness about her; she held her head with an arrogant tilt and her make-up accentuated the startling greenness of her eyes. Sodden with drink as she was, she had a bold-faced shamelessness that I could well imagine appealed to all that was base in men. She embraced us in a sardonic smile.

"I can't say you seem so terribly pleased to see me," she said.

"I heard you were in Paris," said Isabel lamely, a chilly smile on her face.

"You might have called me. I'm in the phone book."

"We haven't been here very long."

Gray came to the rescue.

"Are you having a good time over here, Sophie?"

"Fine. You went bust, Gray, didn't you?"

His face flushed a deeper red.

"Yes."

"Tough on you. I guess it's pretty grim in Chicago right now. Lucky for me I got out when I did. For Christ's sake why doesn't that bastard bring us something to drink?"

"He's just coming," I said, seeing the waiter threading his way through the tables with glasses and a bottle of wine on a tray.

My remark drew her attention to me.

"My loving in-laws kicked me out of Chicago. Said I was gumming up their f—— reputations." She giggled savagely. "I'm a remittance man."

The champagne came and was poured up. With a shaking hand she raised a glass to her lips.

"To hell with stuffed shirts," she said. She emptied the glass and glanced at Larry. "You don't seem to have much to say for yourself, Larry."

He had been looking at her with an impassive face. He had not taken his eyes off her since she had appeared. He smiled amiably.

"I'm not a very talkative guy."

The music struck up again and a man came over to us. He was a tallish fellow and well built, with a great hooked nose, a mat of shining black hair and great sensual lips. He looked like an evil Savonarola. Like most of the men there he wore no collar and his tight-fitting coat was closely buttoned to give him a waist.

"Come on, Sophie. We're going to dance."

"Go away. I'm busy. Can't you see I'm with friends?"

"*J'm en fous de tes amis.* To hell with your friends. You're dancing."

He took hold of her arm but she snatched it away.

"*Fous moi la paix, espèce de con,*" she cried with sudden violence.

"*Merde.*"

"*Mange.*"

Gray did not understand what they were saying, but I saw that Isabel, with that strange knowledge of obscenity that the most virtuous women seem to possess, understood perfectly and her face went hard with a frown of disgust. The man raised his arm with his hand open, the horny hand of a workman, and was about to slap her, when Gray half raised himself from his chair.

"*Allaiz vous ong,*" he shouted, with his execrable accent.

The man stopped and threw Gray a furious glance.

"Take care, Coco," said Sophie, with a bitter laugh. "He'll lay you out cold."

The man took in Gray's great height and weight and strength. He shrugged his shoulders sullenly and, throwing a filthy word at us, slunk off. Sophie giggled drunkenly. The rest of us were silent. I refilled her glass.

"You living in Paris, Larry?" she asked after she had drained it.

"For the present."

It's always difficult to make conversation with a drunk, and there's no denying it, the sober are at a disadvantage with him. We went on talking for a few minutes in a dreary, embarrassed way. Then Sophie pushed back her chair.

"If I don't go back to my boy friend he'll be as mad as hell. He's a sulky brute, but Christ, he's a good screw." She staggered to her feet. "So long, folks. Come again. I'm here every night."

She pushed her way through the dancers and we lost sight of her in the crowd. I almost laughed at the icy scorn on Isabel's classic features. None of us said a word.

"This is a foul place," said Isabel suddenly. "Let's go."

I paid for our drinks and for Sophie's champagne and we trouped out. The crowd was on the dance floor and we got out without remark. It was after two, and to my mind time to go to bed, but Gray said he was hungry, so I suggested that we should go to Graf's in Montmartre and get something to eat. We were silent as we drove up. I sat beside Gray to direct him. We reached the garish restaurant. There were still people sitting on the terrace. We went in and ordered bacon and eggs and beer. Isabel, outwardly at least, had regained her composure. She congratulated me, somewhat ironically perhaps, on my acquaintance with the more disreputable parts of Paris.

"You asked for it," I said.

"I've thoroughly enjoyed myself. I've had a grand evening."

"Hell," said Gray. "It stank. And Sophie."

Isabel shrugged an indifferent shoulder.

"D'you remember her at all?" she asked me. "She sat next to you the first night you came to dinner with us. She hadn't got that awful red hair then. It's natural colour is dingy beige."

I threw my mind back. I had a recollection of a very young girl with blue eyes that were almost green and an attractive tilt to her head. Not pretty, but fresh and ingenuous, with a mixture of shyness and pertness that I found amusing.

"Of course I remember. I liked her name. I had an aunt called Sophie."

"She married a boy called Bob Macdonald."

"Nice fellow," said Gray.

"He was one of the best-looking boys I ever saw. I never understood what he saw in her. She married just after I did. Her parents were divorced and her mother married a Standard Oil man in China. She lived with her father's people at Marvin and we used to see a lot of her then, but after she married she dropped out of our crowd somehow. Bob Macdonald was a lawyer, but he wasn't making much money, and they had a walk-up apartment on the North Side. But it wasn't that. They didn't want to see anybody. I never saw two people so crazy about one another. Even after they'd been married two or three years and had a baby they'd go to the pictures and he'd sit with his arm round her waist and she with her head on his shoulder just like lovers. They were quite a joke in Chicago."

Larry listened to what Isabel said, but made no comment. His face was inscrutable.

"What happened then?" I asked.

"One night they were driving back to Chicago in a little open car they had and they had the baby with them. They always had to take the baby along because they hadn't any help, Sophie did everything herself, and anyway they worshipped it. And a bunch of drunks in a great sedan driving at eighty miles an hour crashed into them head on. Bob and the baby were killed outright, but Sophie only had concussion and a rib ·or two broken. They kept it from her as long as they could that Bob and the baby were dead, but at last they had to tell her. They say it was awful. She nearly went crazy. She shrieked the place down. They had to watch her night and day and once she nearly succeeded in jumping out of the window. Of course we did all we could, but she seemed to hate us. After she came out of the hospital they put her in a sanatorium and she was there for months."

"Poor thing."

"When they let her go she started to drink, and when she was drunk she'd go to bed with anyone who asked her. It was terrible for her in-laws. They're very nice quiet people and they hated the scandal. At first we all tried to help her, but it was impossible; if you asked her to dine she'd arrive plastered and she was quite likely to pass out before the evening was over. Then she got in with a rotten crowd and we had to drop her. She was arrested once for driving a car when she was drunk. She was with a dago she'd picked up in a speak-easy and it turned out that he was wanted by the cops."

"But had she money?" I asked.

"There was Bob's insurance; the people who owned the car that smashed into them were insured and she got something from them. But it didn't last long. She spent it like a drunken sailor and in two years she was broke. Her grandmother wouldn't have her back at Marvin. Then her in-laws said they'd make her an allowance if she'd go and live abroad. I suppose that's what she's living on now."

"The wheel comes full circle," I remarked. "There was a time when the black sheep of the family was sent from my country to America; now apparently he's sent from your country to Europe."

"I can't help feeling sorry for her," said Gray.

"Can't you?" said Isabel coolly. "I can. Of course it was a shock and no one could have sympathized with Sophie more than I did. We'd known one another always. But a normal person recovers from a thing like that. If she went to pieces it's because there was a rotten streak in her. She was naturally unbalanced; even her love for Bob was exaggerated. If she'd had character she'd have been able to make something of life."

"If pots and pans . . . Aren't you very hard, Isabel?" I murmured.

"I don't think so. I have common sense and I see no reason to be sentimental about Sophie. God knows, no one could be more devoted to Gray and the babes than I am, and if they were killed in a motor accident I should go out of my mind, but sooner or later I'd pull myself together. Isn't that what you'd wish me to do, Gray, or would you prefer me to get blind every night and go to bed with every apache in Paris?"

Gray then came as near to making a humorous remark as I ever heard him.

"Of course I'd prefer you to hurl yourself on my funeral pyre in a new Molyneux dress, but as that's not done any more, I guess the best thing you could do would be to take to bridge. And I'd like you to remember not to go an original no-trump on less than three and a half to four quick tricks."

It was not the occasion for me to point out to Isabel that her love for her husband and her children, though sincere enough, was scarcely passionate. Perhaps she read the thought that was passing through my mind, for she addressed me somewhat truculently.

"What have you got to say?"

"I'm like Gray, I'm sorry for the girl."

"She's not a girl, she's thirty."

"I suppose it was the end of the world for her when her husband and her baby were killed. I suppose she didn't care what became of her and flung herself into the horrible degradation of drink and promiscuous copulation to get even with life that had treated her so cruelly. She'd lived in heaven and when she lost it she couldn't put up with the common earth of common men, but in despair plunged headlong into hell. I can imagine that if she couldn't drink the nectar of the gods any more she thought she might as well drink bathroom gin."

"That's the sort of thing you say in novels. It's nonsense and you know it's nonsense. Sophie wallows in the gutter because she likes it. Other women have lost their husbands and children. It wasn't that that made her evil. Evil doesn't spring from good. The evil was there always. When that motor accident broke her defences it set her free to be herself. Don't waste your pity on her; she's now what at heart she always was."

All this time Larry had remained silent. He seemed to be in a brown study and I thought he hardly heard what we were saying. Isabel's words were followed by a brief silence. He began to speak, but in a strange, toneless voice, as though not to us, but to himself; his eyes seemed to look into the dim distance of past time.

"I remember her when she was fourteen with her long hair brushed back off her forehead and a black bow at the back, with her freckled, serious face. She was a modest, high-minded, idealistic child. She read everything she could get hold of and we used to talk about books."

"When?" asked Isabel, with a slight frown.

"Oh, when you were out being social with your mother. I used to go up to her grandfather's and we'd sit under a great elm they had there and read to one another. She loved poetry and wrote quite a lot herself."

"Plenty of girls do that at that age. It's pretty poor stuff."

"Of course it's a long time ago and I daresay I wasn't a very good judge."

"You couldn't have been more than sixteen yourself."

"Of course it was imitative. There was a lot of Robert Frost in it. But I have a notion it was rather remarkable for so young a girl. She had a delicate ear and a sense of rhythm. She had a feeling for the sounds and scents of the country, the first softness of spring in the air and the smell of the parched earth after rain."

"I never knew she wrote poetry," said Isabel.

"She kept it a secret, she was afraid you'd all laugh at her. She was very shy."

"She's not that now."

"When I came back from the war she was almost grown-up. She'd read a lot about the condition of the working classes and she'd seen something of it for herself in Chicago. She'd got on to Carl Sandburg and was writing savagely in free verse about the misery of the poor and the exploitation of the working classes. I daresay it was rather commonplace, but it was sincere and it had pity in it and aspiration. At that time she wanted to become a social worker. It was moving, her desire for sacrifice. I think she was capable of a great deal. She wasn't silly or mawkish, but she gave one the impression of a lovely purity and a strange loftiness of soul. We saw a lot of one another that year."

I could see that Isabel listened to him with growing exasperation. Larry had no notion that he was driving a dagger in her heart and with his every detached word twisting it in the wound. But when she spoke it was with a faint smile on her lips.

"How did she come to choose you for her confidant?"

Larry looked at her with his trustful eyes.

"I don't know. She was a poor girl among all of you who had plenty of dough, and I didn't belong. I was there just because Uncle Bob practiced at Marvin. I suppose she felt that gave us something in common."

Larry had no relations. Most of us have at least cousins whom we may hardly know, but who at least give us a sense that we are part of the human family. Larry's father had been an only son, his mother an only daughter; his grandfather on one side, the Quaker, had been lost at sea when still a young man and his grandfather on the other side had neither brother nor sister. No one could be more alone in the world than Larry.

"Did it ever occur to you that Sophie was in love with you?" asked Isabel.

"Never," he smiled.

"Well, she was."

"When he came back from the war as a wounded hero half the girls in Chicago had a crush on Larry," said Gray in his bluff way.

"This was more than a crush. She worshipped you, my poor Larry. D'you mean to say you didn't know it?"

"I certainly didn't and I don't believe it."

"I suppose you thought she was too high-minded."

"I can still see that skinny little girl with the bow in her hair and her serious face whose voice trembled with tears when she read that ode of Keats' because it was so beautiful. I wonder where she is now."

Isabel gave a very slight start and threw him a suspicious enquiring glance.

"It's getting frightfully late and I'm so tired I don't know what to do. Let's go."

(iii)

On the following evening I took the Blue train to the Riviera and two or three days later went over to Antibes to see Elliott and give him news of Paris. He looked far from well. The cure at Montecatini had not done him the good he expected, and his subsequent wanderings had exhausted him. He found a baptismal font in Venice and then went on to Florence to buy the triptych he had been negotiating for. Anxious to see these objects duly placed, he went down to the Pontine Marshes and put up at a miserable inn where the heat had been hard to bear. His precious purchases were a long time on the way, but determined not to leave till he had accomplished his purpose, he stayed on. He was delighted with the effect when at last everything was in order, and he showed me with pride the photographs he had taken. The church, though small, had dignity, and the restrained richness of the interior was proof of Elliott's good taste.

"I saw an early Christian sarcophagus in Rome that took my fancy and I deliberated a long time about buying it, but in the end I thought better of it."

"What on earth did you want with an early Christian sarcophagus, Elliott?"

"To put myself in it, my dear fellow. It was of a very good design and I thought it would balance the font on the other side of the entrance, but those early Christians were stumpy little fellows and I wouldn't have fitted in. I wasn't going to lie there till the Last Trump with my knees doubled up to my chin like a foetus. Most uncomfortable."

I laughed, but Elliott was serious.

"I had a better idea. I've made all arrangements, with some difficulty, but that was to be expected, to be buried in front of the altar at the foot of the chancel steps, so that when the poor peasants of the Pontine Marshes come up to take Holy Communion they'll clump over my bones with their heavy shoes. Rather chic, don't you think? Just a plain stone slab with my name on it and a couple of dates. *Si monumentum quoeris, circumspice.* If you seek his monument, look around, you know."

"I do know enough Latin to understand a hackneyed quotation, Elliott," I said tartly.

"I beg your pardon, my dear fellow. I'm so accustomed to the crass ignorance of the upper classes, I forgot for the moment that I was talking to an author."

He scored.

"But what I wanted to say to you was this," he continued. "I've left proper instructions in my will, but I want you to see they're carried out. I will *not* be buried on the Riviera among a lot of retired colonels and middle-class French people."

"Of course I'll do what you wish, Elliott, but I don't think we need plan for anything like that for many years to come."

"I'm getting on, you know, and to tell you the truth I shan't be sorry to go. What are those lines of Landor's? I've warmed both hands . . ."

Though I have a bad verbal memory, the poem is very short and I was able to repeat it.

> *"I strove with none, for none was worth my strife.*
> *Nature I loved, and, next to Nature, Art;*
> *I warmed both hands before the fire of Life;*
> *It sinks, and I am ready to depart."*

"That's it," he said.

I could not but reflect that it was only by a violent stretch of the imagination that Elliott could fit the stanza to himself.

"It expresses my sentiments exactly," he said, however. "The only thing I could add to it is that I've always moved in the best society in Europe."

"It would be difficult to squeeze that into a quatrain."

"Society is dead. At one time I had hopes that America would take the place of Europe and create an aristocracy that the *hoi polloi* would respect, but the depression has destroyed any chance of that. My poor country is becoming hopelessly middle-class. You wouldn't believe it, my dear fellow, but last time I was in America a taxi driver addressed me as brother."

But though the Riviera, still shaken by the crash of '29, was not what it was, Elliott continued to give parties and go to parties. He had never frequented Jews, making an exception only for the family of Rothschild, but the grandest parties were being given now by members of the chosen race, and when there was a party Elliott could not bear not to go to it. He wandered through these gatherings, graciously shaking the hand of one or kissing that of another, but with a kind of forlorn detachment like an exiled royalty who felt a trifle embarrassed to find himself in such company. The exiled royalties, however, had the time of their lives and to meet a film star seemed the height of their ambitions. Nor had Elliott ever looked with approval on the modern practice of treating members of the theatrical profession as persons whom you met socially, but a retired actress had built herself a sumptuous residence in his immediate neighbourhood and kept open house. Cabinet ministers, dukes, great ladies stayed with her for weeks on end. Elliott became a constant visitor.

"Of course it's a very mixed crowd," he told me, "but one doesn't have to talk to people one doesn't want to. She's a compatriot of mine and I feel I ought to help her out. It must be a relief to her house guests to find someone who can talk their own language."

Sometimes he was obviously so far from well that I asked him why he didn't take things more easily.

"My dear fellow, at my age one can't afford to fall out. You don't think that I've moved in the highest circles for nearly fifty years without realizing that if you're not seen everywhere you're forgotten."

I wondered if he realized what a lamentable confession he was then making. I had not the heart to laugh at Elliott any more; he seemed to me a profoundly pathetic object. Society was what he lived for, a party was the breath of his nostrils, not to be asked to one was an affront, to be alone was a mortification; and, an old man now, he was desperately afraid.

So the summer passed. Elliott spent it scurrying from one end of the Riviera to the other, lunching in Cannes, dining in Monte Carlo and exercising all his ingenuity to fit in a tea party here and a cocktail party there; and however tired he felt, taking pains to be affable, chatty and amusing. He was full of gossip and you could trust him to know the details of the latest scandal before anyone but the parties immediately concerned. He would have stared at you with frank amazement had you suggested to him that his existence was futile. He would have thought you distressingly plebeian.

(iv)

The autumn came and Elliott decided to go to Paris for a while, partly to see how Isabel, Gray and the children were getting on, and partly to make what he called *acte de présence* in the capital. Then he meant to go to London to order some new clothes and incidentally to look up some old friends. My own plan was to go straight to London, but he asked me to drive up with him to Paris and since that is an agreeable thing to do I consented and, having done so, saw no reason why I should not spend at least a few days in Paris myself. We made the journey by easy stages, stopping at places where the food was good; Elliott had something the matter with his kidneys and drank nothing but Vichy, but always insisted on choosing my half-bottle of wine for me and, too good-natured to grudge me a pleasure he could not share, got a genuine satisfaction out of my enjoyment of a fine vintage. He was so generous that I had difficulty in persuading him to let me pay my share of the expenses. Though I grew a little tired of his stories of the great whom he had known in the past I liked the trip. Much of the country we passed through, just touched with the beginning of its autumn beauty, was very lovely. Having lunched at Fontainebleau, we did not arrive in Paris till afternoon. Elliott dropped me at my modest, old-fashioned hotel and went round the corner to the Ritz.

We had warned Isabel of our arrival, so I was not surprised to find a note from her awaiting me, but I was surprised at its contents.

"Come round the moment you get in. Something terrible has happened. Don't bring Uncle Elliott. For God's sake come as soon as you can."

I am not less curious than anyone else, but I had to have a wash and put on a clean shirt; then I took a taxi and went round to the apartment in the Rue St. Guillaume. I was shown into the drawing-room. Isabel sprang to her feet.

"Where have you been all this time? I've been waiting for hours."

It was five o'clock and, before I could answer, the butler brought in the tea things. Isabel, her hands clenched, watched him with impatience. I couldn't imagine what was the matter.

"I've only just arrived. We dawdled over lunch at Fontainebleau."

"God, how slow he is. Maddening!" said Isabel.

The man placed the salver with the teapot and the sugar basin and the cups on the table and with what really was exasperating deliberation arranged around it plates of bread and butter, cake and cookies. He went out and closed the door behind him.

"Larry's going to marry Sophie Macdonald."

"Who's she?"

"Don't be so stupid," cried Isabel, her eyes flashing with anger. "That drunken slut we met at that filthy café you took us to. God knows why you took us to a place like that. Gray was disgusted."

"Oh, you mean your Chicago friend?" I said, ignoring her unjust reproach. "How d'you know?"

"How should I know? He came and told me himself yesterday afternoon. I've been frantic ever since."

"Supposing you sat down, gave me a cup of tea and told me all about it."

"Help yourself."

She sat behind the tea table and watched me irritably while I poured myself out a cup. I made myself comfortable in a small sofa by the fireplace.

"We haven't seen so much of him lately, since we came back from Dinard, I mean; he came up there for a few days, but wouldn't stay with us, he stayed at a hotel. He used to come down to the beach and play with the children. They're crazy about him. We played golf at St. Briac. Gray asked him one day if he'd seen Sophie again.

" 'Yes, I've seen her several times,' he said.

" 'Why?' I asked.

" 'She's an old friend,' he said.

" 'If I were you I wouldn't waste my time on her,' I said.

"Then he smiled. You know how he smiles, as though he thought what you'd said funny, though it isn't funny at all.

" 'But you're not me,' he said.

"I shrugged my shoulders and changed the conversation. I never gave the matter another thought. You can imagine my horror when he came here and told me they were going to be married.

" 'You can't, Larry,' I said. 'You can't.'

" 'I'm going to,' he said as calmly as if he said he was going to have a second helping of potatoes. 'And I want you to be very nice to her, Isabel.'

" 'That's asking too much,' I said. 'You're crazy. She's bad, bad, bad.' "

"What makes you think that?" I interrupted.

Isabel looked at me with flashing eyes.

"She's soused from morning till night. She goes to bed with every tough who asks her."

"That doesn't mean she's bad. Quite a number of highly respected citizens get drunk and have a liking for rough trade. They're bad habits, like biting one's nails, but I don't know that they're worse than that. I call a person bad who lies and cheats and is unkind."

"If you're going to take her part I'll kill you."

"How did Larry meet her again?"

"He found her address in the phone book. He went to see her. She was sick, and no wonder, with the life she leads. He got a doctor and had someone in to look after her. That's how it started. He says she's given up drink; the damned fool thinks she's cured."

"Have you forgotten what Larry did for Gray? He's cured him, hasn't he?"

"That's different. Gray wanted to be cured. She doesn't."

"How d'you know?"

"Because I know women. When a woman goes to pieces like that she's done for; she can never get back. If Sophie's what she is, it's because she was like that always. D'you think she'll stick to Larry? Of course not. Sooner or later she'll break out. It's in her blood. It's a brute she wants, that's what excites her, and it's a brute she'll go after. She'll lead Larry a hell of a life."

"I think that's very probable, but I don't know what you can do about it. He's going into this with his eyes open."

"*I* can do nothing about it, but you can."

"I?"

"Larry likes you and he listens to what you say. You're the only person who has any influence over him. You know the world. Go to him and tell

168

him that he can't make such a fool of himself. Tell him that it'll ruin him."

"He'll only tell me that it's no business of mine and he'll be quite right."

"But you like him, at least you're interested in him, you can't sit by and let him make a hopeless mess of his life."

"Gray's his oldest and most intimate friend. I don't think it'll do any good, but I should have thought Gray was the best person to speak to him."

"Oh, Gray," she said impatiently.

"You know it may not turn out so badly as you think. I've known two or three fellows, one in Spain and two in the East, who married whores and they made them very good wives. They were grateful to their husbands, for the security they gave them, I mean, and they of course knew what pleases a man."

"You make me tired. D'you think I sacrificed myself to let Larry fall into the hands of a raging nymphomaniac?"

"How did *you* sacrifice yourself?"

"I gave Larry up for the one and only reason that I didn't want to stand in his way."

"Come off it, Isabel. You gave him up for a square-cut diamond and a sable coat."

The words were hardly out of my mouth when a plate of bread and butter came flying at my head. By sheer luck I caught the plate, but the bread and butter was scattered on the floor. I got up and put the plate back on the table.

"Your uncle Elliott wouldn't have thanked you if you'd broken one of his Crown Derby plates. They were made for the third Duke of Dorset and they're almost priceless."

"Pick up the bread and butter," she snapped.

"Pick it up yourself," I said, seating myself again on the sofa.

She got up and, fuming, picked up the scattered pieces.

"And you call yourself an English gentleman," she exclaimed, savagely.

"No, that's a thing I've never done in all my life."

"Get the hell out of here. I never want to see you again. I hate the sight of you."

"I'm sorry for that, because the sight of you always gives me pleasure. Have you ever been told that your nose is exactly like that of the Psyche in the museum of Naples, and that's the loveliest representation of virginal beauty that ever existed. You've got exquisite legs, so long and shapely, and I never cease to be surprised at them, because they were thick and lumpy when you were a girl. I can't imagine how've you managed it."

"An iron will and the grace of God," she said angrily.

"But of course your hands are your most fascinating feature. They're so slim and so elegant."

"I was under the impression you thought them too big."

"Not for your height and build. I'm always amazed at the infinite grace with which you use them. Whether by nature or by art you never make a gesture without imparting beauty to it. They're like flowers sometimes and sometimes like birds on the wing. They're more expressive than any words you can say. They're like the hands in El Greco's portraits; in fact, when I look at them I'm almost inclined to believe Elliott's highly improbable story of your having an ancestor who was a Spanish grandee."

She looked up crossly.

"What are you talking about? That's the first I've heard of it."

I told her about the Count de Lauria and Queen Mary's maid of honour from whose issue in the female line Elliott traced his descent. Meanwhile Isabel contemplated her long fingers and her manicured, painted nails with complacency.

"One must be descended from someone," she said. Then with a tiny chuckle, giving me a mischievous look in which no trace of rancour remained, she added, "You lousy bastard."

So easy is it to make a woman see reason if you only tell her the truth.

"There are moments when I don't positively dislike you," said Isabel.

She came and sat on the sofa beside me and, slipping her arm through mine, leant over to kiss me. I withdrew my cheek.

"I will not have my face smeared with lipstick," I said. "If you want to kiss me, kiss me on the lips, which is what a merciful Providence intended them for."

She giggled and, her hand turning my head towards her, with her lips pressed a thin layer of paint on mine. The sensation was far from unpleasant.

"Now you've done that, perhaps you'll tell me what it is you want."

"Advice."

"I'm quite willing to give you that, but I don't think for a moment you'll take it. There's only one thing you can do and that is to make the best of a bad job."

Flaring up again, she snatched her arm away and, getting up, flung herself into a chair on the other side of the fireplace.

"I'm not going to sit by and let Larry ruin himself. I'll stick at nothing to prevent him from marrying that slut."

"You won't succeed. You see, he's enthralled by one of the most powerful emotions that can beset the human breast."

"You don't mean to say you think he's in love with her?"

"No. That would be trifling in comparison."

"Well?"

"Have you ever read the New Testament?"

"I suppose so."

"D'you remember how Jesus was led into the wilderness and fasted forty days? Then, when he was a-hungered, the devil came to him and said: If thou be the son of God, command that these stones be made bread. But Jesus resisted the temptation. Then the devil set him on a pinnacle of the temple and said to him: If thou be the son of God, cast thyself down. For angels had charge of him and would bear him up. But again Jesus resisted. Then the devil took him into a high mountain and showed him the kingdoms of the world and said that he would give them to him if he would fall down and worship him. But Jesus said: Get thee hence, Satan. That's the end of the story according to the good simple Matthew. But it wasn't. The devil was sly and he came to Jesus once more and said: If thou wilt accept shame and disgrace, scourging, a crown of thorns and death on the cross thou shalt save the human race, for greater love hath no man than this, that a man lay down his life for his friends. Jesus fell. The devil laughed till his sides ached, for he knew the evil men would commit in the name of their redeemer."

Isabel looked at me indignantly.

"Where on earth did you get that?"

"Nowhere. I've invented it on the spur of the moment."

"I think it's idiotic and blasphemous."

"I only wanted to suggest to you that self-sacrifice is a passion so overwhelming that beside it even lust and hunger are trifling. It whirls its victim to destruction in the highest affirmation of his personality. The object doesn't matter; it may be worth while or it may be worthless. No wine is so intoxicating, no love so shattering, no vice so compelling. When he sacrifices himself man for a moment is greater than God, for how can God, infinite and omnipotent, sacrifice himself? At best he can only sacrifice his only begotten son."

"Oh, Christ, how you bore me," said Isabel.

I paid no attention.

"How can you suppose that common sense or prudence will have any effect on Larry when he's in the grip of a passion like that? You don't know what he's been seeking all these years. I don't know either, I only suspect. All these years of labour, all these experiences he garnered weigh nothing in the balance now they're set against his desire—oh, it's more than a desire, his urgent, clamorous need to save the soul of a wanton woman whom he'd known as an innocent child. I think you're right, I think he's undertaking a hopeless job; with his acute sensibility he'll suffer the tortures of the damned; his life's work, whatever it may be, will remain undone. The ignoble Paris killed Achilles by shooting an arrow in his heel. Larry lacks just that touch of ruthlessness that even the saint must have to win his halo."

"I love him," said Isabel. "God knows, I ask nothing of him. I expect nothing. No one could love anyone more unselfishly than I love him. He's going to be so unhappy."

She began to cry and, thinking it would do her good, I let her be. I diverted myself idly with the idea that had sprung so unexpectedly into my mind. I played with it. I couldn't but surmise that the devil, looking at the cruel wars that Christianity has occasioned, the persecutions, the tortures Christian has inflicted on Christian, the unkindness, the hypocrisy, the intolerance, must consider the balance sheet with complacency. And when he remembers that it has laid upon mankind the bitter burden of the sense of sin that has darkened the beauty of the starry night and cast a baleful shadow on the passing pleasures of a world to be enjoyed, he must chuckle as he murmurs: give the devil his due.

Presently Isabel took a handkerchief from her bag and a mirror and, looking at herself, carefully wiped the corner of her eyes.

"Damned sympathetic, aren't you?" she snapped.

I looked at her pensively, but did not answer. She powdered her face and painted her lips.

"You said just now you suspected what he's been after all these years. What did you mean?"

"I can only guess, you know, and I may be quite wrong. I think he's been seeking for a philosophy, or maybe a religion, and a rule of life that'll satisfy both his head and his heart."

Isabel considered this for a moment. She sighed.

"Don't you think it's very strange that a country boy from Marvin, Illinois, should have a notion like that?"

"No stranger than that Luther Burbank who was born on a farm in Massachusetts should have produced a seedless orange or that Henry Ford who was born on a farm in Michigan should have invented a Tin Lizzie."

"But those are practical things. That's in the American tradition."

I laughed.

"Can anything in the world be more practical than to learn how to live to best advantage?"

Isabel gave a gesture of lassitude.

"What do you want me to do?"

"You don't want to lose Larry altogether, do you?"

She shook her head.

"You know how loyal he is: if you won't have anything to do with his wife he won't have anything to do with you. If you've got any sense you'll make friends with Sophie. You'll forget the past and be as nice to her as you can be when you like. She's going to be married and I suppose she's buying some clothes. Why don't you offer to go shopping with her? I think she'd jump at it."

Isabel listened to me with narrowed eyes. She seemed intent upon what I was saying. For a moment she pondered, but I could not guess what was passing through her mind. Then she surprised me.

"Will you ask her to lunch? It would be rather awkward for me after what I said to Larry yesterday."

"Will you behave if I do?"

"Like an angel of light," she answered with her most engaging smile.

"I'll fix it up right away."

There was a phone in the room. I soon found Sophie's number, and after the usual delay which those who use the French telephone learn to put up with patiently, I got her. I mentioned my name.

"I've just arrived in Paris," I said, "and heard that you and Larry are going to be married. I want to congratulate you. I hope you'll be very happy." I smothered a cry as Isabel, who was standing by me, gave the soft of my arm a vicious pinch. "I'm only here for a very short time and I wonder if you and Larry will come and lunch with me the day after tomorrow at the Ritz. I'm asking Gray and Isabel and Elliott Templeton."

"I'll ask Larry. He's here now." There was a pause. "Yes, we shall be glad to."

I fixed an hour, made a civil remark, and replaced the receiver on its stand. I caught an expression in Isabel's eyes that caused me some misgiving.

"What are you thinking?" I asked her. "I don't quite like the look of you."

"I'm sorry; I thought that was the one thing about me you did like."

"You haven't got some nefarious scheme that you're hatching, Isabel?"

She opened her eyes very wide.

"I promise you I haven't. As a matter of fact I'm terribly curious to see what Sophie looks like now Larry has reformed her. All I hope is that she won't come to the Ritz with a mask of paint on her face."

My little party did not go too badly. Gray and Isabel arrived first; Larry and Sophie Macdonald five minutes later. Isabel and Sophie kissed each other warmly and Isabel and Gray congratulated her on her engagement. I caught the appraising sweep of the eyes with which Isabel took in Sophie's appearance. I was shocked at it. When I saw her in that dive in the Rue de Lappe, outrageously painted, with hennaed hair, in the bright green coat, though she looked outrageous and was very drunk, there was something provocative and even basely alluring in her; but now she looked drab and, though certainly a year or two younger than Isabel, much older. She still had that gallant tilt of her head, but now, I don't know why, it was pathetic. She was letting her hair go back to its natural colour and it had the slatternly look that hair has when it has been dyed and left to grow. Except for a streak of red on her lips she had no make-up on. Her skin was rough and it had an unhealthy pallor. I remembered how vividly green her eyes had looked, but now they were pale and gray. She wore a red dress, obviously brand-new, with hat, shoes and bag to match; I don't pretend to know anything about women's clothes, but I had a feeling that it was fussy and too elaborate for the occasion. On her breast was a piece of showy artificial jewellery such as you buy in the Rue de Rivoli. Beside Isabel, in black silk, with a string of cultured pearls round her neck and in a very smart hat, she looked cheap and dowdy.

I ordered cocktails, but Larry and Sophie refused them. Then Elliott arrived. His progress through the vast foyer was, however, impeded by the hands he had to shake and the hands he had to kiss as he saw one person after the other whom he knew. He behaved as though the Ritz were his private house and he were assuring his guests of his pleasure that they had been able to accept his invitation. He had been told nothing about Sophie except that she had lost her husband and child in a motor accident and was now going to marry Larry. When at last he reached us he congratulated them both with the elaborate graciousness of which he was a master. We went in to the dining-room and since we were four men and two women I placed Isabel and Sophie opposite one another at the round table, with Sophie between Gray and myself; but the table was small enough for the conversation to be general. I had already ordered the luncheon and the wine waiter came along with the wine card.

"You don't know anything about wine, my dear fellow," said Elliott. "Give me the wine card, Albert." He turned over the pages. "I drink nothing but Vichy myself, but I can't bear to see people drink wine that isn't perfect."

He and Albert, the wine waiter, were old friends and after an animated discussion they decided on the wine I should give my guests. Then he turned to Sophie.

"And where are you going for your honeymoon, my dear?"

He glanced at her dress and an almost imperceptible raising of his eyebrows showed me that he had formed an unfavourable opinion of it.

"We're going to Greece."

"I've been trying to get there for ten years," said Larry, "but somehow I've never been able to manage it."

"It ought to be lovely at this time of year," said Isabel, with a show of enthusiasm.

She remembered, as I remembered, that that was where Larry proposed to take her when he wanted her to marry him. It seemed to be an *idée fixe* with Larry to go to Greece on a honeymoon.

The conversation flowed none too easily and I would have found it a difficult row to hoe if it hadn't been for Isabel. She was on her best behaviour. Whenever silence seemed to threaten us and I racked my brain for something fresh to talk about, she broke in with facile chatter. I was grateful to her. Sophie hardly spoke except when she was spoken to and then it seemed an effort to her. The spirit had gone out of her. You would have said that something had died in her and I asked myself if Larry wasn't putting her to a strain greater than she could support. If as I suspected she had doped as well as drunk, the sudden deprivation must have worn her nerves to a frazzle. Sometimes I intercepted a look between them. In his I saw tenderness and encouragement, but in hers an appeal that was pathetic. It may be that Gray with his sweetness of disposition instinctively felt what I thought I saw, for he began to tell her how Larry had cured him of the headaches that had incapacitated him and went on to say how much he had depended on him and how much he owed him.

"Now I'm fit as a flea," he continued. "As soon as ever I can get a job I'm going back to work. I've got several irons in the fire and I'm hoping to land something before very long. Gosh, it'll be good to be back home again."

Gray meant well, but what he had said was perhaps not very tactful if, as I supposed, Larry to cure Sophie of her aggravated alcoholism had used with her the same method of suggestion—for that to my mind was what it was—that had been successful with Gray.

"You never have headaches now, Gray?" asked Elliott.

"I haven't had one for three months and if I think one's coming on I take hold of my charm and I'm all right." He fished out of his pocket the ancient coin Larry had given him. "I wouldn't sell it for a million dollars."

We finished luncheon and coffee was served. The wine waiter came up and asked whether we wanted liqueurs. We all refused except Gray, who said he would have a brandy. When the bottle was brought Elliott insisted on looking at it.

"Yes, I can recommend that. That'll do you no harm."

"A little glass for Monsieur?" asked the waiter.

"Alas, it's forbidden me."

Elliott told him at some length that he was having trouble with his kidneys and that his doctor would not allow him to drink alcohol.

"A tear of zubrovka could do Monsieur no harm. It's well known to be very good for the kidneys. We have just received a consignment from Poland."

"Is that true? It's hard to get nowadays. Let me have a look at a bottle."

The wine waiter, a portly, dignified creature with a long silver chain round his neck, went away to fetch it, and Elliott explained that it was the Polish form of vodka but in every way vastly superior.

"We used to drink it at the Radziwills' when I stayed with them for the shooting. You should have seen those Polish princes putting it away; I'm not exaggerating when I tell you that they'd drink it by the tumbler without turning a hair. Good blood, of course; aristocrats to the tips of their fingers. Sophie, you must try it, and you too, Isabel. It's an experience no one can afford to miss."

The wine waiter brought the bottle. Larry, Sophie and I refused to be tempted, but Isabel said she would like to try it. I was surprised, for habitually she drank very little and she had had two cocktails and two or three glasses of wine. The waiter poured out a glass of pale green liquid and Isabel sniffed it.

"Oh, what a lovely smell."

"Hasn't it?" cried Elliott. "That's the herbs they put in it; it's they that give it its delicate taste. Just to keep you company I'll have a drop. It can't hurt me for once."

"It tastes divine," said Isabel. "It's like mother's milk. I've never tasted anything so good."

Elliott raised his glass to his lips.

"Oh, how it brings back the old days. You people who never stayed with the Radziwills don't know what living is. That was the grand style. Feudal, you know. You might have thought yourself back in the Middle Ages. You were met at the station by a carriage with six horses and postilions. And at dinner a footman in livery behind every person."

He went on to describe the magnificence and luxury of the establishment and the brilliance of the parties; and the suspicion, doubtless unworthy, occurred to me that the whole thing was a put-up job between Elliott and the wine waiter to give Elliott an opportunity to discourse upon the grandeur of this princely family and the host of Polish aristocrats he hobnobbed with in their castle. There was no stopping him.

"Another glass, Isabel?"

"Oh, I daren't. But it is heavenly. I'm so glad to know about it; Gray, we must get some."

"I'll have some sent round to the apartment."

"Oh, Uncle Elliott, would you?" cried Isabel enthusiastically. "You are so kind to us. You must try it, Gray; it smells of freshly mown hay and spring flowers, of thyme and lavender, and it's so soft on the palate and so comfortable, it's like listening to music by moonlight."

It was unlike Isabel to gush inordinately and I wondered if she was a trifle tight. The party broke up. I shook hands with Sophie.

"When are you going to be married?" I asked her.

"The week after next. I hope you'll come to the wedding."

"I'm afraid I shan't be in Paris. I'm leaving for London tomorrow."

While I was saying good-bye to the rest•of my guests Isabel took Sophie aside and talked to her for a minute, then turned to Gray.

"Oh, Gray, I'm not coming home just yet. There's a dress show at Molyneux's and I'm taking Sophie to it. She ought to see the new models."

"I'd love to," said Sophie.

We parted. I took Suzanne Rouvier out to dinner that night and next morning started for England.

(vi)

Elliott arrived at Claridge's a fortnight later and shortly afterwards I dropped in to see him. He had ordered himself several suits of clothes and at what I thought excessive length told me in detail what he had chosen and why. When at last I could get a word in I asked him how the wedding had gone off.

"It didn't go off," he answered grimly.

"What *do* you mean?"

"Three days before it was to take place Sophie disappeared. Larry hunted everywhere for her."

"What an extraordinary thing! Did they have a row?"

"No. Far from it. Everything had been arranged. I was going to give her away. They were taking the Orient Express immediately after the wedding. If you ask me, I think Larry's well out of it."

I guessed that Isabel had told Elliott everything.

"What exactly happened?" I asked.

"Well, you remember that day we lunched at the Ritz with you. Isabel took her to Molyneux's. D'you remember the dress Sophie wore? Deplorable. Did you notice the shoulders? That's how you tell if a dress is well made, by the way it fits over the shoulders. Of course, poor girl, she couldn't afford Molyneux's prices, and Isabel, you know how generous she is, and after all they've known one another since they were children, Isabel offered to give her a dress so that at least she'd have something decent to be married in. Naturally she jumped at it. Well, to cut a long story short, Isabel asked her to come to the apartment one day at three so that they could go together for the final fitting. Sophie came all right, but unfortunately Isabel had to take one of the children to the dentist's and didn't get in till after four and by that time Sophie had gone. Isabel thought she'd got tired of waiting and had gone on to Molyneux's, so she went there at once, but she hadn't come. At last she gave her up and went home again. They were all going to dine together and Larry came along at dinnertime and the first thing she asked him was where Sophie was.

"He couldn't understand it and he rang up her apartment, but there was no reply, so he said he'd go down there. They held dinner up as long as they could, but neither of them turned up and so they had dinner by themselves. Of course you know what Sophie's life was before you ran into her in the Rue de Lappe; that was a most unfortunate idea of yours to take them down there. Well, Larry spent all night going around her old haunts, but couldn't find her anywhere. He went to the apartment time after time, but the *concierge* said she hadn't been in. He spent three days hunting for her. She'd just vanished. Then on the fourth day he went to the apartment again and the *concierge* told him she'd been in and packed a bag and gone away in a taxi."

"Was Larry awfully upset?"

"I didn't see him. Isabel tells me he was rather."

"She didn't write or anything?"

"Nothing."

I thought it over.

"What do you make of it?" I said.

"My dear fellow, exactly what you make of it. She couldn't stick it out; she went on the booze again."

That was obvious, but for all that it was strange. I couldn't see why she had chosen just that moment to skip.

"How is Isabel taking it?"

"Of course she's sorry, but she's a sensible girl and she told me she always thought it would be a disaster if Larry married a woman like that."

"And Larry?"

"Isabel's been very kind to him. She says that what makes it difficult is that he won't discuss it. He'll be all right, you know; Isabel says he was never in love with Sophie. He was only marrying her out of a sort of misguided chivalry."

I could see Isabel putting a brave face on a turn of events that was certainly causing her a great deal of satisfaction. I well knew that next time I saw her she would not fail to point out to me that she had known all along what would happen.

But it was nearly a year before I saw her again and though by that time I could have told her something about Sophie that would have set her thinking, the circumstances were such that I had no inclination to. I stayed in London till nearly Christmas and then, wanting to get home, went straight down to the Riviera without stopping in Paris. I set to work on a novel and for the next few months lived in retirement. I saw Elliott now and then. It was obvious that his health was failing, and it pained me that he persisted notwithstanding in leading a social life. He was vexed with me because I would not drive thirty miles to go to the constant parties he continued to give. He thought it very conceited of me to prefer to sit at home and work.

"It's an unusually brilliant season, my dear fellow," he told me. "It's a crime to shut yourself up in your house and miss everything that's going on. And why you had to choose a part of the Riviera to live in that's completely out of fashion I shan't be able to understand if I live to be a hundred."

Poor nice silly Elliott; it was very clear that he would live to no such age.

By June I had finished the rough draft of my novel and thought I deserved a holiday, so, packing a bag, I got on the cutter from which in summer we used to bathe in the Baie des Fosses and set sail along the coast towards Marseilles. There was only a fitful breeze and for the most part we chugged along with the motor auxiliary. We spent a night in the harbour at Cannes, another at Sainte Maxime, and a third at Sanary. Then we got to Toulon. That is a port I have always had an affection for. The ships of the French fleet give it an air at once romantic and companionable, and I am never tired of wandering about its old streets. I can linger for hours on the quay, watching the sailors on shore leave strolling about in pairs or with their girls, and the civilians who saunter back and forth as though they had nothing in the world to do but enjoy the pleasant sunshine. Because of all these ships and the ferryboats that take the bustling crowd to various points of the vast harbour, Toulon gives you the effect of a terminal to which all the ways of the wide world converge; and as you sit in a café, your eyes a little dazzled by the brightness of sea and sky, your fancy takes golden journeys to the uttermost parts of the earth. You land in a longboat on a coral beach, fringed with coconut palms, in the Pacific; you step off the gangway on to the dock at Rangoon and get into a rickshaw; you watch from the upper deck the noisy, gesticulating crowd of Negroes as your ship is made fast to the pier at Port au Prince.

We got in latish in the morning and towards the middle of the afternoon I landed and walked along the quay, looking at the shops, at the people who passed me and at the people sitting under the awning in the cafés. Suddenly I saw Sophie and at the same moment she saw me. She smiled and said hello. I stopped and shook hands with her. She was by herself at a small table with an empty glass before her.

"Sit down and have a drink," she said.

"You have one with me," I replied, taking a chair.

She wore the striped blue-and-white jersey of the French sailor, a pair of bright red slacks and sandals through which protruded the painted nails of her big toes. She wore no hat, and her hair, cut very short and curled, was of so pale a gold that it was almost silver. She was as heavily made up as when we had run across her at the Rue de Lappe. She had had a drink or two as I judged from the saucers on the table, but she was sober. She did not seem displeased to see me.

"How are all the folks in Paris?" she asked.

"I think they're all right. I haven't seen any of them since that day we all lunched together at the Ritz."

She blew a great cloud of smoke from her nostrils and began to laugh.

"I didn't marry Larry after all."

"I know. Why not?"

"Darling, when it came to the point I couldn't see myself being Mary Magdalen to his Jesus Christ. No, sir."

"What made you change your mind at the last moment?"

She looked at me mockingly. With that audacious tilt of the head, with her small breasts and narrow flanks, in that get-up, she looked like a vicious boy; but I must admit that she was much more attractive than in the red dress, with its dismal air of provincial smartness, in which I had last seen her. Face and neck were deeply burnt by the sun, and though the brownness of her skin made the rouge on her cheeks and the black of her eyebrows more aggressive, the effect in its vulgar way was not without lure.

"Would you like me to tell you?"

I nodded. The waiter brought the beer I had ordered for myself and the brandy and seltzer for her. She lit a *caporal* from one she had just finished.

"I hadn't had a drink for three months. I hadn't had a smoke." She saw my faint look of surprise and laughed. "I don't mean cigarettes. Opium. I felt awful. You know, sometimes when I was alone I'd shriek the place down; I'd say, 'I can't go through with it, I can't go through with it.' It wasn't so bad when I was with Larry, but when he wasn't there it was hell."

I was looking at her and when she mentioned opium I scanned her more sharply; I noticed the pin-point pupils that showed she was smoking it now. Her eyes were startlingly green.

"Isabel was giving me my wedding dress. I wonder what's happened to it now. It was a peach. We'd arranged that I should pick her up and we'd go to Molyneux's together. I will say this for Isabel, what she doesn't know about clothes isn't worth knowing. When I got to the apartment that man they have said she'd had to take Joan to the dentist's and had left a message that she'd be in directly. I went into the living room. The coffee things were still on the table and I asked the man if I could have a cup. Coffee was the only thing that kept me going. He said he'd bring me some and took the empty cups and the coffee pot away. He left a bottle on the tray. I looked at it, and it was that Polish stuff you'd all talked about at the Ritz."

"Zubrovka. I remember Elliott saying he'd send Isabel some."

"You'd all raved about how good it smelt and I was curious. I took out the cork and had a sniff. You were quite right; it smelt damned good. I lit a cigarette and in a few minutes the man came in with the coffee. That was good too. They talk a lot about French coffee, they can have it; give me American coffee. That's the only thing I miss here. But Isabel's coffee wasn't bad, I was feeling lousy, and after I'd had a cup I felt better. I looked at that bottle standing there. It was a terrible temptation, but I said, 'To hell with it, I won't think of it,' and I lit another cigarette. I thought Isabel would be in any minute, but she didn't come; I got frightfully nervous; I hate being kept waiting and there was nothing to read in the room. I started walking about and looking at the pictures, but I kept on seeing that damned bottle. Then I thought I'd just pour out a glass and look at it. It had such a pretty colour."

"Pale green."

"That's right. It's funny, its colour is just like its smell. It's like that green you sometimes see in the heart of a white rose. I *had* to see if it tasted like that, I thought just a taste couldn't hurt me; I only meant to take a sip and then I heard a sound, I thought it was Isabel coming in and I swallowed the glassful because I didn't want her to catch me. But it wasn't Isabel after all. Gosh, it made me feel good, I hadn't felt like that since I'd gone on the wagon. I really began to feel alive again. If Isabel had come in then I suppose I'd be married to Larry now. I wonder how it would have turned out."

"And she didn't come in?"

"No, she didn't. I was furious with her. Who did she think she was, keeping me waiting like that? And then I saw that the liqueur glass was full again; I suppose I must have poured it out without thinking, but, believe it or not, I didn't know I had. It seemed silly to pour it back again, so I drank it. There's no denying it, it was delicious. I felt a different woman; I felt like laughing and I hadn't felt like that for three months. D'you remember that old cissie saying he'd seen fellas in Poland drink it by the tumbler without turning a hair? Well, I thought I could take what any Polish son of a bitch could take and you may as well be hanged for a sheep as a lamb, so I emptied the dregs of my coffee in the fireplace and filled the cup to the brim. Talk of mother's milk—my arse. Then I don't quite know what happened, but I don't believe there was much left in the bottle by the time I was through. Then I thought I'd get out before Isabel came in. She nearly caught me. Just as I got out of the front door I heard Joanie's voice. I ran up the stairs and waited till they were safely in the apartment and then I dashed down and got into a taxi. I told the driver to drive like hell and when he asked where to I burst out laughing in his face. I felt like a million dollars."

"Did you go back to your apartment?" I asked, though I knew she hadn't.

"What sort of a damn fool d'you take me for? I knew Larry would come and look for me. I didn't dare go to any of the places I used to go to, so I went to Hakim's. I knew Larry'd never find me there. Besides, I wanted a smoke."

"What's Hakim's?"

"Hakim's. Hakim's an Algerian and he can always get you opium if you've got the dough to pay for it. He was quite a friend of mine. He'll get you anything you want, a boy, a man, a woman or a nigger. He always has half a dozen Algerians on tap. I spent three days there. I don't know how many men I didn't have." She began to giggle. "All shapes, sizes and colours. I made up for lost time all right. But you know, I was scared. I didn't feel safe in Paris, I was afraid Larry'd find me, besides I hadn't got any money left, those bastards you have to pay them to go to bed with you, so I got out, I went back to the apartment and gave the *concierge* a hundred francs and told her if anyone came and asked for me to say I'd gone away. I packed my things and that night I took the train to Toulon. I didn't feel really safe till I got here."

"And have you been here ever since?"

"You betcha, and I'm going to stay here. You can get all the opium you want, the sailors bring it back from the East, and it's good stuff, not that muck they sell you in Paris. I've got a room at the hotel. You know, the Commerce et la Marine. When you go in there at night the corridors just reek of it." She sniffed voluptuously. "Sweet and acrid, and you know they're smoking in their rooms, and it gives you a nice homey feeling. And they don't mind who you take in with you. They come and thump at your door at five in the morning to get the sailors up to go back to their ships, so you don't have to worry about that." And then, without transition: "I saw a book of yours in the store just along the quay; if I'd known I was going to see you I'd have bought it and got you to sign it."

When passing the bookshop I had stopped to look in the window and had noticed among other new books the translation of a novel of mine that had recently appeared.

"I don't suppose it would have amused you much," I said.

"I don't know why it shouldn't. I *can* read, you know."

"And you can write too, I believe."

She gave me a rapid glance and began to laugh.

"Yeah, I used to write poetry when I was a kid. I guess it was pretty terrible, but I thought it fine. I suppose Larry told you." She hesitated for a moment. "Life's hell anyway, but if there is any fun to be got out of it, you're only a god-damn fool if you don't get it." She threw back her head defiantly. "If I buy that book will you write in it?"

"I'm leaving tomorrow. If you really want it, I'll get you a copy and leave it at your hotel."

"That'd be swell."

Just then a naval launch came up to the quay and a crowd of sailors tumbled out of it. Sophie embraced them with a glance.

"That'll be my boy friend." She waved her arm at someone. "You can stand him a drink and then you better scram. He's a Corsican and as jealous as our old friend Jehovah."

A young man came up to us, hesitated when he saw me, but on a beckoning gesture came up to our table. He was tall, swarthy, clean-shaven, with splendid dark eyes, an aquiline nose and raven black, wavy hair. He did not look more than twenty. Sophie introduced me as an American friend of her childhood.

"Dumb but beautiful," she said to me.

"You like 'em tough, don't you?"

"The tougher the better."

"One of these days you'll get your throat cut."

"I wouldn't be surprised," she grinned. "Good riddance to bad rubbish."

"One's going to speak French, isn't one?" the sailor said sharply.

Sophie turned upon him a smile in which there was a trace of mockery. She spoke a fluent and slangy French, with a strong American accent, but this gave the vulgar and obscene colloquialisms that she commonly used a comic tang, so that you could not help but laugh.

"I was telling him that you were beautiful, but to spare your modesty I was saying it in English." She addressed me. "And he's strong. He has the muscles of a boxer. Feel them."

The sailor's sullenness was dispelled by the flattery and with a complacent smile he flexed his arm so that the biceps stood out.

"Feel it," he said. "Go on, feel it."

I did so and expressed a proper admiration. We chatted for a few minutes. I paid for the drinks and got up.

"I must be going."

"It's nice to have seen you. Don't forget the book."

"I won't."

I shook hands with them both and strolled off. On my way I stopped at the bookshop, bought the novel and wrote Sophie's name and my own. Then, because it suddenly occurred to me and I could think of nothing else, I wrote the first line of Ronsard's lovely little poem which is in all the anthologies:

"Mignonne, allons voir si la rose. . . ."

I left it at the hotel. It is on the quay and I have often stayed there because when you are awakened at dawn by the clarion that calls the men on night leave back to duty the sun rising mistily over the smooth water of the harbour invests the wraithlike ships with a shrouded loveliness. Next day we sailed for Cassis, where I wanted to buy some wine, and then to Marseilles to take up a new sail that we had ordered. A week later I got home.

(vii)

I found a message from Joseph, Elliott's manservant, to tell me that Elliott was ill in bed and would be glad to see me, so next day I drove over to Antibes. Joseph, before taking me up to see his master, told me that Elliott had had an attack of uremia and that his doctor took a grave view of his condition. He had come through it and was getting better, but his kidneys were diseased and it was impossible that he should ever completely recover. Joseph had been with Elliott for forty years and was devoted to him, but though his manner was regretful it was impossible not to notice the inner satisfaction with which, like so many members of his class, catastrophe in the house filled him.

"*Ce pauvre monsieur,*" he sighed. "Evidently he had his manias but at bottom he was good. Sooner or later one must die."

He spoke already as though Elliott were at his last gasp.

"I'm sure he's provided for you, Joseph," I said grimly.

"One must hope it," he said mournfully.

I was surprised when he ushered me into the bedroom to find Elliott very spry. He was pale and looked old, but was in good spirits. He was shaved and his hair was neatly brushed. He wore pale blue silk pyjamas, on the pocket of which were embroidered his initials surmounted by his count's crown. These, much larger and again with the crown, were heavily embroidered on the turned-down sheet.

I asked him how he felt.

"Perfectly well," he said cheerfully. "It's only a temporary indisposition. I shall be up and about again in a few days. I've got the Grand Duke Dimitri lunching with me on Saturday and I've told my doctor he must put me to rights by then at all costs."

I spent half an hour with him and on my way out asked Joseph to let me know if Elliott had a relapse. I was astonished a week later when I went to lunch with one of my neighbours to find him there. Dressed for a party, he looked like death.

"You oughtn't to be out, Elliott," I told him.

"Oh, what nonsense, my dear fellow. Frieda is expecting the Princess Mafalda. I've known the Italian royal family for years, ever since poor Louisa was *en poste* at Rome, and I couldn't let poor Frieda down."

I did not know whether to admire his indomitable spirit or to lament that at his age, stricken with mortal illness, he should still retain his passion for society. You would never have thought he was a sick man. Like a dying actor when he has the grease paint on his face and steps on the stage, who forgets for the time being his aches and pains, Elliott played his part of the polished courtier with his accustomed assurance. He was infinitely amiable, flatteringly attentive to the proper people and amusing with that malicious irony at which he was an adept. I think I had never seen him display his social gift to greater advantage. When the Royal Highness had departed (and the grace with which Elliott bowed, managing to combine respect for her exalted rank with an old man's admiration for a comely young woman, was a sight to see) I was not surprised to hear our hostess tell him that he had been the life and soul of the party.

A few days later he was in bed again and his doctor forbade him to leave his room. Elliott was exasperated.

"It's too bad this should happen just now. It's a particularly brilliant season."

He reeled off a long list of persons of importance who were spending the summer on the Riviera.

I went to see him every three or four days. Sometimes he was in bed, but sometimes he lay on a chaise longue in a gorgeous dressing-gown. He seemed to have an inexhaustible supply of them, for I do not remember that I ever saw him in the same one twice. On one of these occasions, it was the beginning of August by now, I found Elliott unusually quiet. Joseph had told me when he let me into the house that he seemed a little better; I was surprised then that he was so listless. I tried to amuse him with such gossip of the coast as I had picked up, but he was plainly uninterested. There was a slight frown between his eyes, and a sullenness in his expression that was unusual with him.

"Are you going to Edna Novemali's party?" he asked me suddenly.

"No, of course not."

"Has she asked you?"

"She's asked everybody on the Riviera."

The Princess Novemali was an American of immense wealth who had married a Roman prince, but not an ordinary prince such as go for two a penny in Italy, but the head of a great family and the descendant of a *condottière* who had carved out a principality for himself in the sixteenth century. She was a woman of sixty, a widow, and since the Fascist regime demanded too large a slice of her American income to suit her, she had left Italy and built herself, on a fine estate behind Cannes, a Florentine villa. She had brought marble from Italy with which to line the walls of her great reception rooms and imported painters to paint the ceilings. Her pictures, her bronzes were uncommonly fine and even Elliott, though he didn't like Italian furniture, was obliged to admit that hers was magnificent. The gardens were lovely and the swimming-pool must have cost a small fortune. She entertained largely and you never sat down to less than twenty at table. She had arranged to give a fancy-dress party on the night of the August full moon and although it was still three weeks ahead nothing else was being talked of on the Riviera. There were to be fireworks and she was bringing down a coloured orchestra from Paris. The exiled royalties were telling one another with envious admiration that it would cost her more than they had to live on for a year.

"It's princely," they said.

"It's crazy," they said.

"It's in bad taste," they said.

"What are you going to wear?" Elliott asked me.

"But I told you, Elliott, I'm not going. You don't think I'm going to dress myself up in fancy dress at my time of life."

"She hasn't asked me," he said hoarsely.

He looked at me with haggard eyes.

"Oh, she will," I said coolly. "I daresay all the invitations haven't gone out yet."

"She's not going to ask me." His voice broke. "It's a deliberate insult."

"Oh, Elliott, I can't believe that. I'm sure it's only an oversight."

"I'm not a man that people overlook."

"Anyhow you wouldn't have been well enough to go."

"Of course I should. The best party of the season! If I were on my death-bed I'd get up for it. I've got the costume of my ancestor, the Count de Lauria, to wear."

I did not quite know what to say and so remained silent.

"Paul Barton was in to see me just before you came," Elliott said suddenly.

I cannot expect the reader to remember who this was, since I had to look back myself to see what name I had given him. Paul Barton was the young American whom Elliott had introduced into London society and who had aroused his hatred by dropping him when he no longer had any use for him. He had been somewhat in the public eye of late, first because he had adopted British nationality and then because he had married the daughter of a news-paper magnate who had been raised to the peerage. With this influence be-hind him and with his own adroitness it was evident that he would go far. Elliott was very bitter.

"Whenever I wake up in the night and hear a mouse scratching away in the wainscot I say, 'That's Paul Barton climbing.' Believe me, my dear fellow, he'll end up in the House of Lords. Thank God, I shan't be alive to see it."

"What did he want?" I asked, for I knew as well as Elliott that this young man did nothing for nothing.

"I'll tell you what he wanted," said Elliott, snarling. "He wanted to borrow my Count de Lauria costume."

"Nerve!"

"Don't you see what it means? It means he knew Edna hadn't asked me and wasn't going to ask me. She put him up to it. The old bitch. She'd never have got anywhere without me. I gave parties for her. I introduced her to everyone she knows. She sleeps with her chauffeur; you knew that of course. Disgusting! He sat there and told me that she's having the whole garden illuminated and there are going to be fireworks. I love fireworks. And he told me that Edna was being pestered by people who were asking for invitations, but she had turned them all down because she wanted the party to be really brilliant. He spoke as though there were no question of my being invited."

"And are you lending him the costume?"

"I'd see him dead and in hell first. I'm going to be buried in it." Elliott, sitting up in bed, rocked to and fro like a woman distraught. "Oh, it's so unkind," he said. "I hate them, I hate them all. They were glad enough to make a fuss of me when I could entertain them, but now I'm old and sick they have no use for me. Not ten people have called to inquire since I've been laid up, and all this week only one miserable bunch of flowers. I've done everything for them. They've eaten my food and drunk my wine. I've run their errands for them. I've made their parties for them. I've turned myself inside out to do them favours. And what have I got out of it? Nothing, nothing, nothing. There's not one of them who cares if I live or die. Oh, it's so cruel." He began to cry. Great heavy tears trickled down his withered cheeks. "I wish to God I'd never left America."

It was lamentable to see that old man, with the grave yawning in front of him, weep like a child because he hadn't been asked to a party, shocking and at the same time almost intolerably pathetic.

"Never mind, Elliott," I said, "it may rain on the night of the party. That'll bitch it."

He caught at my words like the drowning man we've all heard about at a straw. He began to giggle through his tears.

"I've never thought of that. I'll pray to God for rain as I've never prayed before. You're quite right; that'll bitch it."

I managed to divert his frivolous mind into another channel and left him, if not cheerful, at least composed. But I was not willing to let the matter rest, so on getting home I called up Edna Novemali and, saying I had to come to Cannes next day, asked if I could lunch with her. She sent a message that she'd be pleased but there'd be no party. Nevertheless when I arrived I found ten people there besides herself. She was not a bad sort, generous and hospitable, and her only grave fault was her malicious tongue. She could not help saying beastly things about even her intimate friends, but she did this because she was a stupid woman and knew no other way to make herself interesting. Since her slanders were repeated she was often not on speaking terms with the objects of her venom, but she gave good parties and most of them found it convenient after a while to forgive her. I did not want to expose Elliott to the humiliation of asking her to invite him to her big do and so waited to see how the land lay. She was excited about it and the conversation at luncheon was concerned with nothing else.

"Elliott will be delighted to have an opportunity to wear his Philip the Second costume," I said as casually as I could.

"I haven't asked him," she said.

"Why not?" I replied with an air of surprise.

"Why should I? He doesn't count socially any more. He's a bore and a snob and a scandalmonger."

Since these accusations could with equal truth be brought against her, I thought this a bit thick. She was a fool.

"Besides," she added, "I want Paul to wear Elliott's costume. He'll look simply divine in it."

I said nothing more, but determined by hook or by crook to get poor Elliott the invitation he hankered after. After luncheon Edna took her friends out into the garden. That gave me the chance I was looking for. On one occasion I had stayed in the house for a few days and knew its arrangement. I guessed that there would still be a number of invitation cards left over and that they would be in the secretary's room. I whipped along there, meaning to slip one in my pocket, write Elliott's name on it and post it. I knew he was much too ill to go, but it would mean a great deal to him to receive it. I was taken aback when I opened the door to find Edna's secretary at her desk. I had expected her to be still at lunch. She was a middle-aged Scotch woman, called Miss Keith, with sandy hair, a freckled face, pince-nez and an air of determined virginity. I collected myself.

"The Princess is taking the crowd around the garden, so I thought I'd come in and smoke a cigarette with you."

"You're welcome."

Miss Keith spoke with a Scottish burr and when she indulged in the dry humour which she reserved for her favourites she so broadened it as to make her remarks extremely amusing, but when you were overcome with laughter she looked at you with pained surprise as though she thought you daft to see anything funny in what she said.

"I suppose this party is giving you a hell of a lot of work, Miss Keith," I said.

"I don't know whether I'm standing on my head or on my heels."

Knowing I could trust her, I went straight to the point.

"Why hasn't the old girl asked Mr. Templeton?"

Miss Keith permitted a smile to cross her grim features.

"You know what she is. She's got a down on him. She crossed his name out on the list herself."

"He's dying, you know. He'll never leave his bed again. He's awfully hurt at being left out."

"If he wanted to keep in with the Princess he'd have been wiser not to tell everyone that she goes to bed with her chauffeur. And him with a wife and three children."

"And does she?"

Miss Keith looked at me over her pince-nez.

"I've been a secretary for twenty-one years, my dear sir, and I've made it a rule to believe all my employers as pure as the driven snow. I'll admit that when one of my ladies found herself three months gone in the family way when his lordship had been shooting lions in Africa for six, my faith was sorely tried, but she took a little trip to Paris, a very expensive little trip it was too, and all was well. Her ladyship and I shared a deep sigh of relief."

"Miss Keith, I didn't come here to smoke a cigarette with you, I came to snitch an invitation card and send it to Mr. Templeton myself."

"That would have been a very unscrupulous thing to do."

"Granted. Be a good sport, Miss Keith. Give me a card. He won't come and it'll make the poor old man happy. You've got nothing against him, have you?"

"No, he's always been very civil to me. He's a gentleman, I will say that for him, and that's more than you can say for most of the people who come here and fill their fat bellies at the Princess's expense."

All important persons have about them someone in a subordinate position who has their ear. These dependents are very susceptible to slights and, when they are not treated as they think they should be, will by well-directed shafts, constantly repeated, poison the minds of their patrons against those who have provoked their animosity. It is well to keep in with them. This Elliott knew better than anybody and he had always a friendly word and a cordial smile for the poor relation, the old maidservant or the trusted secretary. I was sure he had often exchanged pleasant badinage with Miss Keith and at Christmas had not forgotten to send her a box of chocolates, a vanity case or a handbag.

"Come on, Miss Keith, have a heart."

Miss Keith fixed her pince-nez more firmly on her prominent nose.

"I am sure you wish me to do nothing disloyal to my employer, Mr. Maugham, besides which the old cow would fire me if she found out I'd disobeyed her. The cards are on the desk in their envelopes. I am going to look out of the window partly to stretch my legs which are cramped from sitting too long in one position and also to observe the beauty of the prospect.

What happens when my back is turned neither God nor man can hold me responsible for."

When Miss Keith resumed her seat the invitation was in my pocket.

"It's been nice to see you, Miss Keith," I said, holding out my hand. "What are you wearing at the fancy-dress party?"

"I am a minister's daughter, my dear sir," she replied. "I leave such foolishness to the upper classes. When I have seen that the representatives of the *Herald* and the *Mail* get a good supper and a bottle of our second-best champagne, my duties will be terminated and I shall retire to the privacy of my bedchamber with a detective story."

(viii)

A couple of days later, when I went to see Elliott, I found him beaming.

"Look," he said, "I've had my invitation. It came this morning."

He took the card out from under his pillow and showed it to me.

"It's what I told you," I said. "You see, your name begins with a T. The secretary has evidently only just reached you."

"I haven't answered yet. I'll do it tomorrow."

I had a moment's fright at that.

"Would you like me to answer it for you? I could post it when I leave you."

"No, why should you? I'm quite capable of answering invitations myself."

Fortunately, I thought, the envelope would be opened by Miss Keith and she would have the sense to suppress it. Elliott rang the bell.

"I want to show you my costume."

"You're not thinking of going, Elliott?"

"Of course I am. I haven't worn it since the Beaumonts' ball."

Joseph answered the bell and Elliott told him to bring the costume. It was in a large flat box, wrapped in tissue paper. There were long white silk hose, padded trunks of cloth of gold slashed with white satin, a doublet to match, a cloak, a ruff to wear round the neck, a flat velvet cap and a long gold chain from which hung the order of the Golden Fleece. I recognized it as a copy of the gorgeous dress worn by Philip the Second in Titian's portrait at the Prado, and when Elliott told me it was exactly the costume the Count de Lauria had worn at the wedding of the King of Spain with the Queen of England I could not but think that he was giving rein to his imagination.

On the following morning while I was having breakfast I was called to the telephone. It was Joseph to tell me that Elliott had had another attack during the night and the doctor, hurriedly summoned, doubted whether he would last through the day. I sent for the car and drove over to Antibes. I found Elliott unconscious. He had resolutely refused to have a nurse, but I found one there, sent for by the doctor from the English hospital between Nice and Beaulieu, and was glad to see her. I went out and telegraphed to Isabel. She and Gray were spending the summer with the children at the inexpensive seaside resort of La Baule. It was a long journey and I was afraid they would not get to Antibes in time. Except for her two brothers, whom he had not seen for years, she was Elliott's only living relative.

But the will to live was strong in him or it may be that the doctor's medicaments were effective, for during the course of the day he rallied. Though shattered, he put on a bold front and amused himself by asking the nurse indecent questions about her sex life. I stayed with him most of the afternoon and next day, on going to see him again, found him, though very weak, sufficiently cheerful. The nurse would only let me stay with him a short time. I was worried not to have received an answer to my telegram. Not knowing Isabel's address at La Baule I had sent it to Paris and feared that the *concierge* had delayed to forward it. It was not till two days later that I got a reply to say that they were starting at once. As ill luck would have it, Gray and Isabel were on a motor trip in Brittany and had only just had my wire. I looked up the trains and saw that they could not arrive for at least thirty-six hours.

Early next morning Joseph called me again to tell me that Elliott had had a very bad night and was asking for me. I hurried over. When I arrived Joseph took me aside.

"Monsieur will excuse me if I speak to him on a delicate subject," he said to me. "I am of course a freethinker and believe all religion is nothing but a conspiracy of the priests to gain control over the people, but Monsieur knows what women are. My wife and the chambermaid insist that the poor gentleman should receive the last sacraments and evidently the time is growing short." He looked at me in rather a shamefaced way. "And the fact remains, one never knows, perhaps it is better, if one's got to die, to regularize one's situation with the Church."

I understood him perfectly. However freely they mock, most Frenchmen, when the end comes, prefer to make their peace with the faith that is part of their blood and bones.

"Do you want me to suggest it to him?"

"If Monsieur would have the goodness."

It was not a job I much fancied, but after all Elliott had been for many years a devout Catholic, and it was fitting that he should conform to the obligations of his faith. I went up to his room. He was lying on his back, shrivelled and wan, but he was perfectly conscious. I asked the nurse to leave us alone.

"I'm afraid you're very ill, Elliott," I said. "I was wondering, I was wondering if you wouldn't like to see a priest?"

He looked at me for a minute without answering.

"D'you mean to say I'm going to die?"

"Oh, I hope not. But it's just as well to be on the safe side."

"I understand."

He was silent. It is a terrible moment when you have to tell someone what I had just told Elliott. I could not look at him. I clenched my teeth because I was afraid I was going to cry. I was sitting on the edge of the bed, facing him, with my arm outstretched for support.

He patted my hand.

"Don't be upset, my dear fellow. *Noblesse oblige,* you know."

I laughed hysterically.

"You ridiculous creature, Elliott."

"That's better. Now call up the bishop and say that I wish to make my confession and receive Extreme Unction. I would be grateful if he'd send the Abbé Charles. He's a friend of mine."

The Abbé Charles was the bishop's vicar general whom I have had occasion to mention before. I went downstairs and telephoned. I spoke to the bishop himself.

"Is it urgent?" he asked.

"Very."

"I will attend to it at once."

The doctor arrived and I told him what I had done. He went up with the nurse to see Elliott and I waited on the ground floor in the dining-room. It is only twenty minutes' drive from Nice to Antibes and little more than half an hour later a large black sedan drew up at the door. Joseph came to me.

"*C'est Monseigneur en personne, Monsieur,*" he said in a flurry. "It's the bishop himself."

I went out to receive him. He was not as usual accompanied by his vicar general, but, why I did not know, by a young abbé who bore a casket that contained, I supposed, the utensils needed to administer the sacrament. The chauffeur followed with a shabby black valise. The bishop shook hands with me and presented his companion.

"How is our poor friend?"

"I'm afraid he's very ill, Monseigneur."

"Will you be so obliging as to show us into a room where we can enrobe."

"The dining-room is here, Monseigneur, and the drawing-room is on the next floor."

"The dining-room will do very well."

I ushered him in. Joseph and I waited in the hall. Presently the door opened and the bishop came out, followed by the abbé holding in both hands the chalice on which rested a little platter on which lay the consecrated wafer. They were covered by a cambric napkin so fine that it was transparent. I had never seen the bishop but at a dinner or luncheon party, and a very good trencherman he was, who enjoyed his food and a glass of good wine, telling funny and sometimes ribald stories with verve. He had struck me then as a sturdy, thickset man of no more than average height. Now, in surplice and stole, he looked not only tall, but stately. His red face, puckered as a rule with malicious yet kindly laughter, was grave. There was in his appearance nothing left of the cavalry officer he had once been; he looked, what indeed he was, a great dignitary of the Church. I was hardly surprised to see Joseph cross himself. The bishop inclined his head in a slight bow.

"Conduct me to the sick man," he said.

I made way for him to ascend the stairs before me, but he bade me precede him. We went up in a solemn silence. I entered Elliott's room.

"The bishop has come himself, Elliott."

Elliott struggled to raise himself to a sitting position.

"Monseigneur, this is an honour I did not venture to expect."

"Do not move, my friend." The bishop turned to the nurse and me. "Leave us." And then to the abbé: "I will call you when I am ready."

The abbé glanced around and I guessed that he was looking for a place to set down the chalice. I pushed aside the tortoise-shell-backed brushes on the dressing-table. The nurse went downstairs and I led the abbé into the adjoining room which Elliott used as a study. The windows were open to the blue sky and he went over and stood by one of them. I sat down. A race of Stars was in progress and their sails gleamed dazzling white against the azure. A big schooner with a black hull, her red sails spread, was beating up against the breeze towards the harbour. I recognized her for a lobster boat, bringing a catch from Sardinia to supply the gala dinners at the casinos with a fish course. Through the closed door I could hear the muffled murmur of voices. Elliott was making his confession. I badly wanted a cigarette, but feared the abbé would be shocked if I lit one. He stood motionless, looking out, a slender young man, and his thick waving black hair, his fine dark eyes, his olive skin revealed his Italian origin. There was the quick fire of the South in his aspect and I asked myself what urgent faith, what burning desire had caused him to abandon the joys of common life, the pleasures of his age and the satisfaction of his senses, to devote himself to the service of God.

Suddenly the voices in the next room were still and I looked at the door. It was opened and the bishop appeared.

"Venez," he said to the priest.

I was left alone. I heard the bishop's voice once more and I knew he was saying the prayers that the Church has ordained should be said for the dying. Then there was another silence and I knew that Elliott was partaking of the body and the blood of Christ. From I know not what feeling, inherited, I suppose, from far away ancestors, though not a Catholic I can never attend Mass without a sense of tremulous awe when the little tinkle of the servitor's bell informs me of the Elevation of the Host; and now, similarly, I shivered as though a cold wind ran through me, I shivered with fear and wonder. The door was opened once more.

"You may come in," said the bishop.

I entered. The abbé was covering the cup and the little gilt plate on which had lain the consecrated wafer with the cambric cloth. Elliott's eyes shone.

"Conduct Monseigneur to his car," he said.

We descended the stairs. Joseph and the maids were waiting in the hall. The maids were crying. There were three of them and one after the other they came forward and, dropping to their knees, kissed the bishop's ring. He blessed them with two fingers. Joseph's wife nudged him and he advanced, fell to his knees too and kissed the ring. The bishop faintly smiled.

"You are a freethinker, my son?"

I could see Joseph making an effort over himself.

"Yes, Monseigneur."

"Do not let it trouble you. You have been a good and faithful servant to your master. God will overlook the errors of your understanding."

I went out into the street with him and opened the door of his car. He gave me a bow and as he stepped in smiled indulgently.

"Our poor friend is very low. His defects were of the surface; he was generous of heart and kindly towards his fellow men."

(*ix*)

Thinking that Elliott might want to be alone after the ceremony in which he had taken part, I went up to the drawing-room and began to read, but no sooner had I settled myself than the nurse came in to tell me that he wanted to see me. I climbed the flight of stairs to his room. Whether owing to a shot that the doctor had given him to help him to support the ordeal before him or whether owing to excitement of it, he was calmly cheerful and his eyes were bright.

"A great honour, my dear fellow," he said. "I shall enter the kingdom of

195

heaven with a letter of introduction from a prince of the Church. I fancy that all doors will be open to me."

"I'm afraid you'll find the company very mixed," I smiled.

"Don't you believe it, my dear fellow. We know from Holy Writ that there are class distinctions in heaven just as there are on earth. There are seraphim and cherubim, archangels and angels. I have always moved in the best society in Europe and I have no doubt that I shall move in the best society in heaven. Our Lord has said: The House of my Father hath many mansions. It would be highly unsuitable to lodge the *hoi polloi* in a way to which they're entirely unaccustomed."

I suspected that Elliott saw the celestial habitations in the guise of the châteaux of a Baron de Rothschild with eighteenth-century panelling on the walls, Buhl tables, marquetry cabinets and Louis Quinze suites covered with their original *petit point*.

"Believe me, my dear fellow," he went on after a pause, "there'll be none of this damned equality in heaven."

He dropped off quite suddenly into a doze. I sat down with a book. He slept off and on. At one o'clock the nurse came in to tell me that Joseph had luncheon ready for me. Joseph was subdued.

"Fancy Monseigneur the Bishop coming himself. It is a great honour he has done our poor gentleman. You saw me kiss his ring?"

"I did."

"It's not a thing I would have done of myself. I did it to satisfy my poor wife."

I spent the afternoon in Elliott's room. In the course of it a telegram came from Isabel to say that she and Gray would arrive by the Blue Train next morning. I could hardly hope they would be in time. The doctor came. He shook his head. Towards sunset Elliott awoke and was able to take a little nourishment. It seemed to give him a momentary strength. He beckoned to me and I went up to the bed. His voice was very weak.

"I haven't answered Edna's invitation."

"Oh, don't bother about that now, Elliott."

"Why not? I've always been a man of the world; there's no reason why I should forget my manners as I'm leaving it. Where is the card?"

It was on the chimney piece and I put it in his hand, but I doubt whether he could see it.

"You'll find a pad of writing paper in my study. If you'll get it I'll dictate my answer."

I went into the next room and came back with writing materials. I sat down by the side of his bed.

"Are you ready?"

"Yes."

His eyes were closed, but there was a mischievous smile on his lips and I wondered what was coming.

"Mr. Elliott Templeton regrets that he cannot accept Princess Novemali's kind invitation owing to a previous engagement with his Blessed Lord."

He gave a faint, ghostly chuckle. His face was of a strange blue-white, ghastly to behold, and he exhaled the nauseating stench peculiar to his disease. Poor Elliott who had loved to spray himself with the perfumes of Chanel and Molyneux. He was still holding the purloined invitation card and, thinking it incommoded him, I tried to take it out of his hand, but he tightened his grip on it. I was startled to hear him speak quite loudly.

"The old bitch," he said.

These were the last words he spoke. He sank into a coma. The nurse had been up with him all the previous night and looked very tired, so I sent her to bed, promising to call her if necessary, and said I would sit up. There was indeed nothing to do. I lit a shaded lamp and read till my eyes ached and then, turning it off, I sat in darkness. The night was warm and the windows wide open. At regular intervals the flash of the lighthouse swept the room with a passing glimmer. The moon, which when full would look upon the vacuous, noisy gaiety of Edna Novemali's fancy-dress party, set, and in the sky, a deep, deep blue, the countless stars shone with their terrifying brilliance. I think I may have dropped off into a light sleep, but my senses were still awake, and I was suddenly startled into intense consciousness by a hurried, angry sound, the most awe-inspiring sound that anyone can hear, the death rattle. I went over to the bed and by the gleam of the lighthouse felt Elliott's pulse. He was dead. I lit the lamp by his bedside and looked at him. His jaw had fallen. His eyes were open and before closing them I stared into them for a minute. I was moved and I think a few tears trickled down my cheeks. And old, kind friend. It made me sad to think how silly, useless and trivial his life had been. It mattered very little now that he had gone to so many parties and had hobnobbed with all those princes, dukes and counts. They had forgotten him already.

I saw no reason to wake the exhausted nurse and so returned to my chair by the window. I was asleep when she came in at seven. I left her to do whatever she thought fit and had breakfast, then I went to the station to meet Gray and Isabel. I told them that Elliott was dead and since there was no room for them in his house asked them to stay with me, but they preferred to go to a hotel. I went back to my own house to have a bath, shave and change.

In the course of the morning Gray called me to say that Joseph had given them a letter addressed to me that Elliott had entrusted to him. Since it might contain something for my eyes alone I said I would drive over at once, and so less than an hour later I once more entered the house. The letter, marked on the envelope: *To be delivered immediately after my death,* contained instructions for his obsequies. I knew that he had set his heart on being buried in the church that he had built and I had already told Isabel. He wished to be embalmed and mentioned the name of the firm to which the operation should be given. "I have made enquiries," he continued, "and I am informed that they make a very good job of it. I trust you to see that it is not scamped. I desire to be dressed in the dress of my ancestor the Count de Lauria, with his sword by my side and the order of the Golden Fleece on my breast. I leave the choice of my coffin to you. It should be unpretentious but suitable to my position. In order to give no one unnecessary trouble I desire that Thomas Cook and Son should make all arrangements for the transportation of my remains and that one of their men should accompany the coffin to its final resting place."

I remembered that Elliott had said he wanted to be buried in that fancy dress of his, but took it for a passing whim and I had not thought he meant it seriously. Joseph was insistent that his wishes be carried out and there seemed no reason why they should not be. The body was duly embalmed and then I went with Joseph to dress it in those absurd clothes. It was a gruesome business. We slipped his long legs into the white silk hose and pulled the cloth of gold trunks over them. It was a job to get his arms through the sleeves of the doublet. We fixed the great starched ruff and draped the satin cape over his shoulders. Finally we placed the flat velvet cap on his head and the collar of the Golden Fleece round his neck. The embalmer had rouged his cheeks and reddened his lips. Elliott, the costume too large now for his emaciated frame, looked like a chorus man in an early opera of Verdi's. The sad Don Quixote of a worthless purpose. When the undertaker's men had put him in the coffin I laid the property sword down the length of his body, between his legs, with his hands on the pommel as I have seen the sword laid on the sculptured tomb of a Crusader.

Gray and Isabel went to Italy to attend the funeral.

CHAPTER SIX

(*i*)

I FEEL IT RIGHT to warn the reader that he can very well skip this chapter without losing the thread of such story as I have to tell, since for the most part it is nothing more than the account of a conversation that I had with Larry. I should add, however, that except for this conversation I should perhaps not have thought it worth while to write this book.

(*ii*)

That autumn, a couple of months after Elliott's death, I spent a week in Paris on my way to England. Isabel and Gray, after their grim journey to Italy, had returned to Brittany, but were now once more settled in the apartment in the Rue St. Guillaume. She told me the details of his will. He had left a sum of money for Masses to be said for his soul in the church he had built and a further sum for its upkeep. He had bequeathed a handsome amount to the Bishop of Nice to be spent on charitable purposes. He had left me the equivocal legacy of his eighteenth-century pornographic library and a beautiful drawing by Fragonard of a satyr engaged with a nymph on a performance that is usually conducted in private. It was too indecent to hang on my walls and I am not one to gloat upon obscenity in private. He had provided generously for his servants. His two nephews were to have ten thousand dollars each and the residue of his estate went to Isabel. What this amounted to she did not tell me and I did not inquire; I gathered from her complacency that it was quite a lot of money.

For long, ever since he had regained his health, Gray had been impatient to go back to America and get to work again, and though Isabel was comfortable enough in Paris, his restlessness had affected her too. He had for some time been in communication with his friends, but the best opening that presented itself was contingent on his putting in a considerable amount of capital. That he had not got, but Elliott's death had put Isabel in possession of very much more than was needed and Gray with her approval was starting negotiations with the view, if everything turned out as well as it was represented, of leaving Paris and going to look into the matter for himself. But before that was possible there was much to attend to. They had to come to a reasonable agreement with the French Treasury over the inheritance tax.

They had to get rid of the house at Antibes and the apartment in the Rue St. Guillaume. They had to arrange for a sale at the Hôtel Drouot of Elliott's furniture, pictures and drawings. They were valuable and it seemed wise to wait till spring when the great collectors were likely to be in Paris. Isabel was not sorry to spend another winter there; the children by now could chatter French as easily as they could chatter English and she was glad to let them have a few more months at a French school. They had grown in three years and were now long-legged, skinny, vivacious little creatures, with little at present of their mother's beauty, but with nice manners and an insatiable curiosity.

So much for that.

(iii)

I met Larry by chance. I had asked Isabel about him and she told me that since their return from La Baule they had seen little of him. She and Gray had by now made a number of friends for themselves, people of their own generation, and they were more often engaged than during the pleasant weeks when the four of us were so much together. One evening I went to the Théâtre Français to see *Bérénice*. I had read it of course, but had never seen it played and since it is seldom given I was unwilling to miss the opportunity. It is not one of Racine's best plays, for the subject is tenuous to support five acts, but it is moving and contains passages that are justly famous. The story is founded on a brief passage in Tacitus: Titus, who loved Bérénice, Queen of Palestine, with passion and who even, as was supposed, had promised her marriage, for reasons of state sent her away from Rome during the first days of his reign in despite of his desires and in despite of hers. For the Senate and the people of Rome were violently opposed to their Emperor's alliance with a foreign queen. The play is concerned with the struggle in his breast between love and duty, and when he falters, it is Bérénice who in the end, assured that he loves her, confirms his purpose and separates herself from him forever.

I suppose only a Frenchman can appreciate to the full the grace and grandeur of Racine and the music of his verse, but even a foreigner, once he has accustomed himself to the periwigged formality of the style, can hardly fail to be moved by his passionate tenderness and by the nobility of his sentiment. Racine knew as few have done how much drama is contained in the human voice. To me at all events the roll of those mellifluous Alexandrines is a sufficient substitute for action, and I find the long speeches, working up with infinite skill to the expected climax, every bit as thrilling as any hair-raising adventure of the movies.

There was an interval after the third act and I went out to smoke a cigarette in the foyer over which presides Houdon's Voltaire with his toothless, sardonic grin. Someone touched me on the shoulder. I turned round, perhaps with a slight movement of annoyance, for I wanted to be left with the exaltation with which those sonorous lines had filled me, and saw Larry. As always, I was glad to see him. It was a year since I had set eyes on him and I suggested that at the end of the play we should meet and have a glass of beer together. Larry said he was hungry, for he had had no dinner, and proposed that we should go to Montmartre. We found one another in due course and stepped out into the open. The Théâtre Français has a musty fug that is peculiar to it. It is impregnated with the body odour of those unnumbered generations of sour-faced, unwashed women called *ouvreuses* who show you to your seat and domineeringly await their tip. It was a relief to get into the fresh air, and since the night was fine we walked. The arc lamps in the Avenue de l'Opéra glared so defiantly that the stars above, as though too proud to compete, shrouded their brightness in the dark of their infinite distance. As we walked we spoke of the performance we had just seen. Larry was disappointed. He would have liked it to be more natural, the lines spoken as people naturally speak and the gestures less theatrical. I thought his point of view mistaken. It was rhetoric, magnificent rhetoric, and I had a notion that it should be spoken rhetorically. I liked the regular thump of the rhymes; and the stylized gestures, handed down in a long tradition, seemed to me to suit the temper of that formal art. I could not but think that that was how Racine would have wished his play to be played. I had admired the way in which the actors had contrived to be human, passionate and true within the limitations that confined them. Art is triumphant when it can use convention as an instrument of its own purpose.

We reached the Avenue de Clichy and went into the Brasserie Graf. It was not long past midnight and it was crowded, but we found a table and ordered ourselves eggs and bacon. I told Larry I had seen Isabel.

"Gray will be glad to get back to America," he said. "He's a fish out of water here. He won't be happy till he's at work again. I daresay he'll make a lot of money."

"If he does it'll be due to you. You not only cured him in body, but in spirit as well. You restored his confidence in himself."

"I did very little. I merely showed him how to cure himself."

"How did you learn to do that little?"

"By accident. It was when I was in India. I'd been suffering from insomnia and happened to mention it to an old Yogi I knew and he said he'd soon settle that. He did just what you saw me do with Gray and that night I slept as I hadn't slept for months. And then, a year later it must have been, I was in the Himalayas with an Indian friend of mine and he sprained his ankle. It was impossible to get a doctor and he was in great pain. I thought I'd try to do what the old Yogi had done, and it worked. You can believe it or not, he was completely relieved of the pain." Larry laughed. "I can assure you, no one was more surprised than I. There's nothing to it really; it only means putting the idea into the sufferer's mind."

"Easier said than done."

"Would it surprise you if your arm raised itself from the table without any volition of yours?"

"Very much."

"It will. My Indian friend told people what I'd done when we got back to civilization and brought others to see me. I hated doing it, because I couldn't quite understand it, but they insisted. Somehow or other I did them good. I found I was able to relieve people not only of pain but of fear. It's strange how many people suffer from it. I don't only mean fear of closed spaces and fear of heights, but fear of death and what's worse, fear of life. Often they're people who seem in the best of health, prosperous, without any worry, and yet they're tortured by it. I've sometimes thought it was the most besetting humour of men, and I asked myself at one time if it was due to some deep animal instinct that man has inherited from that primeval something that first felt the thrill of life."

I was listening to Larry with expectation, for it was not often that he spoke at any length, and I had an inkling that for once he felt communicative. Perhaps the play we had just seen had released some inhibition and the rhythm of its sonorous cadences, as music will, had overcome his instinctive reserve. Suddenly I realized that something was happening to my hand. I had not given another thought to Larry's half-laughing question. I was conscious that my hand no longer rested on the table, but was raised an inch above it without my willing it. I was taken aback. I looked at it and saw that it trembled slightly. I felt a queer tingling in the nerves of my arm, a little jerk, and my hand and forearm lifted of themselves, I to the best of my belief neither aiding nor resisting, until they were several inches from the table. Then I felt my whole arm being raised from the shoulder.

"This is very odd," I said.

Larry laughed. I made the slightest effort of will and my hand fell back on to the table.

"It's nothing," he said. "Don't attach any importance to it."

"Were you taught that by the Yogi you spoke to us about when you first came back from India?"

"Oh no, he had no patience with that kind of thing. I don't know whether he believed that he possessed the powers that some Yogis claim to have, but he would have thought it puerile to exercise them."

Our eggs and bacon arrived and we ate them with good appetite. We drank our beer. We neither of us spoke. He was thinking of I knew not what and I was thinking of him. We finished. I lit a cigarette and he lit a pipe.

"What made you go to India in the first place?" I asked abruptly.

"Chance. At least I thought so at the time. Now I'm inclined to think it was the inevitable outcome of my years in Europe. Almost all the people who've had most effect on me I seem to have met by chance, yet looking back it seems as though I couldn't but have met them. It's as if they were waiting there to be called upon when I needed them. I went to India because I wanted a rest. I'd been working very hard and wished to sort out my thoughts. I got a job as a deck hand on one of those pleasure-cruise ships that go around the world. It was going to the East and through the Panama Canal to New York. I hadn't been to America for five years and I was home-sick. I was depressed. You know how ignorant I was when we first met in Chicago all those years ago. I'd read an awful lot in Europe and seen a lot, but I was no nearer than when I started to what I was looking for."

I wanted to ask him what that was, but had a feeling that he'd just laugh, shrug his shoulders and say it was a matter of no consequence.

"But why did you go as a deck hand?" I asked instead. "You had money."

"I wanted the experience. Whenever I've got waterlogged spiritually, when-ever I've absorbed all I can for the time, I've found it useful to do something of that sort. That winter, after Isabel and I broke off our engagement, I worked in a coal mine near Lens for six months."

It was then that he told me of those incidents that I have narrated in a previous chapter.

"Were you sore when Isabel threw you over?"

Before he answered he looked at me for some time with those strangely black eyes of his that seemed then to look inwards rather than out.

"Yes. I was very young. I'd made up my mind that we were going to marry. I'd made plans for the life that we were going to lead together. I expected it to be lovely." He laughed faintly. "But it takes two to make a marriage just as it takes two to make a quarrel. It had never occurred to me that the life I offered Isabel was a life that filled her with dismay. If I'd had any sense I'd never have suggested it. She was too young and ardent. I couldn't blame her. I couldn't yield."

It's just possible that the reader will remember that on his flight from the farm, after that grotesque encounter with the farmer's widowed daughter-in-law, he had gone to Bonn. I was anxious to get him to continue, but knew I must be careful not to ask more direct questions than I could help.

"I've never been to Bonn," I said. "When I was a boy I spent some time as a student at Heidelberg. It was, I think, the happiest time of my life."

"I liked Bonn. I spent a year there. I got a room in the house of the widow of one of the professors at the university who took in a couple of boarders. She and her two daughters, both of them middle-aged, did the cooking and the housework. I found my fellow boarder was a Frenchman and I was disappointed at first because I wanted to speak nothing but German; but he was an Alsatian and he spoke German, if not more fluently, with a better accent than he spoke French. He was dressed like a German pastor and I was surprised to find out after a few days that he was a Benedictine monk. He'd been granted leave of absence from his monastery to make researches at the university library. He was a very learned man, but he didn't look it any more than he looked like my idea of a monk. He was a tall, stout fellow, with sandy hair, prominent blue eyes and a red, round face. He was shy and reserved and didn't seem to want to have anything much to do with me, but he was very polite in a rather elaborate way and always took a civil part in the conversation at table; I only saw him then; as soon as we had finished dinner he went back to work at the library, and after supper, when I sat in the parlour improving my German with whichever of the two daughters wasn't washing up, he retired to his room.

"I was surprised when one afternoon, after I'd been there at least a month, he asked me if I'd care to take a walk with him. He said he could show me places in the neighbourhood that he didn't think I'd be likely to discover for myself. I'm a pretty good walker, but he could outwalk me any day. We must have covered a good fifteen miles on that first walk. He asked me what I was doing in Bonn and I said I'd come to learn German and get to know something about German literature. He talked very intelligently. He said he'd be glad to help me in any way he could. After that we went for walks two or three times a week. I discovered that he'd taught philosophy for some years. When I was in Paris I'd read a certain amount, Spinoza and Plato and Descartes, but I hadn't read any of the great German philosophers and I was only too glad to listen while he talked about them. One day, when we'd made an excursion across the Rhine and were sitting in a beer garden drinking a glass of beer, he asked me if I was a Protestant.

" 'I suppose so,' I said.

"He gave me a quick look and I thought I saw in his eyes the glimmer of a smile. He began to talk about Aeschylus; I'd been learning Greek, you know, and he knew the great tragedians as I could never hope to know them. It was inspiring to hear him. I wondered why he'd suddenly asked me that question. My guardian, Uncle Bob Nelson, was an agnostic, but he went to church regularly because his patients expected it of him and sent me to Sunday school for the same reason. Martha, our help, was a rigid Baptist and she used to frighten my childhood by telling me of the hell fire to which the sinner would be condemned to all eternity. She took a real delight in picturing to me the agonies that would be endured by the various people in the village whom for some reason or other she had had it in for.

"By winter I'd gotten to know Father Ensheim very well. I think he was rather a remarkable man. I never saw him vexed. He was good-natured and kindly, far more broad-minded than I would have expected, and wonderfully tolerant. His erudition was prodigious and he must have known how ignorant I was, but he used to talk to me as though I were as learned as he. He was very patient with me. He seemed to want nothing but to be of service to me. One day, I don't know why, I had an attack of lumbago and Frau Grabau, my landlady, insisted on putting me to bed with hot-water bottles. Father Ensheim, hearing I was laid up, came into my room to see me after supper. Except that I was in a good deal of pain I felt perfectly well. You know what bookish people are, they're inquisitive about books, and as I put down the book I was reading when he came in, he took it up and looked at the title. It was a book about Meister Eckhart that I'd found at a bookseller's in the town. He asked me why I was reading it, and I told him I'd been going through a certain amount of mystical literature and told him about Kosti and how he'd aroused my interest in the subject. He surveyed me with his prominent blue eyes and there was a look in them that I can only describe as amused tenderness. I had the feeling that he found me rather ridiculous, but felt so much loving-kindness towards me that he didn't like me any the less. Anyhow I've never much minded if people thought me a bit of a fool.

"'What are you looking for in these books?' he asked me.

"'If I knew that,' I answered, 'I'd at least be on the way to finding it.'

"'Do you remember my asking you if you were a Protestant? You said you supposed so. What did you mean by that?'

"'I was brought up as one,' I said.

"'Do you believe in God?' he asked.

"I don't like personal questions and my first impulse was to tell him that was no business of his. But there was so much goodness in his aspect that I felt it impossible to affront him. I didn't know what to say; I didn't want to answer yes and I didn't want to answer no. It may have been the pain I was suffering that enabled me to speak or it may have been something in him. Anyhow I told him about myself."

Larry hesitated for a moment and when he went on I knew he wasn't speaking to me but to the Benedictine monk. He had forgotten me. I don't know what there was in the time or the place that enabled him to speak, without my prompting, of what his natural reticence had so long concealed.

"Uncle Bob Nelson was very democratic and he sent me to the high school at Marvin. It was only because Louisa Bradley nagged him into it that when I was fourteen he let me go to St. Paul's. I wasn't very good at anything, either at work or games, but I fitted in all right. I think I was an entirely normal boy. I was crazy about aviation. Those were the early days of flying and Uncle Bob was as excited about it as I was; he knew some of the airmen and when I said I wanted to learn to fly he said he'd fix it for me. I was tall for my age and when I was sixteen I could easily pass for eighteen. Uncle Bob made me promise to keep it a secret, because he knew everyone would be down on him like a ton of bricks for letting me go, but as a matter of fact he helped me to get over to Canada and gave me a letter to someone he knew, and the result was that by the time I was seventeen I was flying in France.

"They were terrible gimcrack planes we flew in then and you practically took your life in your hands each time you went up. The heights we got to were absurd, judged by present standards, but we didn't know any better and thought it wonderful. I loved flying. I couldn't describe the feeling it gave me, I only knew I felt proud and happy. In the air, 'way up, I felt that I was part of something very great and very beautiful. I didn't know what it was all about, I only knew that I wasn't alone any more, by myself as I was, two thousand feet up, but that I belonged. I can't help it if it sounds silly. When I was flying above the clouds and they were like an enormous flock of sheep below me I felt that I was at home with infinitude."

Larry paused. He gazed at me from the caverns of his impenetrable eyes, but I did not know whether he saw me.

"I'd known that men had been killed by the hundred thousand, but I hadn't seen them killed. It didn't mean very much to me. Then I saw a dead man with my own eyes. The sight filled me with shame."

"Shame?" I exclaimed involuntarily.

"Shame, because that boy, he was only three or four years older than me, who'd had such energy and daring, who a moment before had had so much vitality, who'd been so good, was now just mangled flesh that looked as if it had never been alive."

I didn't say anything. I had seen dead men when I was a medical student and I had seen many more during the war. What had dismayed me was how trifling they looked. There was no dignity in them. Marionettes that the showman had thrown into the discard.

"I didn't sleep that night. I cried. I wasn't frightened for myself; I was indignant; it was the wickedness of it that broke me. The war came to an end and I went home. I'd always been keen on mechanics and if there was nothing doing in aviation, I'd intended to get into an automobile factory. I'd been wounded and had to take it easy for a while. Then they wanted me to go to work. I couldn't do the sort of work they wanted me to do. It seemed futile. I'd had a lot of time to think. I kept on asking myself what life was for. After all it was only by luck that I was alive; I wanted to make something of my life, but I didn't know what. I'd never thought much about God. I began to think about him now. I couldn't understand why there was evil in the world. I knew I was very ignorant; I didn't know anyone I could turn to and I wanted to learn, so I began to read at haphazard.

"When I told Father Ensheim all this he asked me: 'Then you've been reading for four years? Where have you got?'

" 'Nowhere,' I said.

"He looked at me with an air of such radiant benignity that I was confused. I didn't know what I'd done to arouse so much feeling in him. He softly drummed his fingers on the table as though he were turning a notion over in his mind.

" 'Our wise old Church,' he said then, 'has discovered that if you will act as if you believed belief will be granted to you; if you pray with doubt, but pray with sincerity, your doubt will be dispelled; if you will surrender yourself to the beauty of that liturgy the power of which over the human spirit has been proved by the experience of the ages, peace will descend upon you. I am returning to my monastery in a little while. Why don't you come and spend a few weeks with us? You can work in the fields with our lay brothers; you can read in our library. It will be an experience no less interesting than working in a coal mine or on a German farm.'

" 'Why do you suggest it?' I asked.

" 'I've been observing you for three months,' he said. 'Perhaps I know you better than you know yourself. The distance that separates you from faith is no greater than the thickness of a cigarette paper.'

"I didn't say anything to that. It gave me a funny sort of feeling, as though someone had got hold of my heartstrings and were giving them a tug. At last I said I'd think about it. He dropped the subject. For the rest of Father Ensheim's stay in Bonn we never spoke of anything connected with religion again, but as he was leaving he gave me the address of his monastery and told me if I made up my mind to come I had only to write him a line and he'd make arrangements. I missed him more than I expected. The year wore on and it was midsummer. I liked it well enough in Bonn. I read Goethe and Schiller and Heine. I read Hölderlin and Rilke. Still I wasn't getting anywhere. I thought a lot of what Father Ensheim had said and at last I decided to accept his offer.

"He met me at the station. The monastery was in Alsace and the country was pretty. Father Ensheim presented me to the abbot and then showed me to the cell that had been assigned to me. It had a narrow iron bed, a crucifix on the wall, and by way of furniture only the barest necessities. The dinner bell rang and I made my way to the refectory. It was a huge vaulted chamber. The abbot stood at the door with two monks, one of whom held a basin and the other a towel, and the abbot sprinkled a few drops of water on the hands of the guests by way of washing them and dried them with the towel one of the two monks handed him. There were three guests besides myself, two priests who were passing that way and had stopped off for dinner and an elderly, grouchy Frenchman who was making a retreat.

"The abbot and the two priors, senior and junior, sat at the head of the room, each at his separate table; the fathers along the two sides of the walls, while the novices, the lay brothers and the guests sat at tables in the middle. Grace was said and we ate. A novice took up his position near the refectory door and in a monotonous voice read from an edifying work. When we had finished grace was said again. The abbot, Father Ensheim, the guests and the monk in charge of them went into a small room where we had coffee and talked of casual things. Then I went back to my cell.

"I stayed there three months. I was very happy. The life exactly suited me. The library was good and I read a great deal. None of the fathers tried in any way to influence me, but they were glad to talk to me. I was deeply impressed by their learning, their piety and their unworldliness. You mustn't think it was an idle life they led. They were constantly occupied. They farmed their own land and worked it themselves and they were glad to have my help. I enjoyed the splendour of the services, but the one I liked best of all was Matins. It was at four in the morning. It was wonderfully moving to sit in the church with the night all around you while the monks, mysterious in their habits, their cowls drawn over their heads, sang with their strong male voices the plain song of the liturgy. There was something reassuring in the regularity of the daily round, and notwithstanding all the energy that was displayed, notwithstanding the activity of thought, you had an abiding sense of repose."

Larry smiled a trifle ruefully.

"Like Rolla, I've come too late into a world too old. I should have been born in the Middle Ages when faith was a matter of course; then my way would have been clear to me and I'd have sought to enter the order. I couldn't believe. I wanted to believe, but I couldn't believe in a God who wasn't better than the ordinary decent man. The monks told me that God had created the world for his glorification. That didn't seem to me a very worthy object. Did Beethoven create his symphonies for his glorification? I don't believe it. I believe he created them because the music in his soul demanded expression and then all he tried to do was to make them as perfect as he knew how.

"I used to listen to the monks repeating the Lord's Prayer; I wondered how they could continue to pray without misgiving to their heavenly father to give them their daily bread. Do children beseech their earthly father to give them sustenance? They expect him to do it, they neither feel gratitude to him for doing so nor need to, and we have only blame for a man who brings children into the world that he can't or won't provide for. It seemed to me that if an omnipotent creator was not prepared to provide his creatures with the necessities, material and spiritual, of existence he'd have done better not to create them."

"Dear Larry," I said, "I think it's just as well you weren't born in the Middle Ages. You'd undoubtedly have perished at the stake."

He smiled.

"You've had a great deal of success," he went on. "Do *you* want to be praised to your face?"

"It only embarrasses me."

"That's what I should have thought. I couldn't believe that God wanted it either. We didn't think much in the air corps of a fellow who wangled a cushy job out of his C.O. by buttering him up. It was hard for me to believe that God thought much of a man who tried to wangle salvation by fulsome flattery. I should have thought the worship most pleasing to him was to do your best according to your lights.

"But that wasn't the chief thing that bothered me: I couldn't reconcile myself with that preoccupation with sin that, so far as I could tell, was never entirely absent from the monks' thoughts. I'd known a lot of fellows in the air corps. Of course they got drunk when they got a chance, and had a girl whenever they could and used foul language; we had one or two bad hats: one fellow was arrested for passing rubber cheques and was sent to prison for six months; it wasn't altogether his fault; he'd never had any money before, and when he got more than he'd ever dreamt of having, it went to his head. I'd known bad men in Paris and when I got back to Chicago I knew more, but for the most part their badness was due to heredity, which they couldn't help, or to their environment, which they didn't choose: I'm not sure that society wasn't more responsible for their crimes than they were. If I'd been God I couldn't have brought myself to condemn one of them, not even the worst, to eternal damnation. Father Ensheim was broad-minded; he thought that hell was the deprivation of God's presence, but if that is such an intolerable punishment that it can justly be called hell, can one conceive that a good God can inflict it? After all, he created men, if he so created them that it was possible for them to sin, it was because he willed it. If I trained a dog to fly at the throat of any stranger who came into my back yard, it wouldn't be fair to beat him when he did so.

"If an all-good and all-powerful God created the world, why did he create evil? The monks said, so that man by conquering the wickedness in him, by resisting temptation, by accepting pain and sorrow and misfortune as the trials sent by God to purify him, might at long last be made worthy to receive his grace. It seemed to me like sending a fellow with a message to some place and just to make it harder for him you constructed a maze that he had to get through, then dug a moat that he had to swim and finally built a wall that he had to scale. I wasn't prepared to believe in an all-wise God who hadn't common sense. I didn't see why you shouldn't believe in a God who hadn't created the world, but had to make the best of the bad job he'd found, a being enormously better, wiser and greater than man, who strove with the evil he hadn't made and who might be hoped in the end to overcome it. But on the other hand I didn't see why you should.

"Those good fathers had no answers that satisfied either my head or my heart to the questions that perplexed me. My place was not with them. When I went to say good-bye to Father Ensheim he didn't ask me whether I had profited by the experience in the way he had been so sure I would. He looked at me with inexpressible kindness.

"'I'm afraid I've been a disappointment to you, Father,' I said.

"'No,' he answered. 'You are a deeply religious man who doesn't believe in God. God will seek you out. You'll come back. Whether here or elsewhere only God can tell.'

(*iv*)

"I settled down in Paris for the rest of the winter. I knew nothing of science, and I thought the time had come when I must acquire at least a nodding acquaintance with it. I read a lot. I don't know that I learnt much except that my ignorance was abysmal. But I knew that before. When the spring came I went to the country and stayed at a little inn on a river near one of those beautiful old French towns where life doesn't seem to have moved for two hundred years."

I guessed that this was the summer Larry had spent with Suzanne Rouvier, but I did not interrupt him.

"After that I went to Spain. I wanted to see Velasquez and El Greco. I wondered if art could point out the way to me that religion hadn't. I wandered about a bit and then came to Seville. I liked it and thought I'd spend the winter there."

I had myself been to Seville when I was twenty-three and I too had liked it. I liked its white, tortuous streets, its cathedral, and the wide-spreading plain of the Guadalquivir; but I liked also those Andalusian girls with their grace and their gaiety, with their dark shining eyes, the carnation in their hair stressing its blackness and by the contrast itself more vivid; I liked the rich colour of their skins and the inviting sensuality of their lips. Then indeed to be young was very heaven. When Larry went there he was only a little older than I had been and I could not but ask myself whether it was possible that he had remained indifferent to the lure of those enchanting creatures. He answered my unspoken question.

"I ran across a French painter I'd known in Paris, a fellow called Auguste Cottet who'd kept Suzanne Rouvier at one time. He'd come to Seville to paint and was living with a girl he'd picked up there. He asked me to go with them one evening to Eretania to listen to a *flamenco* singer and they brought along with them a friend of hers. She was the prettiest little thing you ever saw. She was only eighteen. She'd got into trouble with a boy and had had to leave her native village because she was going to have a baby. The boy was doing his military service. After she had the baby she put it out to nurse and got a job in the tobacco factory. I took her home with me. She was very gay and very sweet, and after a few days I asked her if she'd like to come and live with me. She said she would, so we took a couple of rooms in a *casa de huéspedes,* a bedroom and a sitting-room. I told her she could leave her job, but she didn't want to, and that suited me because it left me my days to myself. We had the use of the kitchen, so she used to make my breakfast for me before she went to work and then at midday she'd come back and cook the lunch and in the evening we'd dine at a restaurant and go to a movie or to some place to dance. She looked upon me as a lunatic because I had a rubber bath and insisted on having a cold sponge every morning. The baby was farmed out in a village a few miles from Seville and we used to go and see it on Sundays. She made no secret of the fact that she was living with me to make enough money to furnish the lodging in a tenement they were going to take when her boy friend was through with his military service. She was a dear little thing and I'm sure she's made her Paco a good wife. She was cheerful, good-tempered and affectionate. She looked upon what you delicately call sexual congress as a natural function of the body like any other. She took pleasure in it and she was happy to give pleasure. She was of course a little animal, but a very nice, attractive, domesticated animal.

"Then one evening she told me that she'd had a letter from Paco in Spanish Morocco, where he was doing his service, to say that he was to be released and would arrive in Cadiz in a couple of days. She packed her belongings next morning, slipped her money in her stocking and I took her to the station. She gave me a hearty kiss as I put her into the railway carriage, but she was too excited at the thought of seeing her lover again to have a thought for me and I'm pretty sure that before the train was well out of the station she'd forgotten my existence.

"I stayed on in Seville and in the fall I set out on the journey that landed me in India."

(v)

It was getting late. The crowd had thinned out and only a few tables were occupied. The people who had been sitting there because they had nothing else to do had gone home. Those who had been to a play or a picture and had come to have a drink or a bite to eat had left. Now and then latecomers straggled in. I saw a tall man, evidently an Englishman, come in with a young rough. He had the long, washed-out face with thinning wavy hair of the British intellectual and evidently suffered from the delusion common to many that when you are abroad no one you know at home can possibly recognize you. The young rough greedily ate a great plate of sandwiches while his companion watched him with amused benevolence. What an appetite! I saw one man whom I knew by sight because we went to the same barber's at Nice. He was stout, elderly and gray-haired, with a puffy red face and heavy pouches under his eyes. He was a Middle Western banker who had left his native city after the crash rather than face an investigation. I do not know whether he had committed any crime; if he had, he was perhaps too small fry to put the authorities to the trouble of extraditing him. He had a pompous manner and the false heartiness of a cheap politician, but his eyes were frightened and unhappy. He was never quite drunk and never quite sober. He was always with some harlot who was obviously getting all she could out of him, and he was now with two painted middle-aged women who treated him with a mockery they didn't trouble to conceal while he, only half understanding what they said, giggled fatuously. The gay life! I wondered if he wouldn't have done better to stay at home and take his medicine. One day women would have squeezed him dry and then there would be nothing left for him but the river or an overdose of veronal.

Between two and three there was a slight increase of custom and I supposed the night clubs were closing their doors. A bunch of young Americans strolled in, very drunk and noisy, but they didn't stay long. Not far from us two fat, sombre women, tightly fitted into mannish clothes, sat side by side, drinking whiskies and sodas in gloomy silence. A party in evening dress put in an appearance, what they call in French *gens du monde,* who had evidently been doing the rounds and now wanted a spot of supper to finish up with. They came and went. My curiosity had been excited by a little man, quietly dressed, who had been sitting there for an hour or more with a glass of beer in front of him reading the paper. He had a neat black beard and wore pince-nez. At last a woman came in and joined him. He gave her a nod devoid of friendliness and I conjectured that he was annoyed because she had kept him waiting. She was young, rather shabby, but heavily painted, and looked very tired. Presently I noticed her take something out of her bag and hand it to him. Money. He looked at it and his face darkened. He addressed her in words I could not hear, but from her manner I guessed they were abusive, and she seemed to be making excuses. Suddenly he leant over and gave her a resounding smack on the cheek. She gave a cry and began to sob. The manager, drawn by the disturbance, came up to see what was the matter. It looked as if he were telling them to get out if they couldn't behave. The girl turned on him and shrilly, so that one heard every word, told him in foul language to mind his own business.

"If he slapped my face it's because I deserved it," she cried.

Women! I had always thought that to live on a woman's immoral earnings you must be a strapping flashy fellow with sex appeal, ready with your knife or your gun; it was astonishing that such a puny creature, who might have been a lawyer's clerk from his appearance, could get a footing in such an overcrowded profession.

(*vi*)

The waiter who had served us was going off duty and to get his tip presented the bill. We paid and ordered coffee.

"Well?" I said.

I felt that Larry was in the mood to talk and I knew that I was in the mood to listen.

"Aren't I boring you?"

"No."

"Well, we got to Bombay. The ship was stopping there for three days to give the tourists a chance to see the sights and make excursions. On the third day I got the afternoon off and went ashore. I walked about for a while, looking at the crowd: what a conglomeration! Chinese, Mohammedans, Hindus, Tamils as black as your hat; and those great humped bullocks with their long horns that draw the carts! Then I went to Elephanta to see the caves. An Indian had joined us at Alexandria for the passage to Bombay and the tourists were rather sniffy about him. He was a fat little man with a brown round face and he wore a thick tweed suit of black and green check and a clerical collar. I was having a breath of air on deck one night and he came up and spoke to me. I didn't want to talk to anyone just then, I wanted to be alone; he asked me a lot of questions and I'm afraid I was rather short with him. Anyhow I told him I was a student working my passage back to America.

" 'You should stop off in India,' he said. 'The East has more to teach the West than the West conceives.'

" 'Oh yes?' I said.

" 'At any rate,' he went on, 'be sure you go and see the caves at Elephanta. You'll never regret it.' " Larry interrupted himself to ask me a question. "Have you ever been to India?"

"Never."

"Well, I was looking at the colossal image with its three heads which is the great sight at Elephanta and wondering what it was all about when I heard someone behind me say: 'I see you've taken my advice.' I turned round and it took me a minute to recognize who it was that had spoken to me. It was the little man in the heavy check suit and the clerical collar, but now he was wearing a long saffron robe, the robe, I knew later, of the Ramakrishna Swamis; and instead of the funny, spluttering little guy he'd been before, he was dignified and rather splendid. We both stared at the colossal bust.

" 'Brahma, the Creator,' he said. 'Vishnu the Preserver and Siva the Destroyer. The three manifestations of the Ultimate Reality.'

" 'I'm afraid I don't quite understand,' I said.

" 'I'm not surprised,' he answered, with a little smile on his lips and a twinkle in his eyes, as though he were gently mocking me. 'A God that can be understood is no God. Who can explain the Infinite in words?'

"He joined the palms of his hands together and with just the indication of a bow strolled on. I stayed looking at those three mysterious heads. Perhaps because I was in a receptive mood, I was strangely stirred. You know how sometimes you try to recall a name; it's on the tip of your tongue, but you just can't get it: that was the feeling I had then. When I came out of the caves I sat for a long while on the steps and looked at the sea. All I knew about Brahmanism were those verses of Emerson and I tried to remember them. It exasperated me that I couldn't and when I went back to Bombay I went into a bookshop to see if I could find a volume of poetry that had them in. They're in the *Oxford Book of English Verse*. D'you remember them?

> "*They reckon ill who leave me out;*
> *When me they fly, I am the wings;*
> *I am the doubter and the doubt,*
> *And I the hymn the Brahmin sings.*

"I had supper in a native eating-house and then, as I didn't have to be on board till ten, I went and walked on the Maidan and looked at the sea. I thought I'd never seen so many stars in the sky. The cool was delicious after the heat of the day. I found a public garden and sat on a bench. It was very dark there and silent white figures flitted to and fro. That wonderful day, with the brilliant sunshine, the coloured, noisy crowds, the smell of the East, acrid and aromatic, enchanted me; and like an object, a splash of colour that a painter puts in to pull his composition together, those three enormous heads of Brahma, Vishnu and Siva gave a mysterious significance to it all. My heart began to beat like mad because I'd suddenly become aware of an intense conviction that India had something to give me that I had to have. It seemed to me that a chance was offered to me and I must take it there and then or it would never be offered me again. I made up my mind quickly. I decided not to go back to the ship. I'd left nothing there but a few things in a grip. I walked slowly back to the native quarter and looked about for a hotel. I found one after a while and took a room. I had the clothes I stood up in, some loose cash, my passport and my letter of credit; I felt so free, I laughed out loud.

"The ship was sailing at eleven and just to be on the safe side I stayed in my room till then. I went down to the quay and watched her pull out. After that I went to the Ramakrishna Mission and routed out the Swami who'd spoken to me at Elephanta. I didn't know his name, but I explained that I wanted to see the Swami who'd just arrived from Alexandria. I told him I'd decided to stay in India and asked him what I ought to see. We had a long talk and at last he said he was going to Benares that night and asked me if I'd like to go with him. I jumped at it. We went third-class. The carriage was full of people eating and drinking and talking and the heat was terrific. I didn't get a wink of sleep and next morning I was pretty tired, but the Swami was as fresh as a daisy. I asked him how come and he said: 'By meditation on the formless one; I found rest in the Absolute.' I didn't know what to think, but I could see with my own eyes that he was as alert and wide awake as though he'd had a good night's sleep in a comfortable bed.

"When at last we got to Benares a young man of my own age came to meet my companion and the Swami asked him to find me a room. His name was Mahendra and he was a teacher at the university. He was a nice, kindly, intelligent fellow and he seemed to take as great a fancy to me as I took to him. That evening he took me out in a boat on the Ganges; it was a thrill for me, very beautiful with the city crowding down to the water's edge, and awe-inspiring; but next morning he had something better to show me, he fetched me at my hotel before dawn and took me out on the river again. I saw something I could never have believed possible, I saw thousands upon thousands of people come down to take their lustral bath and pray. I saw one tall gaunt fellow, with a mass of tangled hair and a great ragged beard, with nothing but a jock-strap to cover his nakedness, stand with his long arms outstretched, his head up, and in a loud voice pray to the rising sun. I can't tell you what an impression it made on me. I spent six months in Benares and I went over and over again on the Ganges at dawn to see that strange sight. I never got over the wonder of it. Those people believed not halfheartedly, not with reservation or uneasy doubt, but with every fibre of their being.

"Everyone was very kind to me. When they discovered I hadn't come to shoot tigers or to buy or sell anything, but only to learn, they did everything to help me. They were pleased that I should wish to learn Hindustani and found teachers for me. They lent me books. They were never tired of answering my questions. Do you know anything about Hinduism?"

"Very little," I answered.

"I should have thought it would interest you. Can there be anything more stupendous than the conception that the universe has no beginning and no end, but passes everlastingly from growth to equilibrium, from equilibrium to decline, from decline to dissolution, from dissolution to growth, and so on to all eternity?"

"And what do the Hindus think is the object of this endless recurrence?"

"I think they'd say that such is the nature of the Absolute. You see, they believe that the purpose of creation is to serve as a stage for the punishment or reward of the deeds of the soul's earlier existences."

"Which presupposes belief in the transmigration of souls."

"It's a belief held by two thirds of the human race."

"The fact that a great many people believe something is no guarantee of its truth."

"No, but at least it makes it worthy of consideration. Christianity absorbed so much of Neo-Platonism, it might very easily have absorbed that too, and in point of fact there was an early Christian sect that believed in it, but it was declared heretical. Except for that Christians would believe in it as confidently as they believe in the resurrection of Christ."

"Am I right in thinking that it means that the soul passes from body to body in an endless course of experience occasioned by the merit or demerit of previous works?"

"I think so."

"But you see, I'm not only my spirit but my body, and who can decide how much I, my individual self, am conditioned by the accident of my body? Would Byron have been Byron but for his club foot, or Dostoyevski Dostoyevski without his epilepsy?"

"The Indians wouldn't speak of an accident. They would answer that it's your actions in previous lives that have determined your soul to inhabit an imperfect body." Larry drummed idly on the table and, lost in thought, gazed into space. Then, with a faint smile on his lips and a reflective look in his eyes, he went on. "Has it occurred to you that transmigration is at once an explanation and a justification of the evil of the world? If the evils we suffer are the result of sins committed in our past lives we can bear them with resignation and hope that if in this one we strive towards virtue our future lives will be less afflicted. But it's easy enough to bear our own evils, all we need for that is a little manliness; what's intolerable is the evil, often so unmerited in appearance, that befalls others. If you can persuade yourself that it is the inevitable result of the past you may pity, you may do what you can to alleviate, and you should, but you have no cause to be indignant."

"But why didn't God create a world free from suffering and misery at the beginning when there was neither merit nor demerit in the individual to determine his actions?"

"The Hindus would say that there was no beginning. The individual soul, co-existent with the universe, has existed from all eternity and owes its nature to some prior existence."

"And does the belief in the transmigration of souls have a practical effect on the lives of those who believe it? After all, that is the test."

"I think it has. I can tell you of one man I knew personally on whose life it certainly had a very practical effect. The first two or three years I was in India I lived mostly in native hotels, but now and then someone asked me to stay with him and once or twice I lived in grandeur as the guest of a maharajah. Through one of my friends in Benares I got an invitation to stay in one of the smaller northern states. The capital was lovely; 'a rose-red city half as old as time.' I was recommended to the Minister of Finance. He'd had a European education and had been to Oxford. When you talked to him you got the impression of a progressive, intelligent and enlightened man; and he had the reputation of being an extremely efficient minister and a clever, astute politician. He wore European clothes and was very natty in appearance. He was rather a nice-looking fellow, a little on the stout side as Indians tend to become in middle age, with a close-cropped, neat moustache. He often asked me to go to his house. He had a large garden and we'd sit under the shade of great trees and talk. He had a wife and two grown-up children. You'd have taken him for just the ordinary, rather commonplace Anglicized Indian and I was staggered when I found out that in a year, when he reached the age of fifty, he was going to resign his profitable position, dispose of his property to his wife and children and go out into the world as a wandering mendicant. But the most surprising part was that his friends, and the maharajah, accepted it as a settled thing and looked upon it not as an extraordinary proceeding but as a very natural one.

"One day I said to him: 'You, who are so liberal, who know the world, who've read so much, science, philosophy, literature—do you in your heart of hearts believe in reincarnation?'

"His whole face changed. It became the face of a visionary.

"'My dear friend,' he said, 'if I didn't believe in it life would have no meaning for me.'"

"And do you believe in it, Larry?" I asked.

"That's a very difficult question to answer. I don't think it's possible for us Occidentals to believe in it as implicitly as these Orientals do. It's in their blood and bones. With us it can only be an opinion. I neither believe in it nor disbelieve in it."

He paused for a moment and with his face resting on his hand looked down at the table. Then he leant back.

"I should like to tell you of a very strange experience I had once. I was practicing meditation one night in my little room at the Ashrama as my Indian friends had taught me to do. I had lit a candle and was concentrating my attention on its flame, and after a time, through the flame, but quite clearly, I saw a long line of figures one behind the other. The foremost was an elderly lady in a lace cap with gray ringlets that hung down over her ears. She wore a tight black bodice and a black silk flounced skirt —the sort of clothes, I think, they wore in the seventies, and she was standing full face to me in a gracious, diffident attitude, her arms hanging straight down her sides with the palms towards me. The expression on her lined face was kindly, sweet and mild. Immediately behind her, but sideways so that I saw his profile, with a great hooked nose and thick lips, was a tall gaunt Jew in a yellow gabardine with a yellow skullcap on his thick dark hair. He had the studious look of a scholar and an air of grim and at the same time passionate austerity. Behind him, but facing me and as distinct as though there were no one between us, was a young man with a cheerful ruddy countenance, whom you couldn't have taken for anything but an Englishman of the sixteenth century. He stood firmly on his feet, his legs a little apart, and he had a bold, reckless, wanton look. He was dressed all in red, grandly as though it were a court dress, with broad-toed velvet shoes on his feet and a flat velvet cap on his head. Behind those three there was an endless chain of figures, like a queue outside a movie house, but they were dim and I couldn't see what they looked like. I was only aware of their vague shapes and of the movement that passed through them like wheat waving in a summer breeze. In a little while, I don't know whether it was in a minute, or five, or ten, they faded slowly into the darkness of the night and there was nothing but the steady flame of the candle."

Larry gave a little smile.

"Of course it may be that I'd fallen into a doze and dreamt. It may be that my concentration on that feeble flame had induced a sort of hypnotic condition in me and that those three figures that I saw as distinctly as I see you were recollections of pictures preserved in my subconscious. But it may be that they were myself in past lives. It may be that I was not so very long ago an old lady in New England and before that a Levantine Jew and somewhere back, soon after Sebastian Cabot had sailed from Bristol, a gallant at the Court of Henry Prince of Wales."

"What eventually happened to your friend of the rose-red city?"

"Two years later I was down south at a place called Madura. One night in the temple someone touched me on the arm. I looked around and saw a bearded man with long black hair, dressed in nothing but a loincloth, with the staff and the begging bowl of the holy man. It was not till he spoke that I recognized him. It was my friend. I was so astounded that I didn't know what to say. He asked me what I'd been doing and I told him; he asked me where I was going and I said to Travancore; he told me to go and see Shri Ganesha. 'He will give you what you're looking for,' he said. I asked him to tell me about him, but he smiled and said I'd find out all that was necessary for me to know when I saw him. I'd got over my surprise by then and asked him what he was doing in Madura. He said he was making a pilgrimage on foot to the holy places of India. I asked him how he ate and how he slept. He told me that when anyone offered him shelter he slept on the veranda, but otherwise under a tree or in the precincts of a temple; and as for food, if people offered him a meal he ate it and if they didn't he went without. I looked at him: 'You've lost weight,' I said. He laughed and answered that he felt all the better for it. Then he said good-bye to me—it was funny to hear that guy in a loincloth say, 'Well, so long, old chap'—and stepped into that part of the temple where I couldn't follow him.

"I stayed in Madura for some time. I think it's the only temple in India in which the white man can walk about freely so long as he doesn't enter the holy of holies. At nightfall it was packed with people. Men, women and children. The men, stripped to the waist, wore dhoties, and their foreheads, and often their chests and arms, were thickly smeared with the white ash of burnt cow dung. You saw them making obeisance at one shrine or another and sometimes lying full length on the ground, face downwards, in the ritual attitude of prostration. They prayed and recited litanies. They called to one another, greeted one another, quarrelled with one another, heatedly argued with one another. There was an ungodly row, and yet in some mysterious way God seemed to be near and living.

"You pass through long halls, the roof supported by sculptured columns, and at the foot of each column a religious mendicant is seated; each has in front of him a bowl for offerings or a small mat on which the faithful now and again throw a copper coin. Some are clad; some are almost naked. Some look at you vacantly as you pass; some are reading, silently or aloud, and appear unconscious of the streaming throng. I looked for my friend among them; I never saw him again. I suppose he proceeded on the journey to his goal."

"And what was that?"

"Liberation from the bondage of rebirth. According to the Vedantists the self, which they call the atman and we call the soul, is distinct from the body and its senses, distinct from the mind and its intelligence; it is not part of the Absolute, for the Absolute, being infinite, can have no parts, but the Absolute itself. It is uncreated; it has existed from eternity and when at last it has cast off the seven veils of ignorance will return to the infinitude from which it came. It is like a drop of water that has arisen from the sea and in a shower has fallen into a puddle, then drifts into a brook, finds its way into a stream, after that into a river, passing through mountain gorges and wide plains, winding this way and that, obstructed by rocks and fallen trees, till at last it reaches the boundless seas from which it rose."

"But that poor little drop of water, when it has once more become one with the sea, has surely lost its individuality."

Larry grinned.

"You want to taste sugar, you don't want to become sugar. What is individuality but the expression of our egoism? Until the soul has shed the last trace of that it cannot become one with the Absolute."

"You talk very familiarly of the Absolute, Larry, and it's an imposing word. What does it actually signify to you?"

"Reality. You can't say what it is; you can only say what it isn't. It's inexpressible. The Indians call it Brahman. It's nowhere and everywhere. All things imply and depend upon it. It's not a person, it's not a thing, it's not a cause. It has no qualities. It transcends permanence and change; whole and part, finite and infinite. It is eternal because its completeness and perfection are unrelated to time. It is truth and freedom."

"Golly," I said to myself, but to Larry: "But how can a purely intellectual conception be a solace to the suffering human race? Men have always wanted a personal God to whom they can turn in their distress for comfort and encouragement."

"It may be that at some far distant day greater insight will show them that they must look for comfort and encouragement in their own souls. I myself think that the need to worship is no more than the survival of an old remembrance of cruel gods that had to be propitiated. I believe that God is within me or nowhere. If that's so, whom or what am I to worship— myself? Men are on different levels of spiritual development, and so the imagination of India has evolved the manifestations of the Absolute that are known as Brahma, Vishnu, Siva and by a hundred other names. The Absolute is in Isvara, the creator and ruler of the world, and it is in the humble fetish before which the peasant in his sun-baked field places the offering of a flower. The multitudinous gods of India are but expedients to lead to the realization that the self is one with the supreme self."

I looked at Larry reflectively.

"I wonder just what it was that attracted you to this austere faith," I said.

"I think I can tell you. I've always felt that there was something pathetic in the founders of religion who made it a condition of salvation that you should believe in them. It's as though they needed your faith to have faith in themselves. They remind you of those old pagan gods who grew wan and faint if they were not sustained by the burnt offerings of the devout. Advaita doesn't ask you to take anything on trust; it asks only that you should have a passionate craving to know Reality; it states that you can experience God as surely as you can experience joy or pain. And there are men in India today—hundreds of them for all I know—who have the certitude that they have done so. I found something wonderfully satisfying in the notion that you can attain Reality by knowledge. In later ages the sages of India in recognition of human infirmity admitted that salvation may be won by the way of love and the way of works, but they never denied that the noblest way, though the hardest, is the way of knowledge, for its instrument is the most precious faculty of man, his reason."

(*vii*)

I must interrupt myself to make it plain that I am not attempting here to give anything in the nature of a description of the philosophical system known as Vedanta. I have not the knowledge to do so, but even if I had this would not be the proper place for it. Our conversation was a long one and Larry told me a great deal more than I have felt it possible to set down in what after all purports to be a novel. My concern is with Larry. I would not have touched on such an intricate subject at all except that it seemed to me that without at least some slight account of his speculations and the singular experiences that were perhaps occasioned by them I could not give plausibility to the line of conduct which he was led to adopt and with which I shall presently acquaint the reader. It irks me that I cannot hope with any words of mine to give an idea of the pleasantness of his voice that invested even his most casual utterances with persuasiveness or of the constant change in his expression, from grave to gently gay, from reflective to playful, that accompanied his thoughts like the ripple of a piano when the violins with a great sweep sing the several themes of a concerto. Although he spoke of serious things he spoke of them quite naturally, in a conversational tone, with a certain diffidence, perhaps, but without any more constraint than if he had been speaking of the weather and the crops. If I have given the impression that there was anything didactic in his manner the fault is mine. His modesty was as evident as his sincerity.

There was no more than a sprinkling of people in the café. The roisterers had long since departed. The sad creatures who make a business of love had gone to their sordid dwellings. Now and then a tired-looking man came in to have a glass of beer and a sandwich, or one, who seemed only half awake, for a cup of coffee. White-collar workers. One had been on a night shift and was going home to bed; the other, roused by the call of an alarm clock, was on his unwilling way to the long day's labour. Larry appeared as unconscious of the time as of the surroundings. I have found myself in the course of my life in many strange situations. More than once I have been within a hair's breadth of death. More than once I have touched hands with romance and known it. I have ridden a pony through Central Asia along the road that Marco Polo took to reach the fabulous lands of Cathay; I have drunk a glass of Russian tea in a prim parlour in Petrograd while a soft-spoken little man in a black coat and striped trousers told me how he had assassinated a grand duke; I have sat in a drawing-room in Westminster and listened to the serene geniality of a piano trio of Haydn's while the bombs were crashing without; but I do not think I have ever found myself in a stranger situation than when I sat on the red-plush seats of that garish restaurant for hour after hour while Larry talked of God and eternity, of the Absolute and the weary wheel of endless becoming.

(viii)

Larry had been silent for a few minutes, and unwilling to hurry him, I waited. Presently he gave me a friendly little smile as though he had suddenly once more become aware of me.

"When I got down to Travancore I found I needn't have asked for information about Shri Ganesha. Everyone knew of him. For many years he'd lived in a cave in the hills, but finally he'd been persuaded to move down to the plain where some charitable person had given him a plot of land and had built a little adobe house for him. It was a long way from Trivandrum, the capital, and it took me all day, first by train and then by bullock cart, to get to the Ashrama. I found a young man at the entrance of the compound and asked him if I could see the Yogi. I'd brought with me the basket of fruit which is the customary gift to offer. In a few minutes the young man came back and led me into a long hall with windows all around it. In one corner Shri Ganesha sat in the attitude of meditation on a raised dais covered with a tiger skin. 'I've been expecting you,' he said. I was surprised, but supposed my friend of Madura had told him something about me. But he shook his head when I mentioned his name. I presented my fruit and he told the young man to take it away. We were left alone and he looked at me without speaking. I don't know how long the silence lasted. It might have been for half an hour. I've told you what he looked like; what I haven't told you is the serenity that he irradiated, the goodness, the peace, the selflessness. I was hot and tired after my journey, but gradually I began to feel wonderfully rested. Before he'd said another word I knew that this was the man I'd been seeking."

"Did he speak English?" I interrupted.

"No. But, you know, I'm pretty quick at languages, I'd picked up enough Tamil to understand and make myself understood in the South. At last he spoke.

" 'What have you come here for?' he asked.

"I began to tell him how I'd come to India and how I'd passed my time for three years; how, on report of their wisdom and sanctity, I'd gone to one holy man after another and had found no one to give me what I looked for. He interrupted me.

" 'All that I know. There is no need to tell me. What have you come here for?'

" 'So that you may be my Guru,' I answered.

" 'Brahman alone is the Guru,' he said.

"He continued to look at me with a strange intensity and then suddenly his body became rigid, his eyes seemed to turn inwards and I saw that he'd fallen into the trance which the Indians call Samadhi and in which they hold the duality of subject and object vanishes and you become Knowledge Absolute. I was sitting cross-legged on the floor, in front of him, and my heart beat violently. After how long a time I don't know he sighed and I realized that he had recovered normal consciousness. He gave me a glance sweet with loving-kindness.

" 'Stay,' he said. 'They will show you where you may sleep.'

"I was given as a dwelling place the shack in which Shri Ganesha had lived when first he came down to the plain. The hall in which he now passed both day and night had been built when disciples gathered around him and more and more people, attracted by his fame, came to visit him. So that I mightn't be conspicuous I adopted the comfortable Indian dress and got so sunburnt that unless your attention was drawn to me you might have taken me for a native. I read a great deal. I meditated. I listened to Shri Ganesha when he chose to talk; he didn't talk very much, but he was always willing to answer questions and it was wonderfully inspiring to listen to him. It was like music in your ears. Though in his youth he had himself practiced very severe austerities he did not enjoin them on his disciples. He sought to wean them from the slavery of selfhood, passion and sense and told them that they could acquire liberation by tranquillity, restraint, renunciation, resignation, by steadfastness of mind and by an ardent desire for freedom. People used to come from the near-by town three or four miles away, where there was a famous temple to which great crowds flocked once a year for a festival; they came from Trivandrum and from far-off places to tell him their troubles, to ask his advice, to listen to his teaching; and all went away strengthened in soul and at peace with themselves. What he taught was very simple. He taught that we are all greater than we know and that wisdom is the means to freedom. He taught that it is not essential to salvation to retire from the world, but only to renounce the self. He taught that work done with no selfish interest purifies the mind and that duties are opportunities afforded to man to sink his separate self and become one with the universal self. But it wasn't his teaching that was so remarkable; it was the man himself, his benignity, his greatness of soul, his saintliness. His presence was a benediction. I was very happy with him. I felt that at last I had found what I wanted. The weeks, the months passed with unimaginable rapidity. I proposed to stay either till he died and he told us that he did not intend very much longer to inhabit his perishable body, or till I received illumination, that state when you have at last burst the bonds of ignorance, and know with a certainty there is no disputing that you and the Absolute are one."

"And then?"

"Then, if what they say is true, there is nothing more. The soul's course on earth is ended and it will return no more."

"And is Shri Ganesha dead?" I asked.

"Not so far as I know."

As he spoke he saw what was implied in my question and gave a light laugh. He went on after a moment's hesitation, but in such a manner as led me at first to suppose that he wished to avoid answering the second question that he well knew was on the tip of my tongue, the question, of course, whether he had received illumination.

"I didn't stay at the Ashrama continuously. I was lucky enough to make the acquaintance of a native forestry officer whose permanent residence was on the outskirts of a village at the foot of the mountains. He was a devotee of Shri Ganesha and when he could get away from his work came and spent two or three days with us. He was a nice fellow and we had long talks. He liked to practice his English on me. After I'd known him for some time, he told me that the forestry service had a bungalow up in the mountains and if ever I wanted to go there to be by myself he would give me the key. I went there now and then. It was a two-day journey; first you had to go by bus to the forestry officer's village, then you had to walk, but when you got there it was magnificent in its grandeur and its solitude. I took what I could in a knapsack on my back and hired a bearer to carry provisions for me, and I stayed till they were exhausted. It was only a log cabin with a cookhouse behind it and for furniture there was nothing but a trestle bed on which to put your sleeping mat, a table and a couple of chairs. It was cool up there and at times it was pleasant to light a fire at night. It gave me a wonderful thrill to know that there wasn't a living soul within twenty miles of me. At night I used often to hear the roar of a tiger or the racket of elephants as they crashed through the jungle. I used to take long walks in the forest. There was one place where I loved to sit because from it I saw the mountains spread before me and below, a lake to which at dusk the wild animals, deer, pig, bison, elephant, leopard came to drink.

"When I'd been at the Ashrama just two years I went up to my forest retreat for a reason that'll make you smile. I wanted to spend my birthday there. I got there the day before. Next morning I awoke before dawn and I thought I'd go and see the sunrise from the place I've just told you about. I knew the way blindfold. I sat down under a tree and waited. It was night still, but the stars were pale in the sky, and day was at hand. I had a strange feeling of suspense. So gradually that I was hardly aware of it light began to filter through the darkness, slowly, like a mysterious figure slinking between the trees. I felt my heart beating as though at the approach of danger. The sun rose."

Larry paused and a rueful smile played on his lips.

"I have no descriptive talent, I don't know the words to paint a picture, I can't tell you, so as to make you see it, how grand the sight was that was displayed before me as the day broke in its splendour. Those mountains with their deep jungle, the mist still entangled in the treetops, and the bottomless lake far below me. The sun caught the lake through a cleft in the heights and it shone like burnished steel. I was ravished with the beauty of the world. I'd never known such exaltation and such a transcendent joy. I had a strange sensation, a tingling that arose in my feet and travelled up to my head, and I felt as though I were suddenly released from my body and as pure spirit partook of a loveliness I had never conceived. I had a sense that a knowledge more than human possessed me, so that everything that had been confused was clear and everything that had perplexed me was explained. I was so happy that it was pain and I struggled to release myself from it, for I felt that if it lasted a moment longer I should die; and yet it was such rapture that I was ready to die rather than forego it. How can I tell you what I felt? No words can tell the ecstasy of my bliss. When I came to myself I was exhausted and trembling. I fell asleep.

"It was high noon when I woke. I walked back to the bungalow, and I was so light at heart that it seemed to me that I hardly touched the ground. I made myself some food, gosh, I was hungry, and I lit my pipe."

Larry lit his pipe now.

"I dared not think that this was illumination that I, Larry Darrell of Marvin, Illinois, had received when others striving for it for years, with austerity and mortification, still waited."

"What makes you think that it was anything more than a hypnotic condition induced by your state of mind combined with the solitude, the mystery of the dawn and the burnished steel of your lake?"

"Only my overwhelming sense of its reality. After all it was an experience of the same order as the mystics have had all over the world through all the centuries. Brahmins in India, Sufis in Persia, Catholics in Spain, Protestants in New England; and so far as they've been able to describe what defies description they've described it in similar terms. It's impossible to deny the fact of its occurrence; the only difficulty is to explain it. If I was for a moment one with the Absolute or if it was an inrush from the subconscious of an affinity with the universal spirit which is latent in all of us, I wouldn't know."

Larry paused for an instant and threw me a quizzical glance.

"By the way, can you touch your little finger with your thumb?" he asked.

"Of course," I said with a laugh, proving it with the appropriate action.

"Are you aware that that's something that only man and the primates can do? It's because the thumb is opposable to the other digits that the hand is the admirable instrument it is. Isn't it possible that the opposable thumb, doubtless in a rudimentary form, was developed in the remote ancestor of man and the gorilla in certain individuals, and was a characteristic that only became common to all after innumerable generations? Isn't it at least possible that these experiences of oneness with Reality that so many diverse persons have had point to a development in the human consciousness of a sixth sense which in the far, far future will be common to all men so that they may have as direct a perception of the Absolute as we have now of the objects of senses?"

"And how would you expect that to affect them?" I asked.

"I can as little tell you that as the first creature that found it could touch its little finger with its thumb could have told you what infinite consequences were entailed in that insignificant action. So far as I'm concerned I can only tell you that the intense sense of peace, joy and assurance that possessed me in that moment of rapture abides with me still and that the vision of the world's beauty is as fresh and vivid now as when first my eyes were dazzled by it."

"But Larry, surely your idea of the Absolute forces you to believe that the world and its beauty are merely an illusion—the fabric of Maya."

"It's a mistake to think that the Indians look upon the world as an illusion; they don't; all they claim is that it's not real in the same sense as the Absolute. Maya is only a speculation devised by those ardent thinkers to explain how the Infinite could produce the Finite. Samkara, the wisest of them all, decided that it was an insoluble mystery. You see, the difficulty is to explain why Brahman, which is Being, Bliss and Intelligence, which is unalterable, which ever is and forever maintains itself in rest, which lacks nothing and needs nothing and so knows neither change nor strife, which is perfect, should create the world. Well, if you ask that question the answer you're generally given is that the Absolute created the world in sport without reference to any purpose. But when you think of flood and famine, of earthquake and hurricane and all the ills that flesh is heir to, your moral sense is outraged at the idea that so much that is shocking can have been created in play. Shri Ganesha had too much kindliness of heart to believe that; he looked upon the world as the expression of the Absolute and as the overflow of its perfection. He taught that God cannot help creating and that the world is the manifestation of his nature. When I asked how, if the world was a manifestation of the nature of a perfect being, it should be so hateful that the only reasonable aim man can set before him is to liberate himself from its bondage, Shri Ganesha answered that the satisfactions of the world are transitory and that only the Infinite gives enduring happiness. But endless duration makes good no better, nor white any whiter. If the rose at noon has lost the beauty it had at dawn, the beauty it had then was real. Nothing in the world is permanent, and we're foolish when we ask anything to last, but surely we're still more foolish not to take delight in it while we have it. If change is of the essence of existence one would have thought it only sensible to make it the premise of our philosophy. We can none of us step into the same river twice, but the river flows on and the other river we step into is cool and refreshing too.

"The Aryans when they first came down into India saw that the world we know is but an appearance of the world we know not; but they welcomed it as gracious and beautiful; it was only centuries later, when the exhaustion of conquest, when the debilitating climate had sapped their vitality so that they became a prey to invading hordes, that they saw only evil in life and craved for liberation from its return. But why should we of the West, we Americans especially, be daunted by decay and death, hunger and thirst, sickness, old age, grief and delusion? The spirit of life is strong in us. I felt more alive then, as I sat in my log cabin smoking my pipe, than I had ever felt before. I felt in myself an energy that cried out to be expended. It was not for me to leave the world and retire to a cloister, but to live in the world and love the objects of the world, not indeed for themselves, but for the Infinite that is in them. If in those moments of ecstasy I had indeed been one with the Absolute, then, if what they said was true, nothing could touch me and when I had worked out the karma of my present life I should return no more. The thought filled me with dismay. I wanted to live again and again. I was willing to accept every sort of life, no matter what its pain and sorrow; I felt that only life after life, life after life could satisfy my eagerness, my vigour and my curiosity.

"Next morning I started down the mountain and the day after arrived at the Ashrama. Shri Ganesha was surprised to see me in European clothes. I'd put them on at the forestry officer's bungalow when I started uphill because it was colder there and hadn't thought to change them.

"'I've come to bid you farewell, master,' I said. 'I am going back to my own people.'

"He did not speak. He was sitting, as ever, cross-legged on the tiger skin on the dais. A stick of incense burnt in the brazier before it and scented the air with its faint fragrance. He was alone as he had been on the first day I saw him. He looked at me with an intensity so piercing that I had the impression he saw into the deepest recesses of my being. I know he knew what had happened.

"'It is well,' he said. 'You have been gone long enough.'

"I went down on my knees and he gave me his blessing. When I rose to my feet my eyes were filled with tears. He was a man of noble and saintly character. I shall always look upon it as a privilege to have known him. I said good-bye to the devotees. Some had been there for years; some had come after me. I left my few belongings and my books, thinking they might be useful to someone, and with my knapsack on my back, in the same old slacks and brown coat I had arrived in, a battered topee on my head, I trudged back to the town. A week later I boarded a ship at Bombay and landed at Marseilles."

Silence fell upon us as we pursued our separate reflections; but, tired though I was, there was one more point which I very much wanted to put to him, and it was I who finally spoke.

"Larry, old boy," I said, "this long quest of yours started with the problem of evil. It was the problem of evil that urged you on. You've said nothing all this time to indicate that you've reached even a tentative solution of it."

"It may be that there is no solution or it may be that I'm not clever enough to find it. Ramakrishna looked upon the world as the sport of God. 'It is like a game,' he said. 'In this game there are joy and sorrow, virtue and vice, knowledge and ignorance, good and evil. The game cannot continue if

sin and suffering are altogether eliminated from the creation.' I would reject that with all my strength. The best I can suggest is that when the Absolute manifested itself in the world evil was the natural correlation of good.
You could never have had the stupendous beauty of the Himalayas without
the unimaginable horror of a convulsion of the earth's crust. The Chinese
craftsman who makes a vase in what they call eggshell porcelain can give
it a lovely shape, ornament it with a beautiful design, stain it a ravishing
colour and give it a perfect glaze, but from its very nature he can't make it
anything but fragile. If you drop it on the floor it will break into a dozen
fragments. Isn't it possible in the same way that the values we cherish in
the world can only exist in combination with evil?"

"It's an ingenious notion, Larry. I don't think it's very satisfactory."

"Neither do I," he smiled. "The best to be said for it is that when you've
come to the conclusion that something is inevitable all you can do is to
make the best of it."

"What are your plans now?"

"I've got a job of work to finish here and then I shall go back to America."

"What to do?"

"Live."

"How?"

He answered very coolly, but with an impish twinkle in his eyes, for he
knew very well how little I expected such a reply.

"With calmness, forebearance, compassion, selflessness and continence."

"A tall order," I said. "And why continence? You're a young man; is it
wise to attempt to suppress what with hunger is the strongest instinct of
the human animal?"

"I am in the fortunate position that sexual indulgence with me has been a
pleasure rather than a need. I know by personal experience that in nothing
are the wise men of India more dead right than in their contention that
chastity intensely enhances the power of the spirit."

"I should have thought that wisdom consisted in striking a balance between the claims of the body and the claims of the spirit."

"That is just what the Indians maintain that we in the West haven't done.
They think that we with our countless inventions, with our factories and
machines and all they produce, have sought happiness in material things,
but that happiness rests not in them, but in spiritual things. And they think
the way we have chosen leads to destruction."

"And are you under the impression that America is a suitable place to
practice the particular virtues you mentioned?"

"I don't see why not. You Europeans know nothing about America. Because we amass large fortunes you think we care for nothing but money. We care nothing for it; the moment we have it we spend it, sometimes well and sometimes ill, but we spend it. Money is nothing to us; it's merely the symbol of success. We are the greatest idealists in the world; I happen to think that we've set our ideal on the wrong objects; I happen to think that the greatest ideal man can set before himself is self-perfection."

"It's a noble one, Larry."

"Isn't it worth while to try to live up to it?"

"But can you for a moment imagine that you, one man, can have any effect on such a restless, busy, lawless, intensely individualistic people as the people of America? You might as well try to hold back the waters of the Mississippi with your bare hands."

"I can try. It was one man who invented the wheel. It was one man who discovered the law of gravitation. Nothing that happens is without effect. If you throw a stone in a pond the universe isn't quite the same as it was before. It's a mistake to think that those holy men of India lead useless lives. They are a shining light in the darkness. They represent an ideal that is a refreshment to their fellows; the common run may never attain it, but they respect it and it affects their lives for good. When a man becomes pure and perfect the influence of his character spreads so that they who seek truth are naturally drawn to him. It may be that if I lead the life I've planned for myself it may affect others; the effect may be no greater than the ripple caused by a stone thrown in a pond, but one ripple causes another, and that one a third; it's just possible that a few people will see that my way of life offers happiness and peace, and that they in their turn will teach what they have learnt to others."

"I wonder if you have any idea what you're up against, Larry. You know, the Philistines have long since discarded the rack and stake as a means of suppressing the opinions they feared: they've discovered a much more deadly weapon of destruction—the wisecrack."

"I'm a pretty tough guy," smiled Larry.

"Well, all I can say is that it's damned lucky for you that you have a private income."

"It's been of great use to me. Except for that I shouldn't have been able to do all I've done. But my apprenticeship is over. From now on it can only be a burden to me. I shall rid myself of it."

"That would be very unwise. The only thing that may make the kind of life you propose possible is financial independence."

"On the contrary, financial independence would make the life I propose meaningless."

231

I couldn't restrain a gesture of impatience.

"It may be all very well for the wandering mendicant in India; he can sleep under a tree and the pious are willing enough to acquire merit by filling his begging bowl with food. But the American climate is far from suitable for sleeping out in the open, and though I don't pretend to know much about America, I do know that if there's one thing your countrymen are agreed upon it's that if you want to eat you must work. My poor Larry, you'd be sent to the workhouse as a vagrant before ever you got into your stride."

He laughed.

"I know. One must adapt oneself to one's environment and of course I'd work. When I get to America I shall try to get a job in a garage. I'm a pretty good mechanic and I don't think it ought to be difficult."

"Wouldn't you then be wasting energy that might be more usefully employed in other ways?"

"I like manual labour. Whenever I've got waterlogged with study I've taken a spell of it and found it spiritually invigorating. I remember reading a biography of Spinoza and thinking how silly the author was to look upon it as a terrible hardship that in order to earn his scanty living Spinoza had to polish lenses. I'm sure it was a help to his intellectual activity, if only because it diverted his attention for a while from the hard work of speculation. My mind is free when I'm washing a car or tinkering with a carburetor and when the job's done I have the pleasant sensation of having accomplished something. Naturally I wouldn't want to stay in a garage indefinitely. It's many years since I was in America and I must learn it afresh. I shall try to get work as a truck driver. In that way, in course of time, I should be able to travel from end to end of the country."

"You've forgotten perhaps the most important use of money. It saves time. Life is so short, and there's so much to do, one can't afford to waste a minute; and just think how much you waste, for instance, in walking from place to place instead of going by bus and in going by bus instead of by taxi."

Larry smiled.

"True enough and I hadn't thought of it, but I could cope with that difficulty by having my own taxi."

"What d'you mean by that?"

"Eventually I shall settle in New York, among other reasons because of its libraries; I can live on very little, I don't mind where I sleep and I'm quite satisfied with one meal a day; by the time I've seen all I want to of

America I should be able to have saved enough to buy a taxi and become a taxi driver."

"You ought to be shut up, Larry. You're as crazy as a loon."

"Not at all. I'm very sensible and very practical. As an owner-driver I would need to work only for as many hours as would provide for my board and lodging and for the depreciation on the car. The rest of my time I could devote to other work and if I wanted to go anywhere in a hurry I could always go in my taxi."

"But, Larry, a taxi is just as much of a possession as a government bond," I said, to tease him. "As an owner-driver you'd be a capitalist."

He laughed.

"No. My taxi would be merely the instrument of my labour. It would be an equivalent to the staff and the begging bowl of the wandering mendicant."

On this note of banter our conversation ended. I had noticed for some time that people were coming into the café with greater frequency. One man in evening dress sat down not far from us and ordered himself a substantial breakfast. He had the tired but satisfied mien of one who looks back upon a night of amorous dalliance with complacency. A few old gentlemen, early risers because old age needs little sleep, were drinking their *café au lait* with deliberation while through thick-lensed spectacles they read the morning paper. Younger men, some of them neat and spruce, others in threadbare coats, hurried in to devour a roll and swallow a cup of coffee on their way to a shop or an office. An old crone entered with a pile of newspapers and went around offering them for sale, vainly as far I could see, at the various tables. I looked out of the great plate-glass windows and saw that it was broad daylight. A minute or two later the electric light was turned off except at the rear of the huge restaurant. I looked at my watch. It was past seven o'clock.

"What about a spot of breakfast?" I said.

We had croissants, all crisp and hot from the bakers, and *café au lait*. I was tired and listless, and felt certain I looked like the wrath of God, but Larry seemed as fresh as ever. His eyes were shining, there wasn't a line on his smooth face, and he didn't look a day more than twenty-five. The coffee revived me.

"Will you allow me to give you a piece of advice, Larry? It's not anything I give often."

"It's not anything I often take," he answered with a grin.

"Will you think very carefully before you dispossess yourself of your very small fortune? When it's gone, it's gone forever. A time may come when

233

you'll want money very badly, either for yourself or for somebody else, and then you'll bitterly regret that you were such a fool."

There was a glint of mockery in his eyes as he answered, but it was devoid of malice.

"You attach more importance to money than I do."

"I can well believe it," I answered tartly. "You see, you've always had it and I haven't. It's given me what I value almost more than anything else in life—independence. You can't think what a comfort it's been to me to think that if I wanted to I could tell anyone in the world to go to hell."

"But I don't want to tell anyone in the world to go to hell, and if I did, the lack of a bank balance wouldn't prevent me. You see, money to you means freedom; to me it means bondage."

"You're an obstinate brute, Larry."

"I know. I can't help it. But in any case I have plenty of time to change my mind if I want to. I'm not going back to America till next spring. My friend Auguste Cottet, the painter, has lent me a cottage at Sanary and I'm going to spend the winter there."

Sanary is an unpretentious seaside resort on the Riviera, between Bandol and Toulon, and it is frequented by artists and writers who do not care for the garish mummery of St. Tropez.

"You'll like it if you don't mind its being as dull as ditchwater."

"I have work to do. I've collected a lot of material and I'm going to write a book."

"What's it about?"

"You'll see when it comes out," he smiled.

"If you'd like to send it to me when it's finished I think I can get it published for you."

"You needn't bother about that. I have some American friends who run a small press in Paris and I've arranged with them to print it for me."

"But you can't expect a book brought out like that to have any sale and you won't get any reviews."

"I don't care if it's reviewed and I don't expect it to sell. I'm only printing enough copies to send to my friends in India and the few people I know in France who might be interested in it. It's of no particular importance. I'm only writing it to get all that material out of the way, and I'm publishing it because I think you can only tell what a thing's like when you see it in print."

"I see the point of both those reasons."

We had finished our breakfast by now and I called the waiter for the bill. When it came I passed it over to Larry.

"If you're going to chuck your money down the drain you can damn well pay for my breakfast."

He laughed and paid. I was stiff from sitting for so long and as we walked out of the restaurant my sides ached. It was good to get into the fresh clean air of the autumn morning. The sky was blue, and the Avenue de Clichy, a sordid thoroughfare by night, had a mild jauntiness, like a painted, haggard woman walking with a girl's springy step, that was not displeasing. I signalled a passing taxi.

"Can I give you a lift?" I asked Larry.

"No. I shall walk down to the Seine and have a swim at one of the baths, then I must go to the Bibliothèque, I've got some research to do there."

We shook hands and I watched him cross the road with his long-legged, loose stride. I, being made of stuff less stern, stepped into the taxi and returned to my hotel. When I got into my sitting-room I noticed that it was after eight.

"This is a nice hour for an elderly gentleman to get home," I remarked disapprovingly to the nude lady (under a glass case) who had since the year 1813 been lying on the top of the clock in what I should have thought was a position of extreme discomfort.

She continued to look at her gilt bronze face in a gilt bronze mirror and all the clock said was: tick, tick. I turned on a hot bath. When I had lain in it till it was tepid, I dried myself, swallowed a sleeping tablet and taking to bed with me Valéry's *Le Cimitière Marin*, which happened to be on the night table, read till I fell asleep.

CHAPTER SEVEN

(i)

ONE MORNING, SIX MONTHS LATER, in April, I was busy writing in my study on the roof of my house at Cap Ferrat when a servant came up to say that the police of St. Jean (my neighbouring village) were below and wished to see me. I was vexed at being interrupted and could not imagine what they wanted. My conscience was at ease and I had already given my subscription to the Benevolent Fund. In return I had received a card, which I kept in my car so that if I was stopped for exceeding the speed limit or found parked on the wrong side of a street I could unostentatiously let it be seen while producing my driving licence and so escape with an indulgent caution. I thought it more likely then that one of my servants had been the victim of an anonymous denunciation, that being one of the amenities of French life, because her papers were not in order; but being on good terms with the local cops, whom I never allowed to leave my house without a glass of wine to speed them on their way, I anticipated no great difficulty. But they, for they worked in pairs, had come on a very different errand.

After we had shaken hands and inquired after our respective healths, the senior of the two, he was called a *brigadier* and had one of the most imposing moustaches I ever saw, fished a notebook out of his pocket. He turned over the pages with a dirty thumb.

"Does the name Sophie Macdonald say something to you?" he asked.

"I know a person of that name," I replied cautiously.

"We have just been in telephonic communication with the police station at Toulon and the chief inspector requests you to betake yourself there [*vous prie de vous y rendre*] without delay."

"For what reason?" I asked. "I am only slightly acquainted with Mrs. Macdonald."

I jumped to the conclusion that she had got into trouble, probably connected with opium, but I didn't see why I should be mixed up in it.

"That is not my affair. There is no doubt that you have had dealings with this woman. It appears that she has been missing from her lodging for five days and a body has been fished out of the harbour which the police have reason to believe is hers. They want you to identify it."

A cold shiver passed through me. I was not, however, too much surprised. It was likely enough that the life she led would incline her in a moment of depression to put an end to herself.

"But surely she can be identified by her clothes and her papers."

"She was found stark naked with her throat cut."

"Good God!" I was horrified. I reflected for an instant. For all I knew the police could force me to go and I thought I had better submit with good grace. "Very well. I will take the first train I can."

I looked up a timetable and found that I could catch one that would get me to Toulon between five and six. The *brigadier* said he would phone the chief inspector to that effect and asked me on my arrival to go straight to the police station. I did no more work that morning. I packed a few necessary things in a suitcase and after luncheon drove to the station.

On presenting myself at the headquarters of the Toulon police I was immediately ushered into the room of the chief inspector. He was sitting at a table, a heavy, swarthy man of saturnine appearance whom I took to be a Corsican. He threw me, perhaps from force of habit, a suspicious glance; but noticing the ribbon of the Legion of Honour, which I had taken the precaution to put in my buttonhole, with an unctuous smile asked me to sit down and proceeded to make profuse apologies for having been obliged to incommode a person of my distinction. Adopting a similar tone, I assured him that nothing could make me happier than to be of service to him. Then we got down to brass tacks and he resumed his brusque, rather insolent manner. Looking at some papers before him, he said:

"This is a dirty business. It appears that the woman Macdonald had a very bad reputation. She was a drunkard, a dope fiend and a nymphomaniac. She was in the habit of sleeping not only with sailors off the ships, but with the riffraff of the town. How does it happen that a person of your age and respectability should be acquainted with such a character?"

I was inclined to tell him that it was no business of his, but from a diligent perusal of hundreds of detective stories I have learnt that it is well to be civil with the police.

"I knew her very little. I met her when she was a girl in Chicago, where she afterwards married a man of good position. I met her again in Paris a year or so ago through friends of hers and mine."

I had been wondering how on earth he had ever connected me with Sophie, but now he pushed forward a book.

"This volume was found in her room. If you will kindly look at the dedication you will see that it hardly suggests that your acquaintance with her was as slight as you claim."

It was the translation of that novel of mine that she had seen in the bookshop window and asked me to write in. Under my own name I had written *"Mignonne, allons voir si la rose,"* because it was the first thing that occurred to me. It certainly looked a trifle familiar.

"If you are suggesting that I was her lover, you are mistaken."

"It would be no affair of mine," he replied, and then with a gleam in his eye: "And without wishing to say anything offensive to you I must add that from what I have heard of her proclivities I should not say you were her type. But it is evident that you would not address a perfect stranger as *mignonne*."

"That line, *monsieur le commissaire,* is the first of a celebrated poem by Ronsard, whose works I am certain are familiar to a man of your education and culture. I wrote it because I felt sure she knew the poem and would recall the following lines, which might suggest to her that the life she was leading was, to say the least of it, indiscreet."

"Evidently I have read Ronsard at school, but with all the work I have to do I confess that the lines you refer to have escaped my memory."

I repeated the first stanza and knowing very well he had never heard the poet's name till I mentioned it, had no fear that he would recall the last one which can hardly be taken as an incitement to virtue.

"She was apparently a woman of some education. We found a number of detective stories in her room and two or three volumes of poetry. There was a Baudelaire and a Rimbaud and an English volume by someone called Eliot. Is he known?"

"Widely."

"I have no time to read poetry. In any case I cannot read English. If he is a good poet it is a pity he doesn't write in French, so that educated people could read him."

The thought of my chief inspector reading *The Waste Land* filled me with pleasure. Suddenly he pushed a snapshot towards me.

"Have you any idea who that is?"

I immediately recognized Larry. He was in bathing trunks, and the photograph, a recent one, had been taken, I guessed, during the summer part of which he had spent with Isabel and Gray at Dinard. My first impulse was to say I did not know, for I wanted nothing less than to get Larry mixed up in this hateful business, but I reflected that if the police discovered his identity my assertion would look as if I thought there was something to hide.

"He's an American citizen called Laurence Darrell."

"It was the only photograph found among the woman's effects. What was the connection between them?"

"They both came from the same village near Chicago. They were childhood friends."

"But this photograph was taken not long ago, I suspect at a seaside resort in the North or on the West of France. It would be easy to discover the exact place. What is he, this individual?"

"An author," I said boldly. The inspector slightly raised his bushy eyebrows and I guessed that he did not attribute high morality to members of my calling. "Of independent means," I added to make it sound more respectable.

"Where is he now?"

Again I was tempted to say I didn't know, but again decided that it would only make things awkward if I did. The French police may have many faults, but their system enables them to find anyone they want to without delay.

"He's living at Sanary."

The inspector looked up and it was clear that he was interested.

"Where?"

I had remembered Larry telling me that Auguste Cottet had lent him his cottage and on my return at Christmas had written to ask him to come and stay with me for a while, but as I fully expected he had refused. I gave the inspector his address.

"I'll telephone to Sanary and have him brought here. It might be worth while to question him."

I could not but see that the inspector thought that here might be a suspect, but I was only inclined to laugh; I was convinced that Larry could easily prove that he had nothing to do with the affair. I was anxious to hear more about Sophie's lamentable end, but the inspector only told me in somewhat greater detail what I already knew. Two fishermen had brought the body in. It was a romantic exaggeration of my local policeman's that it was stark naked. The murderer had left girdle and brassière. If Sophie had been dressed in the same way as I had seen her he had had to strip her only of her slacks and her jersey. There was nothing to identify her and the police had inserted a description in the local paper. This had brought a woman to the station who kept a small rooming-house in a back street, what the French call a *maison de passe,* to which men could bring women or boys. She was an agent of the police, who liked to know who frequented her house and what for. Sophie had been turned out of the hotel on the quay at which she was living when I ran across her because her conduct was more scandalous than even the tolerant proprietor could put up with. She had offered to engage a room with a tiny sitting-room beside it in the house of the woman I have just mentioned. It was more profitable to let it two or three times a night for short periods, but Sophie offered to pay so handsomely that the woman consented to rent it to her by the month. She came to the police station now to state that her tenant had been absent for several days; she had not bothered, thinking she had gone for a trip to Marseilles or to Villefranche, where ships of the British fleet had lately arrived, an event that always attracted women, young and old, from all along the coast; but she had read the description of the deceased in the paper and thought it might apply to her tenant. She had been taken to see the body and after a trifling hesitation declared it was that of Sophie Macdonald.

"But if the body's been identified what do you want me for?"

"Madame Bellet is a woman of high honorability and excellent character," said the inspector, "but she may have reasons for identifying the dead woman that we do not know; and in any case I think she should be seen by someone who was more closely connected with her so that the fact may be confirmed."

"Do you think you have any chance of catching the murderer?"

The inspector shrugged his massive shoulders.

"Naturally we are making enquiries. We have questioned a number of persons at the bars she used to go to. She may have been killed out of jealousy by a sailor whose ship has already left the port or by a gangster for whatever money she had on her. It appears that she always had on her a sum that would seem large to a man of that sort. It may be that some people have a strong suspicion who the culprit is, but in the circles she moved in it is unlikely that anyone will speak unless it is to his advantage. Consorting with the bad characters she did, such an end as she has come to was only too probable."

I had nothing to say to this. The inspector asked me to come next morning at nine o'clock, by which time he would have seen "this gentleman of the photograph," after which a policeman would take us to the morgue to see the body.

"And how about burying her?"

"If after identifying the body you claim it as friends of the deceased and are prepared to undertake the expense of the funeral yourselves, you will receive the necessary authorization."

"I'm sure that Mr. Darrell and I would like to have it as soon as possible."

"I quite understand. It is a sad story and it is better that the poor woman should be laid to rest without delay. And that reminds me that I have here the card of an undertaker who will arrange the matter for you on reasonable terms and with despatch. I will just write a line on it so that he may give you every attention."

I was pretty sure he would get a rake-off on the amount paid, but I thanked him warmly, and when he had ushered me out with every expression of esteem I went forthwith to the address on the card. The undertaker was brisk and businesslike. I chose a coffin, neither the cheapest nor the most expensive, accepted his offer to get me two or three wreaths from a florist of his acquaintance—"to save monsieur a painful duty and out of respect for the dead," he said—and arranged for the hearse to be at the morgue at two o'clock next day. I could not but admire his efficiency when he told me that I need not trouble to see about a grave, he would do all that was necessary, and "Madame was a Protestant, I assume," furthermore he would, if I wished it, have a pastor waiting at the cemetery to read the burial service. But since I was a stranger and a foreigner he was sure that I would not take it amiss if he asked me to be good enough to give him a cheque in advance. He named a larger sum than I had expected, evidently expecting me to beat him down, and I discerned a look of surprise, perhaps even of disappointment, on his face when I took out my cheque book and wrote out a cheque without demur.

I took a room at a hotel and next morning returned to the police station. I was kept waiting for some time and then was bidden to go into the chief inspector's office. I found Larry, looking grave and distressed, sitting in the chair I had sat in the day before. The inspector greeted me with joviality. I might have been a long-lost brother.

"Well, *mon cher monsieur,* your friend has answered all the questions it was my duty to put him with the utmost frankness. I have no reason to disbelieve his statement that he had not seen this poor woman for eighteen months. He has accounted for his movements during the last week in a perfectly satisfactory manner as well as for the fact that his photograph was found in her room. It was taken at Dinard and he happened to have it in his pocket one day when he was lunching with her. I have had excellent reports of the young man from Sanary and I am besides, I say it without vanity, a good judge of character myself; I am convinced that he is incapable of committing a crime of this nature. I have ventured to offer him my sympathy that a friend of his childhood, brought up with all the advantages of a healthy family life, should have turned out so badly. But such is life. And now, my dear gentlemen, one of my men will accompany you to the morgue and when you have identified the body, your time is at your own disposal. Go and have a good lunch. I have a card here of the best restaurant in Toulon and I will just write a word on it which will assure you of the *patron's* best attention. A good bottle of wine will do you both good after this harrowing experience."

He was by now positively beaming with good will. We walked to the mortuary with a policeman. They were not doing a lively business in that establishment. There was a body on one slab only. We went up to it and the mortuary attendant uncovered the head. It was not a pleasant sight. The sea water had taken the curl out of the dyed silvery hair and it was plastered dankly on the skull. The face was horribly swollen and it was ghastly to look at, but there was no doubt that it was Sophie's. The attendant drew the covering sheet down to show us what we both would rather not have seen, the horrid gash across the throat that stretched from ear to ear.

We went back to the station. The chief inspector was busy, but we said what we had to say to an assistant; he left us and presently returned with the necessary papers. We took them to the undertaker.

"Now let's have a drink," I said.

Larry hadn't uttered a word since we left the police station to go to the mortuary except on our return there to declare that he identified the body as that of Sophie Macdonald. I led him down to the quay and we sat at the café at which I had sat with her. A strong mistral was blowing and the harbour, usually so smooth, was flecked with white foam. The fishing-boats were gently rocking. The sun shone brightly and, as always happens with a mistral, every object in sight had a peculiar sparkling sharpness as though you looked at it through glasses focussed with more than common accuracy. It gave an impression of a nerve-racking, throbbing vitality to what you saw. I drank a brandy and soda, but Larry never touched the one I had ordered for him. He sat in moody silence and I did not disturb him.

Presently I looked at my watch.

"We'd better go and have something to eat," I said. "We've got to be at the mortuary at two."

"I'm hungry, I didn't have any breakfast."

Having judged from his appearance that the chief inspector knew where the food was good, I took Larry to the restaurant he had told us of. Knowing that Larry seldom ate meat, I ordered an omelette and a grilled lobster and then, asking for the wine list, chose, again following the policeman's counsel, a vintage wine. When it appeared I poured out a glass for Larry.

"You damn well drink it," I said. "It may suggest a topic of conversation to you."

He obediently did as I bade him.

"Shri Ganesha used to say that silence also is conversation," he murmured.

"That suggests a jolly social gathering of intellectual dons at the University of Cambridge."

"I'm afraid you'll have to stand the racket of this funeral by yourself," he said. "I haven't any money."

"I'm quite prepared to do that," I answered. Then the implication of his remark hit me. "You haven't been and gone and done it really?"

He did not answer for a moment. I noticed the whimsical, teasing glint in his eyes.

"You haven't got rid of your money?"

"Every cent except what I need to last me till my ship comes in."

"What ship?"

"The man who has the next cottage to mine at Sanary is the Marseilles agent of a line of freighters that run from the Near East to New York. They've cabled him from Alexandria that they've had to put a couple of men off there sick from a ship that's coming on to Marseilles and asked him to get two more to take their place. He's a buddy of mine and he's promised to get me on. I'm giving him my old Citroën as a parting present. When I step on board I shall have nothing but the clothes I stand up in and a few things in a grip."

"Well, it's your own money. You're free, white and twenty-one."

"Free is the right word. I've never been happier or felt more independent in my life. When I get to New York I shall have my wages and they'll carry me on till I can get a job."

"What about your book?"

"Oh, it's finished and printed. I made a list of people I wanted it sent to and you ought to get a copy in a day or two."

"Thank you."

There was not much more to say and we finished our meal in amiable silence. I ordered coffee. Larry lit a pipe and I a cigar. I looked at him thoughtfully. He felt my eyes upon him and threw me a glance; his own were lit with an impish twinkle.

"If you feel like telling me I'm a damned fool, don't hesitate. I wouldn't in the least mind."

"No, I don't particularly feel like that. I was only wondering if your life wouldn't have fallen into a more perfect pattern if you'd married and had children like everybody else."

He smiled. I must have remarked twenty times on the beauty of his smile, it was so cosy, trustful and sweet, it reflected the candour, the truthfulness of his charming nature, but I must do so once again, for now, besides all that, there was in it something rueful and tender.

"It's too late for that now. The only woman I've met whom I could have married was poor Sophie."

I looked at him with amazement.

"Can you say that after all that's happened?"

"She had a lovely soul, fervid, aspiring and generous. Her ideals were greathearted. There was even at the end a tragic nobility in the way she sought destruction."

I was silent. I did not know what to make of these strange assertions.

"Why didn't you marry her then?" I asked.

"She was a child. To tell you the truth, it never occurred to me when I

243

used to go over to her grandfather's and we read poetry together under the elm tree that there was in that skinny brat the seed of spiritual beauty."

I could not but think it surprising that at this juncture he made no mention of Isabel. He could not have forgotten that he had been engaged to her and I could only suppose that he regarded the episode as a foolishness without consequence of two young things not old enough to know their own minds. I was ready to believe that the suspicion had never so much as fugitively crossed his mind that ever since she had been eating her heart out for him.

It was time for us to go. We walked to the square where Larry had left his car, very shabby now, and drove to the mortuary. The undertaker was as good as his word. The businesslike efficiency with which everything was accomplished, under that garish sky, with the violent wind bending the cypresses of the cemetery, added a last note of horror to the proceedings. When it was all over the undertaker shook hands with us cordially.

"Well, gentlemen, I hope you are satisfied. It went very well."

"Very well," I said.

"Monsieur will not forget that I am always at his disposition if he has need of my services. Distance is no object."

I thanked him. When we came to the gate of the cemetery Larry asked me if there was anything further I wanted him for.

"Nothing."

"I'd like to get back to Sanary as soon as possible."

"Drop me at my hotel, will you?"

We spoke never a word as we drove. When we arrived I got out. We shook hands and he went off. I paid my bill, got my bag and took a taxi to the station. I too wanted to get away.

(iii)

A few days later I started for England. My intention had been to go straight through, but after what had happened I particularly wanted to see Isabel and so decided to stop in Paris for twenty-four hours. I wired to her to ask if I could come in late in the afternoon and stay to dinner; when I reached my hotel I found a note from her to say that she and Gray were dining out, but that she would be very glad to see me if I would come not before half past five as she had a fitting.

It was chilly and raining off and on quite heavily, so that I presumed Gray would not have gone to Mortefontaine to play golf. This did not suit me very well, since I wanted to see Isabel alone, but when I arrived at the

244

apartment the first thing she said was that Gray was at the Travellers playing bridge.

"I told him not to be too late if he wanted to see you, but we're not dining till nine, which means we needn't get there before nine-thirty, so we've got plenty of time for a good talk. I've got all sorts of things to tell you."

They had sublet the apartment and the sale of Elliott's collection was to take place in a fortnight. They wanted to attend it and were moving into the Ritz. Then they were sailing. Isabel was selling everything except the modern pictures that Elliott had had in his house at Antibes. Though she didn't much care for them she thought quite rightly that they would be a prestige item in their future home.

"It's a pity poor Uncle Elliott wasn't more advanced. Picasso, Matisse and Rouault, you know. I suppose his pictures are good in their way, but I'm afraid they'll seem rather old-fashioned."

"I wouldn't bother about that if I were you. Other painters will come along in a few years and Picasso and Matisse won't seem any more up to date than your Impressionists."

Gray was in the process of concluding his negotiations and with the capital provided by Isabel was to enter a flourishing business as vice-president. It was connected with oil and they were to live at Dallas.

"The first thing we shall have to do is to find a suitable house. I want a nice garden so that Gray can have somewhere to potter about when he comes home from work and I must have a really large living-room so that I can entertain."

"I wonder you don't take Elliott's furniture over with you."

"I don't think it would be very suitable. I shall make it all modern, with perhaps just a little touch of Mexican here and there to give it a note. As soon as I get to New York I'll find out who is the decorator everyone's going to now."

Antoine, the manservant, brought in a tray with an array of bottles and Isabel, always tactful, knowing that nine men out of ten are convinced they can mix a better cocktail than any woman (and they're right), asked me to shake a couple. I poured out the gin and the Noilly-Prat and added the dash of absinthe that transforms a dry Martini from a nondescript drink to one for which the gods of Olympus would undoubtedly have abandoned their home-brewed nectar, a beverage that I have always thought must have been rather like Coca-Cola. I noticed a book on the table as I handed Isabel her glass.

"Hulloa," I said. "Here's Larry's book."

"Yes, it came this morning, but I've been so busy, I had a thousand things to do before lunch and I was lunching out and I was at Molyneux's this afternoon. I don't know when I shall have a moment to get down to it."

I thought with melancholy how an author spends months writing a book, and maybe puts his heart's blood into it, and then it lies about unread till the reader has nothing else in the world to do. It was a volume of three hundred pages nicely printed and neatly bound.

"I suppose you know Larry has been in Sanary all the winter. Did you see him by any chance?"

"Yes, we were at Toulon together only the other day."

"Were you? What were you doing there?"

"Burying Sophie."

"She's not dead?" cried Isabel.

"If she hadn't been we'd have had no plausible reason to bury her."

"That's not funny." She paused for a second. "I'm not going to pretend I'm sorry. A combination of drink and dope, I suppose."

"No, she had her throat cut and was thrown into the sea stark naked." Like the *brigadier* at St. Jean I found myself impelled a trifle to exaggerate her undress.

"How horrible! Poor thing. Of course leading the life she did she was bound to come to a bad end."

"That's what the *commissaire de police* at Toulon said."

"Do they know who did it?"

"No, but I do. I think you killed her."

She gave me a stare of amazement.

"What *are* you talking about?" Then with the ghost of a chuckle: "Guess again; I have a cast-iron alibi."

"I ran across her at Toulon last summer. I had a long talk with her."

"Was she sober?"

"Sufficiently. She told me how it happened that she'd disappeared so unaccountably just a few days before she was going to be married to Larry."

I noticed Isabel's face stiffen. I proceeded to tell her exactly what Sophie had told me. She listened warily.

"I've thought of her story a good deal since then and the more I've thought about it the more convinced I am that there's something fishy about it. I've lunched here twenty times and you never have liqueurs for luncheon. You'd been lunching alone. Why should there have been a bottle of zubrovka on the tray with the coffee cup?"

"Uncle Elliott had just sent it to me. I wanted to see if I liked it as much as when I'd had it at the Ritz."

"Yes, I remember how you raved about it then. I was surprised, as you never drink liqueurs anyway; you're much too careful of your figure for that. I had at the time an impression that you were trying to tantalize Sophie. I thought it was just malice."

"Thank you."

"On the whole you're very good at keeping appointments. Why should you have gone out when you were expecting Sophie for something so important to her and interesting to you as a fitting of her wedding dress?"

"She told you that herself. I wasn't happy about Joan's teeth. Our dentist is very busy and I just had to take the time he could give me."

"When one goes to a dentist one makes the next appointment before leaving."

"I know. But he called me up in the morning and said he had to break it, but could give me three o'clock that afternoon instead, so of course I jumped at it."

"Couldn't the governess have taken Joan?"

"She was scared, poor darling, I felt she'd be happier if I went with her."

"And when you came back and found the bottle of zubrovka three parts empty and Sophie gone, weren't you rather surprised?"

"I thought she'd got tired of waiting and gone on to Molyneux's by herself. I couldn't make it out when I went there and they told me she hadn't been."

"And the zubrovka?"

"Well, I did notice that a good deal had been drunk. I thought Antoine had drunk it and I very nearly spoke to him about it, but Uncle Elliott was paying for him and he was a friend of Joseph's, so I thought I'd better ignore it. He's a very good servant and if he takes a little nip now and then who am I to blame him?"

"What a liar you are, Isabel."

"Don't you believe me?"

"Not for a moment."

Isabel got up and walked over to the chimney piece. There was a wood fire and it was pleasant on that dreary day. She stood with one elbow on the mantle shelf in a graceful attitude which it was one of her most charming gifts to be able to assume without any appearance of intention. Like most French women of distinction she dressed in black in the daytime, which peculiarly suited her rich colouring, and on this occasion she wore a dress the expensive simplicity of which displayed to advantage her slender figure. She puffed at her cigarette for a minute.

"There's no reason why I shouldn't be perfectly frank with you. It was most unfortunate that I had to go out and of course Antoine should never have left the liqueur and the coffee things in the room. They ought to have been taken away when I went out. When I came back and saw the bottle was nearly empty of course I knew what had happened, and when Sophie disappeared I guessed she'd gone off on a bat. I didn't say anything about it because I thought it would only distress Larry, and he was worried enough as it was."

"Are you sure the bottle wasn't left there on your explicit instructions?"

"Quite."

"I don't believe you."

"Don't then." She flung the cigarette viciously into the fire. Her eyes were dark with anger. "All right, if you want the truth you can have it and to hell with you. I did it and I'd do it again. I told you I'd stick at nothing to prevent her from marrying Larry. You wouldn't do a thing, either you or Gray. You just shrugged your shoulders and said it was a terrible mistake. You didn't care a damn. I did."

"If you'd left her alone she'd be alive now."

"Married to Larry and he'd be utterly miserable. He thought he'd make a new woman of her. What fools men are! I knew that sooner or later she'd break down. It stuck out a mile. You saw yourself when we were all lunching together at the Ritz how jittery she was. I noticed you looking at her when she was drinking her coffee; her hand was shaking so, she was afraid to take the cup with one hand, she had to put both her hands to it to get it up to her mouth. I noticed her watching the wine when the waiter filled our glasses; she followed the bottle with those horrible washed-out eyes of hers like a snake following the fluttering of a new-fledged chick and I knew she'd give her soul for a drink."

Isabel faced me now, her eyes flashing with passion, and her voice was harsh. She couldn't get the words out quickly enough.

"The idea came to me when Uncle Elliott made all that fuss about that damned Polish liqueur. I thought it beastly, but I pretended it was the most wonderful stuff I'd ever tasted. I was certain that if she got a chance she'd never have the strength to resist. That's why I took her to the dress show. That's why I offered to make her a present of her wedding dress. That day, when she was going to have the last fitting, I told Antoine I'd have the zubrovka after lunch and then I told him I was expecting a lady and to ask her to wait and offer her some coffee and to leave the liqueur in case she fancied a glass. I did take Joan to the dentist's, but of course we hadn't an appointment and he couldn't see us, so I took her to a newsreel. I'd made up my mind that if I found Sophie hadn't touched the stuff I'd make the best of things and try to be friends with her. That's true, I swear it. But when I got home and saw the bottle I knew I'd been right. She'd gone and I'd have bet any money in the world she'd gone for good."

Isabel was actually panting when she finished.

"That's more or less what I imagined had happened," I said. "You see, I was right; you cut her throat as surely as if you'd drawn the knife across it with your own hands."

"She was bad, bad, bad. I'm glad she's dead." She threw herself into a chair. "Give me a cocktail, damn you."

I went over and mixed another.

"You are a mean devil," she said as she took it from me. Then she allowed herself to smile. Her smile was like a child's that knows it's been naughty, but thinks it can wheedle you by its ingenuous charm not to be cross. "You won't tell Larry, will you?"

"I wouldn't dream of it."

"Cross your heart? Men are so untrustworthy."

"I promise you I won't. But even if I wanted to, I shouldn't have an opportunity as I don't suppose I shall ever see him again in my life."

She sat bolt upright.

"What *do* you mean?"

"At this moment he's on a freighter, either as a deck hand or a stoker, on his way to New York."

"You don't mean that? What a strange creature he is! He was up here a few weeks ago for something he had to look up at the public library in connection with his book, but he never said a word about going to America. I'm glad; that means we shall see him."

"I doubt it. His America will be as remote from your America as the Gobi desert."

Then I told her what he had done and what he intended to do. She listened to me open-mouthed. Consternation was written on her face. She interrupted me now and then with an interjection: "He's crazy. He's crazy." When I had finished she hung her head and I saw two tears trickle down her cheeks.

"Now I really have lost him."

She turned away from me and, leaning her face against the back of the chair, wept. Her lovely face was twisted with the grief she did not care to hide. There was nothing I could do. I didn't know what vain, conflicting hopes she had cherished that my tidings had finally shattered. I had a vague notion that to see him occasionally, at least to know that he was part of her world, had been a bond of union, however tenuous, that his action had finally severed so that she knew herself forever bereft. I wondered what unavailing regret afflicted her. I thought it would do her good to cry. I picked up Larry's book and looked at the table of contents. My copy had not arrived when I left the Riviera and I could not now hope to get it for several days. It was not in the least the sort of thing I expected. It was a collection of essays of about the same length as those in Lytton Strachey's *Eminent Victorians,* upon a number of famous persons. The choice he had made puzzled me. There was one on Sulla, the Roman dictator who, having achieved absolute power, resigned it to return to private life; there was one on Akbar, the Mogul conqueror who won an empire; there was one on Rubens, there was one on Goethe and there was one on the Lord Chesterfield of the Letters. It was obvious that each of the essays had needed a tremendous amount of reading and I was no longer surprised that it had taken Larry so long to produce this book, but I could not see why he had thought it worth while to give it so much time or why he had chosen those particular men to study. Then it occurred to me that every one of them in his own way had made a supreme success of life and I guessed that this was what had interested Larry. He was curious to see what in the end it amounted to.

I skimmed a page to see how he wrote. His style was scholarly, but lucid and easy. There was nothing in it of the pretentiousness or the pedantry that too often characterises the writing of the amateur. One could tell that he had frequented the best authors as assiduously as Elliott Templeton frequented the nobility and gentry. I was interrupted by a sigh from Isabel. She sat up and finished with a grimace the cocktail which was now lukewarm.

"If I don't stop crying my eyes'll be terrible and we're going out to dinner tonight." She took a mirror out of her bag and looked at herself anxiously. "Yes, half an hour with an ice bag over my eyes, that's what I want." She powdered her face and reddened her lips. Then she looked at me reflectively. "Do you think any the worse of me for what I did?"

"Would you care?"

"Strange as it may seem to you, I would. I want you to think well of me." I grinned.

"My dear, I'm a very immoral person," I answered. "When I'm really fond of anyone, though I deplore his wrongdoing it doesn't make me less fond of him. You're not a bad woman in your way and you have every grace and every charm. I don't enjoy your beauty any the less because I know how much it owes to the happy combination of perfect taste and ruthless determination. You only lack one thing to make you completely enchanting."

She smiled and waited.

"Tenderness."

The smile died on her lips and she gave me a glance that was totally lacking in amenity, but before she could collect herself to reply Gray lumbered into the room. In the three years he had been in Paris Gray had put on a good many pounds, his face had grown redder and his hair was thinning rapidly, but he was in rude health and in high spirits. He was unaffectedly pleased to see me. Gray's conversation was composed of clichés. However shopworn, he uttered them with an obvious conviction that he was the first person to think of them. He never went to bed, but hit the hay, where he slept the sleep of the just; if it rained, it rained to beat the band and to the very end Paris to him was Gay Paree. But he was so kindly, so unselfish, so upright, so reliable, so unassuming that it was impossible not to like him. I had a real affection for him. He was excited now over their approaching departure.

"Gosh, it'll be great to get into harness again," he said. "I'm feeling my oats already."

"Is it all settled then?"

"I haven't signed on the dotted line yet, but it's on ice. The fella I'm going in with was a roommate of mine at college, and he's a good scout, and I'm dead sure he wouldn't hand me a lemon. But as soon as we get to New York I'll fly down to Texas to give the outfit the once-over, and you bet I'll keep my eyes peeled for a nigger in the woodpile before I cough up any of Isabel's dough."

"Gray's a very good businessman, you know," she said.

"I wasn't raised in a barn," he smiled.

He went on to tell me at somewhat excessive length about the business he was entering, but I understand little of such matters and the only concrete fact I gathered was that he stood a good chance of making a lot of money. He grew so interested in what he was saying that presently he turned to Isabel and said:

"Look here, why shouldn't we cut this lousy party and us three go and have a slap-up dinner at the Tour d'Argent by ourselves?"

"Oh, darling, we can't do that. They're giving the party for us."

"Anyhow I couldn't come now," I interrupted. "When I heard you were fixed up this evening I called up Suzanne Rouvier and arranged to take her out."

"Who's Suzanne Rouvier?" asked Isabel.

"Oh, one of Larry's gals," I said to tease her.

"I always suspected Larry had a little floozie tucked away somewhere," said Gray, with a fat chuckle.

"Nonsense," snapped Isabel. "I know all about Larry's sex life. There isn't any."

"Well, let's have one more drink before we part," said Gray.

We had it and then I said good-bye to them. They came into the hall with me and while I was putting on my coat Isabel slipped her arm through Gray's and, nestling up to him, looked into his eyes with an expression that imitated very well the tenderness I had accused her of lacking.

"Tell me, Gray—frankly—do you think I'm hard-boiled?"

"No, darling, far from it. Why, has anybody been saying you were?"

"No."

She turned her head away so that he shouldn't see, and in a manner that Elliott would certainly have thought very unladylike put out her tongue at me.

"It's not the same thing," I murmured as I stepped out of the door and closed it behind me.

(iv)

When I passed through Paris again the Maturins had gone and other people lived in Elliott's apartment. I missed Isabel. She was good to look at and easy to talk to. She was quick on the uptake and bore no malice. I have never seen her since. I am a poor and dilatory correspondent and Isabel was no letter writer. If she could not communicate with you by telephone or telegram she did not communicate with you. I had a Christmas card from her that Christmas with a pretty picture on it of a house with a Colonial portico surrounded by live oaks, which I took to be the house on the plantation that they had been unable to sell when they wanted the money and which now they were probably willing to keep. The postmark showed that it had been posted at Dallas, so I concluded that the deal had gone through satisfactorily and they were settled there.

I have never been to Dallas, but I suppose that, like other American cities I know, it has a residential district within easy motoring distance of the business section and the country club where the affluent have fine houses in large gardens with a handsome view of hill or dale from the living-room windows. In such a district and in such a house, furnished from cellar to attic in the latest mode by the most fashionable decorator in New York, Isabel certainly dwells. I can only hope that her Renoir, her flower piece by Manet, her landscape by Monet and her Gauguin do not look too dated. The dining-room is doubtless of a convenient size for the women's luncheons which she gives at frequent intervals and at which the wine is good and the food superlative. Isabel learnt a great deal in Paris. She would not have settled on the house unless she had seen at a glance that the living-room would do very well for the sub-deb dances which it would be her pleasant duty to give as her daughters grew older. Joan and Priscilla must be now of a marriageable age. I am sure that they have been admirably brought up; they have been sent to the best schools and Isabel has taken care that they should acquire the accomplishments that must make them desirable in the eyes of eligible young men. Though I suppose Gray by now is still a little redder in the face, more jowly, balder and a good deal heavier, I can't believe that Isabel has changed. She is still more beautiful than her daughters. The Maturins must be a great asset to the community and I have little doubt that they are as popular as they deserve to be. Isabel is entertaining, gracious, complaisant and tactful; and Gray, of course, is the quintessence of the Regular Guy.

(v)

I continued to see Suzanne Rouvier from time to time until an unexpected change in her condition caused her to leave Paris and she too went out of my life. One afternoon, roughly two years after the events that I have just related, having spent an hour pleasantly browsing over the books in the galleries of the Odéon and with nothing to do for a while, I thought I would call on Suzanne. I had not seen her for six months. She opened the door, a pallet on her thumb and a paintbrush between her teeth, clad in a smock covered with paint.

"*Ah, c'est vous, cher ami. Entrez, je vous en prie.*"

I was a little surprised at this formal address, for generally we spoke to one another in the second person singular, but I stepped into the small room that served both as living-room and studio. There was a canvas on the easel.

"I'm so busy, I don't know which way to turn, but sit down and I will go on with my work. I haven't a moment to waste. You wouldn't believe it, but I'm giving a one-man show at Meyerheim's; and I have to get thirty canvases ready."

"At Meyerheim's? That's wonderful. How on earth have you managed that?"

For Meyerheim is not one of those fly-by-night dealers in the Rue de Seine who have a small shop that is always on the verge of closing for lack of money to pay the rent. Meyerheim has a fine gallery on the moneyed side of the Seine and he has an international reputation. An artist whom he takes up is well on the way to fortune.

"Monsieur Achille brought him to see my work and he thinks I have a lot of talent."

"*À d'autres, ma vieille,*" I replied, which I think can best be translated by: "Tell that to the marines, old girl."

She threw me a glance and giggled.

"I'm going to be married."

"To Meyerheim?"

"Don't be an idiot." She put down her brushes and her pallet. "I've been working all day and I deserve a rest. Let us have a little glass of porto and I'll tell you about it."

One of the less agreeable features of French life is that you are apt to be pressed to drink a glass of vinegary port at an unseasonable hour. You must resign yourself to it. Suzanne fetched a bottle and two glasses, filled them and sat down with a sigh of relief.

"I've been standing for hours and my varicose veins are aching. Well, it's like this. Monsieur Achille's wife died at the beginning of this year. She was a good woman and a good Catholic, but he did not marry her from inclination, he married her because it was good business, and though he esteemed and respected her it would be an exaggeration to say that her death left him inconsolable. His son is suitably married and is doing well in the firm and now a marriage has been arranged between his daughter and a count, Belgian it is true, but authentic, with a very pretty château in the neighbourhood of Namur. Monsieur Achille thought his poor wife would not wish the happiness of two young people to be deferred on her account, so the marriage, notwithstanding that they are in mourning, is to take place as soon as the financial arrangements are completed. Evidently Monsieur Achille will be lonely in that large house at Lille, and he needs a woman not only to minister to his comfort, but also to run the important establishment necessary to his position. To cut a long story short, he has asked me to take the place of his poor wife, for as he very reasonably said: 'I married the first time to eliminate competition between two rival firms, and I do not regret it, but there is no reason why I should not marry the second time to please myself.'"

"I congratulate you," said I.

"Evidently I shall miss my liberty. I have enjoyed it. But one has to think of the future. Between ourselves, I don't mind telling you that I shall never see forty again. Monsieur Achille is at a dangerous age; where should I be if he suddenly took it into his head to run after a girl of twenty? And then there is my daughter to think of. She is now sixteen and promises to be as beautiful as her father. I have given her a good education. But it is no good denying facts that stare you in the face; she has neither the talent to be an actress nor the temperament to be a whore like her poor mother: I ask you then, what has she to look forward to? A secretaryship or a job in the post office. Monsieur Achille has very generously agreed that she should live with us and has promised to give her a handsome *dot* so that she can make a good marriage. Believe me, my dear friend, people can say what they like, but marriage still remains the most satisfactory profession a woman can adopt. Obviously when my daughter's welfare was concerned I could not hesitate to accept a proposition even at the cost of certain satisfactions which in any case, as the years go by, I should find it more difficult to obtain; for I must tell you that when I am married I propose to be of a ferocious virtue [*d'une vertu farouche*], for my long experience has convinced me that the only basis of a happy marriage is complete fidelity on both sides."

"A highly moral sentiment, my pretty," I said. "And will Monsieur Achille continue to make his fortnightly visits to Paris on business?"

"*Oh, la, la,* for whom do you take me, my little one? The first thing I said to Monsieur Achille when he asked for my hand was: 'Now listen, my dear, when you come to Paris for your board meetings it is understood that I come too. I am not going to trust you here by yourself.' 'You cannot imagine that I am capable of committing follies at my age,' he answered. 'Monsieur Achille,' I said to him, 'you are a man in the prime of life and no one knows better than I that you have a passionate temperament. You have a fine presence and a distinguished air. You have everything to please a woman; in short I think it better that you should not be exposed to temptation.' In the end he agreed to give up his place on the board to his son, who will come to Paris instead of his father. Monsieur Achille pretended to think me unreasonable, but he was in point of fact enormously flattered." Suzanne gave a sigh of satisfaction. "Life would be even harder for us poor women than it is if it were not for the unbelievable vanity of men."

"All that is very fine, but what has it got to do with your having a one-man show at Meyerheim's?"

"You are a little stupid today, my poor friend. Have I not told you for years that Monsieur Achille is a highly intelligent man? He has his position to think of and the people of Lille are censorious. Monsieur Achille wishes me to take the place in society which as the wife of a man of his importance it will be my right to occupy. You know what these provincials are, they love to poke their long noses in other people's affairs, and the first thing they will ask is: who is Suzanne Rouvier? Well, they will have their answer. She is the distinguished painter whose recent show at the Meyerheim Gallery had a remarkable and well-deserved success. 'Madame Suzanne Rouvier, the widow of an officer in the colonial infantry, has with the courage characteristic of our Frenchwomen for some years supported herself and a charming daughter deprived too soon of a father's care by means of her talent, and we are happy to know that the general public will soon have the opportunity to appreciate the delicacy of her touch and the soundness of her technique at the galleries of the ever perspicacious Monsieur Meyerheim.'"

"What gibberish is that?" I said, pricking up my ears.

"That, my dear, is the advance publicity that Monsieur Achille is putting out. It will appear in every paper in France of any consequence. He has been magnificent. Meyerheim's terms were onerous, but Monsieur Achille accepted them as if they were a bagatelle. There will be a *champagne d'honneur* at the private view and the Minister of Fine Arts, who is under an obligation to Monsieur Achille, will open the exhibition with an eloquent speech in which he will dwell upon my virtues as a woman and my talent as a painter and which he will end with the declaration that the state, whose duty and privilege it is to reward merit, has bought one of my pictures for the national collections. All Paris will be there and Meyerheim is looking after the critics himself. He has guaranteed that their notices will be not only favourable but lengthy. Poor devils, they earn so little, it is a charity to give them an opportunity of making something on the side."

"You've deserved it all, my dear. You've always been a good sort."

"*Et ta soeur,*" she replied, which is untranslatable. "But that's not all. Monsieur Achille has bought in my name a villa on the coast at St. Rafael, so I shall take my place in Lille society not only as a distinguished artist, but as a woman of property. In two or three years he is going to retire and we shall live on the Riviera like gentlefolks [*comme des gens bien*]. He can paddle in the sea and catch shrimps while I devote myself to my art. Now I will show you my pictures."

Suzanne had been painting for several years and she had worked through the manner of her various lovers to arrive at a style of her own. She still could not draw, but she had acquired a pretty sense of colour. She showed me landscapes that she had painted while staying with her mother in the province of Anjou, bits of the gardens at Versailles and the forest at Fontainebleau, street scenes that had taken her fancy in the suburbs of Paris. Her painting was vaporous and unsubstantial, but it had a flowerlike grace and even a certain careless elegance. There was one picture that took my fancy and because I thought she would be pleased I offered to buy it. I cannot remember whether it was called *A Glade in the Forest* or *The White*

Scarf and subsequent examination has left me uncertain to this day. I asked the price, which was reasonable, and said I would take it.

"You're an angel," she cried. "My first sale. Of course you can't have it till after the show, but I'll see that it gets into the papers that you've bought it. After all, a little publicity can do you no harm. I'm glad you've chosen that one, I think it's one of my best." She took a hand mirror and looked at the picture in it. "It has charm," she said, screwing up her eyes. "No one can deny that. Those greens—how rich they are and yet how delicate! And that white note in the middle, that is a real find; it ties the picture together, it has distinction. There's talent there, there can be no doubt of it, there's real talent."

I saw that she was already a long way on the road to being a professional painter.

"And now, my little one, we've gossiped long enough, I must get back to work."

"And I must be going," I said.

"*À propos,* is that poor Larry still among the Redskins?"

For that was the disrespectful way in which she was accustomed to refer to the inhabitants of God's Own Country.

"So far as I know."

"It must be hard for someone like him who is so sweet and gentle. If one can believe the movies life is terrible over there with all those gangsters and cowboys and Mexicans. Not that those cowboys haven't a physical attraction which says something to you. *Oh, la, la.* But it appears that it is *excessively* dangerous to go out into the streets of New York without a revolver in your pocket."

She came to the door to see me out and kissed me on both cheeks.

"We've had some good times together. Keep a good recollection of me."

(*vi*)

This is the end of my story. I have heard nothing of Larry, nor indeed did I expect to. Since he generally did what he proposed, I think it likely that on his return to America he got a job in a garage and then drove a truck till he had acquired the knowledge he wanted of the country from which he had for so many years absented himself. When he had done that he may very well have carried out his fantastic suggestion of becoming a taxi driver: true, it was only a random idea thrown across a café table in jest, but I wouldn't be altogether surprised if he had put it into effect; and I have never since taken a taxi in New York without glancing at the driver on the chance that I might meet Larry's gravely smiling, deep-set eyes. I never have. War broke out. He would have been too old to fly, but he may be once more driving a truck, at home or abroad; or he may be working in a factory. I should like to think that in his leisure hours he is writing a book in which he is trying to set forth whatever life has taught him and the message he has to deliver to his fellowmen; but if he is, it may be long before it is finished. He has plenty of time, for the years have left no mark on him and to all intents and purposes he is still a young man.

He is without ambition and he has no desire for fame; to become anything of a public figure would be deeply distasteful to him; and so it may be that he is satisfied to lead his chosen life and be no more than just himself. He is too modest to set himself up as an example to others; but it may be he thinks that a few uncertain souls, drawn to him like moths to a candle, will be brought in time to share his own glowing belief that ultimate satisfaction can only be found in the life of the spirit, and that by himself following with selflessness and renunciation the path of perfection he will serve as well as if he wrote books or addressed multitudes.

But this is conjecture. I am of the earth, earthy; I can only admire the radiance of such a rare creature, I cannot step into his shoes and enter into his inmost heart as I sometimes think I can do with persons more nearly allied to the common run of men. Larry has been absorbed, as he wished, into that tumultuous conglomeration of humanity, distracted by so many conflicting interests, so lost in the world's confusion, so wistful of good, so cocksure on the outside, so diffident within, so kind, so hard, so trustful and so cagey, so mean, and so generous, which is the people of the United States. That is all I can tell of him: I know it is very unsatisfactory; I can't help it. But as I was finishing this book, uneasily conscious that I must leave my reader in the air and seeing no way to avoid it, I looked back with my mind's eye on my long narrative to see if there was any way in which I could devise a more satisfactory ending; and to my intense surprise it dawned upon me that without in the least intending to I had written nothing more nor less than a success story. For all the persons with whom I have been concerned got what they wanted: Elliott social eminence; Isabel an assured position backed by a substantial fortune in an active and cultured community; Gray a steady and lucrative job, with an office to go to from nine till six every day; Suzanne Rouvier security; Sophie death; and Larry happiness. And however superciliously the highbrows carp, we the public in our heart of hearts all like a success story; so perhaps my ending is not so unsatisfactory after all.